Julia stood up and made to leave, but Danny glanced over and saw that Frank had taken a seat at the end of the pew and was looking hard at the woman. On the other side, Cal had just taken his place, effectively blocking her in.

"We're not here to arrest you, Julia, but we're not going to let you go, either. Your best option is to come with us and we'll get everything ironed out for you," Danny said as he stood. "Let's not make a scene."

She turned to face him directly for the first time. "There won't be any scene."

And with that, she fell straight through the floor.

Danny quickly punched his radio key four times, then bent over to quickly pick up all her clothes. "I hate it when they run," he muttered.

Praise for the MAJESTIC-12 Series

"A smart look at a Cold War in many ways even colder and scarier and deadlier than the one we barely survived."
—*New York Times* bestselling author Harry Turtledove

"A heady blend of super-spies and superpowers, *MJ-12: Inception* is Cold War-era science fiction done right. A taut thriller, and skillfully evocative."
—*New York Times* bestselling author Chris Roberson

"*X-Men* meets *Mission: Impossible*. Martinez takes a concept as simple as 'Super spies that are actually super' and comes away with a hit. Filled with compelling, well-rounded characters, *MJ-12* is my new favorite spy series."
—Michael R. Underwood, author of *Geekomancy* and the Genrenauts series

"The Cold War becomes even more chilling as super-powered Americans are trained to become super-spies in Martinez's new alternate-history thriller. It's morally complex, intense, and so steeped in the 1940s, you can smell the cigarette smoke."
—Beth Cato, author of *Breath of Earth* and *The Clockwork Dagger*

"*MJ-12: Inception* is a thriller that blends the best elements of Cold War-era spy stories, supernatural fantasy, and splashy pulp comics."
—*B&N Sci-Fi & Fantasy Blog*

"*MJ-12: Inception* is Michael J. Martinez doing what he does best: taking a selection of great genres and mashing them up into something fresh and exciting, and quite unlike anything you've read before . . . . Or to put it another way, it's like the *X-Files* and *Heroes* went back in time, dressed up in dinner jackets, lit a fuse, and jumped through a window to the theme from *Mission: Impossible*. Absolutely loved it."

—*Fantasy Faction*

"Martinez made a point to recognize the sacrifices made by those in the intelligence community to protect their nation. . . . the characters were all well-developed, their powers were imaginative, the twists weren't obvious and Martinez did a good job capturing the setting. . . . *MJ-12: Inception* was an enjoyable twist on the superhero genre and I look forward to seeing what happens next."

—*Amazing Stories*

"With *MJ-12: Inception*, Martinez weaves an intense tale of patriotism, Cold War politics, the US spy network, and the nuances of human relationships which I simply couldn't put down."

—*The Qwillery*

"Martinez has me hooked, and I'm anxiously awaiting the next book in the trilogy; I imagine more Variants, more subterfuge, and more world-ending risks are to be revealed. It's good stuff."

—*GeekDad*

"*MJ-12: Inception* is both a complete stand-alone adventure and a thrilling introduction to a richly reimagined Cold War spy-fi series. I eagerly await Michael J. Martinez's next novel featuring the Majestic 12."

—*Mutt Café*

MJ-12

Books by Michael J. Martinez

The Daedalus Series
The Daedalus Incident
The Enceladus Crisis
The Venusian Gambit
The Gravity of the Affair (novella)

MAJESTIC-12
MJ-12: Inception
MJ-12: Shadows

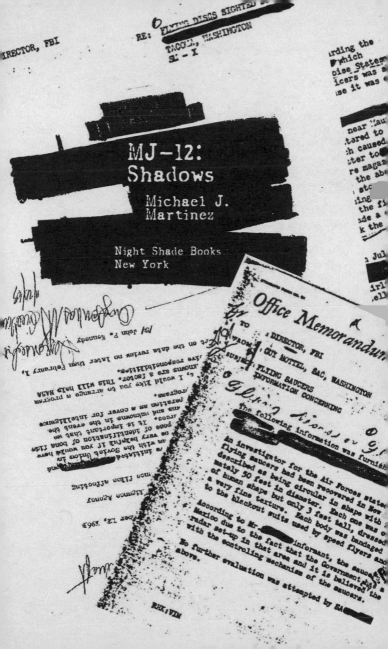

MJ-12:
Shadows

Michael J.
Martinez

Night Shade Books
New York

Night Shade books may be purchased in bulk at special discounts for sales promotion, corporate gifts, fund-raising, or educational purposes. Special editions can also be created to specifications. For details, contact the Special Sales Department, Night Shade Books, 307 West 36th Street, 11th Floor, New York, NY 10018 or info@skyhorsepublishing.com.

Night Shade Books™ is a trademark of Skyhorse Publishing, Inc.®, a Delaware corporation.

Visit our website at www.nightshadebooks.com.

10 9 8 7 6 5 4 3 2 1

Library of Congress Cataloging-in-Publication Data

Names: Martinez, Michael J., author.
Title: MJ-12: shadows: a Majestic-12 thriller / by Michael J. Martinez.
Other titles: MJ-twelve | Shadows
Description: New York: Night Shade Books, [2017]
Identifiers: LCCN 2017006717| ISBN 9781597809269 (hardback: alk. paper) | ISBN 9781597809283 (ebook)
Subjects: LCSH: Paranormal fiction.
Classification: LCC PS3613.A78647 M56 2017 | DDC 813/.6—dc23
LC record available at https://lccn.loc.gov/2017006717

ISBN: 978-1-59780-926-9
Ebook ISBN: 978-1-59780-928-3

Cover design by Lesley Worrell

Printed in Canada

In memory of Joanie.

Author's Note

Throughout the years, the Central Intelligence Agency and the other organizations within the U.S. Intelligence Community have been dedicated to helping keep this nation safe. That said, CIA in particular has a rather blemished track record when it comes to regime change and various dirty deeds. The events in 1949 Syria you'll read about here are, for the most part, historically accurate—without the superpowered covert agents, of course. The United States has a long history of covert action and intervention in the Middle East, and the events in Syria described here are perhaps some of the strangest and, in some ways, most egregious. I chose to write about this time and place because it made for a compelling story, first and foremost—but as we think about the ongoing tragedies in Syria today, one can't help but wonder if we were setting the stage for the events of today back in 1949.

The MAJESTIC-12 series is set in the late 1940s, and as such, the characters have some decidedly un-modern views with regard to race, class, and gender. These views were not included merely for historical accuracy but to recognize how far we've come since then—and perhaps highlight how much further we have to go.

SHADOWS

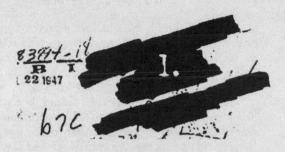

December 24, 1948

Lt. Rudolf Schmidt of the Vienna *Polizei* had seen many things over the course of his short but eventful career. From the *Anschluss* to liberation to occupation, crime continued no matter who was in charge in the city of Mozart, Beethoven, and Freud. There had been crimes when the Turks were at the gate, he was sure, or when the Romans fought off the barbarians.

But he was pretty certain there was no crime quite like this one.

"I tell you, it is impossible," said Josef Franz, director of security for the *Österreichische Postsparkasse*, the Austrian Postal Savings Bank. "These vaults are ten meters below the subbasement, and the walls are lined with foot-thick steel. The elevator is manned at the top and at the bottom, and the stairwell is right next to it. All the exits are covered twenty-four hours a day, seven days a week. There is no way this could have happened!"

Schmidt looked around the bank's main vault, where only Vienna's wealthiest could afford to keep their valuables—for all the good it did them. Money and valuables were strewn about haphazardly—jewels, bank notes, coins. It looked for all the world like someone had thrown a surprise party in the vault, but used gold and jewelry for confetti.

"Well, *HerrDirektor*, it *did* happen, so we must figure out how that is. You say that this happened today? Between when and when?"

"Noon and two p.m. We check the vault itself every two hours," Franz said. He was short and altogether too fat for his position, Schmidt thought. Likely a retired police officer, or even an old Austrian Army veteran who retired before the Nazis came to power. He didn't look like he could secure a shopping bag, let alone a bank. Perhaps he was smart and had others do his bidding. It didn't seem likely, though.

"We are searching the guards' homes, but you say they never left," Schmidt mused, half to himself. "Top-to-bottom search of the bank building itself, of course. Rooftops. Neighboring buildings. All employees and their vehicles." He turned to face the director. "This is no way to spend Christmas Eve. Though perhaps it was the best time to try such a thing. Minds are elsewhere."

"My guards are among the best in all the country," Franz protested. "And I personally performed the noon check of the vault. All was in order. No one was inside."

Schmidt walked gingerly around the looted vault as bank employees attempted to sort through the scattered treasures, pairing them with their private security boxes.

Adding to the mystery was the fact that either the thieves had carefully closed all the looted security boxes before leaving, or had somehow gained entry to them without opening the locks.

"Who would go to the trouble to re-lock all the boxes, yet scatter everything around?" Schmidt wondered aloud. "Takes far too much time."

A different voice answered him. "Perhaps someone who didn't need a key."

Schmidt turned to see two smartly dressed people walking toward him with intent. The man was tall and broad, wearing a suit with a severe, American-style cut. He had short-cropped brown hair and a slight smile, and his dark brown eyes looked as though they'd seen quite a lot—not uncommon after the War, of course. The woman with him—a rarity in and of itself—was thin and pale, with intense green eyes and a mouth that seemed like it might never smile at all. A very dark dress suit with a white blouse added to her funereal aura. She walked right past them into the vault, her heels clicking on the concrete floor, while the man stopped and held out his hand.

"Special Agent Stanley Harper, United States Federal Bureau of Investigation," he said. "We heard this was a crime of . . . particular interest. We're helping out the occupation authority with similar incidents."

Schmidt's eyebrows rose. "Lieutenant Schmidt, Vienna police. A G-man? You have seen other crimes like this?" he asked as he shook the proffered hand.

The FBI man looked around. "Secure room, locked containers . . . yes, we have," he said, his German accent nearly perfect to Schmidt's ears. "Though not on this scale. Whoever is doing this, it seems they have found a new level of ambition."

"Where else?" Schmidt asked.

Harper gave an apologetic smile. "Sorry. I really can't say. Some very interesting places, though. I assume nothing large was taken?"

Schmidt couldn't help but do a double take. "You are very well informed, Agent Harper. Nothing large is missing. There is a Gustav Klimt here worth millions. Vases and urns and other valuables. Only things that are small, easily palmed; those are the ones missing."

"Palmed . . ." the American said, his eyes suddenly lost in thought. He then stooped down to pick up a few coins from the floor, wrapping them completely in his meaty fist. "Huh."

"You have an idea?" Schmidt asked.

Harper smiled and made a show of dropping all the coins—as if he didn't want to be accused of taking anything. "Just an idle thought, *Herr Leutnant*."

Schmidt turned around to see the man's partner—it was strange; he didn't know of any police agency who had women investigators—running her hands across the various safe deposit boxes. She finally stopped and turned back to Harper, giving him a nod.

Harper held out a business card. "Once you're done here, if you wouldn't mind keeping us informed as you proceed?"

"Of course," Schmidt said, taking the card. "You do not wish to look any further?"

"When you've seen what we've seen, you get a lot from one look," the agent replied. "Thank you for your cooperation."

The two turned to leave, but Schmidt hurried after them. "Can you at least give me an idea of what I'm looking for?" he asked, almost plaintively. "The diamonds taken here are worth several million marks."

The woman turned and, to Schmidt's great surprise, did actually smile. "You wouldn't believe us if we told you."

* * *

The two FBI agents walked out of the Austrian Postal Savings Bank—a beautiful, marble-clad Modernist ode to money itself—and onto the evening hustle and bustle of Biberstrasse. "Well? What'd you get?" the man who'd called himself Harper said in English, a slight Boston accent breaking through.

"It's her," the woman replied, stopping to look up at the bank building itself. "Thick walls, small girl. She didn't even need to enter the front door. Only question I have is where she put her clothes."

The bank occupied an entire block in Vienna's historic core. There were no alleys, no place to really hide. If the bank really was hit between noon and two p.m., like the cops said, their suspect's M. O. definitely would've been noticed.

Unless . . .

"She parked," the man said, looking at the cars lining the block. He quickly walked around the corner and saw that there were several cars angled in, with just a couple feet between the fenders and the building's facade. "Here," he said. "She parked here, got ready, and probably just went straight down."

The woman next to him frowned. "There's got to be thirty cars here, Frank."

"Just on this side, too," he replied. "Let's get to work, Zip."

Zipporah Silverman smiled wanly, pulled her coat tight around her, and started walking down the street, running her fingertips idly along the hoods of the parked cars. Zippy was a unique individual—a Variant. Like the very few other Variants in the world, she possessed a paranormal ability. In her case, she could gain a psychic impression of past activities by touching an object, an ability called psychometry. So, she went down the row of cars, looking for the image of the woman she'd seen when she touched the safety deposit boxes in the vault. She stopped at the sixth car in the row. "This one wasn't here until late afternoon," she said. She then crouched to the ground, placing her palm on the asphalt beneath the fender.

Ten seconds later, she stood. "Not here."

They walked farther down the street, finding two others potential candidates, but with the same result. It was only when they turned onto Dominikanerbastei that Zippy found something. She stayed crouched beneath the front hood of a Tatra T87, a beastly V8 luxury sedan with a Deco body and enough wear and tear to place it as a pre-war model.

"She was here," she said softly, both hands pressed to the pavement. "And she didn't go in through the side. She went *under*."

Frank Lodge swore under his breath. "That's new," he muttered. "You get a look at her face?"

Zippy stood and smiled. "Yep. She's a real looker, too. You'd like her."

"Yeah, I go in for the thieving types," Frank cracked. "Let's get moving. Maybe now we can finally track her down."

* * *

The choir at Vienna's St. Stephen's Cathedral sounded truly Heaven-sent. Voices of angels, raised in praise of God Almighty, and with a harmony that Calvin Hooks had never even thought possible, his time in the churches of Tennessee notwithstanding.

He supposed they could use a little rhythm, if he was going to be picky about it, but almost immediately chided himself. He was sure God would be plenty pleased with such a hymn.

The church itself had just reopened a couple weeks prior; fires set during the Soviet takeover of the city had severely damaged the ancient church's roof. And with it being Christmas Eve, there was a fair amount of folks taking refuge against the chill outside. Even the hardest hearts, Cal knew, would find solace in a beautiful old church like this on Christmas.

Then a woman walked by, her heels snapping sharply on the checkerboard marble floor, and Cal's mind immediately shifted. He held a small cigarette case to his mouth. "Got eyes on her, I think," he whispered. "Walking in now, center aisle, right side."

The case vibrated twice in acknowledgement. A few seconds later, a slight blond man wearing glasses brushed past him to follow. Cal watched him go briefly . . . until he realized that the couple across the aisle were staring at him in something akin to shock.

He knew it had nothing to do with his whispering and everything to do with the fact that he was probably one of maybe a half dozen black people in all of Vienna. And it wasn't like German folk—and Austria, Germany . . . they were kind of all the same to him—were exactly keen on Negroes.

Cal sighed and put his eyes back on the target, the blond man, who had taken a seat one row behind the woman. He had to keep his eyes on the target. His ears, though, he'd save for that Christmas carol the choir was singing. *Always good to keep a little bit of the Lord in mind*, he thought.

* * *

Danny Wallace reached down for the kneeler, then got on his knees and folded his hands in front of him, leaning his arms on the back of the pew in front of him. The woman was less than three feet away. She immediately flinched and shifted, and Danny knew then they had the right target—as if the sensation in his mind wasn't confirmation enough.

She was a flaring beacon now that he'd been able to finally get close enough.

"Nice trick at the vault today," he said quietly, trying to suppress a smile. "You're getting pretty daring. You're also starting to develop a pattern, though, and that's a problem."

To her credit, the woman kept herself composed, sitting stock-still with her arms folded and staring straight ahead. "Excuse me?" she said, sounding incongruously pleasant. She was petite and dressed conservatively but quite fashionably for church. Danny knew she could afford it.

"You're rushing things. You think you need to get in and get out, so you're making messes wherever you go. The bank today. The hotel safe in Davos last week. The museum storehouse in Graz two weeks ago. You're just reaching in, grabbing for stuff, throwing it aside if it doesn't interest you. You think you're going to be interrupted at any moment. But you're not thinking about what you *could* do if you were caught."

The woman cracked a small smile. "I'm thinking about it right now," she replied quietly. "But thanks for the tip."

She's going to run, Danny thought. He reached into his pocket and gave his own cigarette case radio three quick taps, the signal for everyone else to get in position. "You have a pretty unique ability, I'll give you that. But I also think you're wasting it on bank jobs and knickknacks."

The woman's smile grew wider. "Ah, so you know a little about me, then. And this is where you try to sell me on joining you for . . . what, exactly? Are you a gangster?"

Danny had to stifle a laugh at her pronunciation—she'd obviously picked up the word at the movie house. "Sorry, nothing so glamorous. But maybe something far more exciting. And useful."

"Ah, a goody-goody," she replied, another line lifted straight from the silver screen. "Let me guess. You want me to fight for you, whoever you are. Why should I? I like my knickknacks."

"Because if you don't, we'll tell your husband exactly why you left him—and where he can find that car and all his mother's jewelry you took on the way out. You want that, Julia Meyer?"

The smile finally faded. "My husband is a pig," she spat. "And his mother is a witch from hell."

"Good," Danny quipped. "Come with me, and we'll cover all your tracks. You'll have to give everything back you haven't spent yet, but you won't be on the hook for it. And we won't tell your family where you are. New life, clean slate."

"I already have a clean slate," Julia remarked. "Nobody can connect me to any of those crimes. And you don't have enough to arrest me—if you did, you would. And you know that handcuffs wouldn't hold me anyway."

"I know, Julia. You're a Variant. Over the past couple years, you've developed a kind of Enhancement that allows you to do extraordinary things. Did you ever in your life imagine that one day you'd be able walk right through walls, to reach through doors without opening them? You're like a ghost. It's a pretty incredible ability."

She continued to stare straight ahead, but her eyebrow cocked up a bit. "A Variant? Is that what you call—do you mean there are others like me? People who can walk through walls?"

"There are others like you, but you're the only one I've met who can do what you do, Julia. But we Variants, we can do extraordinary things."

Julia stood up and made to leave, but Danny glanced over and saw that Frank had taken a seat at the end of the pew and was looking hard at the woman. On the other side, Cal had just taken his place, effectively blocking her in.

"We're not here to arrest you, Julia, but we're not going to let you go, either. Your best option is to come with us and we'll get everything ironed out for you," Danny said as he stood. "Let's not make a scene."

She turned to face him directly for the first time. "There won't be any scene."

And with that, she fell straight through the floor.

Danny quickly punched his radio key four times, then bent over to quickly pick up all her clothes. "I hate it when they run," he muttered.

* * *

Knowing a naked woman might drop from the ceiling at any moment was one thing. Actually seeing it was quite another. So, it took Maggie Dubinsky a few moments before she realized she was truly on deck.

"Wow, your clothes really don't go with you," Maggie said with a broad smile as the woman, now crouched on the floor of the cathedral's crypts, looked up at her wide-eyed.

The woman—Julia Meyer, according to the dossier Maggie had read a few hours before in a nondescript hotel room—immediately took off in a sprint.

"Please stop!" Maggie shouted, her voice echoing off the low stone ceilings and columns of the church's lower level as she took off in pursuit. "We need to talk!"

But Julia wasn't having it, and she wasn't bothering to stop or run around things like columns and tombs, either. Maggie had little chance of keeping up with her, so she had a couple of options—she could activate a device, initially developed by the Soviets, that would temporarily block any Variant from using their Enhancement, or she could simply use her own ability.

The way Julia was running through stuff, though, option one was out. For all Maggie knew, the gizmo could somehow trap her suddenly solid body in the middle of a column or something—and that seemed potentially messy.

Instead, Maggie paused a moment and reached out with her mind, grasping at the flailing red threads that, in her head, visually represented Julia's frayed emotions. Maggie gathered a few of them in a twist . . . and pulled.

She was rewarded with a cry of panic and horror up ahead. Maggie saw that Julia had stopped running and was slowly turning toward her, the look of fear on her face amplified up to a level that few people could contemplate.

"Oh, shit," Maggie muttered, then tried to adjust quickly, reaching for cooler threads of calm and happiness. But it was too late.

Julia ran straight toward Maggie, screaming and wild-eyed, then continued on *through* her and into the very wall of the catacomb.

"*Shit shit shit shit*," Maggie shouted, keying her radio as she ran toward the stairs leading upward. "Subject on the move! Panicked and buck naked!"

Most of the time, a dose of fear administered from Maggie made her targets simply fold like a bad hand, collapsing in a heap and blubbering like babies. But for a scant few—maybe one in twenty or so—that abject fear that Maggie could project triggered a fight-or-flight reflex, and Julia had chosen flight.

Just her luck.

* * *

Danny, Frank, and Cal dashed out of the church, startling several well-dressed families heading into the arched doorway. Despite the bitter cold, the plaza around them was full of pedestrians, but Frank was grateful for both the crowds and the winter weather—it would make Julia Meyer a lot easier to find.

"Commander?" Frank asked, turning to Danny.

The young man's eyes were screwed shut in concentration. "She's . . . here. Under us. But moving really slow."

Higher volumes may lead to reduced movement rates, came the voice of U.S. Army Gen. Mark Davis, who had died three years earlier but somehow also now resided inside Frank's mind, standing at attention for whenever he was needed. *Her Enhancement may have limits. She'll have to surface soon. Keep on her.*

"No shit," Frank muttered. There were times when all the voices and accumulated expertise in his head—a rather morbid gift from those Frank had watched die—was incredibly useful. Other times, they stated the obvious with all the gravity of a Congressional decree.

Danny was already walking into the plaza, Cal at his side. Frank hurried to catch up, passing bakeries and coffeehouses with the most incredible scents coming from inside. Running around Vienna in the depth of winter on Christmas Eve was not how he expected to be living life these days, but then again, his life hadn't been normal in years.

"Wait," Danny said, holding up his hand. "She's right here. She's stopped moving."

Frank started taking off his overcoat just as Maggie and Zippy came running over—Maggie had been in the basement, Zippy at the very back of the cathedral. "Looks like she's reached the end of her rope," Frank said. "Let's hope she—"

Suddenly, the woman from the cathedral practically leapt straight out of the cobblestoned street between them, collapsing back down onto the cold stone, gasping for breath.

Frank immediately threw his overcoat over her. "Maggie, now!"

Maggie produced a small metal disk from her pocket, flipped a toggle switch on it, and slipped it into the pocket of Frank's coat. A moment later, Maggie grimaced. "It's working," she said, distaste written across her face.

Julia Meyer looked up at the five people standing above her. "Who *are* you?" she gasped.

Danny knelt down next to her and smiled, handing over her clothes. "I'm Commander Dan Wallace, United States Navy. We work on a special project back in America called MAJESTIC-12. And like it or not, you just joined the team."

January 20, 1949

*I*t's amazing what a few curtains and some bunting can do, James Forrestal thought as he surveyed the National Guard Armory in Washington, D.C., where the capital's movers and shakers were gathered to celebrate the inauguration of Harry S. Truman, he of the already legendary DEWEY DEFEATS TRUMAN headline. And only the armory was big enough to house all the folks Truman invited. The President wanted a celebration—not for himself but for the country. At least, so he claimed.

Forrestal, however, didn't feel like celebrating.

As he hung back by the bar, Scotch in hand, Forrestal couldn't help but feel a bit guilty. Truman was his boss; the President had named him Secretary of Defense, the first man to hold that newly minted title now that "Secretary of War" sounded a little too aggressive in the horrible aftermath of World War II. Forrestal wanted to be loyal, he really did. But Truman could make it so very, very hard sometimes.

Hell, the whole title change was a symptom of the problem, in Forrestal's view. There were still wars to fight.

"Even you look good in a tux, Jim," came a voice from behind him, breaking him out of his reverie. Forrestal turned to see a big, slightly balding man beaming at him.

"Senator McCarthy," Forrestal said, smiling and shaking the man's hand. "Didn't expect to find you here tonight."

Joseph McCarthy, the junior U.S. Senator from Wisconsin, shrugged. "Only the senators from Utah pass up free drinks. Besides, I'm celebrating the institution, not the man."

The two men clinked glasses at this. "I hope we can still count on you for our military modernization plans, Joe," Forrestal said with a wink. Neither man was particularly keen on reducing the size and makeup of the U.S. armed forces, but that was the Truman administration's stance and Forrestal knew he had to keep his mouth shut publicly, no matter how much he might disagree with the President.

McCarthy's smile evaporated. "You know as well as I do that the Commies are still building up their forces. Why should we roll over? I don't care that Truman and his crew—Acheson and Hillenkoetter and the rest of those idiots—think we can do more with covert action and intelligence-gathering. The Soviets are a threat. Especially if they have Variants!"

Forrestal stiffened at the word and looked around, worry on his face; with his luck, Secretary of State Dean Acheson or CIA Director Roscoe Hillenkoetter would be standing right behind him. "Dammit, Joe, I told you about that in confidence. The very existence of Variants is classified to hell and back, let alone the fact that the Russkies have them too! They could arrest us both for treason for just talking about it!"

McCarthy stepped in a bit closer and put his hand on Forrestal's shoulder. "I know, Jim, but it's not treason. Members of Congress have a right to know about a game-changer like this. You're a true-blue American. And I *am* keeping it under my hat, for the most part."

"For the *most part*?" Forrestal hissed. The Defense Secretary had been deeply worried about the Variants and the implication their very existence had for the nation—and humanity at large—while Truman and Hillenkoetter were busy turning them into super-spies and giving these people, these *weapons*, incredible leeway in their daily activities. Forrestal had confided in McCarthy because he didn't know who else to turn to, and the Wisconsin senator had always been a political ally. Now it seemed McCarthy had been blabbing about the nation's best-kept secret program, and Forrestal felt a knot of worry growing in his gut. "Who else have you brought in?"

"Let's get some air, shall we?"

Forrestal followed the senator as he weaved his way through the dancing crowd. There was a Negro woman on stage, singing her heart out. It was the first time Negroes had even been allowed into an inaugural ball other than to serve drinks. Once upon a time, Forrestal might have found the notion somewhat distasteful. These days, though, he had no choice but to admit that skin color was the least of humanity's worries.

To Forrestal's surprise, McCarthy didn't lead him to the door. Instead, they turned right just before the coat check and headed toward a small, quiet area away from the crowds, where the Secret Service had set up a small command post.

And standing there, chatting with one of the agents, was a short, stocky man with a receding hairline and a face that could be generously described as pugnacious—J. Edgar Hoover, director of the Federal Bureau of Investigation.

"You really oughta think about applying," he was saying to the agent. "What you're doing here, it's fine. It's good and honorable and important. But out there, with the FBI, you're gonna be where the action is, my friend. I promise you that."

"I appreciate that, Director," the young agent said. Forrestal had seen him around the White House before. Young, smart, obviously impressionable.

Hoover turned and nodded curtly at McCarthy and Forrestal. "Son, you mind giving us the room for a minute? Need to have a chat with these fine gentleman. National security. You understand."

The agent scurried away as if he'd seen his shadow, reminding Forrestal just how much pull Hoover had in this town.

"Good to see you, Jim," Hoover said as they shook hands. "Been ages. I'm glad Joe here brought us together."

Forrestal smiled, but inside he wasn't quite sure if he shared that sentiment. Truman had been absolutely insistent that Hoover be kept out of the MAJESTIC-12 project at all costs, a move with which Forrestal actually agreed.

Nobody in the White House was sure whether Hoover would want his *own* Variants as agents, or if he'd simply round them up and throw them in a hole as a danger to humanity. He was capable of either option, and Forrestal felt Hoover was too much of a loose cannon and political empire-builder to be trusted. But here he was, and the knot in Forrestal's stomach tightened up a few notches.

"I assume, then, that Joe has told you a few things," Forrestal ventured.

Hoover raised an eyebrow and smiled. "Just enough. Honestly, Jim, it scares the crap out of me. This shit's right out of the funny pages, right? Superpowered people—American citizens—being rounded up and turned into secret agents for Hillenkoetter and the CIA? It's crazy, is what it is."

"Director, please understand, there are less than a dozen people in government who know about these Variants," Forrestal said. "If word were ever to get back to the President—"

Hoover cut him off with a wave of his hand. "I'm not doing anything with this right now, Jim. I promise you that. It's just important that people *know* about it. Do you seriously think that Harry is prepared for when—and it's *when*, not *if*—these Variants get the idea in their heads to do something stupid? To make a move that threatens America? To try to take over?"

"There are contingencies in place, Director. I've reviewed them myself. If the Variants do any of those things, they get put down. Simple as that," Forrestal said with all the fervor of a politician protecting his turf—which he was.

"And I'm glad to hear it. Really glad. But all the same, the FBI is going to be looking out for these people now too. Wouldn't hurt to have a few of them on our side. Checks and balances—isn't that what we're celebrating tonight?" Hoover said, barking out a laugh for emphasis.

McCarthy eyed the director with suspicion; it was obvious to Forrestal that this was news to the senator. "How exactly are you going to do that?" he said.

"Well, I was going to ask Jim here about that," Hoover replied. "I mean, how many of these people do you have now?"

Forrestal shrugged. "We have eight fully up and running. More in the training program. Just brought one in a couple weeks ago."

"And how do you find them?"

Forrestal knew then and there he had to decide just how much to trust Hoover, and whether he might eventually end up as ally, rival, or enemy. He hadn't told McCarthy about Subject-1 and their ability to locate other Variants. He didn't even know who Subject-1 was—only the President and Hillenkoetter knew that. And the very existence of this Variant homing pigeon was perhaps America's greatest advantage against the Soviets and their own Variant program.

So, he lied.

"Analysis, mostly," Forrestal said. "We keep an eye out for unusual reports in the papers. Strange activity, mysterious crimes, that sort of thing. Field scouts will then go and check them out. It's police work, really. Your boys ought to be pretty good at it."

Hoover nodded. "They are indeed, Jim. I already started looking. And I'm gonna keep you updated as we go. I hope you'll extend me the same courtesy."

"Of course, Director," Forrestal said. "I'm glad you're taking the initiative here. Appreciate it."

The two shook hands as McCarthy beamed at them both, obviously pleased with himself. Forrestal would later give the ambitious politician as stern a talking-to as he could manage, knowing that the bastard had a vote on his budgets.

After some further pleasantries and the promise of fishing at some nebulous point in the future, Forrestal was left to his own devices and returned to the glittering hall. He watched the President and First Lady take a turn on the dance floor, Truman smiling that big, toothy grin of his. Forrestal grabbed a flute of champagne from a passing waiter and downed it in one shot, trying to ease his nerves.

Truman wasn't a bad man, not in the least. But he was a goddamn haberdasher from the middle of nowhere who got swept up in a two-bit political machine in Missouri. He got sent to Congress to do other men's bidding, and Roosevelt had chosen him to be his vice-president for more of the same. Truman talked a good game, with that whole "buck stops here" nonsense. But deep down, Forrestal knew that he just wasn't up to the task. Not with humanity's position at the top of the food chain under threat.

Of course, Forrestal wasn't a fool. He knew that Hoover would have eventually found out; the damn man had ears everywhere. And there were a couple of pertinent bits of information that Forrestal still kept to himself. He knew in his bones that Variants were a threat, but he preferred them in the right hands—his hands. Hoover would have to hit the jackpot to find a Variant before MAJESTIC-12 did.

But in case those Variants did wander off the reservation, Forrestal figured it was better to have men like McCarthy and Hoover—men who weren't afraid to act—in his corner.

Overall, despite the initial surprise and with lingering reservations about Hoover, Forrestal decided he was fine with how the evening had gone. He grabbed another Scotch and headed outside for some air, not noticing the pair of eyes that had been on him the entire evening.

3.

January 25, 1949

Julia Meyer had never seen a place so desolate in her entire life.

Her plane—a creaky, god-awful cargo hauler—had landed on a huge, dried-out lake bed, white as salt and stretching for miles in all directions until it bumped up against sandy desert mountains. There were buildings—short and squat except for the couple they used to store airplanes—and a few scattered encampments away from the main base that she had seen from the air.

Her handler—not quite a captor, certainly not a friend, and she was still unsure if he'd ever be her boss—had called the place Area 51 and said that its very existence was one of the United States's foremost secrets. And even though she'd only known Danny Wallace for a short period of time, she'd quickly come to understand he wasn't a man to exaggerate.

So, it made sense that Area 51 was where they trained Variants to become full-blown spies.

Julia knew her worth in this, of course. A spy who could walk through walls was valuable. There were others with different Enhancements—another unusual term Danny used to describe these strange powers. There was a woman who could look into the past through physical touch. A man with extraordinary powers to both heal and harm. And of course, she had already found herself at the mercy of the woman who could play with emotions like a puppeteer controlled a marionette. Julia swore that if she ever saw Maggie again, she would avoid her at all costs.

"Let's go," Danny said, grabbing his duffel bag and nodding toward hers. Julia gathered her things and followed the navy man—now dressed in a khaki uniform—off the plane and into a waiting jeep.

"Any final questions?" he asked as the driver put the vehicle into gear and headed for one of the buildings.

"No," she replied, repeating the verbal agreement they'd already made several times over. "You will take me to your scientists for analysis of my ability for a few days, then I will go to one of the training places here to work on the things that will make me a spy. And when you feel you can trust me, you will take this thing off my leg."

This thing was the damned electronic device that the Maggie woman had used on her in Vienna. It blocked her ability completely. Danny had decided to handcuff it to her ankle after she tried to make a break for it at the Keflavik air field in Iceland on their way back.

Julia was still skeptical of the entire affair, but she'd run out of alternative options for the time being. She would play along for now. Besides, the training he promised her could make any future endeavors even more lucrative.

"You behave yourself, you get the jewelry off," Danny said. She hated how he thought he was being clever, calling her shackle *jewelry*. "Now we'll have a bit of paperwork first, and—driver, what the hell is going on over there? Three o'clock."

Julia looked to where Danny was pointing, in the distance off to the right, where a number of heavy trucks were driving off down a road that led into the mountains. It was a very large caravan and seemed to include heavy equipment as well as numerous people. Even from far off, Julia could see a few of the people were wearing white lab coats.

"No idea, sir," the young driver shouted over the airflow around the jeep. "Bunch of trucks from the carpool got requisitioned, is all I know."

Danny looked around him until his eyes fixed on the largest building on base. It looked very important, with its own security fence. Julia noticed that the cargo doors to the building were opened.

"Shit! Follow those trucks, sergeant!" Danny ordered. Immediately, the jeep swerved and headed for the line of vehicles. "We get any visitors while I was gone?"

"I drove General Montague in just yesterday, sir," the driver replied.

Danny sat back in his seat with a worried grimace on his face—an uncharacteristic look for a man Julia had heretofore only seen as being quietly competent. "What is it?" she asked.

"Don't know yet, and you're probably not cleared for it," he replied.

* * *

Danny stewed for the entire hour it took the convoy to head over the mountains. They were heading toward one of the nuclear test sites; that, combined with Major General Bob Montague's arrival, was cause for worry.

Danny was nominal commander of Area 51's Variant research and training program, but that was due more to necessity rather than the appropriate rank—there were only so many people cleared for TOP SECRET-MAJIK stuff, after all. Montague was one of them, but he already had a full-time job commanding the air base in Albuquerque. Mostly, the general left Danny to his own devices, but every now and then, he'd get to asking unusually pointed questions about individual Variants or other related topics, leading Danny to believe the general was likely being fed intel by someone on base or elsewhere inside MAJESTIC-12.

Of course, Danny could've simply been paranoid, and he accepted that as part of the job description. But there were days . . .

The convoy rolled to a stop on a hillside overlooking another valley. About two miles down, he could just make out a number of technicians standing around an impossibly bright light.

Measuring only six feet across, that light was somehow an impossibility of physics, a pure white nothingness that could be moved by magnetic fields but was otherwise immune to any attempts to alter it. Danny had discovered it in 1945, in the ruins of Hiroshima, and since transporting it to the United States, they'd been able to determine that the pulses of radio waves and radiation it threw off regularly were ultimately connected to and very likely the actual source of the Variants' powers.

How and why this was happening, nobody knew. The best physicists in the world were stumped. Einstein had once told an Area 51 researcher that such a thing was unequivocally impossible. And yet there it was.

Now Danny just had to figure out what the hell it was doing off base and on a nuclear testing range.

He jumped out of the jeep and turned to his driver. "Take Miss Meyer back to base. Put her in containment holding until I get back. That shackle on her ankle does not come off under any circumstances whatsoever. Understood?"

Danny didn't wait for the reply. Instead, he marched off toward the rest of the caravan of vehicles, looking for anybody who could explain what was happening. Thankfully, he found a friend before anyone else.

"Commander!"

Dr. Detlev Bronk, one of the world's foremost—actually, he was the only one—biophysicists came rushing up to greet Danny. Bronk was a reedy man with slicked-back gray hair, with a propensity for wearing both Hawaiian shirts and, usually, an amused look on his face.

"What's going on, Det?" Danny demanded as he continued to stride forward to where he assumed the brass would be.

"Schreiber managed to talk Montague into another test of the vortex," Bronk said, falling in beside Danny. "You're not going to like it."

"They already nuked the vortex at sea last year. How badly am I not going to like it?"

"I lodged a formal protest with the President as soon as I found out. But they kept me in the dark so long, I doubt it'll get there in time," Bronk said, handing Danny a pair of binoculars. "Take a look."

Danny stopped to put the binoculars to his eyes. He surveyed the vortex—a team of engineers were dismantling the frame of the magnetic field generator they'd used to transport it there. Others were inspecting what Danny presumed to be a nuclear weapon atop a three-story wooden derrick.

And there was a man in all black talking to a man who was seated in—and tied to—a chair.

"What the hell?" Danny muttered. "Is this what I think it is?" He looked over at Bronk, who responded only with a grave look on his face.

He didn't wait for a response. Danny took off at a sprint, his glasses nearly falling off his face. He stopped only as he approached Montague, who was talking to a thin, severe-looking man in a white lab coat. It was all he could do to adhere to military protocol and salute first.

"Commander Wallace, reporting for duty," he snapped. "May I ask what's going on, sir?"

Montague fixed him with a grandfatherly smile, though one tinged with the knowledge of what was coming next. "Commander, good to see you back. I trust the Meyer extraction went well."

"Yes, sir. Miss Meyer is heading to base as we speak, sir. Now if I may, as to my original question?"

Montague sighed. "Commander, Dr. Schreiber here sent me his research request in your absence. I understand the reasoning why you denied his request before—and to his credit, he included that in his request to me. We subsequently arrived at an alternate solution, so I approved it."

Danny's eyes grew wide. "A solution, sir?"

Montague turned and nodded toward the valley below. "That man is a convicted murderer. He's due to be hanged in two weeks. We've offered him a quicker, easier sentence as well as compensation for his ailing mother. And now maybe his death will do even more good, beyond serving justice."

Danny opened his mouth to argue, but Montague held up his hand. "Decision's been made, Commander." And with that, Montague walked off, leaving Danny with Dr. Kurt Schreiber, one of MAJESTIC-12's top scientists.

Before that, Schreiber had been one of Adolf Hitler's top scientists.

"You really, really just want to kill someone, don't you," Danny hissed.

Schreiber merely smiled. "The only difference between what happened at Hiroshima and our nuclear test last year was the fact that, in Japan, people died. If the vortex exhibits any changes during this test, then my theory will be proven correct. If not, then a man already sentenced to die will have at least helped us learn more."

"And I'll ask this yet again, Doctor—how the hell do you even quantify the effect of a person's death? There's nothing scientific about this theory!"

"On the contrary, Commander, it is quite scientific. In physics, we believe that there is no lost energy in the universe. Energy simply changes form into something else. So, what happens to the energy that animates a man in life? The energy that animates his mind? His soul? We do not know, but we know that the energy does not simply dissolve. It goes *somewhere*. And so, now we will see if this particular energy has an effect on our vortex."

Danny opened his mouth to argue further, but thought better of it. "Go over my head again, Doctor, and I'll see that you spend time in the brig for insubordination."

He walked back to where Bronk had settled in next to a series of dials and readouts. "Well?" Bronk asked.

"Pointless," Danny said. "They already decided. It's happening."

Bronk grimaced. "It's immoral. Though I suppose they feel they're clever by using a convict like this."

Danny looked down at the instruments, primed to record the passing of a human being not by eulogy but by radiation and radio pulses. "Too clever."

"You don't have to be here for this," Bronk said. "Schreiber's men can handle it. Montague has the military side of things under control."

"No, I need to be here now. See it through. And if Schreiber is right, I have to figure out how to stop him from executing more people with nukes."

* * *

An hour later, with the observers ten miles away and well upwind, Danny watched as Schreiber pressed a big red button. Of course it had to be a big red button. It probably gave the Nazi a little thrill to press it, the bastard.

Fifteen seconds later, the sky was lit up by blinding nuclear fire. A man's life ended with the ultimate finality—there would be nothing left of him at all, or the chair he sat in, or the ropes that bound him. Nothing except a slightly darker patch of earth already blackened by unnatural heat.

Schreiber didn't even act like he noticed. He was too busy watching his instruments, dials and needles and ticker tapes of data that only a handful of people in the entire world knew how to read.

"Well?" Montague snapped, Danny right at his side.

The Nazi turned and smiled—a smile that sent a chill right up Danny's spine. "There is something here, yes, that we have not seen before," Schreiber said. "A little variance in the radiation patterns that we were not expecting. It is—wait."

The dials and ticker tapes suddenly went nuts.

"What is it?" Danny demanded, all pretense of military decorum gone.

"The vortex, it is issuing another pulse. A strong one!" Schreiber exulted. "It has responded!"

"Responded?" Montague asked. "What horseshit is this?"

Schreiber made a visible effort to compose himself. "It would seem, gentlemen, that the energy expended by this man's death—which had a measurable impact on the vortex—may have prompted the vortex itself to respond with one of the energy bursts that created Variants in the first place."

Danny frowned. "Or maybe it's just coincidence. We've studied this thing for three years now. Still can't predict when or why it does that. It just does."

"It would be an incredible coincidence, Commander, as you no doubt know," Schreiber responded, giving the Navy man a hard-eyed look.

The two stared each other down a moment longer until Montague interrupted. "We have a bearing and altitude of that pulse, Doctor?"

Schreiber finally turned and looked over his readouts, making calculations on a small notepad he kept in his pocket at all times. "Southeast, General. Fairly high altitude. Hard to say without more data."

Montague turned to Danny. "Get your team ready just in case."

"Yes, sir," Danny replied. "And if I may, I strongly suggest that no further experiments with human life be taken until all of the data is thoroughly analyzed. Maybe it's coincidence, maybe it's not. But I don't think we should gamble on it."

The general nodded. "Agreed. Doctor, this should keep you busy awhile. And I'm sure Commander Wallace here will keep you honest."

"I'm sure he will, General," Schreiber said, still smiling.

Danny glared at Schreiber, then fixed Montague with an equally withering look. "Permission to begin work on my report on today's events. *Sir.*"

Montague smirked slightly before turning away from Danny. "Granted. Dismissed," he said breezily before turning his back to talk to Schreiber once more.

Danny stormed off, red-faced with anger. He would make damned sure that everyone in Washington who was cleared for MAJESTIC-12 knew of such a callous disregard for life.

February 3, 1949

Unlike in most other meeting spaces, the man in charge in the White House Cabinet Room never sat at the head of the long, angular table that dominated the room. The President always sat in the very middle, with his back to the windows overlooking the grounds. It made sense, of course, in that nearly everybody in the room had clear sightlines to the President, and the latter could see whoever was talking.

But for Admiral Roscoe Hillenkoetter, the director of the Central Intelligence Agency, there was something amiss about the setup. It had pestered and annoyed him for months—ever since he'd taken over the job, really—until one day it finally hit him.

The pecking order was all botched up.

At normal tables, you'd have the President at the head, followed by his closest aides on either side, continuing on all the way down to the other end, where you might find some junior deputy cabinet secretary hiding behind a notepad. But in the Cabinet Room, that sense of order and power was lost.

Did the man directly across the table from the President— in this case, that goddamn blowhard Jim Forrestal—carry the same weight as Hillenkoetter himself, directly to the President's left? Or were both trumped by Secretary of State Dean Acheson, who sat at Truman's right hand? And Forrestal himself was flanked by Air Force General Hoyt Vandenberg on his left, and Army Secretary Gordon Gray on the right. So, where did *they* stand?

Hillenkoetter hated Washington for so many reasons, but this particular mind game was high up on his list.

"All right, then," Truman said, nodding at Hillenkoetter's deputy, who had just wrapped up the latest intelligence briefing. "Hilly, how are we doing with the Soviet nuclear program? I know Uncle Joe wants an A-bomb, and I want us to be ready when he gets there."

Hillenkoetter cleared his throat. This was a question he was getting tired of repeatedly answering. But this was the President of the United States. "We're still working on it, Mr. President. We're monitoring all their top scientists, as well as the ones they nabbed from the Germans. They seem to have set up shop out in the Kazakh Soviet, near the Chinese and Mongolian borders. No-man's-land, really. Tough to infiltrate. All we can do is send the planes overhead as often as we can get 'em fueled."

"Mr. President," Forrestal interrupted. "We know they're there; we know what they're doing. We've done enough sitting around and keeping watch. We should be taking action."

Hillenkoetter shook his head and looked over at Truman, who had a long-suffering smile on his face.

"Jim, we've been over this," the President said. "Spy planes are one thing. Getting an actual force over there? Dropping a bomb? That's an act of war against the Soviet Union."

"So, we get the Chinese Nationalists to do it, or fund a rising of the Kazakh people," Forrestal pressed.

Hillenkoetter stepped back into the fray. "And how's that going with your Operation NIGHTINGALE, Jim?"

Forrestal frowned sharply. NIGHTINGALE was a Defense Department "special"—one of Forrestal's pet projects, even though it really was a program that probably should've fallen under the CIA's purview. The whole thing was an attempt to train and arm Ukrainian nationals to fight back against the Soviet Union, to create an internal insurrection that, Forrestal hoped, would blossom into a costly and distracting civil war inside the U.S.S.R. The problem was, the Ukrainian nationals Forrestal recruited were Nazi collaborators and sympathizers, more than a few of whom belonged on trial at Nuremburg rather than being trained to fight on behalf of the United States.

"Operation NIGHTINGALE is proceeding as planned, Director," Forrestal snapped. "Training went well, and they're now preparing for insertion into the Ukraine to begin gathering support and material."

Truman leaned back in his chair. "All right, all right. Jim, you keep me posted on the Ukraine. But we're not going to barge into—where is it, Kazakh?—guns blazing. Hilly, are there any special assets we can deploy to help get more out of the Reds' nuclear program?"

"Special assets" was Truman's particular code word for "Variants." For a while, the President had been in favor of using Variants sparingly in the field. But after recent successes outside Prague and elsewhere, the President seemed to be asking about them more and more frequently—which worried Hillenkoetter.

"We're more than a year away from infiltrating the Soviet nuclear program, Mr. President," Hillenkoetter said truthfully. "Their security is just as good as ours was on the Manhattan Project, if not more so. And fully trained physicists don't just pop up overnight. Stalin is very good at keeping close tabs on useful people."

Acheson coughed slightly, his little way of gaining the floor. "I'm sorry, Admiral, but we're going to need better from CIA on this. Surely, you've read the Dulles report."

Hillenkoetter frowned. The Dulles report was a damning broadside against the CIA that criticized the quality of intelligence, the quality of its operatives and analysts, and Hillenkoetter's own leadership. It was the work of Allen Dulles, a Republican lawyer with ties to folks from the old O.S.S. and the new Pentagon. Hillenkoetter had been politically cornered by Forrestal into cooperating with Dulles and his researchers, yet another example that the role of CIA Director was far more political than it needed to be. The results were as Hillenkoetter had expected from the get-go. After all, it was no great secret that Dulles, himself an O.S.S. veteran, had long wanted his name engraved on Hillenkoetter's door.

"I have, Mr. Secretary, and we're still studying it," Hillenkoetter replied. "Off the top of my head, though, we can't give you better intelligence without better assets on the ground. And we can't give you better assets on the ground without better people, but we can't get *them* because A) we don't have an official budget from Congress, so we're left scrounging for leftovers from the Marshall Plan and the Pentagon; and B) Frank Wisner over at OPC is actually outbidding us for talent because he can use the State Department's budget.

"As for criticism of my leadership," Hillenkoetter concluded, sitting up straight, "well, I serve at the pleasure of the President. Always have, always will. I'm not worried about impressing Allen Dulles. I'm worried about getting the best intel I can get."

Hillenkoetter leaned back and gauged the faces around the room. Acheson seemed, if not chagrined, at least appeased, while Forrestal just scowled. Truman, however, looked pleased. "We've got something cooking that'll help get you the budget you need, Hilly. From there, you can take that report, follow through on the recommendations, and get the CIA up to speed."

That was probably the best Hillenkoetter could expect in terms of support. "Yes, Mr. President."

Truman nodded, and turned his National Security Council's attention to other matters. Hillenkoetter listened as attentively as he could manage but couldn't help but find his thoughts drifting. For one, it was his intel that formed the basis of the discussion, and he knew it cold. And he remained worried about any number of other things—the Russian nuclear program, instability in the Middle East, tensions in Berlin and Vienna . . . it was a long, long list.

Finally, Truman ended the meeting with a smile and his usual "Thank you, gentlemen," but tapped Hillenkoetter on the shoulder as the others began to file out—the CIA Director was to remain there. Vandenberg, Gray, and

Forrestal also stayed behind, which meant there could only be one topic at hand—MAJESTIC-12.

"All right, then, let's get down to it," Truman said simply. "How are your trainees coming along, Hilly?"

Hillenkoetter sat up and folded his hands on the table. "Our First Team is back from Vienna with a new recruit— I'm told she can walk through walls, but she's an Austrian national, so we're taking our time vetting her. You'll have the report on her at your desks when you get back to the office. Our Second Team is almost ready to be cleared. And the others are still undergoing training with their Enhancements—most of them remain too unpredictable to use in real-world situations."

"And what's this business about nuclear testing and a convicted murderer?" Truman asked sharply. "Area 51 is starting to sound more like the Wild West. That's not how I want things done around here, Hilly."

Forrestal cleared his throat. "Actually, that's something both Hilly and I signed off on, Mr. President. I know it sounds unorthodox, but we need to better understand the phenomenon we have at Area 51. And our preliminary data is promising. We're making progress."

Truman turned to Hillenkoetter with surprise. "You actually agreed with Jim on this?"

The CIA Director nodded. "I've already gotten an earful from the commander on the ground, but yes."

Truman sat back in his chair and ran a hand over his balding head. "Well, hell. I suppose if it worked . . . but let me tell you this, all of you." The President sat up straight again. "No more of that nonsense. I don't care if it's Hitler's brother you want to use, nobody authorizes any further deaths but me, and I'm going to want to see a mountain of evidence that it's necessary. Are we clear, gentlemen?"

Nods and murmurs floated around the ornate room and settled heavily onto Hillenkoetter's already burdened conscience. He'd known what Schreiber was up to and what Danny's reaction would be, and made the decision anyway. He knew it would haunt him for a very long time. What was worse, of course, was that Schreiber really seemed to be on to something. Even worse than *that*, the scientist seemed to be enjoying it a little too much.

"All right. Now, I have a request from Dean Acheson here that you already responded to, Hilly. He's got a couple of his OPC boys in Damascus who say they need some help from your shop, but Frank Wisner wasn't happy with your reply? What's going on?" Truman asked.

This is not my day, Hillenkoetter thought. The State Department's Office of Policy Coordination was a dirty-tricks department designed to disrupt Soviet machinations overseas without resorting to outright warfare. Some called it "creative diplomacy," but Hillenkoetter knew it was more about propaganda, buying off local politicians, and creating scandals—all with the air of plausible deniability. Plus, Hillenkoetter knew instinctively OPC should be under CIA's direct control, even if Truman had created it as a kind of joint office with CIA and State. It turned out to be a Frankenstein experiment with muddy bureaucracy at its core.

But then again, most of what they were doing now was experimental. There'd never been a peacetime agency devoted solely to intelligence-gathering, let alone an office in any civilian agency devoted to dirty tricks.

"I gave him plenty of options, Mr. President. I've got a dozen different agents he can choose from. Not sure why he hasn't yet, frankly," Hillenkoetter said.

"Any of the Variants on the list you gave him?" Vandenberg asked.

"No, and before you ask, I'd prefer to keep them out of this," Hillenkoetter replied. "They're too valuable to use in things like this Damascus mess OPC has brewing."

Truman raised an eyebrow. "This 'Damascus mess' isn't run-of-the-mill stuff, Hilly. We could seal off the Med coast entirely, keep Uncle Joe stuck in the Black Sea. Plus, we'd lock up all the oil they're exporting. There's a strong national interest at play here."

Hillenkoetter looked around the room and saw nods—and a small smile from Jim Forrestal that made him want to punch the man in the teeth. "So, we're going to use Variants on OPC missions now? We just got through discussing the Russian nuclear program—I need them ready to move on any lead we get there. Isn't that more important?"

Truman stood, with everyone else in the room on their feet an instant later. "You have enough Variants that we don't have to choose one or the other, Hilly. I'm ordering you to send some of your agents to Damascus to help out. I'll leave the duration up to you and the OPC's man on the ground. The OPC folks won't know what they are, so they'll have to keep a low profile but still get the job done. Let's see what they can do. Understood?"

The CIA Director could barely mutter a "Yes, sir" before Truman left the room, the others filing out in his wake.

"And get me more on those Russian nukes!" Truman called out as he exited. "I won't be caught flat-footed!"

Hillenkoetter suddenly wished he was back at sea, rather than adrift in Washington.

CENTRAL INTELLIGENCE AGENCY MEMORANDUM

DATE: February 3, 1949
CLASSIFICATION: TOP SECRET-MAJIK
TO: POTUS, SECDEF Forrestal, SECUSA Gray, GEN Vandenberg
FROM: DCI Hillenkoetter
CC: LCDR Wallace (USN), Dr. Detlev Bronk
RE: Second Team overview

The following report details MAJESTIC-12 staff and evaluators' opinions on the individual Variants currently assigned to MJ-12 Second Team. Overall, we believe this team is near operational efficiency and may be ready for assignment in a matter of weeks.

While the evaluators believe this team will coalesce well, with Enhancements that complement each other, CMDR Wallace believes pairing Second Team individuals with more experienced agents—Variant or otherwise—may also prove fruitful.

CHRISTINA VANOVERBEKE

BIOGRAPHY: Vanoverbeke (DOB 3.21.17, Bowling Green, Ky.) was working as a lounge singer in New York prior to discovering her Enhancement. Her parents are alive, she has a brother and sister, and she is twice divorced. Her career success was limited prior to her Enhancement and subsequent discovery by MAJESTIC-12.

ENHANCEMENT: Vanoverbeke has the super-physical ability to leap great distances in any direction. Her forward
leap has been measured at 776 feet, with her vertical
maximum was measured at 547 feet. These leaps are also
quite rapid and high speed—she can cover ground quickly
and sustainably for several minutes, and climb mountains
in a half-dozen leaps if need be. Furthermore, her body
suffers no damage from the speed or impact of her movements; an explanation for this effect, which defies basic
physics, has not been reached.

DRAWBACKS: Initially, Vanoverbeke had trouble with spontaneous effects, much like other Variants; her ability
would manifest at inopportune moments. Training has mit-
igated this somewhat, but it remains an issue for the time
being. Our analysis indicates these spontaneous effects
may not be fully controlled.

TRAINING: Upon entering training, Vanoverbeke had a
minimal high-school education and slightly below-aver-
age physical fitness. Her spycraft skills have improved
considerably, though she has drawn attention to herself and her looks at times when such is inappropriate.
Her physical skills have improved slightly, though her
Enhancement does not seem tied to her fitness. Her firearms skills are slightly above-average.

EVALUATION: Vanoverbeke's Enhancement lends itself well
to reconnaissance and movement. She also has a talent
for social interaction and infiltration based on charm
and looks, though the evaluators recommend against covering her as a singer, as her talent is somewhat wanting

(hence her relative lack of success in that area). Combat
operations are not recommended, except for scouting.

TIMOTHY SORENSEN

BIOGRAPHY: Sorensen (DOB 6.12.12, Milwaukee, Wis.) was an
electrician in St. Paul, Minn., prior to his Enhancement.
He is married (wife Jessica) with two junior-high-school
children (Bill and Amy), who remain in the St. Paul area.
Parents deceased. High-school education and vocational
training. Sorensen owns his own business, which has since
been sold to augment his government salary.

ENHANCEMENT: Sorensen has the ability to essentially
turn invisible. His skin changes color and texture to
match his background, and also seems to bend light waves.
In shadow or darkness, he can move freely without detection. In bright light or within crowds, his form may
appear as a blur or silhouette if he moves too quickly.
This ability may be kept "on" even while Sorensen sleeps
or is rendered unconscious. It does not, however, mitigate
any sounds he might make.

DRAWBACKS: Sorensen's clothing and items carried do not
become invisible when he does. Thus, Sorensen must be
completely naked and unencumbered prior to activating
his power, thus preventing him from entering his Variant
state while observed. Even the smallest item, such as his
wedding ring, stands out.

TRAINING: Sorensen has a keen mind, with aptitudes in science, mechanics, and engineering. His physical fitness is somewhat above-average, and his training in hand-to-hand and firearms has gone well. His spycraft lessons have been less successful, as he is somewhat unsubtle and, at times, clumsy. Extra training in silent movement has been recommended.

EVALUATION: Reconnaissance and infiltration likely will be Sorensen's strengths, though this will be of limited use until means are developed for him to render carried items invisible as well. He may also serve well in combat operations, particularly while invisible. Social interactions are not a strength; though he is friendly enough, he remains too straightforward and "folksy" for such work.

RICHARD YAMATO

BIOGRAPHY: Yamato (DOB 9.4.30, Sacramento, Calif.) is of Japanese ancestry, and was interned with his family during the war. They returned to their home after the war, and Yamato was about to start his final year of high school in 1948 before his Enhancement took hold. His parents and three siblings remain in Sacramento, and he has told them he enlisted in the United States Army. (Note that this cover may take work, as Yamato's family remains somewhat embittered by their internment experience, as does Yamato.)

ENHANCEMENT: Yamato has the ability to generate and release exceptional amounts of electricity from his body. Over the course of his training, Yamato has produced currents as low as 7.26 milliamps and as high as 10.316 amps, with voltages ranging from 0.37V to 2,127V. In simple terms, he can produce effects ranging from mere static electricity to an overload that could theoretically cause a localized blackout in an urban area.

As part of his training, he has learned to generate shocks that can incapacitate the average person for several minutes, but he can also thoroughly destroy living tissue with greater outputs. Yamato can transmit electricity with a touch, or can cause arcs of electricity to erupt from his body, with a directed range of up to 75 yards. However, the further he is from a target, the less subtle his emanations become. At distant ranges, he can only produce high—voltage, high—ampere lightning arcs.

Yamato has a limited ability to affect existing electrical systems; he can cause burnout quickly, but less subtle manipulation has been only partially successful. While he is immune to the electricity his body generates, all other forms of electrical exposure harm him normally. The source of his electrical generation and output remains unknown at this time.

DRAWBACKS: Yamato's presence among electrical devices can at times prompt small malfunctions——a blown lightbulb in a lamp, a brownout in a home, a loss of power in a car battery. These occurrences can be random, though the evaluators the-orize that they may be related to his emotional state.

TRAINING: Yamato is a bright student with an aptitude for history, language, and tactics. He already speaks Japanese and English fluently, and has taken on Chinese and Spanish since arriving for training. His physical fitness and skills are above average, and he has taken to physical training and combat practice. He has shown occasional flashes of minor insubordination, likely a result of his youth and background.

EVALUATION: Evaluators believe Yamato would be an exceptional combatant, given his Enhancement. Despite his facility with language and a certain innate charm, his Asian background and young age would make it diffi-cult for him to engage in non—combat covert activities. When the idea of covert action in Asian countries came up, Yamato noted that he would be an ill fit in any country other than Japan. In his words: "We may all look alike to you, pal, but trust me, I set one foot in China and they're gonna know I'm not from around there." Evaluators also note that Yamato may need additional supervision due to his attitude and past insubordination.

JULIA MEYER

BIOGRAPHY: Meyer (DOB 4.23.15, Strasbourg, Austria) is an Austrian national and former homemaker. She is

estranged from her husband and family and has no children. Most recently, she had engaged in major thefts
and other criminal activity throughout central Europe,
thanks to the nature of her Enhancement. She has the
equivalent of a high-school education and was a pho-
tography and fine art model before meeting her husband
prior to the war.

ENHANCEMENT: Meyer has the ability to become immaterial, and can move through solid objects. This allows her
to walk through walls and sink through floors with ease,
and she can move underground or through other solids for
as long as she can hold her breath. (She does not need to
hold her breath while immaterial so long as her respira-
tory system is not occupying the same space as a solid.)
She remains visible during this process. Tests on any
number of materials have yet to result in a limitation to
this ability, and she also is immune to fire, electricity
and other energies while immaterial. Furthermore, she can
control the ability to the point where only parts of her
body, such as a hand and arm, become immaterial while the
rest of her stays corporeal.

DRAWBACKS: As with Sorensen's Enhancement, Meyer's
clothing and carried items do not become immaterial with
her--with one exception. Small items that she can clasp
in her hand--items that can be completely surrounded
by her corporeal form--will phase with her and become
effectively immaterial. This facilitated much of her criminal activity. Otherwise, when she becomes immaterial,

her clothing sloughs off her completely and, again, she remains visible to observers.

TRAINING: Having just joined the MAJESTIC-12 program, Meyer is still being assessed. However, her recent activities have given her practical insights into aspects of spycraft and security. She is of average fitness and intelligence.

EVALUATION: Meyer's ability has already proven useful in infiltration, as well as exfiltration of small, easily palmed objects, and she has shown creativity in her recent activities. She also possesses above-average social skills, along with fluency in German, Russian, and English. However, as an Austrian national, her loyalty remains in question; she remains with MAJESTIC-12 under threat of arrest in Austria, though she appears to have warmed to her trainers during her short time in training. Regardless, evaluators recommend careful supervision in any field activities, and field supervisors should have the necessary equipment on hand to neutralize her in case of unauthorized conduct.

February 9, 1949

Danny watched as Julia walked through the Marine Corps obstacle course without breaking stride—or without climbing or crawling, or without getting muddy, or without even cowering under the gunfire overhead from the handful of MAJIK-cleared trainers on either side of the usually treacherous gauntlet.

She just walked, completely naked under the high desert sun at Area 51, oblivious to it all and looking slightly bored with the exercise. Through the barbed wire, through the climbing walls, through the ropes and mud and dummy landmines.

Danny sighed. She wasn't *supposed* to use her Enhancement. The others on her team certainly weren't, even though their specific skills wouldn't be much help to them in this instance. Tim Sorensen, an electrician from St. Paul, had a natural camouflage in his skin so that he could fade into any background; Christina Vanoverbeke, a one-time cabaret singer in New York who could defy gravity with massive leaps and—potentially—even flight, though she hadn't gotten to that point yet; and Rick Yamato, a Japanese teenager who had spent three years in the internment camp at Tule Lake, California, during the war and developed the ability to generate and channel electrical impulses. Zipporah Silverman—Zippy—had been the fourth member of this particular team until the death of Ellis Longstreet in the woods outside Prague last year, when she was transferred to the First Team.

Danny closed his eyes a moment. He'd spent the war as an intelligence analyst. He'd never lost a man under his command until Ellis. The team had been trying to transport a defecting intelligence officer from Prague to Munich when they were set upon by a squad of Soviet Variants— the defector turned out to have been a double agent, and the Soviets had also been receiving intel from a man on the inside at Area 51—a Marine officer and a friend of Danny's from the war.

Danny had executed the traitor in Berlin later that year, and left his body for the Reds to find. It was a harsh thing to do, and Danny wished he'd felt more guilty about it, but he really didn't. The traitor—Danny couldn't bring himself to call him by name anymore—wasn't a Variant. He'd been *scared* of Variants and their potential to change the world.

But Ellis wasn't just a man under Danny's command— they were both Variants. Out of every million people, maybe only one or two would end up with Enhancements, affected somehow by the pulses created by the two white vortexes they knew of in existence: one Danny had found at Hiroshima and transported to Nevada, and the second Frank had seen in Berlin right after the war. So, Danny knew personally just how special Variants were. He wanted to protect them and help them—and the best way, it seemed, to keep the government from deciding they were dangerous and needed to be hunted down was to join their side. That, more than anything else, was Danny's goal for MAJESTIC-12. Yes, he'd taken an oath to serve his country, and so he would. But if he ever had to choose between his country and Variants, well . . . he was happy he'd found a way to avoid that choice. Hopefully for a good long time.

"Meyer, come here!"

The shout came from Maj. John Hamilton, a Marine officer who had served with the O.S.S., the office that had become the CIA. Hamilton was nearly six and a half feet tall, with blond hair and good looks that made him seem like some kind of Viking god. He'd been a commercial sailor prior to the war, with several round-the-world trips under his belt, before hunkering down with Communist insurgents in Yugoslavia to fight the Nazis.

He was a fine replacement for Danny's former-friend-turned-traitor, so long as Danny approved him wandering off base for a few weeks at a time. While he was known on base as John Hamilton, the rest of the world knew him as Sterling Hayden, a rising star in Hollywood. Danny—with Director Hillenkoetter's bemused approval—allowed Hamilton his acting career, so long as he kept it to only one or two films a year. It was a good trade-off: with his military and O.S.S. training, along with his years as a guerilla fighter and his acting ability, Hamilton was just about perfect for the job of getting Variants up to speed.

Plus, Danny liked having him around. He walked over to where Hamilton was giving Julia a good old-fashioned chewing-out as only a Marine could.

"When I goddamn tell you to run the course, you goddamn fucking run the course like God intended—with a rifle in your hand, in the mud like the rest of them!" Hamilton yelled as he bent down slightly to get in the young woman's face. "You don't go prancing off naked as a jaybird and walking through the goddamn walls!"

Julia looked scared—Hamilton could be pretty intense—but did her best to look cool. "But if I don't need to worry about walls, why should I?"

Danny smiled. This was a recurring theme with Julia, who had obviously gotten used to getting whatever she wanted by simply taking it and walking away through the nearest wall. He reached into his pocket for another of the null-zone generators—a bit of technology stolen from the Russians, and one of the only high points of the botched Prague mission. "Because when I turn this on," Danny said, holding the boxy device in his hand and flipping the switch, "you can't walk through anything anymore. We have these. The Russians have these. So, what happens when you can't use your Enhancement? *That's* why we're training you."

Julia frowned. "I see."

"Get your goddamn clothes on and do it again," Hamilton growled. "And if you don't beat everyone else's time, you'll do it again just to be sure. Move it."

With an outsized sigh, Julia turned and sauntered back to the start of the course, where her uniform and boots remained on the ground in the spot where she'd sloughed through them.

"She's a fine-looking woman, I'll say that," Hamilton said with a smile, his tough-guy act gone in an instant.

"I suppose she is," Danny said, a bit indifferently. "Remember the rules, Hollywood. Save it for when you're on leave for the next film."

Hamilton smiled. "It'll be a Western. *El Paso*. I get to be the bad guy this time. We start shooting in a few months. Meantime, will you get that girl some clothes that'll stick to her?"

Danny laughed. "I have Mrs. Stevens working on it. You know how she is, though. Million little projects going on all at once. Tough to get her to focus."

"She's a housewife, Danny. Why's a housewife working here? Hell, she asked for my autograph last week!"

The two began walking back toward the course, where Hamilton prepared to spray fire over Julia's head as she did the course again—properly this time. "Mrs. Stevens is a certified genius, John. Her IQ tests were off the charts, and she seems to gain a few points each time we test her, even with all new questions. She'll soon be smarter than Einstein."

Hamilton laughed and shook his head as he prepared his rifle. "How the hell do you even command someone like that? Doesn't she question everything?"

"Not yet," Danny said. "Certainly keeps me on my toes, though."

"Yeah, well, these folks ever decide they've had enough of this—you know, as a group? Gonna be hard to keep 'em in check." Hamilton then looked over at Julia, who was just now lacing up her boots. "Get a move on, Meyer! I ain't got all fucking day!"

Danny gave the tall Marine a slap on the back. "I trust you got a handle on them, John. I'm going to be off on assignment with First Team in a couple weeks. Shouldn't be away for more than a month. Montague will be spending more time here, but I'm leaning on you to keep things going."

Julia began crawling through the mud under strings of barbed wire, her dummy rifle in hand and a heavy pack on her back. Hamilton squeezed off a few rounds over her head that made her flinch. "Roger that, Commander. Where you going?"

"Can't say, other than I'll have a great tan when I get back. Thanks, John."

Danny headed back toward his jeep and driver, leaving Hamilton to fantasize about sand, palm trees, beaches, and girls in swimsuits. At least he had the sand part right.

The young Air Force private drove Danny past the small mini-camp that housed the Second Team of four Variants. There were three such camps around Groom Lake, a dried lakebed in the Nevada mountains. Each camp had individual quarters for the Variants, a mess hall that also served as classroom and gymnasium—and a guard installation to support at least twenty MPs. Each was surrounded by a one-mile perimeter of barbed wire, and there was a guard tower in the middle with excellent sightlines. There were at least two miles of desert between each of the camps and the main Area 51 base, where scientific research around the vortex continued.

That was also where most of the paperwork surrounding MAJESTIC-12 got done. Secret projects, Danny found, required a lot of pencil-pushing. Requisitions had to be made through at least a few dozen different channels in time-consuming, roundabout ways. Personnel had to be screened and assigned to areas according to their clearances—Danny, Hamilton, Mrs. Stevens, and Schreiber were the only ones fully aware of everything that went on at Area 51. The people studying the Variants had no clue about the vortex, and vice versa. And the MPs knew well enough to keep their noses out of everything that didn't have to do with perimeter security and guarding the "trainees."

As Danny's jeep pulled up to the main base at Area 51, which was dominated by a huge hangar housing the vortex and other scientific gear, he wondered just how long something this *big* could remain this secret. They had layered several different stories under different classifications for MAJESTIC-12—one of the false cover stories even had to do with a recovered "alien flying saucer," which had been Danny's idea. But still, there were over 150 people at Area 51 now, and some of them would surely say something at some point. There was a naked woman walking through walls in broad daylight, for crying out loud.

The jeep pulled up to the administrative building, and Danny hopped out and headed inside. He and the MAJESTIC-12 sponsors had done everything possible to secure both the Variants and their secrets. It would have to do; he had more pressing matters to worry about, especially since he was heading to Damascus in a couple weeks.

But it turned out that when Danny got to his office, there was one more matter of concern waiting for him.

"General Montague, sir!" Danny said, quickly coming to attention and snapping off a salute. "Didn't expect you here, sir."

Montague returned the salute and extended his hand. "Heard you were heading out of town, figured we should powwow before you do."

Danny shook the general's hand and took a seat behind his desk. Montague was cleared for MAJESTIC-12, of course, given that he had nominal command of Area 51; Danny was technically Montague's deputy but had independent operational command of the Variant assets as well. It was a messy situation, and it wasn't always clear just how much Montague knew. But Danny was damn sure Montague wasn't copied in on his Damascus orders.

Secret government conspiracies were a pain in the ass in more ways than one.

"Of course, General. Major Hamilton will have operational command of the Variants, answerable to myself and DCI Hillenkoetter while I'm gone. He'll continue to have responsibility for Area 51 security as well, answerable to you, of course," Danny said evenly.

"And the scientific inquiries?" Montague asked.

"Variant training and assessment will still go through Detlev Bronk, while any work on the vortex will continue to be conducted by Dr. Schreiber. Both of them remain under my command, and I report directly to DCI Hillenkoetter on these matters," Danny replied. To an outsider, the MAJESTIC-12 organizational chart would look perfectly Byzantine, but Danny knew quite well whom to report to on what. Very little of it involved directly reporting to Montague, though the Navy man was sure the Air Force general would like that changed.

"And while you're away, Commander?"

Danny frowned slightly at this. "That has yet to be determined, General. It's one of the queries I have out to Director Hillenkoetter right now, in fact."

Montague nodded and sat back in his chair. "Since I'm responsible for this base, I obviously know about the Russian you have here. POSEIDON is his code name, yes?"

POSEIDON was a Russian MGB agent—a Variant, in fact—captured by MAJESTIC-12 Variants in Istanbul the previous year. POSEIDON had the ability to "pull" objects toward him at high speeds, a kind of psychokinetic Enhancement. He couldn't push them away, oddly, but that didn't matter when fully grown men could be yanked through the air with a single thought.

Until the null-zone generators were captured from the Russians and refined, POSEIDON had been kept in a special underground cell the size of several football fields, and almost constantly drugged to the point where he couldn't use his Enhancement. Now, however, they simply kept a null-zone generator just outside his cell at all times, rendering him powerless but also giving him a small semblance of his life back.

"Yes. What about him, sir?" Danny asked, his brow furrowed.

"How has your interrogation and study of him been going?"

Danny paused but recognized that Montague had the clearance to hear the details; he just didn't need to readily provide them. "We've been able to establish a baseline on his Enhancement in terms of range and impact, and we've regularly sat down for conversations. We haven't gotten very far, of course. He's not in the mood to cooperate much, given that we kept him drugged up for the better part of four months."

"And how is that study and interrogation going to continue while you're gone, Commander?" Montague asked, a little too pointedly for Danny's taste.

"Dr. Bronk will take the lead on both counts, sir."

Montague seemed to think about this for a moment, then smiled. "All right, Commander. I expect a full report on all activities here before you go, including who's responsible for what during your absence." The general rose, and Danny quickly followed suit. "I'll have a look around before I go. Anything else you wish to report?"

Danny thought a moment. "Looks like Second Team may be cleared for operations in a few weeks, sir. We may need some more air assets on standby if we have two full teams going."

Montague nodded. "Noted. Thank you, Commander."

Danny saluted, and Montague gave a half-wave in return on his way out, leaving the young Navy man to sit back down at his desk, worried. Montague occasionally asked about individual Variants, but more out of curiosity than anything else. The only real reason the two-star was involved in MAJESTIC-12 at all was because he had nominal command over the old Indian Springs Army Air Force Station that ultimately became Area 51. It was his Air Force personnel who kept the place secure, kept the scientists and Variants fed, and provided all the infrastructure needed to keep the place going.

But Danny also knew quite well that Montague was Jim Forrestal's eyes and ears at Area 51, and that Forrestal and Danny's boss, Director Hillenkoetter, had little respect for each other.

Danny got up and headed out of his office to go see his clerk, who immediately snapped to attention. "You know where Dr. Bronk is, Airman?" Danny asked.

"Labs, I think, sir. Said he was going to talk to Mrs. Stevens."

Danny nodded and returned the man's salute before walking off once more, this time out of the administrative building and into the main labs, passing through two sets of ID checks and a pat-down before he was allowed to walk freely inside the massive hangar-sized building. Danny was perhaps the most widely recognized person at Area 51, but even still, they took security seriously.

He paused to look in on the main lab, where the anomaly was housed. It remained utterly inscrutable—a six-foot-by-six-foot swirl of white light in the middle of the room that, surprisingly, gave off little actual light. A series of magnetic containment generators, little two-by-two boxes hooked up to the electrical plant, sat on the floor, surrounding it. For whatever reason, the vortex always remained 37.473 inches above the ground, hovering, no matter how or when they moved it. Even when moved to other buildings or even ships, it stayed exactly that high above the decking.

It was a calamity of physics. Even Albert Einstein, consulted discreetly the previous year, said it had no business existing. And yet there it was.

A handful of techs sat at consoles, monitoring radio and radiation emissions. The techs looked bored; the vortex would randomly erupt in a burst of invisible emissions and swirl a bit more from time to time, but there was no discernible schedule to it. And so they waited. Meanwhile, Schreiber and his team likely were elsewhere in the building, concocting new experiments they hoped would finally get this impossible phenomenon to spill its secrets.

Hopefully, Schreiber wouldn't try to kill anyone else. At least the executive order had been clear on that.

Danny continued on down the hall and up a flight of stairs, heading toward one of the smaller labs and looking through each glass-paned door until he spied Bronk talking with Mrs. Stevens in her lab. Danny smiled; nothing put him in a good mood like being around her quirky genius.

"How's my world-conquering super-laser coming, Mrs. Stevens?" Danny asked as he entered the lab—the cleanest and most neatly organized laboratory west of the Mississippi. Everything had a file folder, every file had a neat stack or a cabinet. Every piece of equipment was in its place, every pen neatly lined up in a row on a worktable. Everything—right down to the blank notebooks and paperclips—had a designated location, cleanly labeled in a crisp, elegant hand.

"Commander!" Mrs. Stevens said, her pearly white smile broad. "I'd hoped you might stop by. I was just telling Dr. Bronk here how much I'm enjoying my time these days. So many fun little challenges you've given me lately! Why, I could be in here all day if I didn't have to head home to make Mr. Stevens dinner!"

Mrs. Stevens was thin and blonde, hair perfectly coiffed and pinned into an elaborate updo. She wore a red-and-white dress that had a distinct "alpine maiden" look to it, with poofed-up sleeves and broad skirts, matching it with sensible two-inch patent leather heels and a string of pearls. Danny had been invited over for a dinner party once, and he knew full well that Mrs. Stevens could turn Army rations into a gourmet feast if need be.

She also happened to be an off-the charts, genuine genius, courtesy of her own Enhancement. She was a Variant as well and, for the past year, an engineer and inventor of the highest caliber.

"How is Mr. Stevens getting along?" Danny asked as he gently took her extended hand. The only way to get Mrs. Stevens to work for MAJESTIC-12 was to allow her to continue to mother-hen her husband and two kids. So, Danny had hired the husband to do maintenance around the less-secure parts of the base, and the two kids had joined a handful of others—children of other scientists and officers—as playmates and classmates in a tiny one-room school near the administrative building.

"Oh, he likes it fine, just fine, Commander. It's far more interesting than his old factory job. He likes that he's thinking on his feet every day, solving all those little maintenance problems. It's so good for him!"

Danny wondered for a moment just how a sturdy, working-class man like Mr. Stevens was coping with his wife's newfound intellect, but knew far better than to ask. "I'm glad, Mrs. Stevens. So, what are we up to today?"

She dashed over to a cupboard near her worktable and withdrew a neatly folded bundle of cloth. "Well, I think I might have a solution for you on those Variants with those pesky cellular-matter reactions," she said, unfolding the cloth.

"Come again?" Danny asked.

Bronk took pity on him. "Julia and Tim. The ones who have to be naked for their abilities to function properly."

"Oh, right. You know, I only asked you about that a couple days ago," Danny said.

"Well, Mrs. Stevens here thought it imperative that we protect the modesty of our fellow guests, especially poor Julia," Bronk replied, a half-grin on his long face. "Besides, it'll help with operational readiness."

"Fair enough. What'cha got, Mrs. Stevens?"

Danny saw that the lady was blushing slightly as she began; she occasionally got flustered with certain language like, apparently, the word "naked."

"Well, as you know, the null-field devices we got from the Soviets use a mix of radio and non-ionized radiation across a broad spectrum to create pockets of space in which Variant Enhancements don't work. So, that was my first idea—gosh, if we can stop Enhancements from happening, can we create matter that works *with* Enhancements as well through the same methods? I mean, it seemed so simple!"

"Sure," Danny said slowly, playing along as if he followed purely for her benefit. He wasn't a physicist and knew only that the null-field devices worked. Bronk had tried to explain it once, and Danny had quit on him after five minutes.

"So, here you have a cloth with some insulated metallic threads running through it," she went on, holding up a two-foot-square piece of dark fabric. "I went ahead and compared the data we got on those vortex emissions—you know, when it acts all funny—and cross-referenced it with the emissions from the null-field device. Well, I asked one of the boys to do that. I don't like being around those things, you understand."

"Of course," Danny assured her. "Nobody does."

"Anyhoo, I hypothesized that if we altered those emissions and then channeled the energy into a more contained matrix—this cloth—we might have a material that would actually adopt the characteristics of a Variant's enhancement. Now, it wouldn't do me or Mr. Hooks any good, of course, but for Mr. Sorensen and especially poor Miss Meyer, well, it might help them out a lot!"

Danny reached out and felt the fabric between his fingers. "So, you're saying that when Tim camouflages or Julia walks through a wall, this would go with them?"

"Well, we'd have to test it, but sure. I think so," Mrs. Stevens said brightly. "That's the idea, anyways. In fact, we might even be able to make pockets to allow Miss Meyer to carry things with her. Wouldn't that be nice?"

Danny smiled broadly. "That it would, ma'am. That it would. Tell you what—why don't you take this down to the training area where Tim and Julia are. Tell Major Hamilton I sent you. Let's give it a whirl and see if it works. Sound good?"

Mrs. Stevens looked at the clock. "Hmmm . . . sure, Commander. I can scoot down there and back before dinner, I think. But I should get going! If you gentlemen will excuse me?"

The two men agreed, and Mrs. Stevens carefully packed up the cloth and an altered null-zone generator before heading out the door, her heels clicking smartly down the hall.

"I love that girl," Bronk said after she was gone. "I want to put her and Wernher von Braun in a room together for a day or two. We'll be sending men to Jupiter inside of a week."

Danny smiled at that but quickly turned serious. "We might have a problem. Montague just showed up, and he's sniffing around POSEIDON. He knew I was leaving."

Bronk scowled and ran a hand across his balding gray head. "Well, nelly. That's a problem. You think he's going to try to pull rank again?"

"I don't doubt it. I'm going to talk with Hamilton, too, but between the two of you, I want to be damn sure that Montague doesn't go near POSEIDON. More importantly, I don't want Schreiber near him, either. If anything goes squirrelly, you get on the horn to Foggy Bottom and let Hillenkoetter know ASAP. Got it?"

"Yeah, I got it," Bronk said, leaning up against a worktable with a sigh. "You know, we gotta get Mrs. Stevens on the vortex. Think about what she could do with it. We'd have the damn thing cracked in a week."

"I know, but we can't," Danny said. This wasn't the first time Bronk had brought up the idea. "Direct presidential order: no known Variants are to be in the same room as that vortex. Period."

"All right, but can I at least show her some more data? You saw just now what she did with the numbers I gave her."

Danny thought about this for a moment, then smiled. "Well, it's not a *direct* violation of any orders. Just keep it under your hat. Let's see what she can do."

FROM: DCI HILLENKOETTER
TO: LCMR WALLACE USN, LT LODGE USA, MR. HOOKS CIA,
MISS DUBINKSY CIA, MISS SILVERMAN CIA
CC: MR. COPELAND OPC, MR. MEADE OPC
RE: DAMASCUS OPERATION
CLASSIFICATION: TOP SECRET

YOU ARE HEREBY ORDERED TO TRAVEL TO DAMASCUS, SYRIA,
AS PART OF A CIA-OPC JOINT OPERATION UNDER COMMAND
OF MR. COPELAND. THE PURPOSE OF THE OPERATION IS:

- TO DENY PORTS OF CALL TO SOVIET FORCES ALONG THE
  EASTERN MEDITERRANEAN COAST.

- TO SECURE OIL RESERVES FROM TRANSJORDAN, IRAQ,
  AND SAUDI ARABIA TO MEDITERRANEAN PORTS UNDER
  NOMINAL U.S. OR ALLIED CONTROL.

YOU WILL ASSIST MR. COPELAND AND MR. MEADE IN
ENCOURAGING THE CURRENT PRESIDENT OF SYRIA, SHUKRI
AL-QUWATLI, TO CLOSE OFF DIPLOMACY AND TRADE WITH
THE U.S.S.R., AND TO APPROACH ISRAEL FOR POSSIBLE PEACE
TALKS.

BARRING THIS, YOU WILL SUPPORT MR. COPELAND AND
MR. MEADE IN PROVIDING ADVICE TO SYRIAN COL. HUSNI
AL-ZA'IM, ONE OF THE COUNTRY'S MILITARY LEADERS AND
A LEADING CANDIDATE TO BECOME THE NATION'S NEXT
PRESIDENT.

UNDER NO CIRCUMSTANCES ARE YOU TO PROVIDE ANY DIRECT
SUPPORT TO EITHER AL-QUWATLI OR AL-ZA'IM, OR BE
IDENTIFIED AS WORKING FOR THE UNITED STATES IN ANY
CAPACITY BEYOND DIPLOMATIC.

YOU WILL BE PROVIDED WITH DIPLOMATIC CREDENTIALS AT
THE LEGATION IN DAMASCUS, AND WILL BE REQUIRED TO
REPORT TO JAMES KEELEY, HEAD OF THE LEGATION, AS
REQUIRED. KEELEY IS CLEARED FOR ALL OPC ACTIVITY, BUT
IS NOT WITHIN THE CHAIN OF COMMAND.

THE SUCCESS OF YOUR MISSION WILL BE DETERMINED BY
THE IMPLEMENTATION OF STABLE PRO-U.S. POLICIES BY THE
SYRIAN GOVERNMENT.

(SIGNED) HILLENKOETTER.

ADDENDUM
TOP SECRET-MAJIK
MAJESTIC-12 EYES ONLY
FROM: DCI HILLENKOETTER
TO: WALLACE, LODGE, HOOKS, DUBINKSY, SILVERMAN
CC: POTUS, SECDEF FORRESTAL
RE: DAMASCUS OPERATION

COPELAND, MEADE, AND KEELEY ARE NOT MAJIK-CLEARED.
ANY MAJESTIC-12 KNOWLEDGE, INCLUDING KNOWLEDGE OF
YOUR ENHANCEMENTS AND YOUR NATURE AS VARIANTS, MUST
REMAIN CONFIDENTIAL. ANY USE OF YOUR ABILITIES IN THE

COURSE OF OPERATIONS IN SYRIA MUST BE DONE WITHOUT
THEIR KNOWLEDGE.

FURTHERMORE, YOUR ABILITIES AND NATURE MUST BE
KEPT FROM ALL SYRIAN NATIONALS, FROM OTHER FOREIGN
NATIONALS, AND FROM ANY OTHER U.S. CITIZENS IN YOUR
AREA OF OPERATIONS. CONTACT WITH AGENTS OF THE U.S.S.R.
AND OTHER COMMUNISTS MUST BE KEPT TO A MINIMUM.

FINALLY, ANY VARIANTS ENCOUNTERED IN THE COURSE
OF YOUR DUTIES MUST BE CONTACTED, ASSESSED, AND, IF
POSSIBLE, BROUGHT TO THE UNITED STATES. THIS SUPERCEDES
ALL OTHER ORDERS REGARDING THE DAMASCUS OPERATION
AND ANY OPC AUTHORITY.

LCMR WALLACE IS ASSIGNED TO THIS OPERATION ONLY
TO ASSIST IN THE SEARCH FOR UNKNOWN OR OPPOSITION
VARIANT OPERATIVES IN THE DAMASCUS REGION. ONCE
THIS SEARCH IS CONCLUDED, HE IS CLEARED TO RETURN TO
AREA 51 TO CONTINUE OTHER MAJESTIC-12 DUTIES. IN HIS
ABSENCE, LT LODGE WILL BE IN COMMAND OF MAJESTIC-12
ASSETS IN DAMASCUS, REPORTING TO DCI HILLENKOETTER
AND LCMR WALLACE ON ALL RELATED MATTERS.

(SIGNED) HILLENKOETTER

6.

February 22, 1949

Maggie stepped out into the cool afternoon air and was immediately grateful for the light coat she'd lugged all the way from Washington. All the photos she'd seen of Damascus showed men in Arab robes, camels, and palm trees, so she assumed that she'd be stepping into a sweltering desert, like something out of *Lawrence of Arabia*. Instead, like nearly every other airport she'd seen, she emerged out of customs and into a swarm of people speaking half a dozen different languages, all trying to find a ride into the city.

And it was chilly! She bundled her blue coat around her and adjusted the bright-red hat she'd bought for the occasion. She was posing as an American diplomat's fiancée, excited to rejoin her love here at the edge of the Middle East, though thinking of Frank as anything other than a colleague was something of a stretch. Nice guy, sure, but a little too muscle-bound and meatheaded sometimes. Plus, she doubted any woman could compete with the ghosts in that man's head.

She smiled as she walked out into the sun and saw a palm tree—finally!—and a horse-drawn cart being loaded with crates and boxes, fighting for space with cars and trucks of seemingly every vintage made since Henry Ford started production. Looking around, she tried to find her own ride, but found there were enough white faces mixed in with the Arab-looking folks to make it more difficult than she'd thought. *At least they won't be wearing fezzes or headscarves,* she thought bleakly as she craned her neck to see above the crowd.

"Miss Jones! Miss Jones! Is that you?"

It look a moment for Maggie to register that yes, here in Damascus, that was her name—Maggie Jones. She'd have to work on that, she thought as she turned toward the voice. A somewhat short, round-faced man with dark round glasses and slicked-back hair ambled up to her with a genial smile on his face, one hand in the pocket of his rumpled, off-the-rack suit, the other hand extended. "Miss Jones! There you are!"

She smiled and turned, gently taking his hand in a way she hoped would be appropriately demure. "My hero! Thank you for rescuing me. You must be Mr. Copeland?"

"Yes, yes, Miles Copeland from the consulate. So glad you made it! Frank will be terribly pleased to see you again. How was the trip?" he asked, deftly grabbing her suitcase and motioning for her to follow as he made his way through the throng.

"Oh, you know. Washington to Halifax to Iceland to Scotland to Paris to Venice to Istanbul to here. I surely hope I don't have to travel in an airplane again anytime soon!" she said airily, slipping into the role a little better now. "Is the consulate far? I am hoping to freshen up."

Copeland stopped next to a rather dispirited-looking Volkswagen, popping the front hood and heaving her suitcase inside. "Depends on traffic," he said with a smirk. "It's market day. But you'll definitely get to see the sights."

Maggie saw there were two others already in the car—one was a rather wiry, muscular man sitting in the passenger seat, and the other was Frank Lodge, in the back. She nonetheless waited for Copeland to open the door for her, as she imagined "Maggie Jones" would expect of any man.

"When'd you get in, Frank?" she asked as she settled in.

"This morning—went through Rome and had some delays. Maggie, this is Stephen Meade," Frank said, nodding toward the front of the car.

The man in the passenger seat turned and extended a hand. He seemed compact yet strong, with a weathered, tanned face that could've been on a cigarette ad. "Pleasure to meet you, Miss Dubinsky. I hear tell you're quite the asset."

Maggie shook hands—he had a strong grip that she could tell was held back for her expense. Through her Enhancement, she could also tell he already had taken a bit of a fancy to her, and she resisted the urge to tamp it down in his head. "I get by," she said shortly. "And call me Miss Jones. I have enough trouble keeping the names straight."

Meade nodded and turned back toward the front of the car without another word. Copeland got in, gunned the engine—"gunned" being a relative term for what surely had to be the sickliest vehicle in Damascus—and swerved into traffic with all the gusto of a practiced cabbie.

"Nice outfit," Frank remarked. "You usually don't get all fancied up."

"Playing the part. I had a friend help me pick it out."

Frank arched his eyebrow and smiled. "You have girly friends now?"

Maggie frowned. Frank didn't need to know that it was really just a super-helpful girl at Woodward & Lothrop in downtown D.C. "You could use a good makeover yourself, pal. That suit of yours looks beat to hell."

Frank smiled, and Maggie caught Copeland and Meade trading a look, their amusement palpable to her senses. She didn't care; she wasn't going to keep the lady act up for a minute longer than she had to.

"All right, mission briefing time," Copeland said. "We know for sure nobody's going to listen in on a moving car. You two all read up?"

Frank nodded. "Your buddy Colonel Za'im is trying to stir up opposition against President al-Quwatli, hoping he can take over. If we back him, he'll then be in a position to clamp down on any efforts by the Reds to stick their noses in the Middle East."

"And he'll also approve the Trans-Arabian Pipeline project," Maggie added. "That means a short trip to the Med for all that oil in Saudi Arabia. So, how's your buddy making out?"

Copeland maneuvered deftly between a tram and a camel as the car entered the outskirts of Damascus proper. "He's got enough of the army with him to make a proper move, what with al-Quwatli's mishandling of the war with Israel last year. But they need a reason. Al-Quwatli is still pretty popular on the street, even though the politicos wish he hadn't run for reelection last year. He's been cozying up to the Syrian Communist Party lately and, well, we can't have that. But that doesn't matter to the army—they need something more damning to hang their hat on."

Maggie watched out the window as they drove, noting the beautiful array of stone buildings—some new, some looking as old as time—huddled together on the narrow streets. Colorful awnings stretched over stands of fruit and trinkets for the people strolling by. There were men in full Bedouin robes, men in dapper suits and fezzes, women in swaths of cloth that covered all but their eyes, and ladies in the smartest fashion this side of Paris. Signs in English, French, and Arabic all fought for attention amid the bustle. "And we're here to give them the reason," she said absently. "Without making it look like the U.S. is involved because, at the moment, most of the Middle East hates us for Israel."

"*And* for all the colonialism," Meade reminded her. "They hate the French and British far more, but we got lumped right in there with 'em. There's a strong Arab nativist movement going on. Toss the Turks, toss the French, toss the British, toss everybody. Us, too."

"And the Russians?" Frank asked.

"Different story there," Copeland said, a touch of frustration evident in his voice. "The Reds are seen as being more like the Arabs—once ruled by elites, having taken power for themselves. There's still some mistrust, but the Syrians just don't have the bad history with Russia that they've had with the West."

"And we're sure that Za'im is gonna play ball?" Frank asked. "Seems like he's going against the tide here."

"Husni al-Za'im got his start in the Ottoman Army, then went into the occupation French forces before finally siding with the nationalists and ending up in charge of the Syrian military, such as it is," Meade replied. "He's far more of a secularist than a lot of the Arab nativists. Syria has a strong Christian minority, some Jews—a mix of everybody, really. He wants a modern state with no official view on religion or ethnicity, unlike a lot of other folks who want the whole thing to be driven by Muslims. Za'im's a Kurd from up by the Turkish border. He's a Western guy, very level-headed. He'll be fine."

Copeland muttered something ugly under his breath as he nearly avoided a collision with a bicyclist carrying a ridiculously large basket strapped to his back. "Like you said, Miss Jones, we need something he can hang his hat on. Al-Quwatli won the election because he was seen as a hero of Syrian independence and a steady hand at the helm. We have to shake that perception, make him look like he's not in control."

"And how do we do that?" Maggie asked.

She could sense the satisfaction emanating from Copeland. "You're gonna love it."

* * *

Cal sat upright as Lorraine Copeland refilled his teacup. "Really, ma'am. I can manage just fine myself. You should sit down and rest some."

The young blonde, at least seven months pregnant by Cal's guess, simply smiled at him as she finished pouring. "Nonsense, Mr. Hooks," she said in a light Scottish accent. "You're a guest in my home, and I'll not leave any of Miles's friends to fend for themselves. Honestly, I'm delighted for the company."

Cal leaned back and returned the smile, marveling at the hospitality. Crying shame he had to travel halfway around the world to be treated this well in a white woman's home, but he was grateful for it regardless. Maybe it was because she was European, or maybe because he was an official guest of the American Consulate.

"Well, you got that fine young man to take care of," Cal said as Lorraine finally and carefully took a seat. "Named after his daddy?"

"Miles the Third and three times the trouble," she laughed. "Oh, that boy. So glad we have Haya to help me out with things. I just can't keep up with him these days. Little whirlwind, he is."

Cal remembered the little blond boy's curiosity when he'd arrived the previous day, his flights having taken him through Africa en route to Damascus. He'd been covered as an African businessman seeking investment in Ethiopia, the former Italian holding on the Horn of Africa. This was Cal's first outing without explicit diplomatic protection, which made him distinctly nervous, but Copeland had assured him the consulate would step in to help if things got sticky.

"So, how'd a young man like you end up working with, well . . . your particular agency?" Lorraine asked.

"Well, I ain't that young, ma'am, but thank you for saying so," Cal said, remembering that he looked a good twenty years younger than his actual age, thanks to his Enhancement. "They just needed someone with my skills, I suppose. And there are times when having a Negro around is a good thing—either I draw all the attention away from other folks, or nobody pays attention and I do what needs doing."

"You're like me, then," she said with a mischievous grin. "Miles has people in and out of here at all hours, but I'm the one who does what needs doing."

"And you're mighty fine at it. It's a wonderful home."

That wasn't just a shallow compliment; Cal really loved the place. The house was the light beige of desert clay, with a central courtyard featuring a small fountain that gurgled quietly into a brightly tiled basin. Tile work adorned the trim around the place, and creeping vines kept things looking lush. Inside, parquet wood floors and arched windows brought in breezes, while fans—likely a critical necessity during the summer—hung motionless from the high ceilings. Overall, it was a small, modest house but well appointed.

They'd been enjoying the courtyard earlier, but the evening chill had driven them inside to Copeland's study, which was adorned with French furniture, and the walls were lined with books. A Decca turntable had pride of place on a beautifully wrought credenza next to a radio. There were a fair number of albums there as well, mostly jazz. A trumpet stood on a stand next to the credenza—Copeland had already boasted of the time he played fourth trumpet with the Glenn Miller Orchestra. Cal was more of a Dizzy Gillespie fan, but that still seemed pretty good.

Cal looked up to see Danny and Zippy come in. "They're here, finally," Danny said. "Miles said they had some traffic. Be here in a moment."

Zippy went over to Lorraine. "How's the little one doing today?" she asked with a smile.

"He's a kicker, this one," she replied. "Or she, I suppose, but no girl would bat me around like this one."

Danny was wearing his U.S. Navy-issued shipboard khakis—he had official cover as a defense attaché—while Zippy wore a dark-gray lady's suit. She was covered as a reporter from *The Palestine Post* in Jerusalem, which Cal figured was a right fine idea, given how reporters were always poking their noses into things.

"How was your walk around town?" Cal asked Danny with an arched eyebrow. *Any other Variants around?*

Danny wrinkled his brow a bit as he took a seat and waved away Lorraine as she tried to get up to pour more tea. "It was fine, I guess. May want to check it out again tomorrow."

Cal couldn't get a read on what that might've meant, but was distracted as Copeland and Meade entered the study with Frank and Maggie in tow. Cal shook hands with his newly arrived teammates, and was surprised when Maggie gave him a brief hug. That wasn't really her thing, but maybe she was still playing her cover.

"Lorraine, darling, why don't you check on little Miles for a bit," Copeland said. "I'm afraid we have some things to discuss."

Lorraine smiled and stood, gratefully taking Zippy's offered hand, then excused herself quickly. Cal figured Miles had a fair number of interesting folks at his house. Meanwhile, Copeland walked over and put a record on the turntable—Cal was delighted to see it was Coleman Hawkins' "Picasso"—and soon the sounds of the master saxophonist provided background music to their discussion. "Just in case there are ears out there," Copeland said with a smile.

Drinks were poured—Copeland had some Scotch and gin stowed on one of his bookshelves—and then Copeland sat down at his desk and lit a cigarette, waving the others toward the sofas and chairs around the room.

"All right, let's get to it. In one week, al-Quwatli is having a diplomatic reception at the Syrian House of Representatives. That's our next, best chance to have a meaningful sit-down with Za'im and a couple of his supporters. Two of you should be there so we have the numbers. Who's coming?"

Frank looked around. "We could probably only get away with one of the ladies, not both. So, how about me and Maggie? Or do you think Zippy would be better, Danny?"

"I think Zippy would be better off," Danny said. "Maggie can get a bead on him during the reception. Cal and I will do the perimeter work. Sound good?"

"Fine," Copeland said. "Colonel Meade here will join you on watch. And I think Miss Silverman will be great. We can add in the pressure to get an armistice with Israel going."

"And what else will we be discussing?" Zippy asked.

"Well, every time we meet, I make sure we get commitments on the big three, as I like to call them: keeping the Reds out, peace with Israel, and getting the TAPline done. No doubt Za'im will ask for money—he *always* asks for money. But aside from a little bit of a slush fund, we're not committing anything until he's settled in as president. We're not throwing good money after bad."

"Anything else?" Frank asked.

"We want to be sure, of course, that his coup planning is going well, and we'll pore over it afterward to see if there's any holes we can help plug," Copeland said. "And finally, we'll get to our own operation, which I think will tip the scales against al-Quwatli and give Za'im the excuse he needs to take over."

"Right," Danny said, leaning forward with interest. "And what is this op, exactly?"

Copeland smiled. "It's kind of an open secret that I'm the American you talk to when you *really* want to get things done. Jim Keeley is the official envoy here, though al-Quwatli still hasn't let him present his credentials—it's been months. That's another reason we're doing this; al-Quwatli isn't even listening to our official envoys, let alone me or anyone from England or France.

"So, anyway, like I said, I'm kind of the operations guy, and most of the folks in the Syrian government know I'm probably the liaison to State and CIA. I don't mind—Meade here has a deeper cover. It's good to have a figurehead. And that's what we're going to use in a few weeks when we trick the Syrian government into raiding my house."

The words hung silently in the room for several long moments before Cal couldn't take it anymore. "You mean to say, Mr. Copeland, you're going to try to get the Syrians to actually break in? Right here?"

Copeland grinned. "That's exactly right, Mr. Hooks. Like I said, they know I handle some of the intelligence work. All I have to do is make it known that I have some intel here at the house, something that has to do with the Syrian government itself. I'm thinking something on the Ba'ath Party, which al-Quwatli hates. Everybody hates the Ba'athists. He's going to want to know exactly what's going on and how much I know, and he'll send some goons to try to grab it from my safe here," he said, pointing to a squat metal box in the corner of the room.

Frank furrowed his brow. "And how, exactly, can you be sure that the government's going to go for this? I mean, you're an accredited diplomat. They can't be seen breaking in here, no matter how badly they want the intel."

"Exactly, Mr. Lodge! That's exactly the point. If we catch them in the act, then we'll have the goods on al-Quwatli and expose him as paranoid and weak. It'll encourage the opposition parties to back Za'im's coup and definitely encourage other countries to eventually recognize his government afterward. As for getting them to do it, well, Za'im is going to help take care of that for us. He has some people close to al-Quwatli who can nudge him in the right direction."

Cal looked over to his teammates, all in some state of disbelief except for Maggie, who simply had a smirk on her face. Of all his teammates, Cal figured Maggie would be the one to find the humor in such a terrible idea.

Zippy cleared her throat. "Excuse me, Mr. Copeland, but what about Lorraine and little Miles? They can't be here when this happens."

"Oh, we've thought of that," Copeland said. "She's heading over the mountains to Beirut to visit friends. It's an easy drive, nothing at all to worry about there, Miss Silverman."

"And so when the Syrians break in, we just . . . grab 'em?" Danny asked.

"Like a police sting, exactly." Copeland looked at his watch. "Excuse me a minute. I want to say good night to Miles before we get on with the planning."

Copeland got up and hurried out of the room, leaving the Variants looking at Meade, who simply shrugged. "He's crazy, but believe me, I was in O.S.S. during the war. You'd be surprised how often crazy works."

Danny frowned. "You know, I was originally going to be here for a few days, but now I think I'm going to stay until this op is done," he told the others. "Honestly, I think it's insane, but Colonel Meade here has a pretty good reputation. If he's on board, we can do it. But I want to see it through."

"That all?" Cal asked.

"No. I need to do some more recon before this goes down," Danny said, looking him squarely in the eye. "Not entirely sure the coast is clear."

Meade sat up at this. "We have the Reds well accounted for, Commander," he said pointedly. "I've personally lined up all the best anti-Communist guys in the Syrian Army. We have this in hand."

"I'm sure you do, Colonel," Danny replied. "But they're not the only ones I'm worried about. And before you ask, no, you're not cleared for it."

February 28, 1949

Frank was grateful the Syrians didn't seem to place high value on the tuxedo, but the three-piece suit he'd reluctantly put on wasn't significantly better. It didn't help that there were multiple opinions floating through his head at any given moment, from the sartorial advice of a Turkish academic (*I think tweed, yes? For authority*) to the lament of a WWII commando (*Your range of motion is shot to hell, and if it goes down in here, you're gonna die unless you lose the jacket*).

As he surveyed the room closely, Frank couldn't help but wonder if his control over his ability was slipping somehow. Since he'd picked up the knack for absorbing the memories, skills, and knowledge of the recently deceased four years earlier, comments like the ones jostling around inside his head usually came when faced with a direct application of that knowledge—combat, mechanical repair, surgery. Only then would the appropriate voice and memory chime in, as if the deceased were whispering instructions in his ear.

Honestly, it was handy. Frank had access to at least several PhDs' worth of know-how, the skills of the best fighters, drivers, pilots, and strategists in the military, and the ability to survive and thrive in nearly any climate and geography known to man. He was up to seventeen different languages as of Friday, when he'd sat at the bedside of a Kurdish woman who'd been hit by a car. Before then, he hadn't even known there was such a language as Kurdish. Now he was a fluent speaker and knew more about the culture than the guys back at the Smithsonian did.

The thing about the languages was that, somehow, the whispers in his ear were never there. Frank just *knew* Kurdish. And Arabic. And Hebrew, Russian, Spanish, French, Flemish, German, Turkish, Czech, Icelandic, and others.

He didn't know how it worked or why. It just did. But lately, well, all those voices seemed to have opinions on things only tangentially related to the skills he had absorbed. He'd learned to pick and choose what he wanted, but still . . . stuff slipped through. Like about the suit he was wearing.

Over the past several months, Frank had taken to saying "good night" to the voices before his head hit the pillow in the small but comfortable apartment the CIA rented for him in Foggy Bottom. He'd occasionally say "good morning" too. It was almost a challenge to the people he was carrying around with him. So far, they were silent in the face of such modest pleasantries. He figured he'd shit a brick if they actually started replying. Maybe they knew that.

"Frank," Danny said. "You all right?"

Smiling, Frank turned to his boss. "Yeah, sorry. Situational assessment. Had to do some sifting in my head. Apparently, this suit jacket is gonna get me killed if it goes south in here."

Danny smiled back. "Yeah, well, apparently Za'im has his men covering the place pretty well. I half-expect him to try the coup here and now, but Copeland's really trying to pull this off without bloodshed," he whispered, the clink of glasses and convivial chatter masking his words.

"Ambitious," Frank replied. "Never heard of a coup without blood on the streets. How's your own situational assessment going?"

For the past week, Danny had been hitting the streets of Damascus, covering the bulk of the city by foot and bicycle. His Enhancement—known only to a few Variants, the CIA Director, and the President himself—was that if he concentrated hard enough, he could locate other Variants. It was Danny who'd rounded up the entire group that turned into the MAJESTIC-12 program. Hell, he could walk into a mid-sized city and make a beeline for a Variant sitting at a bar in the most nondescript neighborhood. Frank had seen him do it.

But this time was different. Danny had caught a "flicker" of something in Damascus—a Variant whose presence only registered for a short moment—on his first night in town. No other Variant had ever produced such a signal in Danny's mind. He'd been searching ever since but to no avail.

"Nothing new," Danny sighed. "We're the only five Variants in town. And I don't think there are any null-zone generators here, either. The Soviets have bigger fish to fry."

"You hope," Frank grumbled.

"I hope," Danny agreed. "Where are our people?"

Frank nodded toward the room. "My fiancée, Miss Jones, is over there being charming toward some Syrian politicians, and they're eating it up. I would have expected nothing less. Then our African trade ambassador there is primarily staying out of the way by the snacks table. I think he's going to try to get his missus to make Syrian lamb safiha when he gets back, because he's been putting them away at a good clip."

"We gotta get Cal out there more," Danny muttered.

"Ain't his thing, Commander," Frank replied, a surge of protectiveness coming over him. "He's an honest man who just wants to do the right thing, and that isn't what this is by any stretch."

Danny sighed. "And Zippy?"

"Just saw her a moment ago. She's been talking to everyone, got her little notebook out and everything. Shaking a lot of hands, too. Very touchy-feely. Where'd she go?"

Frank felt a hand on his shoulder. "Right here," Zippy replied. "Care to comment on Syrian-Israeli relations for *The Jerusalem Post*, gentlemen?"

"Relations would be a great thing to have," Danny said. "But don't quote me on that. What's the scoop?"

Zippy deftly slid her notebook and pen into her purse. "Well, I'd say maybe one in five parliamentarians would be willing to make peace with Israel so long as all the Israeli gains in the 1948 war were given back. The other four would be quite happy to try to invade again."

"And?" Danny prompted.

"Three members of Parliament are having affairs with other women, one with another *man*, the dirty boy. Two others are on the take, along with at least a third of the senior military officers present. Some of the bribes are us—I saw Copeland in one of 'em—and some aren't us, which means it's either the British, French, Soviets, or . . . well, OK, could be anybody."

Frank marveled at Zippy's Enhancement. Danny called her ability *psychometry*, which he defined as the ability to glean information about a person or object just from touch. She was getting pretty good at looking for intel, just as Frank had learned how to focus his death watch experiences so that he got only the skills or knowledge he wanted. The drawback for Zippy, though, was that she could never really shut it off. Hence the gloves she usually wore when she wasn't on duty.

"That reporter cover's pretty handy," Danny said. "Let's get over to Copeland. I think we're gonna start the show in a few."

"We know how the colonel's feeling?" Frank asked as they started toward Copeland, who was holding court among several Syrians and, apparently, telling some pretty good jokes.

"Maggie says he's angry and nervous," Zippy replied. "Apparently, al-Quwatli didn't show up for this one, and Za'im thought he would. Now he's wondering what the hell the President is up to."

"Great, angry coup leader," Frank muttered. "This'll be fun."

Copeland excused himself and walked over to Frank and Zippy just as Danny faded away into the crowd. "You two ready?" he asked cheerily.

"Sure," Frank replied. "Where to?"

Copeland smiled and walked toward one of the exits of the large, ceremonial foyer and down a corridor. A few guests mingled on the sidelines, and some of them seemed to note their passing with just a touch more than casual interest. Several of the voices in Frank's head took interest.

Male, mid-thirties, Arabic descent, unarmed, English-made watch. Looking at Zippy. No threat.

Female, late twenties, Caucasian, Turkish-made dress, French-made shoes. Either English or French. Likely from the consulate, possible ally.

Male, late thirties, Caucasian, shoulder mount, Russian-tailored suit. We'll see him again. Not an ally.

Frank glanced back at the guy with the bad Russian suit, who looked like he was glaring at them as they passed, but he'd already turned a corner to rejoin the party. "Who was the sourpuss back there?" Frank whispered.

"Karilov," Copeland replied, his voice a touch too loud for Frank's tastes. "Soviet Consulate. Probably my opposite number. Not much of a talker. Now, Vasiliev, his boss? Great fellow, really. I think he likes the game as much as I do. Much more interesting than Keeley."

"You're social with the Soviet consul?" Zippy asked incredulously.

"Well, sure, Miss Silverman. We all go to the same parties. We all visit the same politicians. We attend sessions of Parliament and go to major court hearings and all those things. It's just rude not to be social. Vasiliev isn't rude. Karilov is. Ah, here we are."

By now, they were alone in a side corridor, in a maze of offices surrounding the parliamentary chamber. Copeland opened the door and immediately smiled at the two Syrian Army officers inside. "Evening, fellows. He knows we're coming," Copeland said.

They were ushered into the room—a secretary's anteroom—and quickly frisked by one of the officers as the other stood with his hand on his holstered pistol. Even

Zippy was frisked, and her purse searched—they were nothing if not thorough.

Frank looked over at Zippy, but she alleviated his concern with a glance—she hadn't gleaned anything particularly troublesome from the guard. Copeland, meanwhile, was already heading for the inner office.

"Colonel al-Za'im, it is wonderful to see you again, my friend."

Behind the desk, a large man in a garish military uniform rose to take Copeland's hand. Za'im was taller than average and built like a brick house—thick and stocky, no neck, balding hair, full face. Frank couldn't help but think that he looked like Edward G. Robinson, the actor who defined gangsters in the movies.

"Who are these people?" Za'im asked in passable, accented English. "Your friends from Washington you told me about?"

"Why, yes, Colonel, this is—"

Frank interrupted with a raised hand and a step forward. "You can call me Frank, Colonel. And this here is Miss Silver. And if it's all right with you, we'll leave it at that. You understand, of course."

Za'im smiled slightly, and Frank relaxed. He wasn't going to let his real name get around, and he figured a truncated "Silver" rather than "Silverman" would go over better with the Syrian military leadership—the same leadership that got their asses handed to them by the Israelis just the year before.

"Of course. Mr. Frank, Miss Silver. We thank you for your support of the Syrian people," Za'im said, almost as if he were bored. "May I present Colonels al-Hinnawi and al-Shishakli, my friends and fellow Syrian patriots."

Everybody shook hands cordially. Al-Hinnawi was, if anything, stockier and more dour looking than his boss, while al-Shishakli was quite different—tall, lean, with a politician's smile and a clever look about him. Al-Shishakli gave both the newcomers a thorough once-over behind his smile and his patrician-sounding "A pleasure to meet you."

Chairs were brought in, seats were taken. "Now, Mr. Copeland, how will these individuals help retake our nation from the criminal al-Quwatli? You know it was terrible supplies, inferior weapons, and unreasonable orders that prompted our defeat last year—certainly not the heart of the Syrian soldier! Can you help us with the supplies and weapons? We can handle the orders, of course."

Copeland sighed and smiled. "My friend, you know that the United States cannot directly give you arms and supplies as you prepare to replace a democratically elected government—no matter how terrible that government has become!" he added quickly. "Once you have taken power and set new elections, then we would be happy to discuss a wide variety of aid packages, including rewards for completing the TAPline agreement that the current administration has set aside."

"And so, I ask again, why are these individuals here?" Za'im asked. "This one, Mr. Frank, is he some kind of military advisor? And Miss Silver? Surely not military!" The colonels in the room had a good chuckle at this, while Zippy forced a smile for her audience.

"No, Colonel. These two will be helping me with our little operation at my house. We're still on, yes?" Copeland asked.

"Ah, yes. Our pretext for the rest of the world," Za'im said. "It is clever. And these two will help you catch the thieves we will send to your home?"

"They are both highly trained operatives and will not only assist in capturing the burglars but also in interrogating them to bring the truth of the current administration's involvement to light," Copeland said proudly.

At this, al-Shishakli leaned forward, worry on his face. "Now, understand clearly, Mr. Copeland. We will not stand for any Syrians seriously injured in this operation. You may defend yourself and your home, but we expect the return of our . . . operatives, let's say . . . without lasting damage."

Al-Hinnawi chuckled slightly and spoke in Arabic, which Frank understood quite clearly. "Adib, do you expect him to invite the burglars in for tea? All that matters is that al-Quwatli is blamed. If our men are a little worse off, is that not more believable?"

"I will not have good men harmed if I can help it, not at the hands of these Americans!" al-Shishakli hissed in Arabic. "Colonel al-Za'im, you cannot stress this enough."

Za'im looked at his two subordinates, one on either side, then addressed Copeland in English once more. "Again, casualties are to be avoided, and we would prefer no lasting harm to anyone involved. But capturing the burglars in the act is most important."

"We can do that," Frank reassured him. "Mr. Copeland here has a great plan."

The doors opened again, and a small boy—couldn't have been more than ten to Frank's eye—walked in, dressed like a sheik from *Lawrence of Arabia*, complete with headscarf. He walked over to al-Shishakli, and whispered in his ear.

"Ah, I think it is time to return to the party," the colonel said. "Someone was just asking for you, Colonel al-Za'im."

Za'im nodded and stood. "We will aim for March seventh for our operation," he told Copeland. "A day on either end, perhaps, depending on how quickly al-Quwatli wishes to strike. I will try to send word, but be ready."

Copeland shook hands with all three colonels. "My family will be out of the house starting the second, just to be sure. Good luck to us all."

More pleasantries were exchanged, and the colonels filed out, the little Arab boy in tow. "Who's the kid?" Zippy asked Copeland when they were gone.

"I think he's Shishakli's boy. Learning the family business from the ground up."

"You keep your eye on Shishakli," Frank said to Copeland. "He's the brains of this whole operation."

Copeland smiled. "Very good, Mr. Lodge. You're absolutely right. Now, shall we get back to the party?"

Frank followed Copeland and Zippy back through the halls, wondering just how much Copeland wasn't telling them about his plans—or whether the man was just winging it all along on a cloud of bluster and bullshit.

As Frank approached the bar, he saw Maggie chatting amiably with a number of Syrians and assorted Europeans—she'd bitch about it later something fierce, but you never know who might be useful later on. Cal could learn a thing or two from her.

"A drink, my friend," said the man next to him. "To strong international relations."

Lost in his head, Frank turned to suddenly find the Russian-looking fellow from earlier standing next to him, eying him with a curious smile and holding out a glass of champagne—it was Karilov, from the Soviet embassy. Cursing himself for being careless, Frank nonetheless smiled back and took the proffered glass.

Leningrad accent, came a voice in Frank's head. *College educated, but not in the West.* With so many voices in his head, Frank wasn't always sure who was talking at any given moment, but the information was useful. "I think I'm hearing a Leningrad accent, if I'm not mistaken?" Frank said cordially.

The Russian's eyebrows shot up. "Very impressive, Mister . . ."

"Smith. U.S. State Department. Linguistics. And you are?" Frank asked, trying to sound pleasantly ignorant.

"Karilov. I work at the embassy of the United Soviet Socialist Republics. A pleasure, Mr. Smith." The two shook hands and Frank got the distinct feeling that neither of them believed the other's last name for one second. "So, what brings an expert in Russian languages to Damascus, of all places?"

Frank smiled. "I speak many languages. You'd be surprised."

"I have no doubt. And I see here this evening a few other new faces as well. Very interesting."

Frank looked around with what he hoped passed for an innocuous expression. "Well, my fiancée is over there, but otherwise? I wouldn't know. I imagine there's always a rotating cast of characters around here."

"Indeed, but it is wise to take note. Something for you to consider as you settle into your new position," Karilov said. "There's always someone taking note."

The Russian sketched a little bow, then walked back among the partiers, leaving Frank looking for exits and praying Copeland wasn't as sloppy as he seemed.

March 5, 1949

Alexei Mikhailovich Petrov had heard of men during the Great Patriotic War, wounded men who had lost limbs—hands, arms, feet, legs. He remembered one in particular, a corporal who barely looked old enough to shave, in the bed next to his, shortly after the siege of Stalingrad had been lifted. This corporal had screamed in pain, saying his legs felt as though they were on fire. No amount of vodka or critically short-supplied morphine could bring relief.

All this despite the fact he no longer had legs.

Alexei Mikhailovich remembered this corporal now, because he too was suffering from a lost limb, though one that had always been invisible. His phantom reach, his pull, his Empowerment, as it was called at the Bekhterev Institute—gone. All he had was the memory of it, the mental urge he channeled through the ether that would draw things to him. Weapons, crates, men, even an automobile. All pulled toward him, such strong power at his beck and call.

But these Americans, they had taken it away from him with their infernal device. Alexei Mikhailovich had heard stories of such instruments, but only as rumor in the halls of the Bekhterev Institute, where the Soviet Union housed and trained its *Chempiony Proletariata*—its Champions of the Proletariat. Their intelligence had not been able to confirm that the Americans had discovered the means to nullify Empowerments, but Alexei, like most other Empowereds, had been operating under the assumption.

The Soviet's Istanbul operation had gone horribly, horribly wrong—their intelligence had accounted for only three American Empowereds, and there turned out to be more. The woman in particular, the one who turned fear into a dagger and thrust it into men's hearts, they had not accounted for her. Her anger and rage in the cisterns under the ancient city that night had been something to behold. It was a horror like Alexei had never felt, not even when a Nazi bayonet had pierced his chest, barely missing his heart. No horror was comparable to what that woman could weave.

And then water, a flood, and rock. That was all he remembered after the fear. The rest was a haze, a stupor unlike any other. Floating, barely registering sound and noise, only hunger and a need for light and movement that never came. Weeks, months—the Americans had told him it had not been very long, but he did not believe them. It was months, he was sure of it, because he had wasted away to barely fifty-five kilograms by the time they had revived him, allowed him to eat and talk, read and sleep normally. It took him a week before he could walk again and take a piss like a man should, standing up.

His fury far surpassed his physical condition, but he hid it well. There would be a time when the Americans would slip up, when their nullifying field would collapse or falter and he could reach out again. He would lay waste to all around him on that day, and he savored the possibilities of what he might do and to whom. There was the Navy man, Wallace, who continued to act like his friend—a laughable ruse. And the scientist, Bronk, with his team of white-coated lackeys, studying him like a rat in a maze.

Alexei always acknowledged them. He talked with them about the small things. But he would not divulge information. They knew of Bekhterev; they had even heard of Director Beria's involvement. They had gathered some passable intelligence, he had to admit. But he would not tell them anything more. Not even when they brought that witch down to frighten him. He begged and pleaded, pissed himself, screamed in abject terror, tried to claw his own eyes from his skull—but still he did not relent.

It wasn't for Mother Russia he did this, not really, though he would of course swear otherwise should he ever return. No, he held on because he hated these people and wanted them all to die for what they had done to him.

Even this one, who showed up today. Alexei Mikhailovich had never seen him before, and he suspected it was a new tack the Americans were trying in their attempts to break him.

"Mr. Petrov," the man said in English, taking a seat across from Alexei's cot in the cell's only chair. "Do you know where you are?"

Alexei was startled to hear a German accent, an accent he knew well from Stalingrad. The man was thin and reedy, with slicked-back hair, balding, a cruel mouth and a Roman nose. He wore a suit and a lab coat—a scientist, or so they would have him believe.

"I am a captive of the United States of America, an unlawful captive. I was taken from a neutral country and brought somewhere. I was drugged for a very long time, and now I am kept locked away to be studied for my ability. The rest does not matter."

"Does not matter?" The German smiled. "I should think it matters quite a lot. Would it surprise you to know you are in America itself?"

Alexei considered this and decided he would see what this man's game was. "It would not surprise me. America is a large country, like Russia. Your people, when they visit me, they wear light clothing, they have dust on their shoes. I would say that not only am I in America but I am in the southwestern part of this country. I believe this would include the states called Texas, New Mexico, Arizona, California, Utah, and Nevada."

"Impressive, Mr. Petrov. You've been trained well. In fact, you're absolutely right. But forgive me if I don't tell you exactly where quite yet."

"Yet?" Alexei asked, eyes narrowing. "I have no time for games. Whatever you're here to do, get on with it."

"You have all the time in the world, and I have something you want," the German said.

"There is only one thing I want, and it is something you will not allow."

"Prisoner exchanges happen all the time."

"That is not what I want."

The German's smile grew broader. "Then it is vengeance. An admirable goal."

Alexei stood up from his cot. "Who the hell are you?"

"Not important, though what *is* important is that you keep my visits here to yourself. Do not tell the others who see you here, Commander Wallace and Dr. Bronk."

"Why?" Alexei demanded.

"Because our interests are not aligned with theirs, of course."

"This is a trick. Another way to try to break me." Alexei began to pace. "Have you not done enough to me yet, you bastards?"

The German rose and stepped close to Alexei, lowering his voice to barely a whisper. "There is a vortex here. You know of what I speak. It is here, and so are you. You will be visited by someone else. Some*thing* else. Soon. It calls itself Vanda. And you must listen to what it says."

Without another word, the German walked out of the room, locking the doors behind him. It was only then that Alexei realized that he had come without guards, that this was the slip-up he'd been waiting for. How easy it would have been to overpower the mad German scientist, threaten his life, walk out. Such stupidity! He was a fool, caught off guard by silly mind games!

Then, of course, he realized that this, too, was some sort of test. Perhaps they'd have let him walk out of the cell, only to be tranquilized or even shot in the halls. Another test, another game.

This time seemed different, though. This German was either a canny player or deadly serious. And so when the doors opened and this "Vanda" appeared, Alexei would listen. And then find his advantage.

Maybe, when all was said and done, he would let the German live. He found the man's intensity . . . intriguing.

* * *

"The microphones get fixed?" Master Sergeant Stephen Piscatelli asked the men on duty that night.

"Yes, Master Sergeant," the young airman replied. "Not sure what happened, but seems like they're picking up just fine now. Seems like the prisoner's whispering to himself tonight."

Piscatelli frowned. He'd just looked in on the sleeping prisoner a few minutes ago. There was nobody else in there, and all was quiet. "That's new. You getting any of it?"

The airman picked up the headphones from his console and listened in. "Not really, Master Sergeant. A few words here and there."

Taking a seat next to the airman, Piscatelli slipped on another set of headphones and tried to make something out.

". . . release . . . pull . . . home . . . brothers . . . tall man . . ."

"Who do you suppose 'Vanda' is, Master Sergeant?" the airman asked.

"Probably the poor bastard's girl back home. Maybe his mom. He's been in there a long time. Hell, I give him points for not going cuckoo until now." Piscatelli stood up and tossed the headphones back on the console. "Write it all down and put it in your duty report. Be sure to flag it for the higher-ups."

"Anybody in particular to flag it to, Master Sergeant?"

Piscatelli smiled. "Son, you're at Area 51. You're not even cleared to take a piss next to half these people, let alone know who they are. Just flag it for the next watch."

9.

March 9, 1949

Maggie put her feet up on the chair across from her, enjoying the cool night and the burbling of the courtyard fountain. She had to admit Copeland was doing all right for himself here in Damascus. Back in Washington, a government salary would get you a tiny house in Arlington or a closet-sized apartment in D.C. itself. In Syria, it apparently landed you four bedrooms, a study, formal living and dining, and a couple of locals for the housekeeping, cooking, and nannying.

"Maybe I should be a diplomat," Maggie said absently to Cal, who was sitting next to her, nursing a cup of tea. "I mean, you get to live in a place like this, somewhere exotic. And you know I'd be good at it. I could get 'em to agree to anything. Peace in our time."

Cal smiled and raised his teacup to her. "Ain't no doubt you could, Miss Maggie. You could get old Uncle Joe himself to surrender if you put your mind to it. But that ain't how this game is played."

Maggie regarded Cal coolly. "Maybe it should be."

"No, can't be going around like that. You know it well as I do. Folks get crazy when they see something they don't understand. If average folks get a whiff of us, well, I can't see how that ends well. And if we start taking charge like that, getting folks to do what we want, even for the right reasons? They're gonna be mighty angry."

Cal was right, of course. Maggie often forgot he was a good thirty years older than she was—lately he'd been absorbing enough life energy to stay looking like a hale and hearty twenty-eight or so. Sure, it meant killing a cow once every other week or so to top off with; without any further energy, he would eventually resume his normal age and health. The benefits were worth a trip to the slaughterhouse outside of town every few weeks.

The best part was that Cal wasn't passing judgement, unlike Danny or Frank. Sometimes, Maggie would just say things like that to get a reaction, and she could see the threads of genuine fear in both men as she spoke. Fear for their lives, maybe, or fear of what she could do. Hers was a powerful Enhancement, she knew. Not as long-lasting or versatile as Frank's, not as critical as Danny's, but she could pack a pretty good wallop.

So could Cal. Maybe that was why he wasn't afraid, why they'd had this conversation a dozen times, and each time he saw it as nothing more than what it was—letting off steam. When you can kill someone with a touch, it puts things in perspective. And he wore the responsibility well, too.

"How the hell are you so even-keeled after all this?" she asked. "Seriously. How do you do it?"

Cal shrugged. "I never wanted much, Miss Maggie. I got a woman who loves me and a son I'm proud of—he's decided to be a lawyer. Did I tell you that?"

"No, you didn't. That's wonderful." Maggie could feel the pride pouring off him like a wave.

"My son, the lawyer. Ain't that something. So, I got a family. I got love. We're setting down in Adams Morgan, got a nice little church we go to now. Some nice suppers with the neighbors. Starting to get out into the community, you know? That's always good. Keeps you grounded. Family, faith, and community. Maybe that's the secret."

Maggie felt like crying but instead gave him a smile. "Sounds so simple."

"I always found life's simpler than you think. Of course, ain't nobody talking down to me anymore like they did at the Firestone plant. Washington's different that way, for sure. That helps. Still some stupid crackers here and there, but a whole lot less of 'em than in Tennessee."

Maggie had never given black people much thought before—there weren't that many of them in the tiny Chicago suburb where she grew up, not that many in Mill Valley, either. But knowing Cal made her realize that, despite what she'd been through with her Enhancement, she still had it a lot better than he did 99 percent of the time.

"Maggie, check in," came Frank's voice over the Handie-Talkie on the table. She could sense his annoyance from across the house.

She picked up the radio and keyed it. "Nothing yet. I told you, I'll know when they're in range." Indeed, that was why she and Cal were stationed in the courtyard, in the exact center of Copeland's house—so that she could sense new emotions from anybody approaching the building. She did another little sweep of the area, to the farthest extent of her senses, just to be sure.

"Roger. Out."

This was their third night of sentry duty, and it was getting to be pretty damn dull. Copeland was all nervous energy, to the point where Danny had threatened to tie him to a chair lest he be seen moving around the house. He ended up sitting in his study, in the dark, looking out the window. Danny, Frank, and Zippy were stationed near other windows and doors, quietly monitoring the empty streets around the house, which stood on a corner and abutted two other homes. In a few minutes, Cal would head up to replace Zippy for a spell, and she would come down for tea and more conversation.

Maggie was honestly running out of polite things to say. Maybe she'd start getting impolite and see what happened.

"Maybe there's a knitting circle or something you can join up with," Cal suggested helpfully. "You know, get to know some folks in the area."

Maggie grimaced and resisted the urge to make Cal weep like a little girl. "Not really my thing. I—" She suddenly caught the wave of amusement from Cal and couldn't help but smile. "Oh, you jerk!"

"Maybe there's a knife-skills circle instead." He chuckled. "Target-practice circle? Ladies' boxing?"

Maggie was about to reply with something particularly colorful when something crept into the edge of her perception. She quickly grabbed the radio. "I got two nervous nellies on the street, approaching the intersection from different angles."

Zippy replied first. "Eyes on target. Male, early twenties. Wearing . . . a military uniform?"

Cal sat up straight. "That ain't no burglar."

"And he's got no good reason to be nervous walking down the street," Maggie said.

"Eyes on target two. Male, mid-twenties, army fatigues," Danny said. "Just walking down the street and . . . shit, scoping out the house with binoculars."

Maggie and Cal got up and rushed toward the front of the house, where Danny was stationed in the ground-floor parlor. "He's just standing there? Out in the open?"

Danny shook his head in amazement. "Like a walk in the park. No craft to it at all. What kind of nervous are they?"

Maggie reached out again with her mind, the puce-colored threads of anxiousness visible from afar. "Like . . . the kind of nervous you get before a race or a big game. Like when you're at the top of a diving board about to dive in. Nervous but . . . ready."

The radio crackled again. "Guys, I got three guys in the alley," Frank reported. "Repeat. Three targets in the alley. Fatigues and rifles, heading for the back door."

Danny swore. "Counter-op. Five bucks says they'll plant something incriminating on Copeland. Ten says the Russians are in on it."

Zippy's voice came next. "Three more on my side, total of four. Armed and advancing toward the side door."

Maggie ventured a look out the window and saw that the binoculars guy had been joined by three other soldiers, all similarly armed. "That makes eleven. Squad and leader," she said.

"Pincer move. No way out," Danny said before keying the radio. "Zippy, grab Miles and get him to the courtyard. Frank, meet us there. Move out!"

They quickly dashed through the empty, dark house to the courtyard. Frank had gotten there first and had already shut down the water to the fountain so they could hear better. "Mags, I think you're up. How many can you handle and how close do they need to be?" he asked.

"Maybe all but they'd have to be real close," she said. "Everybody would have to be in the courtyard. And one or two will probably freak out and try something dumb."

"What? What the hell are you talking about?" Copeland said. "They brought a goddamn army! We need to get out of here!"

Frank looked over to Cal, who gave a deep sigh before reaching over to put a hand on Copeland's shoulder. "It's gonna be OK, Mr. Copeland."

Copeland collapsed into Cal's arms, drained of just enough life energy to render him completely unconscious. "Now what?" Cal asked as he propped Copeland in the chair next to the fountain.

Frank and Danny traded a look, Danny acquiescing to Frank's expertise, backed up as it was by the memories of several highly decorated soldiers. "Maggie: you, Miles, and Zippy in the center. Cal and Dan: get over there behind the vines along those columns and stay out of sight. When Maggie switches on, you two need to neutralize any stragglers. Nonlethal. Mags, try not to affect our guys."

"And you?" Maggie asked.

Frank smiled. "I'll take care of whoever doesn't show up here."

With that, Frank jogged off back into the house, while Danny and Cal took their assigned positions. Zippy chambered a round in her pistol.

"Easy there, Calamity Jane," Maggie said, reaching out to assuage Zippy's nervousness. Unlike the rest of the team, Zippy hadn't been in combat before. "Remember your training and let me take care of these guys, OK?"

The younger woman nodded, but the grip on her pistol remained tight. "Right. Just so long as—"

Maggie felt the bullet enter her right calf almost before she heard the shot.

"Fuck!" she yelled as her leg gave out, sending her crashing to the cobblestones. Zippy immediately returned fire, and a soldier fell from the second-floor balcony into the courtyard with a sickening thump.

"*La tatlaquu alnnara!*" came an angry voice from inside the house. Immediately, soldiers started swarming the courtyard, weapons at the ready. Wisely opting for discretion, Zippy gently lowered her pistol to the ground.

Maggie wanted nothing more than to transfer all her pain and anger to the men around her, but knew she had to wait until she could get as many of them as possible. Cal, meanwhile, knelt down over her. "Here, Miss Maggie, let me take care of that for you."

"No, Cal!" she said through gritted teeth. "Witnesses. They saw me go down. They can't see me get up. It can wait. You should've stayed put."

A young man with an imperial bearing and the epaulets of an officer strode into the courtyard, barking out something that sounded angry. A couple of the men pointed to the injured man on the cobblestones, and the officer's face grew darker as he turned to Maggie and the others.

"Who did this?" he demanded in heavily accented English.

Cal stood up and stared the man down. "Who shoots a woman? Where I come from, only criminals and cowards do that. Which was he?"

The officer looked like he was about to chew through his own teeth. "We are here on matters of state security, and we will search these premises until we find what we're looking for."

"You mean these?" Frank shouted from the balcony above. Maggie and the others looked up to see a manila folder in his hands. The fact that his hair was slightly disheveled was the only sign he'd probably taken the folder by force. "Funny thing is," he continued, "I found this on one of your men as he was coming in. The safe's still closed, and the only guy who knows the combination fainted dead away the moment you showed up. So, how do you explain that?"

The officer pointed up at Frank and barked something else in Arabic, and Maggie decided she was done with waiting.

Six men immediately collapsed to the ground, their faces twisted in horror. Three others covered their eyes and began to scream. And the officer turned and made a beeline for the exit, only to be met by Danny, whose crude hand-to-hand made short work of him. Even through her pain and the use of her Enhancement, Maggie could see there were still a few holes in his technique—it was a good thing his opponent wasn't thinking straight.

"Frank?" Danny called out. "Got everyone?"

"Clear," he replied as he came down the stairs. "Two in the study, one in the bedroom. Thought he was going to go through Mrs. Copeland's unmentionables."

One by one, Cal put the still-conscious soldiers to sleep with a touch, and as he did, his appearance changed. He was getting younger, almost as if he were barely twenty-one again. Maggie assumed he was storing up so he could take care of her leg, which couldn't happen soon enough—it hurt like hell.

Her heart sank, though, when she heard Copeland's voice. "What . . . what the . . . what the hell happened here?" Maggie saw the OPC man stagger to his feet and look around the courtyard, now strewn with unconscious and injured soldiers. "Oh, my God. Are any of them dead?"

"Well, we have one injured," Frank retorted. "Maggie took one in the leg from a trigger-happy idiot. Great plan you had there, Miles."

Copeland went pale and ran over to Maggie. "Oh, I'm so sorry. I'm so sorry! I'll call for a doctor immediately! Let me go and I'll get you some help."

Frank brushed past him roughly, dragging the tablecloth off the tea table as he went. "No need," Frank said as he started ripping the cloth into strips. "I'm a doctor."

"You're a *doctor*?" Copeland asked incredulously.

"I'm a lot of things," Frank replied, kneeling down to attend to Maggie's wound. "We'll get this taken care of, at least for now. We can do more later, OK?"

Maggie nodded but started suddenly as she heard another door in the house being broken down—and the clatter of boots on tile. "Now what?" she asked, preparing to harness her abilities once more. But she relaxed as soon as she saw the face from her mission briefings, Col. Husni al-Za'im, enter the courtyard.

"What has happened here?" he demanded loudly. "Is this not the home of an American diplomat?"

Copeland, who had been standing slack-jawed in the middle of the courtyard, suddenly rushed forward. "It was an entire squadron of troops!" he sputtered. "Soldiers! Not just a burglary, but a dozen goddamn soldiers! I—"

Za'im held up his hand to silence Copeland. "You say that these men broke into your home, Mr. Copeland?"

It took a moment, but Copeland finally got the gist; they were to act along for the benefit of the people Za'im had brought with him—a number of officers as well as three or four guys in suits and fezzes who, to Maggie, looked like either government bureaucrats or newspapermen. Maybe both. "Yes, Colonel. These men broke into my home."

Frank finished tying off Maggie's tourniquet, stood up, and walked toward Za'im with the papers he'd found. "I think they were trying to plant these, Colonel," he said. "I imagine the guy over by the door by my C.O., Commander Wallace, could tell you all about it."

Za'im nodded and took the papers from Frank. "Thank you, sir. I assume you and your fellows saw service in the war, which is why you were able to defeat these men, who were not following lawful orders, I can assure you!"

Frank nodded, hoping they all sounded convincing enough. It didn't have to be perfect; it just had to work. "Most of us saw action in the war, Colonel. It was a struggle, but we managed to stop them. I'm sure they heard you coming and panicked as well."

To Maggie's surprise, Za'im gave Frank the barest flutter of a wink before continuing. "Mr. Copeland, I promise you, I will get to the bottom of this travesty. I can only pray to God that elements of the Syrian government were not involved in this; otherwise, severe repercussions will echo throughout the halls of power. I—wait, is that woman shot?"

Shit, Maggie thought. "I'm fine, sir. Really. Just grazed me." Actually, it had punctured a hole clean through, but Maggie wasn't in the mood. She wanted to be back on her feet as soon as she could, and that meant clearing the house and getting a moment alone with Cal to heal her up.

Za'im turned to another officer. "Get a doctor at once! Now! This is horrible! I am so sorry, miss. We will discover who is responsible for this, I promise you!"

Maggie rolled her eyes as Danny came over to help her sit up. "We may have to send you home, Miss Jones, if we can't clear things up quickly," Danny said.

"God *damn* it, Danny, you need me here," she hissed.

Danny could only smile. "Don't worry, Miss Jones. I'll personally attend to your safety on the trip back." He then lowered his voice. "I need to personally tell Hilly what a fucked-up op this is so we can get the rest of the team out. And you obviously can't be seen walking around Damascus anymore."

Maggie sighed. "I'm the damsel in distress."

"You're the damsel," he replied.

"The damsel who kicked nearly everyone's ass in here."

"Yep."

"It's not goddamn fair," she muttered.

10.

March 15, 1949

"Give me one good reason why I shouldn't send every single last one of you back to the States on a leaky freighter," Jim Keeley seethed as he threw a manila folder down on his desk. "You got a woman shot, Miles! A *woman*! What if that was your wife? Or your little boy?!"

Frank watched Copeland's face fall slightly, while Meade just looked ahead stoically. The fact that the two OPC men had waited days to report the "break-in" at Copeland's house to Keeley, the envoy and their ostensible boss, hadn't been a good idea. Frank had told them as much. Not that it mattered at this point.

"The woman was part of a team sent by Foggy Bottom," Copeland replied. Frank knew that neighborhood housed both the CIA and State Department headquarters, so at least there was some wiggle room for the truth in his statement.

"A team for what, Miles?" Keeley demanded. "Or am I not cleared for that? Again?"

Copeland looked down at his hands. "I'm sorry, sir. You're not."

Keeley stared hard at Copeland, as if his gaze could burrow through the other man's skull and find the truth inside his brains. He finally looked over at Frank instead. "And I suppose you can't tell me anything either, Mr. Lodge?"

Frank considered this a moment. Copeland was potentially the worst goddamn spy he'd seen in a while. Half the town knew he wasn't just a diplomatic attaché, and his own boss knew damn well he was reporting to someone higher up the ladder. Copeland should've been recalled months before. Maggie getting herself shot was the only reason his harebrained op had actually worked.

"Miss Jones is fine, Mr. Keeley, sir," Frank said tentatively. "It wasn't as bad as the Syrian doctor made it out to be, but we sent her on home just in case. As for her being here, well, she's a civilian dependent and it didn't work out. No harm done."

Keeley softened a bit. "Look, I'm glad the girl's OK. I'm also glad you got her on a plane out of here with Commander Wallace. But you're still here officially, and Mr. Hooks and God-knows-who-else are still here *un*officially. And I got my phone ringing off the hook for a week straight, alternating between investigators, reporters, Syrian Army officers promising 'support'—whatever that means—and government officials apologizing every hour on the hour." He turned his attention back to Copeland. "I'm not an idiot, Miles. You want al-Quwatli out and al-Za'im in, and you think you can do it with charm and a slush fund. You might even be right. But you came *this* close to killing someone. This is not a goddamn game, do you hear me?"

"Yes, sir," Copeland replied, still looking at his hands.

Keeley regarded him for several long moments, opening his mouth to speak once or twice but failing to find the right words. "Here's what's going to happen," the envoy finally said. "I'm filing an official complaint with CIA and State about your activities, Miles. I know they're in all likelihood the ones who sent Mr. Lodge and his people here in the first place, but I got a feeling you're blowing smoke up their asses back in Washington. And I swear, one more public screwup like this and I'm personally revoking your diplomatic passports and sending you all home, and to hell with what Foggy Bottom wants.

"Now get the hell out."

Copeland opened his mouth to say something, but Meade was already on his feet and had a hand on his colleague's shoulder to keep him quiet. They all quickly filed out, leaving Keeley staring out the window, looking extremely tired.

"He doesn't understand," Copeland muttered as they walked through the office's small secretarial pool. "Everything went perfectly. It just—"

Frank turned on his heel and got in Copeland's face. "First off, shut the fuck up about operational matters in the middle of the goddamn office, you fucking amateur," he whispered. "Second, one of my people got *shot* in your little op, so everything did *not* go perfectly. Third, I figure you have about two weeks to go before the folks in D.C. match up Keeley's report and mine and decide to send you the hell home, so if you have any interest in staying here and playing kingmaker, you better fix this shit fast—and quietly."

Frank stalked off without waiting for a reply, leaving the office—a small suite of rooms above a Persian carpet merchant—and heading downstairs to the busy, dusty street. It was only when he started walking toward the center of town that he realized Meade was following him.

"He's not so bad, you know," he said, catching up to Frank and settling in beside him. "I mean, yeah, he's lucky he's lived this long, but he's smart. He takes chances. I think he can do this."

Meade carried himself with the economy of movement belonging to an experienced soldier. "You know as well as I do that this op was messed up," Frank said. "Shouldn't have happened."

Meade shrugged. "It was the best of a number of bad options, Lodge. We needed a way to quickly cast doubt on al-Quwatli, both at home and abroad. And it worked."

Frank frowned but had to concede the point. The raid had made all the papers back home and was the talk of the town in Damascus. Embassy and consulate security had doubled since the attacks, and more than a few ambassadors had called on al-Quwatli to explicitly guarantee their safety. Meanwhile, Parliament was up in arms trying to get to the bottom of it all, and Za'im was busy stoking the fires further. Just that morning, Frank had caught him on the radio talking about an "assassination list" compiled by the al-Quwatli administration and consisting of opposition leaders, army officers, and a few foreign diplomats.

"What's your status, then?" Frank asked.

"Our friend is working to build support," Meade said, referring to Za'im. "Figure he'll have the whole thing lined up soon. The goal is to do it without shots fired, and I genuinely think he can do it."

"There were *already* shots fired, Steve," Frank reminded him. "Maggie took one in the leg."

"And she looked pissed about it," Meade said with a small smile. "She's a tiger, that one. I admit, I'll miss her."

This actually prompted Frank to crack a smile. "You got no chance, pal. Never seen her give a guy the time of day. She'll kick you much as look at you."

Meade shrugged. "My kind of girl. I imagine she's got some interesting skills to get her attached to your team."

"You have no idea. But because of her injury, she and Wallace are out. And I'm supposed to keep an eye on you now."

"Why did Wallace leave?"

Frank thought back to a short cable the Navy man had received just after the "successful" op at Copeland's house. He'd gone pale, then quickly set it on fire in an ashtray. He and Maggie were then on the next flight out of Damascus. All Danny had told them was that there was something up at Area 51 that needed his attention.

"Probably to go speak to the Director about the crap you got going on around here," Frank replied. "Like I said, I figure you got two weeks to seal the deal and get your guy in the big chair. You think you can manage that?"

Meade stopped at a street corner and checked his watch, just as a nondescript Mercedes-Benz pulled up. "Right on time. You want to find out for yourself?"

Frank peeked in and saw three men in ill-fitting suits in the car. *Military bearing, all with shoulder harnesses, all of local extraction. Mid-forties and up. Senior officers. They were all at the reception.*

"What's this?" Frank asked casually.

"A little city tour. Making a to-do list for later with a little friendly advice from yours truly. Could use your ideas, Frank."

"Five's a crowd," Frank replied. "There's just some stuff I don't want to know."

Meade shrugged. "I'll keep you posted. Two weeks seems good."

The OPC man got in the car, which sped off down the street, leaving Frank to wonder whether Meade could make this whole thing happen despite Copeland, or if he'd have to get Cal and Zippy over the border fast.

Turning back toward Copeland's house, Frank made a mental note to look into buying a car and getting a good map of Syria and Lebanon. Just in case.

11.

March 25, 1949

Danny Wallace hated his dress uniform—he invariably spilled something on the spotless whites within five minutes of putting them on—but figured that if he was going to take on the Secretary of Defense at the White House, he'd better look his best.

Plus, Danny really didn't own a top-flight civilian suit. The only one he had was a couple years old, and frankly, he knew Truman was a bit of a clotheshorse.

Of course, this didn't stop Hillenkoetter from wearing a slightly rumpled, ill-fitting suit over his large, gangly frame, but the Director wasn't the kind of man to care about such things. Between the Dulles report, the Iron Curtain tightening up, and Asia heading south fast, Hilly had more to worry about than his attire.

"The President will see you now," the secretary said, and Danny followed his boss into the Oval Office, where a grim-faced Truman stood to meet them, extending his hand to Hillenkoetter first.

"Damn shame about this, Hilly. Damn shame indeed," Truman said, shaking hands before turning to Danny, who smartly saluted before getting his own handshake. "Really appreciate you being on top of all this, Commander. I know you got a lot on your plate."

"It's my command, Mr. President. Buck stops with me," Danny replied, earning a little smirk from his commander in chief.

Truman waved them to a couch. "We got a few minutes yet before he arrives. Tell me about Syria, son."

Danny cleared his throat. "You read up on the operation, no doubt. Honestly, Mr. President, it was very poorly planned and relied far too much on the unpredictable actions of the Syrian nationals in order to succeed. It was only because of Miss Dubinsky's Enhancement and Lieutenant Lodge's extensive skills that we got out of it as well as we did. If we had been normal agents, we might've been captured or killed."

Truman nodded. "Where's Miss Dubinsky now, Commander?"

"Back here in D.C., Mr. President. She'll be placed back at Area 51 for retraining in a few weeks."

"Very good. We dodged a bullet. You think that Syria thing will work? Seems like the government there's getting more unstable every day."

Danny thought about the last cable he'd received from Frank. Both Copeland and Meade were working feverishly, meeting with coup plotters day and night and digging deep into new plans with newfound seriousness. Even Frank and Cal had been involved, and Zippy was busy working the press angle, writing about how al-Quwatli's administration was unfit to lead the country anymore. "I'm not as worried about the government falling as I am about whether Copeland and Meade have the capability to guide the government that comes after," Danny said.

"That's why I want to keep Lodge, Hooks, and Silverman there a little longer," Hillenkoetter said. "Honestly, they're better trained for contingencies than the OPC guys there."

"Approved," Truman said before Danny could protest. "Good to ride herd on them, better to get their bacon out of the fire in case things go bad. And between you and me, Hilly, I'm getting a little tired of Frank Wisner's OPC messes. I'm thinking of putting the office back under CIA control, soon as it's politically feasible."

"I'd appreciate that, Mr. President," Hillenkoetter said, a quick look of relief crossing his face. "They're far too permissive about what they're allowed to do."

"And you're too conservative, Hilly," the President said, with just enough of an edge beneath his toothy smile. "Find a way where you and Wisner can meet in the middle."

There was a rap on the door, and one of the Secret Service men stuck his head in. "He's here, Mr. President."

"Show him right in, Tommy, thank you."

The three men waited in silence for several long, awkward moments until the secretary opened the door once more and James Forrestal walked in.

"Oh! Didn't know we were having that kind of meeting," Forrestal said as the door closed behind him. "Good to see you again, Wallace."

Wallace saluted Forrestal—he was still the Secretary of Defense, after all—and shook his hand, but didn't otherwise reply. The President's secretary had already ordered coffee, which now sat on the table between the men. Forrestal waited for someone to speak, then shrugged and poured a cup, offering it to Truman. "Mr. President?"

The Missourian waved it away. "We have a problem, Jim. More than one."

Forrestal put down the cup. "What happened?"

Truman looked over to Danny, who nodded and passed a folder Forrestal's way. "We've had a major security breach at Area 51, Mr. Secretary."

Forrestal took the folder and opened it, scanning the cover page. His brow furrowed as he read. "I fail to see how this is a breach, Commander."

"Course you do, Jim. Because you ordered it," Hillenkoetter said. "You ordered a full security review—and pulled all the audio recorders on all the Variants for 'testing'—just as Wallace here was out of town. And we have the call logs from your phone to Area 51 just two hours before Dr. Schreiber went down to visit POSEIDON, even though we'd agreed that those two bastards should never meet."

"I never agreed to that," Forrestal said, his face animated. "I still think it's a mistake. Schreiber's doing fine work on that vortex, and keeping him out of Variant research is dangerous."

"More dangerous than allowing a former Nazi access to humans with superpowers?" Danny snapped before he realized what he'd said.

"*Former* Nazi, and a brilliant mind," Forrestal replied quickly. "We *still* don't know what these . . . these *people* are capable of. And that Bronk guy, he doesn't seem to be getting anywhere on their origins or the extent of their powers or even *why* they have these powers. So, yes, I want the best man for the job, and I think that's Schreiber. So I gave him a chance to check things out. And as Secretary of Defense, I outrank both of you."

"You don't outrank me, Jim," Truman said quietly. "And need I remind you, when it comes to MAJESTIC-12, you and Hilly are on equal footing, and Commander Wallace needs approvals from you *both* to make substantive changes to anything at Area 51." Truman stood up and began to pace, his face reddening. "*And* I personally told you, Jim, that I didn't want the PAPERCLIP man near our Variants. My order. *Mine!* And as of last November, the people of the United States upheld the notion that I should be the one to give the orders; is that not correct?"

"Well, yes, Mr. President, but—"

Truman cut Forrestal off. "No buts, Jim. You're the security breach here. You've shown far too much willingness to go off on your own with regard to MAJESTIC-12. You know what I gotta do now, Jim? I gotta launch a full-on security investigation on you, because you went ahead and violated one of my direct orders."

"I don't think that's strictly necesse—"

"*Necessary?*" Truman thundered. "It's absolutely necessary. You violate my orders on the single most sensitive, top-secret project in United States history, and you don't think you should be held accountable for that? And I know, Jim; I know about Dewey," the President added, waggling a finger at him. "You told me back in November that it was just the press gunning for me, but I had some of my people look into it. You met Governor Dewey last fall and offered to stay on as Defense Secretary for him. What'd you tell him about all this, Jim?"

"Nothing, Mr. President! I swear it!"

Truman stood up straight and visibly tamped down on his anger. "I'll expect your resignation on my desk Monday. After that, I expect you to cooperate fully with the subsequent investigation into your activities around MAJESTIC-12." The President stiffly and formally extended his hand toward the Defense Secretary. "Your country thanks you for your service."

Stunned, Forrestal shook Truman's hand, then turned to look at Hillenkoetter and Danny like a deer in the headlights. "If you'll excuse me, then," he said quietly, then walked to the door of the Oval Office, which opened to let him out.

"Shit," Truman said once he was gone, flopping back down onto the couch. "I hate doing stuff like that."

"Needed to be done, Mr. President," Hillenkoetter said succinctly. "We're gonna have to keep an eye on him. And we can't have Hoover running the investigation, either. Or even the Defense guys."

"I've already figured that out, I think," Truman said. "Secret Service is run through Treasury, so neither Defense nor Justice have any say or any knowledge of what they can do. So, we'll make this a special Secret Service investigation. Just need the right investigators."

"Anybody in mind?" Hillenkoetter asked.

Truman turned to Danny and smiled. "In fact, I do."

12.

March 28, 1949

Danny exited the door of the cargo plane and let the hot desert air hit his face, prompting a smile. He'd never thought he would've been much for deserts, but having spent time at Area 51 for years now, he'd found himself missing its sun and warmth. Less so, however, the headaches.

Major Hamilton was waiting for him and Maggie at the bottom of the stairs. "Didn't expect to see you back here so soon, Maggie," he said.

"Neither did I," Maggie said. "How you doing, Major?"

Danny shot Hamilton a glance. *She's not cleared.* "Keeping busy," the major said cheerily. "Let's get you back to base. We've set up a room for you near the administrative center, where some of the scientists stay."

Her eyebrows shot up. "You mean I don't have to drive the three miles to stay in the barbed-wire playpen?"

"Not this trip, Mags," Danny replied. "Need you handy. You won't be here long."

Maggie looked at him, expecting more information, but Danny didn't feel like repeating himself later, so he motioned for her to walk ahead toward the waiting jeep. "We buttoned up here?" he asked Hamilton quietly when she was out of earshot.

"I think so. Tell you more in a bit."

The five-minute ride to the main base was spent in silence. When they arrived, Danny urged Maggie to settle in and "freshen up," which she seemed to take with some bemusement. Then, with Hamilton in tow, Danny made a beeline for his office, where Detlev Bronk was already waiting for them.

Danny made sure the door was closed before he started talking. "Really good job, gentlemen. I figured Montague would try to pull something while I was gone. Just didn't think Forrestal would involve himself personally."

Hamilton handed over a teletype. "Resigned this morning. Health reasons."

Danny couldn't help but crack a smile. "Hope he's feeling better. Now, what's the latest?"

Bronk went first. "We didn't discover that Schreiber had been visiting POSEIDON until the third or fourth time. Apparently, the last few times he was down there he actually drew blood and then used the samples in various vortex experiments—late at night, while everyone who would have known he was up to something was asleep. Schreiber was a night owl to begin with, so it wasn't seen as such a big deal when he came in to do work at 2 a.m."

Danny frowned. "New rule: at least three people are in the room with the vortex at all times, and I want it locked down between 11 p.m. and 7 a.m. unless specifically requested and signed off on by at least two of the three of us. What else?"

"We're still trying to figure out what the results of his testing were, and if POSEIDON's blood had any effect. I have a team going over the readings now, and all of Schreiber's notes."

"Where's Schreiber now?" Danny asked.

"House arrest," Hamilton said. "We took everything out of his room, searched it, and then gave back only some books and stuff, nothing related to his work. He's out of the picture for now, but he hasn't exactly been completely transparent about what he was up to and whether it worked or not."

"I really wish we could get Mrs. Stevens on the vortex study," Bronk added. "She's far too smart to be creating underwear for Variants."

Danny smiled. "Did the underwear work?"

"Of course it did," Bronk replied. "She even got pockets in 'em."

"Handy. And we may earn some extra trust on this next assignment I have for her. Meantime, I'll need you to take the lead on the vortex and, most importantly, figure out what Schreiber was up to. John, how are we looking on security?"

The tall, good-looking man shrugged. "Nothing beyond that direct call to Schreiber. The rest of Forrestal's orders came through normal channels. We let 'em through and then watched like a hawk. Most of it came from Montague, but he said he was acting under orders from the secretary. So, he's clean."

"Sure he is," Danny remarked. "All right. Great job, gentlemen. Now, if you'll excuse me, I need to do a quick mission briefing for a detached team."

Hamilton stood to go, but turned back. "Detached team?"

"Keeping this one close. Maggie and Mrs. Stevens. Sorry, all I can say."

Hamilton shrugged and left, leaving Bronk to linger a moment. "I thought we were keeping Mrs. Stevens out of fieldwork. She's doing incredible things in the labs here, Dan. Incredible things."

"Not my call, Doc," Danny said, making it clear it wasn't up for further discussion. After Bronk left, he had his clerk run out to find both women. It took fifteen minutes before both of them were sitting in his office and reintroductions were made.

"So what can I do for you two?" Mrs. Stevens said. "I always love creating things for your little business trips." She added little finger-quotes around "business trips" for good measure.

"Well, actually, this time you're the one on the business trip, Mrs. Stevens. I have a sensitive assignment for you and Miss Dubinsky here. I think you'll like it."

Maggie leaned over. "That means you'll hate it," she interpreted.

"I'm sorry, Commander, but I just can't up and leave on some kind of assignment!" Mrs. Stevens protested. "I have several experiments running in my lab right now. And who's going to take care of Mr. Stevens while I'm gone?"

"Mr. Stevens will be given full privileges at the mess hall for the duration of your absence, and we'll have someone come in and clean house every so often," Danny said, making a note to himself to actually deliver on these promises. "If all goes well, you won't be gone very long."

"Well, I'm sorry again, Commander, but when I took this job, it was with the understanding that your assignments wouldn't conflict with my duties at home. My most important duty is to my family, sir!"

Danny shot a look at Maggie, who was ready to burst out giggling. "Mrs. Stevens, I couldn't agree with you more. But this assignment doesn't come from me. It comes from the very top. From President Truman himself."

Mrs. Stevens, who had been sitting up straight with reserved and proper anger, suddenly settled back into her chair. "The President? Why does he even know about little old me?"

"You're a Variant, Mrs. Stevens. He's read dossiers on all of you. More importantly, you're the most intelligent person ever measured in IQ, and this assignment needs your smarts and discernment."

"And what does it need from me?" Maggie asked.

"Your warmth and way with people, of course," Danny cracked. "This isn't a combat op, Mags."

"Damn shame," she replied, earning a look of horror from Mrs. Stevens. "What's the op?"

"What I'm about to tell you is sensitive as hell, and you'll be involved in a domestic matter for the first time. That means that you cannot, repeat *cannot*, allow yourselves to be discovered as Variants under any circumstances. You'll be covered as special Secret Service investigators under a new program for women."

"Do they even *have* women Secret Service agents?" Mrs. Stevens asked.

"They do now," Danny said. "Your job—and yes, this comes from Truman himself—is to investigate potential leaks regarding Area 51 and the MAJESTIC-12 program by the now-former Secretary of Defense, James Forrestal."

For once, Maggie seemed genuinely shocked. "The Defense Secretary sold us out?"

"We don't know that yet, but there have been some activities here at Area 51 under his purview that violated direct orders from the President. Luckily, I had people watching for it while we were in Damascus, and we caught it. But now the President wants a full-on security review, and you two will be part of that."

Mrs. Stevens nodded gravely. "You want me to analyze his behavior and his friendships and acquaintances to find any potential patterns, then see if other people's patterns check out as well."

"Bingo," Danny said.

"And you want me to talk pretty to them," Maggie said.

"Doesn't have to be pretty. But we need the truth," Danny said. "We've worked very, very hard to give Variants a place to live and a chance to serve their country. For all your sakes, you need to find any potential leaks, if only to protect other Variants."

"And if we find a leak?" Mrs. Stevens asked.

"I can only assume it will be dealt with accordingly," Danny replied neutrally. "But I should add, *plugging* the leak is not your purview here. Read me?" He said the last part, looking directly at Maggie.

"Loud and clear," Maggie replied, but Danny knew full well she was fiercely protective of her fellow Variants. In fact, he was counting on it.

13.

March 30, 1949

Ever since Cal had arrived in Syria, the dawn call to prayer woke him up just as the sun was rising. He found it exotic and kind of soothing, and certainly better than the bells of an alarm clock.

Tank treads made a noisy alarm look meek by comparison.

It took a moment for the noise to register, but once he'd figured it out, Cal jumped out of bed and ran to the window, looking down from his second-floor perch onto the dusty street below, where three tanks were rolling through the neighborhood. At the intersection, a couple of soldiers were putting signs up on the street poles. Cal wasn't close enough to read them, and he couldn't have read Arabic either way, but given the circumstances, he figured it wasn't because the circus had come to town.

Cal ran from his room to find Copeland already awake and trying to comfort his pregnant wife and little boy. "You just stay here today, all right? I have some men from the consulate coming over to stand watch. I'm going to have to go do things here, OK?"

"You be careful," Lorraine replied, giving him a kiss. "Don't do anything heroic out there. You run if it gets bad, you hear me?"

"I will, I promise." Copeland smiled as Cal cleared his throat—partly to get attention, and partly to not burst out laughing.

"Is this what I think it is?" Cal asked. "What's the good word?"

Copeland nodded. "This is it. Let's go. Meade's coming around to pick us up."

Ten minutes later, with Cal fully dressed and Frank by his side, they were out the door and in Meade's comfortable BMW 321. The streets were quiet and largely empty except for a handful of storefronts and market stalls where the proprietors were making their prayers, their carpets pointing south-southeast toward Mecca. The Syrian Army, however, was too busy securing major roads and bridges to pray. Cal had studied up on Islam a little bit, and wondered if the soldiers would gain absolution later, or if Za'im had given the country's Christians and Kurds coup duty that morning.

"Well, they're not stopping the prayers," Frank ventured, obviously thinking along similar tracks. "I figure if the people felt threatened or angry, they'd do something about it."

Meade nodded. "We saw a little of that in Turkey and the Balkans during the war. Prayer time trumps most things, but not self-preservation."

Cal couldn't help but smile. "So, what's the plan?"

"Quick trip around town," Meade said. "I want to make sure they went through the to-do list, like the state radio station on your right."

Frank and Cal turned to see a small sandstone building with a large metal transmission tower sprouting up from around and inside it, completely surrounded by soldiers with weapons drawn. So it was across the rest of Damascus: the newspaper, hospitals, power plants, the presidential palace, major intersections, and various military barracks and bases, all locked down tight.

The last stop was Parliament, where a large crowd had gathered at the front steps. Meade pulled over a block away, and the four of them began walking toward the area. They were stopped by a young Syrian Army officer, but a flash of their diplomatic credentials—they didn't even look at Cal's—let them through.

The crowd, as they got close, consisted of government bureaucrats and parliamentarians, many of whom seemed to have dressed up for the occasion—three-piece suits, pocket watches, shined shoes, and velvet fezzes were the order of the day. A fair number of journalists were there as well, trading information and likely playing a big game of telephone. Cal spotted Zippy in the middle of an interview ahead and waited patiently until she was done before heading over.

"Miss Zippy," Cal said quietly. "How you doing this morning?"

To his surprise, she gave him a big smile. "This reporter thing is a lot more fun than I thought it would be. Really easy way to get information without looking suspicious. I'm surprised we don't use it on all our jobs."

Cal shrugged. "I imagine I wouldn't be as good at it as you. I'm no writer. What's the word out there?"

She flipped open her notebook. "Syrian Army is in full control of Damascus, and reports out of Aleppo say the same thing. They say President al-Quwatli was taken into custody—*protective* custody, I should say—and that he's been transported to one of the army barracks for his own safety."

Cal frowned. "Good Lord. They're gonna kill him there."

Zippy shrugged. "Maybe, maybe not. Some of the crowd here still believe he's the father of Syrian independence from France, while others think he's been a terrible president, especially lately. I think we have Copeland to thank for that. But I really don't think killing him would be a good idea. If this group is any indication, they like the fact that nobody's dead. We should try to keep it that way."

"Amen to that, Miss Zippy. I'll pass it along. Anything else?"

"I think they're tired of fighting," she said, seeming sympathetic with the people there. "I think they want peace. Tell Za'im that."

Cal smiled and wandered back toward Frank and the others. Peace would be a fine, fine thing indeed, though the look on Frank's face when he found him wasn't encouraging.

"Za'im isn't here. He's at one of the barracks with al-Quwatli. We're a little worried," Frank said. "Especially Copeland. We don't know which one."

"Zippy says al-Quwatli's at the Mezze Prison barracks. And she says this crowd wouldn't be very keen at all if he ended up dead at the end of all this," Cal said.

Frank dashed off toward Meade, who was in the middle of an animated conversation with three Syrians. Cal kept pace easily and not without a little pride in his borrowed youth—though he always felt a little bad about that, too, no matter how good it felt for a fifty-five-year-old man to keep up with a thirty-year-old trained soldier.

"We gotta go," Frank said, pulling Meade aside. "Za'im's got al-Quwatli at Mezze Prison. We don't want it getting messy."

Meade nodded and, literally pulling Copeland away from another group, dashed back to the car, everyone else in tow. He drove quickly and, at times, dangerously through the still–largely deserted streets of Damascus.

"Was this part of the plan?" Cal asked from the back seat. "Locking down the old president like this?"

Meade's eyes darted to the rearview, but he left the question for Copeland to answer. "No, it wasn't, Mr. Hooks," Copeland said. "The plan was to keep al-Quwatli at the presidential palace and try to convince him to transfer power peaceably in exchange for leading a small, muzzled opposition party. I thought we had agreement on that. Didn't we have agreement on that, Steve?"

Meade shook his head. "Sorry, guys," he said to Cal and Frank. "This must be Miles's first coup. It never goes how you want it to go."

Cal smiled ruefully. "I ain't been at this long, but nothing I've been part of ever went a hundred percent according to plan. May want to drive a bit faster there, Mr. Meade."

A few minutes later, the car pulled up to a gated compound where several Syrian Army soldiers stood guard. They immediately trained their weapons on the car, but Miles frantically waved his diplomatic credentials out the window and, after a few minutes of rapid-fire Arabic, got the guards to radio their superiors. It took less than thirty seconds for the weapons to be lowered and the gate opened.

"At least Za'im remembers who his friends are," Meade said, trying to put up a veneer of good cheer as he aimed the car toward the largest cluster of buildings.

"Or we're loose ends to tie up," Frank said. Cal caught his eye, and Frank opened his coat—he had his CIA-issued gun in a shoulder holster, and the silencer was right there in a pouch next to it. Cal nodded back—his own gun was stowed at the small of his back.

It was also unloaded, except for a single bullet in the chamber. Cal wanted to be damn sure that he didn't rely on a weapon when there could be a better way to solve your problem. Frank would probably chew him out something fierce for it . . . which was why Cal kept his ammo situation to himself. The good Lord had given him the ability to put people to sleep with a touch, steal a bit of life from them in the process, so it stood to reason that nobody had to get killed in most cases.

They'd just pulled up to one of the larger barracks when they spied al-Shishakli outside, al-Hinnawi on one side . . . and a boy not older than maybe ten on the other. Cal recognized the officers from the mission briefings, but . . . "What's that boy doing here?" he mused.

"Apparently, that's Shishakli's kid," Frank said, getting himself out of the car. "I don't even ask anymore."

Miles immediately rushed over and started talking in Arabic. The two officers looked worried, and there were a lot of hands moving about. "Apparently, Za'im's acting up," Frank muttered, translating for Cal. "He brought the President here and meanwhile already moved his family into the presidential palace. He has people cataloging museums and galleries, too."

Cal frowned. "Now ain't the time to redecorate."

A minute later, all four Americans were ushered inside the barracks. But instead of going somewhere more appropriate—an officers' quarters or mess hall, say—they ended up in a bathroom. There they found Za'im pacing, with al-Quwatli tied to a chair and placed in the wide-open shower room.

"Why is he in there?" Copeland asked, more to himself than anyone else.

Nonetheless, Frank answered. "Easy place to wash away the blood, Miles. Now fix this."

When Za'im saw them, he rushed over and gave Miles a huge hug, then heartily shook the hands of Meade and Frank. When he got to Cal, though, the Syrian stopped. "And who is this?" he asked, still smiling but with a wary look in his eye.

"One of ours, Colonel," Frank said calmly. "He's been looking out for you for the past month, watching your back. Just like us."

Za'im's smile grew wider and he extended his hand. "Then you are welcome, African man. I thank you for your service to your country and to mine!"

Cal shook but tried to gauge the look in the man's eye. Za'im was sweating slightly, his movements manic and erratic. It was only then, as he shook Za'im's right hand, that Cal noticed the pistol in his other hand.

"Well, it's my pleasure, Colonel," Cal said slowly, desperately wishing Miss Maggie was still around. "It's real nice to be able to help the Syrian people like this, and without any bloodshed. Can't abide bloodshed when it ain't necessary."

Cal knew it was ham-fisted the moment he said it, but he was no diplomat. Za'im looked at him curiously but then walked back toward the shower room. "Yes, my friend, only a lunatic or criminal would *want* blood to be shed. But there are times, unfortunately, when it is necessary."

Copeland took a step forward. "Colonel, you've won. The army is in control of Damascus. We checked everything—your plan was flawless and executed brilliantly. There's no reason for the President to be tied—"

"*I* am the President!" Za'im shouted, his humor evaporating.

"Yes, of course, Mr. President. My apologies," Copeland said, hands outstretched. "But there's no reason for the *former* president to be killed here today. In fact, it may only make things worse for you if that happens."

Cal looked over to Frank, who stood with his arms crossed over his chest—and one hand burrowed in his jacket. With all the skills and memories Frank had at his command, Cal knew he could probably handle the situation on his own in a matter of seconds. But then all the effort Copeland had put into cultivating Za'im would be lost.

Of course, Cal thought, maybe that wasn't a bad thing.

"Al-Quwatli is a traitor to the Syrian people!" Za'im said, practically shouting. "He gave us our independence only to squander Syrian blood in a fruitless battle against Israel. Had he given us the arms and men we needed, we would all be praying in Jerusalem by now! But he is weak and wants to see a weakened Syria when our country should be the most powerful nation in what you call your 'Middle East.' How can I let him live? How can I let him become the head of the opposition, Mr. Copeland, to have him sniping at me and biting at my ankles all the time? This is no way for a leader to run a country!"

Cal thought furiously. By now, Za'im was standing just a few feet from al-Quwatli, who was sitting with his eyes closed, breathing exaggerated breaths. *He's preparing to die*, Cal thought. *He's making peace with his Maker.*

There had to be another way.

"Mr. President, if I may?" Cal said before he even realized words were coming out of his mouth.

Za'im looked at Cal quizzically. "You disagree, African man?"

Cal frowned. There was a time when being called a lot worse than "African man" was simply a way of life. But being a Variant, with his kind of power, made him a lot less tolerant of it lately. "My name is Calvin Hooks, Mr. President, and maybe there's a third way here, between what had been planned originally and this . . . new plan."

"And what way is this, Mr. Hooks?" Za'im demanded. "How long have you even been in my country?"

"Oh, about a month now," Cal said, slowly walking toward Za'im and al-Quwatli, his hands out. There were half a dozen other Syrian Army men in the room, so Cal figured he'd be riddled with bullets if he made a sudden move to try to even touch Za'im. "But I've done my reading. That there former president is still a symbol to a whole lot of your people, even the ones who are out there celebrating right now that he's gone. Am I right?"

"What of it?" Zai'm asked.

"Well, you kill him, even if you set it up to look like you didn't, well, they're gonna blame you. Now, I'm not a leader, but seems to me it's easier to rule a country where the people like you, rather than a country where they think you killed their George Washington."

"Who? Who is George Washington?"

Cal closed his eyes and cursed himself. "Sorry. Their hero. The father of their country. George Washington was the first president of the United States. This gentleman here is the first president of an independent Syria, am I right? You can't kill a symbol, sir. It's just . . . too big. Too big. They'll get angry and they'll blame you and then you won't be able to do anything else except spend the rest of your days lookin' over your shoulder in fear."

Cal looked over to Frank, who was staring right back, surprised. Cal thought he'd messed up somehow, but Frank gave him a small grin and cocked his head back toward Za'im. *Keep at it.*

"So. Mr. Hooks," Za'im said, walking toward Cal with the gun in his hand by his side. "You are not a leader. You are not even given full rights in your own country. But I respect this, because you know what it is like to be led, and led poorly. What would you have me do?"

Well, damned if I know, Cal thought. "You can't kill him. Doesn't sound like you want him around anymore either, though. Right?"

"This is correct, Mr. Hooks."

"Then kick him out. Exile him," Cal said. "I'm sure the United States would be happy to put him up for a while. Get him out of your hair."

Copeland and Meade looked over at Cal in complete shock, and Cal realized he'd just made a serious promise on behalf of his entire country. Not how he thought his day would've gone.

But Za'im was smiling again. "And I will tell the people he fled. Yes, Mr. Hooks . . . I like this. We can even show them! Shishakli! Get the film crew! We will show al-Quwatli getting into a car and driving off with our American friends here."

Frank stepped forward. "Um, Colonel . . . sorry, Mr. President . . . we shouldn't really be captured on film, you know."

At this, Za'im actually chuckled and put a finger to the side of his nose. "I understand you, sir. I understand you! We will stage it, then. And then you may do whatever you wish with this traitor here. Untie him!"

The Syrians scurried to release al-Quwatli, who had a look on his face that was part utter confusion, part immense relief. Copeland, however, appeared rather put out. "Mr. Hooks, that was not part of the plan," he whispered through gritted teeth.

"Neither was seeing that man executed in a shower," Cal replied under this breath. "Go on and send me home if you want, Mr. Copeland, but I wasn't gonna just sit there and let him do it."

Meade smiled. "Honestly? Best of a bad situation, Miles. And now we get a chance to chat with al-Quwatli for a few days of interviews before we pack him off wherever."

Copeland considered this, then nodded, even if it was begrudgingly. "All right. And yes, this is better than having him executed. Thank you, Mr. Hooks." The OPC man then turned and started speaking Arabic again with Za'im and his officers.

"That was pretty damn good, Cal," Frank said, clapping him on the shoulder. "I'm impressed."

Cal looked down at his hands, which were trembling. "That was mighty stupid, I think."

"It was brave and it saved a man's life," Frank said quietly. "Solved everybody's problems, too."

Cal shook his head. "Yeah, well, except for one problem."

"What's that?"

"What are we gonna do the *next* time Za'im gets antsy?"

Frank grimaced. "No idea. But we better be ready."

A-8

TOP SECRET
EYES ONLY
THE WHITE HOUSE
WASHINGTON

TO: DCI Hillenkoetter, LGEN Vandenberg, SECA Gray,
MAJG Montague, LCDR Wallace, DR Bronk

Gentlemen,

It is my determination that the new Secretary of
Defense will not be cleared for Operation Majestic
Twelve. Gordon Gray, the Secretary of the Army, will join
General Vandenberg as the military representatives on the
project and will assist in the maintenance, upkeep, and
research at Area 51.

It is also my determination that any missions involving
Variant individuals must be personally approved by
the President of the United States. Any changes in the
operations at Area 51 must also be approved by the
President, to avoid additional security issues.

Investigations of potential security breaches in the
wake of Secretary Forrestal's resignation are continuing
under the Director of Central Intelligence.

I would remind you all that sharing any detail of
Majestic Twelve outside those previously approved is an
Act of Treason against the United States, and will be
dealt with as such.

Harry Truman

TOP SECRET
EYES ONLY

14.

April 7, 1949

Maggie Dubinsky sat on the park bench in Lafayette Square, just across the street from the White House, appreciating the hell out of the location. Pennsylvania Avenue was the busiest street in Washington, generating enough noise and movement during the day to effectively shield anyone who was watching.

Yes, there were some Secret Service guys in the park—a couple of all-too-obviously plainclothes mooks who wouldn't pass muster as department store security guards. But they weren't watching for a couple of guys sitting on a park bench. They were looking for active threats to the President.

The threats Maggie was looking for were far more insidious.

It had taken days of combing through Forrestal's confiscated address book and calendar to find times and places where he might've met with someone outside MAJESTIC-12 or the Pentagon, but then that's what Mrs. Stevens was for—finding patterns. She quickly determined that a trip across the river to the White House or Capitol Hill often led to additional business in the city, which made sense. And so they began looking for holes in the schedule—an extra fifteen minutes to half an hour where Forrestal could've made a side trip somewhere in between, off the books.

There were a lot of stops in Georgetown, as it happened, which was on the way back to Virginia but also pretty close to Foggy Bottom, where both the CIA and State Department were. There were also some business cards from restaurants in the neighborhood in Forrestal's address book. From there, they managed to find a hole in Forrestal's schedule around dinner, and a restaurant reservation at the Occidental Grill for the same time.

Then they got to play gumshoe, heading to the restaurant with a veritable who's who of Washington in black-and-white photographs, along with freshly minted Secret Service badges. A waiter identified Frank Wisner as Forrestal's most recent dinner companion there, just two nights before his last meeting with Truman.

After that, they did surveillance on Wisner, who barely left his office—thankfully. When he did, it made it much easier to follow him. And he often came to this park to read a book and have a sandwich. Occasionally, Wisner would also get company—the first time it happened, Maggie wasn't prepared.

This time was different.

A short man in a large fedora and greatcoat walked across the park, and Maggie made him immediately—the wisps of nerves coming off him gave the game away. That said, she admired the effort he took to hide his face, keeping his hat low and his eyes away from others as they approached. Though it wasn't exactly surprising that J. Edgar Hoover would have known a trick or two.

Maggie opened her purse and pressed down on a large button, then grabbed her makeup compact as the portable reel-to-reel started up. The machine was attached to an odd-looking microphone cleverly incorporated into the design of the oversized handbag—a Mrs. Stevens "special" that had taken her all of a day to whip up.

She opened the compact and checked her face. "Eyes on Target One."

A short burst of static flooded her ear before she heard the response. "All right, then. I mean, roger that. Target One," Mrs. Stevens replied. Maggie resisted the urge to look up at the second-story window of Blair House, the presidential guest house, where her fellow Variant was perched with a radio and a few other toys, including a small film camera.

"Sorry. Talk normally. I'm just used to . . . Wait. Target Two confirmed, approaching."

"I see him. I'll patch your audio into the mike so you can hear what's going on," Mrs. Stevens said.

Maggie watched as Frank Wisner sat down next to Hoover, their backs to the White House. "How are you, Director?" Wisner said; Maggie could hear him in her earpiece clear as day.

"I'm pissed off, that's what I am," Hoover said. "We haven't got anything out of anywhere since Jim was fired. How'd those freaks do in Syria?"

Wisner coughed once and cleared his throat. "Honestly, they're pretty well-trained operatives. Nothing in the reports or follow-ups indicates use of strange abilities or events. One of 'em apparently talked Za'im out of shooting his predecessor in the head, but it wasn't the girl. I guess he just made a damn convincing argument."

Maggie's eyes widened. She'd just listened in on the head of the State Department's Office of Policy Coordination and the director of the goddamn FBI talking not only about her but her Enhancement as well.

Suddenly, a flock of pigeons in the immediate vicinity took wing, and two dogs began barking frantically. Maggie realized that she'd let her guard down, and immediately clamped back down on her surge of emotion, doing her best to focus . . . even if she so very badly wanted to make both men die of fright in that moment.

"If we're going to expose these *things* for what they are, Frank, I need more than that. Where's Forrestal now?"

"He went down to his place in Florida, but he's apparently had some kind of breakdown. The family's circling the wagons. Can't get through to him. He's not taking any calls, not even when I pretend to be the President. Heard he may have gone to a hospital, but we just don't know."

Maggie glared daggers at the two men but kept her emotions in check. She was a person, not a thing, despite what Hoover thought. In fact, she was far *more* of a person than he'd ever be. She was different, sure. But she was pretty damn sure she was *better*.

"Visitors?" Hoover asked. "I could head down there for vacation."

"Doubt it," Wisner said. "May be worth a try, but if you're spotted . . ."

"Right. Fine. What about Joe?"

"They gave a short briefing on the Hill about the Syria situation, but it left out pretty much everything, including our office's involvement. So, nothing there."

Maggie pulled out a notepad and wrote: WHO IS JOE? CAPITOL HILL.

"Do you think your men in Syria could capture one of those agents? Lock him down somewhere? Might be our best chance to break this thing wide open," Hoover said.

Even from a distance, Maggie noticed that Wisner looked uncomfortable. "My guys aren't soldiers, Director. They're spies and negotiators and blackmailers and thieves, and they're good at what they do. Word out of Damascus is that the agents supplied by CIA are highly skilled real combat types, even the women. Incredibly talented and dangerous. And, frankly, it raises too many questions."

There was a long silence before Hoover finally stood. "Tell Joe I want him to set up a meeting with some kindred spirits at the Pentagon. Seems like we may need some fire-power here."

Wisner stood as well. "Director, I have to point out that the behavior of the agents in question, well . . . it was exemplary. Throughout this Syria thing, they've been right on point. No problems with them at all. They're good at what they do and every indication is that they are patriotic Americans, just like you and me."

Hoover took a step toward Wisner and practically bumped chests with him. "And how do you know that's not what they *want* you to think? Dammit, man, they are *not human*. They're dangerous! The moment they truly realize just how dangerous they are, how do we stop them? What happens when they decide to join the Reds? Or decide to band together and take over both countries? Or all of humanity? Think about that the next time you get a report on how nice they are!"

Hoover tromped off, steaming, and Wisner slowly walked away in the other direction about a minute later, leaving Maggie stewing on her own bench.

"Well, that wasn't very nice," Mrs. Stevens said over the radio.

Maggie snapped open her compact but caught her reflection before she replied. She never recalled her face looking so cold and angry before, even though that seemed to be her MO ever since she'd become Empowered. "Let's go."

She jabbed her finger into her purse and stopped the tape, then slung it over her shoulder and made for the Capital Grille, a landmark restaurant a block away with large private booths and a discreet staff—perfect for politicking and semi-secret meetings. Much better than a public park.

Mrs. Stevens was waiting for her in a booth when she arrived.

"I ordered highballs. That all right, Maggie? I love highballs. Thought we might celebrate!"

Maggie plopped down in the booth and looked hard at the other woman. "Celebrate what, exactly? The fact that the director of the FBI not only knows about us but sees us as subhuman and wants to kill us because we're a threat?"

Mrs. Stevens's smile evaporated. "Well, when you put it that way. But he didn't say anything about killing us. Just sort of . . . stopping us?"

The waiter came over with the two drinks, and Maggie took a long swig. "Mrs. Stevens . . . good Lord, I don't even know your first name."

Her smile returned immediately. "It's Rose."

"Rose. Look. We are *different* from all other people who've ever lived, OK? You're literally the smartest person alive. I can control people's emotions. Heck, how long do you think it would take just the two of us to assassinate the President if we really put our minds to it?"

Mrs. Stevens looked blank for a moment, then raised her eyebrows. "Maybe about ten minutes? Depends on a number of variables, such as where Truman is in the house, the number of guards, how many—"

Maggie held up her hand. "Rose. It was a rhetorical question. Nobody wants to assassinate the President. But you can see Hoover's point, right? If we wanted to, we could be really dangerous. If the world found out about us, they'd hate us. They'd want to kill us."

"Some would. Maybe some wouldn't. Maybe that's why we're doing all this, to prove our worth and to let people know we're on the right side of things, you know?"

Maggie couldn't help but smile. "You're smart, Rose, but let's not be naive, OK?"

Mrs. Stevens pursed her lips and took a sip of her drink. "All right. Anyway, what do we do?"

"Take over the world before they kill us all?" Maggie said with a smile, but immediately regretted it; the look on Mrs. Stevens's face was pure shock. "Kidding! Kidding. God, I'm kidding, Rose. Sorry. No, we're going to report in to Danny on the secure teletype at Foggy Bottom, and we're going to figure out who Joe on Capitol Hill is. We're also going to warn Frank, Cal, and Zippy to watch their backs out there in Syria, in case Wisner changes his mind. And then we find a way to talk to Forrestal, which won't be easy, with his family running interference. We scare him too much, he'll run to Hoover and that'll prove Hoover right. So, until he moves, we're stuck."

Mrs. Stevens's smile popped right back on her face. "Well, while you were sneaking around the park, I got a bit of good news from our Secret Service man in Florida. Forrestal left his house."

"Left? Where did he go?"

"Well, they had to do a little digging to find out, but seems like he checked himself in at Bethesda Naval Hospital. For exhaustion. And very limited visiting hours for family."

Maggie thought about this for a second. "Limited visiting hours for us, too. But we've gotten into worse places. Shouldn't be too hard."

"What worse places?" Mrs. Stevens asked, leaning forward.

Maggie finally cracked a smile of her own. "You aren't cleared for it. Which means I'm gonna need another couple highballs before I tell you."

15.

April 17, 1949

Diplomacy had never been one of Frank Lodge's strong suits to begin with, but even with one of America's foremost diplomats now residing in his head, he still didn't like playing the part. And yet here he was, dressed in a goddamn suit and sitting in the back seat of Meade's BMW with Copeland and Keeley, on the way to meet with the new President of Syria, Husni al-Za'im.

Cal was sitting up front, dressed in a military uniform this time to make his presence at the meeting more believable. A couple of the military guys stationed at the legation had tossed some angry looks Cal's way, but Meade had stepped in and told them, in no uncertain terms, to mind their own business and, if need be, take orders from Cal.

Frank hoped it wouldn't come to that. He'd honestly never thought much one way or the other about Negroes, given that he was a Bostonian and didn't really come across too many of them. The ones he'd seen in colored units during the war had been fine soldiers, and Frank had done his best to stop his men from engaging in the name-calling and occasional fights that broke out between whites and coloreds.

But Frank saw Cal very differently. Cal had been pissed on his entire life, and yet here he was, a Variant with the amazing power to heal or kill with a single touch. You'd think all that mistreatment would put a man suddenly bestowed with such astonishing capabilities on a very different path. Who wouldn't exact a little justice for all those years of injustice? But Cal was a man of faith, something Frank wished he could understand but didn't. And so, Cal served his country, did as much as he could not to harm anyone too greatly, and took the slings and arrows with a sigh, even with a little smile. Maybe knowing he *could* kill with a touch was enough for him to endure it.

All Frank knew was that if it was him, he'd want to crack some heads.

The car pulled up to Damascus's presidential palace, and a soldier opened the back door of the car for Keeley, Copeland, and Frank, while Cal got out from the shotgun seat and gave a quick look around before flashing Frank an "OK" signal.

"I suppose I'm still going in blind with regard to whatever exactly you did to get Za'im in power, Miles?" Keeley muttered as they entered the spacious building. A little misdirection on the new administration's part had sent the reporters or photographers on a wild-goose chase; there was no one there to cover their arrival.

"Trust me, sir, it's better this way," Copeland said. "Ah, there's Miss Silverman!"

Frank smiled as Zippy Silverman walked over to greet them. She left her kid gloves on as she shook hands—probably wise, given her ability—and paused to give Frank and Cal a hug. They hadn't seen each other for a couple weeks, but she'd regularly left updates and reports at a dead drop conveniently located in a park between Copeland's house and the U.S. legation.

"How you doing, Zip?" Frank asked with a smile. "You look good."

"Reporting suits me," she replied. "And I'm pretty good at it, too. Who knew?"

Keeley stepped over to them. "Excuse me. Who the hell is this?"

Frank put up a calming hand. "Sir, this is Zipporah Silverman. She's one of us, working undercover as a correspondent for *The Jerusalem Post*."

"And as a stringer for the Associated Press now, too," she said, excitement in her voice. "Honestly, the pay's almost better than what I'm getting with—"

"—an agency which shall not be named," Frank finished.

"Right," Zippy said, blushing. "Anyway, I've met the colonel already, so he won't be surprised to see me."

Keeley frowned and stared hard at Frank and Zippy for a minute before turning on his heel and stalking off toward a waiting government official. Frank gave Zippy a small smile. "Nobody tells him anything," Frank said. "Every time I see him, same thing."

"Yeah, well, the Russian ambassador is just as bad," Zippy said as they began walking behind Keeley. "Met him last week. Perfect idiot. It's his number two, Karilov, we should be worried about. They're pretty angry about the coup. He seems to be working some of the opposition legislators hard, some of the military guys who weren't with Za'im. Already laying the groundwork for something."

Frank raised an eyebrow. "You *are* good. Think you can seed some stuff into stories yet?"

"Depends on the seed," she replied. "Not a huge audience here for the *Post*. Mostly intellectuals and government types looking for the next thing to hate about Israel."

"That really bugs you, doesn't it?"

Zippy shrugged. "I'm Jewish, Frank. The Nazis killed so many of us. We've been hated for generations and for no good goddamn reason. Why is everyone surprised that we're now standing up for ourselves and building a country of our own? Don't we deserve it?"

Frank wanted to ask about the "we" part but thought better of it—not the time or the place. "What else on the streets?"

"People are generally OK with Za'im. They feel snakebit after losing the war with Israel last year, and he's promising national pride—without demonizing Israel in the process. He also loosened some of the restrictions on dress—headscarves, fezzes, that sort of thing. Kind of a pro-West move, I think."

"Or pro-Commie," Frank muttered. "Not like the Reds are big on religious dress-up either."

Conversation was halted as they entered the anteroom of the presidential reception hall. There they were

searched—thoroughly—by Za'im's soldiers, and Frank
was grateful he'd left his gun at home. While they were
being patted down, no fewer than four voices in his head
explained in no uncertain terms the best way to dispatch
the six guards in the room with maximum efficiency, and
Frank had to make an effort not to shush them aloud.

After the search, which included confiscating Cal's
sidearm for good measure, the party was ushered into
an opulent room resplendent with the kind of artworks
Frank had seen in Istanbul last year, on a different assignment. Of course, he knew—or rather, the memory of an
Ottoman historian told him—that Syria had been part of
the Ottoman Empire for centuries, and the country was
still shaking off that cultural legacy, along with that of the
French and English, for that matter.

"My friends!" Za'im said, rising from his place at the
head of a long, intricately carved, and polished table. "I
am so very pleased to see you!" He came over, arms wide,
and greeted Copeland with an ebullient hug, ignoring an
increasingly red-faced Keeley.

Thankfully, Copeland remembered his etiquette.
"President al-Za'im, it is good to see you well," he said,
extricating himself from the man's bear hug. "May I present
James Keeley, envoy extraordinary, minister plenipoten-
tiary, and duly appointed representative of the government
and people of the United States of America to the great
Republic of Syria."

Za'im smiled and extended his hand. "Welcome, Mr.
Keeley. My apologies. Your man Mr. Copeland here has
helped save our country from ruin. As have the others here.
On behalf of the Syrian people, I thank you for bringing
peace and prosperity back to our nation."

Keeley shook the new president's hand warily. "On behalf
of the United States, officially, I thank you for receiving me.
We have much to discuss."

"We do! We do! Please sit and take a coffee with me,"
Za'im said.

He's a little manic, said the voice of Jonathan Goldman in Frank's head. Goldman was a head-shrink from Washington whose deathbed Frank had sat at just before the Vienna mission. *Hasn't been getting much sleep, little wild-eyed. Interesting.*

He's not bothering to introduce the others in the room, despite their high ranks, came the voice of Thomas Kincade, a good behind-the-scenes State Department diplomat who'd passed away last February. *He's not used to protocol yet. And yeah, he's looking a little ragged, and not just from putting a government together.*

Frank looked off to the side of the room, where Za'im's aides sat. He immediately recognized al-Hinnawi and al-Shishakli—and Shishakli's kid as well. This time, they'd even got the boy a little military suit of his own, with piping and fringe and everything.

Odd.

Weird.

Unusual.

What the hell? The voices in his head were all on alert now. *Who brings a ten-year-old boy to government meetings? Or coup-planning sessions, for that matter?*

"So, my friends. Mr. Keeley. Does this meeting mean that the United States will officially recognize the legitimacy of our new government on behalf of the Syrian people?"

Keeley smiled, even as the others around the table looked surprised at Za'im's forthrightness. "I'm afraid not, sir. The United States certainly appreciates you acting in the best interests of your people, and has certain expectations that those interests will continue to be upheld."

Za'im's smile narrowed a fraction. "Well, then, speak plainly, Mr. Keeley. What does the United States wish from us before we receive formal recognition?"

"This was a military coup, of course, Mr. Za'im. We expect there will be new elections in short order. We also hope you'll establish peaceful relations with your neighboring states. *All* your neighbors, I should say."

Za'im nodded. "I have no wish to move against Israel at the moment, Mr. Keeley. We have much to do to ensure the welfare of the Syrian people. So long as Israel respects our borders, we will not march on them."

"Those borders are in dispute," Keeley noted. "Are you willing to engage in constructive dialogue and negotiations in order to resolve that dispute? That would go a long way toward recognition."

Za'im thought about this a moment. "I cannot be seen reaching out to Israel for any sort of peace," he said. "Part of what got me here was bitterness over losing the war last year. But if there was an intermediary who could work on our behalf? Then, yes. I would listen to them and I hope they would listen to me. What else?"

This time, Copeland piped up. "The previous administration had stalled its approval for the Trans-Arabian Pipeline. We are hopeful that, as a gesture of goodwill between Syria, the United States, and its Arabian neighbors, you would see fit to approve the TAPline with all due haste."

Za'im nodded and gave Copeland a small smile. "I wondered when you would bring this up. Of course, Syria does not wish to impede progress and commerce. But we would hope that Syria too would benefit from this project, as it is our government that will be called upon to help protect and defend the land on which it sits."

He wants money. Military aid, the diplomat said in Frank's head.

Copeland knew it too. "How much are we talking, my friend?"

Za'im smiled. "See? This is proper negotiating! I would say . . . two hundred million."

Keeley looked shocked, and even Zippy and Cal looked taken aback by the sum. But Copeland merely smiled. "That's quite a lot of money, sir," Copeland said evenly. "Far more than we had discussed previously, I believe."

"Running a country is hard," Za'im said. "There is much work to be done to make Syria great again."

"I'm only authorized to go to fifty million," Copeland insisted.

"One hundred fifty million," Za'im countered.

"Seventy-five."

"One twenty-five."

"Fine, a hundred million even, but that's really all I can do," Copeland said.

Za'im smiled and clapped his hands. "Done!"

"So, does that mean you'll approve the TAPline right away?" Copeland asked.

"Once the United States has recognized the legitimate government of Syria and I have assurances from the highest levels that my hundred million dollars is on the way, then yes," Za'im said. "And I urge your president to hurry, as many other Western nations are waiting to see what the United States does—as are the Soviets."

"Have you received a delegation from the Soviet Union, sir?" Keeley asked neutrally.

"Of course not, Mr. Keeley! I wanted to see my friends here first!"

"Well, we appreciate that," Keeley said.

Za'im smiled. "The Russians are coming tomorrow instead."

Frank couldn't help but chuckle a bit at this. Za'im had used American expertise, assistance, and even a U.S.-led covert operation—a generous term for the fucking mess at Copeland's house the previous month—to bring himself to power but was still playing both sides against each other. It was kind of brilliant. For all his brashness, Za'im at least had the balls to back it up.

"I see. Is there anything else?" Keeley asked.

"Yes, actually. I am hoping you can help me with a small problem I have," Za'im said, looking over at Frank, Cal, and Zippy. "You seem to have some talented individuals well suited to the task."

And here we go, Frank thought. "And what task would that be, sir?" Frank said.

"Have any of you been to Lebanon?" Za'im asked.

FROM: LT LODGE USA
TO: LCMR WALLACE USN, DCI HILLENKOETTER CIA, LTG
VANDENDBERG USAF
CC: MR HOOKS CIA, MISS SILVERMAN CIA, MISS DUBINSKY CIA
DATE: 19 APR 1949
RE: DAMASCUS OPERATION
CLASSIFICATION: TOP SECRET—MAJIK

THIS REQUEST WILL COME THROUGH OFFICIAL CHANNELS FROM
OPC, BUT GIVEN THAT THE REQUEST INCLUDES MAJESTIC-12
ASSETS, WE ARE GIVING OUR OWN UPDATE.

PRESIDENT ZA'IM OF SYRIA HAS ASKED CIA/OPC CHIEF
OF STATION COPELAND TO INVESTIGATE A SITUATION IN
BEIRUT, LEBANON, ON HIS BEHALF, AND HAS SPECIFICALLY
REQUESTED MYSELF, MR HOOKS, AND MISS SILVERMAN FOR
THE JOB, ALONG WITH MR MEADE FROM OPC. THE FOLLOWING
IS OUR VIEW OF THE REQUEST AND OUR RECOMMENDATION.

HISTORICAL BACKGROUND

ORIGINALLY PART OF THE FRENCH MANDATE OF SYRIA, LEBANON
GAINED INDEPENDENCE AS A SOVEREIGN REPUBLIC IN 1943.
THERE ARE THOSE WITHIN SYRIA WHO STILL SEE LEBANON AS
PART OF A "GREATER SYRIA," WITH CULTURAL, RELIGIOUS, AND
ETHNIC TIES. THIS MAY BE RECIPROCATED BY CERTAIN ELEMENTS
WITHIN LEBANON, BUT LIKELY TO A LESSER DEGREE.

IN OTHER WORDS, SYRIANS—POSSIBLY INCLUDING THE
CURRENT GOVERNMENT—MAY SEE UNIFICATION WITH LEBANON
AS A GOAL. THE LEBANESE MAY NOT FEEL THE SAME WAY.

* TOP SECRET *

LEBANON SHARES A BORDER WITH ISRAEL AND SUPPORTED
OTHER ARAB—MUSLIM NATIONS DURING THE 1948 CONFLICT,
THOUGH THE COUNTRY LIMITED ITS SUPPORT LARGELY TO
LOGICSTICS AND STAGING. REGULAR LEBANESE TROOPS DID
NOT INVADE ISRAEL DURING THE CONFLICT.

THE CURRENT GOVERNMENT OF LEBANON IS CONSIDERED
NEUTRAL TO BOTH THE UNITED STATES AND SOVIET UNION.
BY CONSTITUTIONAL LAW, IT INCLUDES REPRESENTATIVES
OF ALL MAJOR RELIGIONS AND ETHNIC GROUPS IN THE
AREA. LEBANON HAS BECOME A TRADING HUB FOR THE
ENTIRE REGION, AND HAS ENJOYED ECONOMIC PROSPERITY
AND A COSMOPOLITAN CULTURE SINCE THE END OF THE
WAR.

ZA'IM'S RELATIONS WITH THE LEBANESE GOVERNMENT
REMAIN TENTATIVE, AS ZA'IM IS NEW TO HIS POSITION AND
THE LEBANESE WORRY ABOUT HIS INTENTIONS. WE ARE TOLD
THE NEW SYRIAN GOVERNMENT HAS REACHED OUT TO THE
LEBANESE GOVERNMENT AND ASSURED THEM OF STATUS QUO
POLICIES TOWARD EACH OTHER.

ANTOUN SAADEH

THE PRESIDENT OF SYRIA HAS REQUESTED CIA/OPC
INVESTIGATION INTO THE ACTIVITIES OF ANTOUN SAADEH,
AN ACTIVIST AND NEWSPAPERMAN IN BEIRUT. SAADEH
IS A PROPONENT OF THE "GREATER SYRIA" MOVEMENT,
WHICH HE SEES STRETCHING FROM SYRIA AND LEBANON
THROUGH TRANSJORDAN, ISRAEL, IRAQ, AND PARTS OF
THE SINAI.

SAADEH IS GREEK ORTHODOX BY BIRTH, AND SEES GREATER
SYRIA AS A MORE SECULAR STATE. SOME OF HIS VIEWS ARE
HIGHLY NATIONALIST, OTHERS HIGHLY SOCIALIST. HIS SYRIAN
SOCIAL NATIONALIST PARTY (SSNP) EMBRACES ELEMENTS OF
BOTH FASCISM AND COMMUNISM, WHILE DENYING LINKS TO
BOTH AND PROCLAIMING ITS PLATFORM TO BE A WHOLLY
NEW INVENTION RATHER THAN A SYNTHESIS.

SAADEH HAS BEEN IN LEBANON FOR NEARLY TWO YEARS,
HAVING BEEN EXILED PRIOR TO LEBANESE INDEPENDENCE.
SINCE HIS RETURN, HE FOUNDED A NEWSPAPER DEVOTED TO
HIS POLITICS AND PHILOSOPHY, AND HAS BEEN RALLYING
CITIZENS AGAINST LEBANON'S GOVERNMENT. ACCORDING
TO ZA'IM, CORROBORATED BY COPELAND'S SOURCES WITHIN
LEBANON, SAADEH MAY BE PLANNING A REVOLUTION OR
COUP AGAINST THE LEBANESE GOVERNMENT IN THE NEAR
FUTURE. THE FREE MARKET ECONOMY IN LEBANON HAS LED
TO POCKETS OF POVERTY AND DISEMPOWERMENT THAT MAY
BE SYMPATHETIC TO SAADEH, AND THERE MAY BE ELEMENTS
OF THE ARMY THAT MAY WISH TO TAKE A MORE MILITANT
STAND AGAINST ISRAEL WHO MAY SUPPORT SAADEH'S
NATIONALIST LEANINGS.

PROPOSED MISSION

ZA'IM WISHES OPC/CIA TO GO TO BEIRUT AND REPORT ON
SAADEH'S ACTIVITES, AND TO PROTECT SAADEH AS NECESSARY
AGAINST ELEMENTS OF THE LEBANESE GOVERNMENT THAT
MAY SEEK TO SHUT HIM DOWN. OUR SUPPORT OF SAADEH WOULD

BE LIMITED TO HIS PERSONAL SECURITY AGAINST LEBANESE
GOVERNMENT INTERVENTION. IF THERE IS A COUP, IT IS
UP TO SAADEH AND HIS REVOLUTIONARIES TO ENSURE ITS
SUCCESS. ZA'IM HAS ALREADY BEEN TOLD THE UNITED STATES
WOULD NOT SUPPORT ANYONE IN SUCH A CIRCUMSTANCE, AND
ZA'IM AGREED, ASKING ONLY THAT WE TRANSPORT SAADEH
TO DAMASACUS SHOULD A COUP ATTEMPT FAIL.

ACCORDING TO COPELAND, THERE IS SOME NATURAL POLITICAL
ALIGNMENT BETWEEN ZA'IM AND SAADEH--A GREATER SYRIA,
FOR EXAMPLE, THAT RELIES LESS ON RELIGION AND MORE
ON A SHARED SOCIAL CONTRACT. IT IS COPELAND'S OPINION
THAT ZA'IM SEEKS TO "HEDGE HIS BETS" IN LEBANON, HOPING
TO PROTECT AND ENCOURAGE A LIKE-MINDED POLITICIAN
WITHOUT AGGRAVATING THE CURRENT GOVERNMENT, UNTIL
SUCH TIME AS ZA'IM IS SECURE ENOUGH IN HIS POSITION TO
EFFECT A UNION WITH LEBANON.

AS A GESTURE OF GOODWILL IN THIS, ZA'IM HAS GIVEN THE
NECESSARY APPROVALS TO BEGIN CONSTRUCTION OF THE
TRANS-ARABIAN PIPELINE (TAPLINE) IN SYRIAN TERRITORY.
HE HAS ALSO OFFERED HIS VERBAL COMMITMENT TO
RESETTLING UP TO 250,000 PALESTINIAN REFUGEES FROM
THEIR FORMER TERRITORIES IN THE STATE OF ISRAEL.

RECOMMENDATIONS

WE BELIEVE ZA'IM WISHES TO CONSOLIDATE POWER IN SYRIA
QUICKLY, AND MAY WISH TO PURSUE A "GREATER SYRIA"

POLICY. UNIFICATION WITH LEBANON MAY BE A FIRST
STEP, AND THIS MAY BE FOLLOWED BY EFFORTS TO ABSORB
TRANSJORDAN, IRAQ, AND ISRAEL. GIVEN ZA'IM'S ALLIANCE
WITH THE UNITED STATES, BROKERED BY COPELAND,
THIS WOULD POSITION A PRO-WESTERN GOVERNMENT AS
THE PREEMINENT POWER IN THE REGION, BUT MAY ALSO
THREATEN ISRAEL.

MISS SILVERMAN, IN SHAKING HANDS WITH ZA'IM AT THE
END OF OUR MOST RECENT ENCOUNTER, HAS DETECTED WHAT
SHE DESCRIBED AS A GREAT DEAL OF PACING AND NERVOUS
ENERGY ON HIS PART, FOLLOWED BY PERIODS OF LETHARGY
AND INERTIA. SHE REMARKED AS THOUGH SHE WAS SHAKING
HANDS WITH TWO DIFFERENT PEOPLE. THIS MAY IMPLY A
MANIC-DEPRESSIVE STATE THAT BEARS CLOSE WATCHING.

WE RECOMMEND THAT MYSELF AND MR HOOKS ACCOMPANY
MR MEADE TO BEIRUT AS PART OF THE RECONAISSANCE ON
SAADEH. THE THREE OF US WOULD BE WELL POSITIONED TO
PROTECT SAADEH IF ABSOLUTELY NECESSARY, BUT WE WOULD
ONLY USE FORCE AS A LAST RESORT. THIS WOULD ALSO
GIVE US THE OPPORTUNITY TO BETTER UNDERSTAND THE
LEBANESE GOVERNMENT AND THE GREATER SYRIA NATION,
AND TO GET A DIFFERENT VIEW OF ZA'IM AS WELL.

WE FURTHER RECOMMEND MISS SILVERMAN REMAIN IN
DAMASCUS UNDER HER CURRENT COVER, WITH COPELAND AS
HER LIAISON. COPELAND HAS BEEN INSTRUCTED IN OUR
CURRENT CONTACT TECHNIQUES, AND HAS BEEN TOLD NOT

TO BREAK FROM THEM UNDER ANY CIRCUMSTANCE. MISS
SILVERMAN WILL CONTINUE TO INVESTIGATE ZA'IM'S
CURRENT MENTAL STATE THROUGH HER COVERAGE OF THE
SYRIAN GOVERNMENT ON BEHALF OF THE JERUSALEM POST
AND AP.

IF MISS DUBINKSY CAN BE SPARED, WE WOULD REQUEST
SHE RETURN TO DAMASCUS UNDER PREVIOUS COVER TO
GAIN FURTHER INFORMATION ON THE CURRENT SYRIAN
GOVERNMENT AND ITS POWER STRUCTURE, ALONGSIDE MISS
SILVERMAN.

FINALLY, WE REQUEST CMDR WALLACE VISIT BEIRUT IN THE
NEAR FUTURE TO ASSIST IN THE SEARCH FOR ANY VARIANTS
IN THE CITY.

(SIGNED) LT FRANK LODGE USA

16

April 27, 1949

Danny smiled as he read over Frank's dispatch along with Hillenkoetter's much more recent response. All MAJESTIC-12 activities were now going through National Command Authority—the President—so Truman himself had to sign off on Frank's plan. To Danny's surprise, Frank got most of what he wanted. He and Cal would go to Beirut to check out Saadeh and see what Za'im saw in the guy, while Zippy would stay behind and keep an eye on things in Damascus.

Truman still had Maggie and Mrs. Stevens investigating the MAJESTIC-12 leaks, but he seemed to be pleased with their progress and was keeping them on the case. Before going to visit with Forrestal himself at Bethesda, though, they needed to follow through on their work to determine the identity of "Joe on Capitol Hill"; Truman remained concerned enough about his former Defense Secretary to spare him interrogation until absolutely necessary.

Checking for possible Variants in Beirut was tempting—especially with the odd shadow-play lingering in his mind after the quick visit to Damascus—but Danny knew he had far too much to do at Area 51.

He slid the dispatches into his secure garbage can—a lidded metal container with a lock and a slot. They'd get burned later. He then turned back to the massive stack of papers and notebooks on his desk, which he'd been going through assiduously for weeks now.

They were Kurt Schreiber's notes. All of them. Going back more than two years.

Danny had never liked the idea of having a former Nazi at Area 51, despite his research into enhanced humans and the success he'd had with the Berlin vortex—in fact, it remained an open question as to whether Schreiber had actually helped usher the vortex into existence or just happened to be at the right place at the right time.

The notebooks were voluminous; Schreiber was a true scientist in that he recorded every single observation about everything. Every experiment on the vortex, every conversation with his fellow scientists, detailed notes on every meeting with the brass. Much of this was in German, which Danny had studied during the war as part of his assignment to Naval Intelligence, but even with that background, a well-thumbed German-English paperback dictionary had come in handy often.

He was amused that Schreiber seemed to refer to Danny as *Welpe* in his notes—"puppy." More troubling was the term he used for Variants: *neue Gotter*, or "new gods." And POSEIDON was noted as *Gottgriff* or "God's grasp." Yet there wasn't much in the way of worship in Schreiber's journals. Rather, it seemed like he believed that the "gods" he talked of were something attainable, perhaps something to aspire to, and that finding a way to understand—or even trigger—the vortex was the key to that ascension.

The MAJESTIC-12 science team had already established a sound theory of causality between the vortex's irregular emissions and the emergence of Variants in the general populace. At seemingly random intervals—usually anywhere between three weeks and four months—the vortex would erupt in a series of broad-spectrum, non-ionized radiation emissions, and once the direction was tracked down, a new Variant would eventually be found. There were some emissions that didn't have a Variant attached yet; the working assumption was that the abilities bestowed were so minor or so unobtrusive that the MAJESTIC-12 program might never locate them. But there was also the pesky question marks around the Variants being discovered who didn't correlate to any known emission, which meant that they were either Enhanced prior to the vortex's arrival at Area 51 from Hiroshima, or were somehow empowered by the Berlin vortex, now in the hands of the Soviets in Leningrad.

But Schreiber was pursuing something very distinct—the *triggering* of the vortex. He'd gotten close when they dropped a test nuke on that poor sap the past winter; the readings he'd recorded were very close to those just prior to an emission, even though an emission had never come.

Schreiber had theories on that, Danny saw as he carefully made his way through the notebooks. He felt that the death toll wasn't high enough. He wanted to place the vortex in the middle of a nuclear test with a larger number of human subjects—to basically see just how many people had to die to purposefully trigger the vortex.

Danny was aghast at this at first, especially once he realized one night, staring up at his ceiling, that if Schreiber had come up with such a theory—the hypothesis that enough deaths would result in triggering the vortex, and thus Enhancement—then the Russians might have also stumbled across something similar.

Schreiber also suspected that Variants could be the key to triggering the vortex, whether it was their presence or even, more permanently, their deaths. If Variants somehow carried the energies of the vortex within them—a theory far from proven, given that no Variant studied showed any kind of non-ionized radiation signature—then those energies could very well trigger a response.

Ultimately, no matter how it happened, Schreiber's clear plan was to turn the vortex into a Variant factory, triggering energy emissions and targeting them into individuals *willing* to be Empowered. He wanted to create super-soldiers with strange paranormal abilities, a veritable army of them.

There was no record of any conversation about this with Forrestal, which didn't surprise Danny too much; even Schreiber would've known not to leave a paper trail behind for something like that. But Danny also didn't find it hard

to imagine that Forrestal would've been hugely intrigued—
and massively appalled as well. Danny didn't know the man
well; from their infrequent interactions, he had a hunch
Forrestal truly feared Variants, but also that he would've
ultimately chosen the super-army over discretion, if only
because he knew the Russians would do the same thing.

Capturing Schreiber in the act had likely saved a lot of
lives, and Bronk believed his notes would give the research
team new avenues to explore. Danny was 100 percent certain that Bronk was no Schreiber, and that was all Danny
could ask for right now.

But there was one part of Schreiber's notes that Danny
couldn't quite decipher, a series of discussions with someone called "Vanda," who Danny couldn't for the life of him
identify. He'd managed to connect all the rest of the names
and cute little nicknames to actual people at Area 51 and
elsewhere, but "Vanda" remained unaccounted for.

The nature of the discussions was pretty esoteric.
Apparently, Schreiber and Vanda had discussed, in great
detail, some of Schreiber's theories about death and the
vortex, which Vanda apparently confirmed and, in a few
cases, expanded upon. Vanda had even suggested that the
vortex wasn't just an unknown phenomenon of physics but
also some sort of gateway.

To what, neither Vanda nor Schreiber knew. There was
speculation about another layer of reality, and a passage
that Danny roughly translated as "shadows dwelling behind
the curtain of our perceptions."

Shadows.

Ever since Damascus, Danny had had shadows on
the brain. What he'd seen in Syria had triggered his
Enhancement in a very unusual, erratic way. There hadn't
been Variants there—he was certain of that—but when he
searched, he could practically *feel* something skittering
away at the edges of his perception. It was disconcerting,
to say the least.

Two days earlier, he'd gone to visit Schreiber in his quarters, where he was being held under house arrest ever

since Danny had returned from Damascus. It wasn't their first visit, and Schreiber had previously acted amused by Danny's line of questions, even sarcastically pretending to play host, offering Danny tea while German classical music played on his phonograph. This time, though, had been different.

"Who is Vanda?" Danny had asked without ceremony.

This caught Schreiber off guard, and he held a cup and saucer in front of him for several long seconds before putting it down on the table. "Commander, do you really think I'm going to help you?" he'd asked.

Danny had shrugged. "You know as well as I do that we have the means to get pretty much any information out of you that we want, Doctor."

"Yes, you do, but you haven't the will to use it," Schreiber had retorted. "The Nazis would've gotten it out of me weeks ago and I would already be dead. The Soviets, the same. But you? You are soft and it is because of that I feel quite comfortable here, thank you.

"And besides," he'd added. "The two most effective Variants you have for this sort of thing are not here, are they? If your precious Maggie were around, she might be able to get me to talk, though I think she would underestimate me, yes? And of course, Frank Lodge could manage, but I wonder if I might yet find a way to keep things from him in death. I would certainly try, anyway, knowing what was coming."

Danny had paused, running through the roster of Variants in his mind, finding Schreiber's conclusions inescapably correct. "Well, then, Doctor," he'd said, standing. "I suppose we'll have to get one of them back and find out. Maggie first, of course. And then if that doesn't work, I'll personally kill you so Frank can get to work."

Schreiber had just smiled his spooky Cheshire Cat smile. "Until then, Commander."

After that, Danny had reported the conversation and his suspicions to Hillenkoetter, who reported back that Danny was to sit on every bit of it—Schreiber's research, his theories about death and triggering the vortex, "Vanda," all of it—until it could be sorted out. If Schreiber was in touch with Montague and Forrestal, then it was possible that other members of MAJESTIC-12 had collaborated with Schreiber, and that meant the number of trustworthy folks was narrowing considerably.

So, Danny sat on it, for the most part. Bronk was helping with the translation and interpretation of Schreiber's notes, but Danny kept the "Vanda" entries to himself. And Hamilton was told only to keep Schreiber under lock and key—and far away from where POSEIDON was being held.

A knock on his office door brought Danny back to the here and now. "Come."

Bronk entered, holding a small box and a couple of notebooks. His thin face was alight with excitement. "Think you need to see this, Dan."

Bronk set the box down on the desk—Danny could feel cold radiating from the little cardboard box, something that looked like it held sugar or flour or something. It looked like it had been in the refrigerator for some reason.

"What's this?" Danny asked.

Bronk opened it, and Danny saw a couple of glass vials inside with dark crimson fluid in them. Blood. "Found this in the infirmary, in the back of the refrigerator there, away from other samples. It was taped down. Looked like it was there a while. I think it's POSEIDON's blood."

Danny's eyes went wide. "How can you tell?"

"These notebooks," Bronk said, holding up one of the composition books. "Came across a passage here in a note from late February. I think Schreiber got POSEIDON to donate some blood to the cause."

"For what?"

"I think he wanted to toss it in the vortex," Bronk said, flipping through the notebook to another passage. "If his theory is correct—that there's an intrinsic relationship between the vortex and the Variants, and that Variants can somehow possess aspects of the vortex's energy—then it stands that the blood might hold traces of that energy and that Variant blood might trigger something in the vortex."

Danny leaned back in his chair, steepling his fingers and thinking. "OK. I want that blood secured until we test it. We'll need to get another sample from POSEIDON to compare. I'll have you do that."

"And then what?"

"Don't know," Danny admitted. "I admit, I'm tempted to see if Schreiber is right. But I'd need more data before I bring that to the folks in Washington."

Bronk nodded. "All right. What about—"

The scientist was interrupted by Danny's Air Force clerk barging into the office. "Commander! We got a situation down at training area two! Major Hamilton is asking you get over there ASAP."

Frowning, Danny bolted up and grabbed his jacket—a linen suitcoat mostly to keep the sun off his arms—and headed out. "Secure those samples, Det," he called out behind him. "Lock it down tight!"

Ten minutes later, Danny was at the gate of TA2, having driven at top speed across the Groom Lake salt flats. Before he even got out of the jeep, he could see the four Variants there—Sorensen, Vanoverbeke, Yamato, and Julia Meyer—sitting on the ground in the middle of the exercise area. They were in training fatigues, soiled and sweaty, each of them looked grimly determined as they stared at their hands or the sand on the ground. Six armed guards surrounded them in a wide circle, while Major Hamilton was yelling at them in his best Marine voice.

Danny got out of the jeep and jogged over. "Major! A word, please."

Hamilton turned his back on the group and walked over, red-faced and furious. "Commander, we got a problem with these yahoos."

"Easy, Hollywood," Danny said with a smile, looking up at the taller man. "What's going on?"

"Mutiny," Hamilton spat. "Just decided about a half-hour ago that they weren't gonna play ball anymore. Dropped to the turf and just sat there. I yelled at them, stripped their privileges, promised holy hell and a dark hole for each of 'em. Nothing. Just sitting there."

Danny nodded. They'd been training Variants at Area 51 for over a year now, and he'd honestly been surprised there hadn't been anything like this before. "They use their abilities at all?"

"Not that I'm aware of. I had a couple of the guys bring null-units over anyway to be sure."

"Smart," Danny allowed. "The other sites?"

"TA One and Three both secure; trainees there still at it. No unusual activity."

"All right. Get the MPs out of here and take the null-units with them. I'm gonna go have a chat with 'em. Keep eyes on us from the tower, but get everyone else out of sight."

Hamilton nodded and gave a shout for the guards, who sullenly stood down and retreated into other areas of the training area. Danny knew well that the guards would have eyes and weapons trained on the group regardless, and that a working null-unit could be tossed among them pretty quickly.

Danny walked over to the four Variants and took a seat on the ground on front of them, crossing his legs Indian-style and giving them a little smile. "All right, you guys. You got something on your minds. I'm listening."

Unsurprisingly, Julia was the first to speak. "We don't want to be here anymore."

Danny nodded. "Care to elaborate on that?"

Yamato spoke up. "I spent the war in internment, Commander. Now it's over, four years gone, and I'm still in internment. Just for a different reason. Meanwhile, California's going gangbusters, lots of jobs, lots of ways to make a good living. I want to go back to that."

"How you going to do that, Rick?" Danny asked.

Yamato nodded over at Sorenson. "Tim's been giving me some tips on being an electrician. He was thinking about heading west before you found him. So, maybe he and I head down to San Diego, set up shop. I got some natural talent there, you know." Smiling, Yamato opened his hand and produced a little arc of white lightning that danced between his fingers.

"That you do," Danny said, still smiling and trying to keep things light. "How are you feeling, Christina?"

Vanoverbeke, a small, slight blonde woman, just shook her head. "I'm not getting any younger, Commander Wallace. So what if I can jump a country mile? Ain't gonna help me get a gig singing. These are my prime years here. That window to Broadway isn't gonna stay open forever."

Danny lowered his head, looking down at the sand. He didn't have the heart to tell Vanoverbeke that all the New York talent scouts had told them she didn't have what it takes to make it on Broadway beyond the chorus; they'd originally thought she might have enough talent to infiltrate potential cultural exchanges between the U.S. and other countries. Even to Danny's untrained ear, she didn't have the pipes for anything other than late-night weekday gigs at semi-respectable cabarets.

"Right. So, you guys want out," Danny said finally. "I've looked at your progress reports. For the most part, you got a handle on things. But not 100 percent, though. Tim, you still tend to phase a little bit when your guard isn't up, yeah?"

Sorensen frowned. "Not as bad as all that," he protested quietly.

"And you, Rick, you still giving folks joy buzzers when you least expect it?" Danny asked. Yamato didn't reply, but his sullen look was answer enough.

"Christina, you can't get a gig anywhere if you're gonna leap into the audience randomly," Danny continued. "And Julia, well, what happens the next time someone sees your hand accidentally pass through a glass at a restaurant? And need I remind you you also have a criminal record in Europe that needs tending to?"

Sorensen, Yamato, and Vanoverbeke looked at Julia with surprise; Danny figured she'd have avoided that detail, and Danny took a little pleasure in dropping it on them.

"Look, I don't want you here if you don't want to be here, but the fact remains that the United States government has invested in you. Money, time, training. We're helping you get a handle on your Enhancements, understand what you can do and how best to control them. We expect you to keep that ability under wraps when you're out and about, and we're prepared to take you back in and keep you locked down if you fail to keep a low profile.

"What's more, we expect to be compensated for all that money, time, and training. That's why we're asking you to get with the program. It's a big commitment, but let's not kid ourselves here. Do you think the government is gonna really let you go if you don't play ball? I hate saying this, but you're *different*. The only reason the government hasn't put you in a deep, dark hole is because you can be *useful*. You've seen a few of our other Variants. They have assignments and jobs to do, yeah. They take a lot of risks. But they draw a good salary. They get down time. They're trusted—and they're trusted because they earned that trust from the powers that be."

Danny stood and brushed the sand and dust off his pants. "I'm gonna let this one go, you guys. No reports here. And you're gonna get up and start following orders. But if you pull this again, I'm gonna have to send this up to Washington, and I am genuinely concerned about what the response will be. Because it won't just be about you four, but it'll be about all the other Variants who are playing ball and being good citizens right now. They got good lives. And you could mess that up for them, all right?"

Danny surveyed each face in turn. Vanoverbeke and Sorensen looked properly chagrined, and Yamato still looked sullen but at least seemed more thoughtful about it. Only Julia still looked at him defiantly. Danny knew she'd be the problem down the road.

"All right. I'm bringing Major Hamilton back here. Get moving and don't let this happen again, OK?"

With that, Danny walked off and met Hamilton halfway back to the guard tower. "I want null-units placed all over this area," Danny ordered quietly. "Wire them up so that you can shut them down when you need to train. Otherwise, they're armed and operative at all times. Clear?"

Hamilton nodded. "It's Meyer, isn't it."

Danny frowned. "She'll come around."

"No, she won't," Hamilton said. "She's gonna break for it, I promise you."

Danny nodded but couldn't bring himself to say any more. Instead, he just walked to his jeep, got in, and gunned the engine.

May 22, 1949

Maggie hated hospitals. Hated them with a passion, really. Even before her Enhancement, she had hated going to hospitals. First her grandfather, then her aunt, and when she was just out of high school, it was her older brother. She went to hospitals to see people suffer, to say goodbyes, to watch over people as they died.

All those memories came flooding back as she walked the fourteenth floor of the Bethesda Naval Hospital, past room after room of sick, wounded, dying men. It was just after midnight, so at least the relatives and visitors weren't there and most everyone was asleep—otherwise, the emotions would've overwhelmed her senses, crippling her with sorrow and worry and desperate hope. Even now, though, the place seemed to be infused with a low-grade, background feeling of depression, as if the walls themselves had seen just about all they could take.

Maggie straightened out her white dress and felt for her little white nurse's hat for what seemed like the millionth time, all the while keeping an eye out for anybody else wandering the halls. The trick, she found, was to look really busy and walk fast, and for the past thirteen floors, it had worked pretty well.

It had taken Mrs. Stevens a couple of days to hatch a plan to get into the place—it was a military facility, after all, and the Navy did a good job of keeping things buttoned up; unlike the joke about killing Truman, Mrs. Stevens was taking this pretty seriously and wanted to insure they would get out undetected as well. So, after hours of watching each entrance from cars and park benches, the genius woman had come up with the idea of getting in through the laundry service.

Bethesda Naval Hospital had its own laundry, of course, but the doctors and nurses had multiple uniforms—surgical clothes, white lab coats, casual military uniforms, dress uniforms. Once a week on Saturday morning, all those clothes were taken out to be properly cleaned. And on Saturday night, all those clothes were sent back pressed and ready to wear. At that point, it was a simple matter to track down the cleaner's location. On Saturday evening—instead of enjoying a night on the town as most sane people would—the two Variants managed to sneak into the truck with the uniforms and rode right into the loading docks at the hospital. From there, Maggie only needed to give the driver a little distraction—a sudden pang of lust for the shift nurse in charge of uniforms—and they hopped out of the truck and snuck right into the building.

Sure, the driver got his face slapped in the process, but Maggie assured herself that, yes, even that was in the national interest.

Maggie had availed herself of a nurse's uniform, while Mrs. Stevens had opted to change into a blue smock used by the janitorial staff, her belief being that while one new face on the nursing staff could be readily dismissed as an oversight, two would stick out like a sore thumb. And besides, who paid any notice to the women emptying the wastebaskets, anyway?

They looped round and round each floor, looking for former Defense Secretary James Forrestal. The newspapers had said he'd checked in with a case of "nervous and physical exhaustion," but the scuttlebutt around town was that he'd gone 'round the bend. Naturally, with that in mind, Maggie and Mrs. Stevens had first visited the psychiatric wards on the first floor—where they found nothing.

"If he's got a cover story for why he's here, they're not gonna put him in with the loonies," Maggie muttered quietly as she joined Mrs. Stevens for an elevator ride on the sixth floor. "Probably gonna be in some VIP area for the muckety-mucks."

"Now, Maggie, it's not nice to call them loonies," Mrs. Stevens chided quietly. "Psychiatry has come a long way."

Maggie just grimaced. "You obviously haven't been committed before," she said, memories of the California mental hospital she'd been committed to leaping to mind. "*Loonies* is being kind. Let's go."

The two decided to split up to cover more ground, making their way through the rest of the floors, checking each of the four wings. Maggie had picked up a couple of boxes of bandages, and as they went around, she placed boxes in different cabinets, picking up similar-looking ones elsewhere. Nobody noticed. The nurses and corpsmen on each floor were uninspired at best, focusing on crossword puzzles or reading for the most part.

Finally, the sixteenth floor was different.

The elevator opened onto the corridor as usual, and as it happened, the car next to Maggie's opened at the same time, Mrs. Stevens exiting it. "Went up a few floors to work my way down," she whispered. "Heard someone say something about special guests on sixteen, so here we are."

Maggie nodded and pointed off to the left, and Mrs. Stevens pushed her wheeled garbage can that way. Maggie walked to the right, noting that the halls in this area of the hospital had better paint and more recent furnishings—a bit of an upgrade from the usual navy-issue metal chairs and desks. At the intersection of the cross-shaped floor, she saw the nurses' desk off to her left, but she kept going, knowing that she'd want to avoid the nurses' station until last, so she could make a quick getaway.

The desk distracted her just enough to miss the Navy corpsman walking toward her from the end of the hall. *Shit.*

"Help you, ma'am?" the corpsman said. He was a young man, uniformed in shipboard khakis, with a sidearm holstered on his hip.

Maggie smiled. "Restocking supplies, Corpsman," she said. "Need to grab a few things." She reached out with her Enhancement, pulling at the strings of early-morning routine calm she found in the man, blunting the dark gray threads of suspicion that had begun to grow.

The corpsman paused a moment. "Diet kitchen's to your right. Other two rooms are off limits, OK?" He smiled at her, and she encouraged the idle interest in her just enough to make him want to please her—without *really* making him want to please her.

"I know," she said smoothly. "Thanks, Corpsman."

The man nodded and went down the corridor, turning toward the nurses' station. Maggie watched him leave just as Mrs. Stevens arrived, pushing her wheeled can before her, the threads of excitement inside her growing. She'd seen him go and had the same question as Maggie: there weren't too many armed corpsmen in the hospital this late, and most were guarding the entrances, so who was this guy guarding?

Maggie purposefully and slowly made her way down the hall, resisting the urge to hustle. At the end of the corridor were four doors leading to a kitchen, an office, a bath, and a numbered patient room.

That last room had a light on.

Maggie nodded in the direction of the room, then reached out with her Enhancement. Inside, there was restlessness. Tiredness, too, with an undercurrent of worry and strain. If she had to guess, whoever was in there was engaged in some sort of relaxing activity that might or might not have been working.

Mrs. Stevens rolled up and eyed the door. "Here?" she whispered.

"Yeah," she replied, then pointed to the bathroom. "Put your can in there."

Maggie slowly tried the door to the patient room. It was unlocked.

With one more quick glance around, Maggie opened it and ducked inside, quickly closing the door behind her, taking care to ensure it latched silently.

She turned to find James Forrestal staring wide-eyed at her.

"You're one of them," he said. "I knew it was only a matter of time."

Maggie smiled and began to quell the growing alarm inside the man. "I am. Just want to talk, Mr. Secretary. It's OK."

Forrestal was in gray pyjamas and a plaid robe, sitting at a desk along the wall. He had a thick book open in front of him, and it looked as though he were taking notes or copying something. His hair was slightly disheveled, but otherwise, he looked perfectly sane.

"You're calming me down, aren't you," he said softly. "So I don't panic."

That's new, Maggie thought. Of course, Forrestal would've seen her file, known all about her. "Yeah, Mr. Secretary. I am. Like I said, just want to talk."

Just then, another door opened, and Mrs. Stevens walked in through the bathroom. "Hello, Mr. Secretary," she said quietly but with a winning smile. "Sure is good to see you well."

Maggie had to tamp down even harder on the man's growing panic. "I know both of you," he said. "And I think I need to call that corpsman back here now."

"Really, it's OK, Mr. Secretary. Jim. Can I call you Jim?" Maggie asked. "We're here on an official investigation. Really."

Forrestal frowned. "If it's so official, why are you sneaking around in the middle of the night?"

"Because we're MAJESTIC-12, Jim. You know as well as we do, we don't officially exist. And even our Secret Service covers wouldn't get us in the door here," Maggie said. "We just need to know who else knows about MAJESTIC-12, that's all."

Forrestal turned and carefully put down his pen, smirking at the page on his desk. "You know any Sophocles?"

Maggie shook her head as she pulled over another chair and had a seat. "Can't say I do."

"This is *Ajax*. Just copying it down. Helps me remember it better. It's about someone who travels too far down a dark road, and what becomes of those close to him." Forrestal smiled. "More or less. I thought it was fitting."

"You think you've traveled down a dark road?" Maggie asked.

Forrestal regarded her with a curious look. "It's amazing what you can do, Miss . . . Dubinsky, is it? Just amazing. You could probably kill me with a thought. And you, Mrs. Stevens, I believe. You could not only figure out how to kill me without a sound but get away with it scot-free. You're literally two of the most powerful people on the planet, and I went along with the crazy idea that we could rein you in. I'm a fool, obviously."

"We're not out to hurt anyone," Maggie said, feeling her own anger rise a bit. "We're serving our country. And at the moment, we're trying to protect the MAJESTIC-12 program and our fellow Variants. We know you talked to people. We just need to know the extent of it. Who's Joe on Capitol Hill?"

Forrestal thought a moment, then smiled at her. "Interesting. I really want to tell you, to make you happy, but it's not enough to compel me to tell you. And I know that telling you will only endanger others."

"Nobody's in danger, Mr. Secretary," Mrs. Stevens said gently. "We just need to find out who knows what, that's all."

"And while it's breaking my heart to keep this from you, I think I still have the wherewithal to do so," Forrestal replied. "Yes. I don't think I'll tell you."

"Why not?" Maggie said, trying everything in her arsenal—lust, sadness, hope—to get him to talk.

"Oh, Miss Dubinsky, I do want to tell you, really. And I'd like to do so much more with you. And . . . my, I'm a mess right now," Forrestal said, running a hand through his hair. "But you see, nobody in MAJESTIC-12 is willing to do what has to be done with the Variants. Nobody's ready to make the tough decisions. Hilly wants to treat you just like anyone else—as if you could treat an A-bomb like a person! And Truman, he's so enamored of you that he can't see straight. The others, well, they got rid of me, so now the others will fall right into line. Can't you see? I had to tell someone else. Checks and balances, Miss Dubinsky. That's what makes our country work. Checks and balances. Someone has to watch the watchmen."

Maggie whispered through gritted teeth; she was done being nice. "Right. So, it's Hoover. And Wisner. Who else?"

Forrestal's eyes grew wide and fearful. "M-McCarthy. Joe McCarthy."

Maggie frowned and turned to Mrs. Stevens. "Who?"

"Wisconsin senator," Mrs. Stevens replied. "Not very popular. Kind of paranoid."

Before Maggie could reply, Forrestal piped up. "Of course he's paranoid! Look at what you're able to do! Look at what you made me say!"

"Easy, Jim," Maggie said, reining in her own anger as she tried to soothe his agitation. "We're just trying to secure the program, that's all. Nobody's gonna get hurt."

"You're dangerous! You and your Variant friends! I see them in the shadows now all the time. Lurking. Moving. It's why I stay up! I can only sleep in the day now, because . . . "

Maggie felt the fear building in Forrestal as his face turned into a mask of horror. He mutely pointed at the corner of the room . . .

. . . where a shadow began to move.

"What the hell?" Maggie whispered.

Suddenly, Forrestal leapt to his feet and, shoving Maggie aside, ran out the main door into the hallway.

"Shit!" Maggie swore, her emotional connection broken. "Move it, Rose!"

The two women dashed after him, but to their surprise, he wasn't in the hallway, making a beeline for the nurses' desk or the corpsman. Instead, he'd gone into the diet kitchen on the other side of the hall.

They dashed in after him, finding him inside a small, closet-sized kitchenette, frantically tying the belt of his bathrobe to a radiator.

A radiator right under an open window.

"Jim! No!" Maggie shouted.

Before she could reach out to calm him, he hurled a small metal coffee pot at her. She dodged, but it managed to graze her forehead. And it was hot.

"Fuck!" she growled. And in that moment, her anger escaped her and filled the room.

Mrs. Stevens' hands flew to cover her mouth as she backed into a counter, trying to get as far from Maggie as the small room would allow.

And Forrestal—wide-eyed and panicked—took one end of the belt in his hand . . .

. . . and jumped out the window.

"No!"

Maggie rushed forward and stuck her head out the window, only to find Forrestal hanging by one hand, grasping the cloth belt for dear life. She grabbed it in the middle and started trying to haul him back in.

"Hang on! We're going to get you back in here, Jim!"

But Forrestal still looked utterly horrified—*insane* might have even been a good word for it—as he looked past Maggie's right shoulder toward the wall of the building.

She turned to look, and saw the vague outline of a human figure in the shadowy corner of the building—sixteen floors up.

Maggie turned back to Forrestal, who looked at her now with anger and fear combined. "Maybe they'll blame you," he whispered.

He let go.

Maggie could do nothing but watch as he fell, landing far below on a roof only a few stories above the ground, his body askew and his legs buckled into horrible angles. She looked for movement, but there was none.

Closing her eyes to rein in her emotions, Maggie then turned to see Mrs. Stevens, still in the corner, eyes wide, tears welling.

"Out. Now," Maggie said quietly. "Get your can and get to the elevator. I'll take the far stairs. Get to the loading dock and get a car running. Meet you there. Go!"

Nodding, Mrs. Stevens fumbled for the door and headed for the bathroom to retrieve her garbage can. To her credit, she walked with only a little bit of a hurry. And it wasn't like the elevators were busy. A moment later, Maggie heard the faint ding of the bell.

That was when she walked out and slowly made her way toward the stairs, well away from the nurses' desk and the corpsman.

It was probably for the best that she didn't encounter anyone on her way to the stairs, because she was in no mood to play nice, and she really didn't want the hassle of leaving screaming, terrified people in her wake.

JAMES FORRESTAL DEAD

Falls to His Death 13 Stories
Up at Naval Hospital

PRESIDENT DECLARES FORMER DEFENSE
SECRETARY A 'WAR CASUALTY'

Doctors Claimed Improvement Prior to Fall

BETHESDA, Md., May 22—
Former Secretary of Defense
James Forrestal fell to his death
early Sunday morning from the
16th floor of the National Naval
Medical Center here. The cause
seems to be suicide.

Mr. Forrestal had apparently
refused his usual sleeping pill
at 1:45 a.m., and was left alone
in his room, where he was reading a passage from Sophocles.
He was later discovered having
fallen from a window in a
kitchen across the hall from his
room, a belt from a bathrobe
found tied to a radiator nearby.

President Truman received
news of Mr. Forrestal's death
early this morning on the radio
and was said to be shocked and
grieved beyond measure. The
White House later put out a
statement saying: "This able
and devoted public servant was
as truly a casualty of war as if
he had died on the firing line."

The National Naval Medical
Center reported Mr. Forrestal's
death as occurring around 2 a.m.
According to the hospital's statement, the window in the 16th floor
diet kitchen was easily opened,
and the screen easily removed.

Mr. Forrestal's body hit a small promontory on the fourth floor, then came to rest on top of a third-floor roof.

The sound of the falling body was heard by Navy Lt. Dorothy Turner, a duty nurse on the seventh floor. She led the investigation that ultimately discovered the tragedy.

Mr. Forrestal, 57, had resigned as Defense Secretary on March 28, and was admitted to the Naval hospital here on April 2 where he was diagnosed with "severe occupational fatigue," something akin to the shell-shocked condition some soldiers experience during wartime. Up until these tragic events, Forrestal's doctors had considered him well on the way to recovery.

A corpsman was assigned to check on the former Defense Secretary every 15 minutes, while a psychiatrist slept in a room across the hall so as to be on call at all times. Neither man reported anything unusual. A full investigation by the Navy has already commenced, though the man's doctors, speaking on condition of anonymity, report that "sudden and acute despondency" can be common in certain mental conditions.

The hospital denied early reports of a person or persons unaccounted for on the 16th floor, attributing a subsequent search of the building at approximately 2:10 a.m. to finding potential witnesses to the tragedy and security of patient welfare.

Forrestal, the nation's first Secretary of Defense, is to be given the honor of burial at Arlington National Cemetery on Wednesday at 11 a.m., and it is believed President Truman himself will lead the mourners.

18.

May 25, 1949

President Truman threw the newspaper on his desk in disgust and looked up at Roscoe Hillenkoetter. "I tell you what, Hilly: I'm about ready to lock them the hell up, you hear me? These girls of yours, these Variants, they knew full well how Jim felt about them. And that's because your boy Wallace wasn't shy about giving *his* opinions. Can you sit there and tell me—tell me to my face, Hilly—that these Variants didn't want to see Jim Forrestal dead? Because that's what it feels like, doesn't it?"

Hillenkoetter adjusted his suit jacket and squirmed a bit on the couch in front of Truman's desk. To Truman's credit, the President was holding this one pretty close to the vest; folks like Hoyt Vandenberg, Detlev Bronk, Vannevar Bush, that prick Montague, none of them knew about it. Just Truman, Hilly, Wallace, and the two girls themselves.

The trick was in ensuring that didn't change.

"I don't know what more I can tell you, Mr. President, I really don't," Hillenkoetter said, taking a puff from a cigarette and placing it back into the ashtray. Being CIA Director was hell on the nerves on a good day, and this wasn't a good day. His wife would kill him if she knew he'd been smoking. "I believe them, pure and simple. Jim Forrestal, God rest him, was going off the deep end. They didn't so much as nudge. In fact, Miss Dubinsky did her level best to try to calm him down, but he was too far gone."

Truman got up and paced the Oval Office. He remained impeccably dressed, but there was an air of frustration and nervousness around him that made him seem rumpled, like somehow his demeanor needed a good ironing. "You know, I bought into this hook, line, and sinker, Hilly, that these Variants of yours, well, that they were just normal people, right? That they were average, everyday patriotic Americans who just happened to be blessed with these strange abilities. You assured me that your program out in Nevada would give them a grounding, a goal, something to keep them going and keep them in check. What if you're wrong? What if *I'm* wrong? Hell, what if Jim Forrestal was right and they're all little Hitlers or Stalins waiting to happen, but this time with goddamn comic book powers?"

Hillenkoetter sighed, then opened the briefcase next to him, pulling out one of the null-area generators and placing it on the coffee table in front of him. "Then let's get 'em in here and find out, sir. You've got a good head for people. They're right outside."

Truman's gaze was fixed on the alarm clock–sized device. "They'll know it's on, right?"

"Most likely."

"So, while that means Miss Dubinsky won't be able to fool with my head, what's it mean for Mrs. Stevens?"

Hillenkoetter leaned back into the couch cushions. "She doesn't really notice it at first, but the intensified mental acuity and rapid reasoning fades pretty quickly. It's only when she's out of range, or the device is turned off, that it all snaps back into place. She doesn't like it, frankly. Says it makes her embarrassed for how dumb she feels."

Truman grimaced. "Seems a cruel thing to block someone from thinking straight."

"Especially the smartest person in the country," Hillenkoetter replied. "Maybe the world."

The President sighed and returned to the chair behind his desk. "All right. Keep that handy, but for now, let's go without it. But if I start acting funny in any way, you flip that thing on, you hear me?"

Hillenkoetter put it back in his briefcase and closed it, leaving it unlocked. "Yes, Mr. President."

Truman nodded, then lifted up his phone. "Send the two ladies in."

A moment later, the right-hand door of the office opened, with a Secret Service agent ushering Maggie Dubinsky and Rose Stevens inside. Hillenkoetter gave them both a quick, practiced once-over: Both wore conservative dresses and suits, practical heels, they'd gotten their hair done up, their makeup was tasteful. So, they at least knew to dress up for the occasion. Mrs. Stevens was looking around with her eyes wide, her mouth slightly open, reminding Hillenkoetter of when he'd first brought Danny Wallace to meet the President a few years prior. Star-struck and nervous.

Maggie Dubinsky seemed like neither of those things, even though she knew full well her ass was on the line. Or maybe it was *because* her ass was on the line. Her face was a mask with a very small, unthreatening smile painted onto it. Her eyes were clear and intently focused— on Hillenkoetter, on Truman, on the hand the President extended to her.

"Miss Dubinsky, Mrs. Stevens," Truman said. "Thank you for seeing me."

Maggie took the President's hand and shook it gently, with only a hairsbreadth more force than a woman in her position might otherwise offer. "It's an honor, sir. We're here to help," she replied, her smile widening just a crack. Hillenkoetter was surprised her entire mask didn't crumble.

Because that was it, wasn't it? He'd read it in the reports about her, time and again. The more you play with emotions, the less you believe in them. If that emotional reality, for want of a better word, was basically made of wet sand, to be molded as you saw fit, then it stood to reason that any emotion would be viewed as false, fleeting, and phony.

Mrs. Stevens, on the other hand, was perfectly effusive, assuring the President that both she and her husband had voted for him against "that horrible Mr. Dewey." Truman thanked her for helping him prove that famous headline wrong, Mrs. Stevens looked like she might pass out in sheer rapture. And she was supposed to be the genius of the bunch?

Truman made a big show of pouring coffee for the ladies—he was as much an emotional chameleon as Maggie, but far better with his masks—and then sat down next to Hilly on the couch facing the two women. "I want to start by thanking you both for your honesty and veracity in your report from the Bethesda hospital," Truman said. "I'm sure it occurred to both of you that you could've made things easier on yourselves if you hadn't."

Maggie's brow furrowed for a split second before the mask fell back into place. "Ah, yes. Well, we saw what we saw, Mr. President. In my experience, anything but the truth tends to make things worse. I told my kindergarteners that back in the day."

Truman smiled, but Mrs. Stevens picked up the thread before he could continue. "And I know, Mr. Truman—I mean, Mr. President, sir—that it's our word against, well, nobody else's. But Miss Dubinsky and I have some ideas about what we saw, and we want to run them by you if we might. Would that be all right, Director Hillenkoetter? Mr. President? If we did that for just a minute or two?"

Truman gave Hillenkoetter a perfectly bemused look before waving his hand at them. "By all means, Mrs. Stevens. I'm curious as to what you have to say."

Mrs. Stevens cleared her throat and sat up a bit straighter on the couch. "Now, before we really dive in here, I know for a fact, Mr. President, that Miss Dubinsky here was not using her Enhancement on that poor man, your friend James Forrestal, before he died. I would swear by it in court."

At this, even Maggie looked surprised. "How do you know that?" she blurted out, her mask shattered and replaced with both concern and even a hint of . . . amusement? Hard to tell on her, Hillenkoetter figured.

"Let's just say you and I shouldn't play cards," Mrs. Stevens replied, patting Maggie's knee lightly. "You have what they call a tell. I've noticed it with many of the Variants whose Enhancements require positive cognition triggers. When you engage your cognition triggers, and I mean you in particular, I can see contraction in your trapezius and a slight widening of the pupils."

All three stared blankly at Mrs. Stevens. "And in English?" Hillenkoetter prodded.

"Oh, right," she said, blushing. "When Maggie uses her Enhancement to change someone's emotions, her neck and shoulder muscles tense up in a particular way, and her eyes change a bit."

Maggie looked at her hard for a moment, then shrugged. "Well, OK, then."

Truman, however, leaned forward with interest. "And you're saying that other Variants have a similar tell?"

"The ones that need to think about their particular Enhancements, yes. Myself, for example, my Enhancement is always on, apparently. I don't really need to think about thinking. Why, that would be pretty silly, wouldn't it? But the others, they each have their own queer little thing that lets me know they're up to something."

"You're very observant, Mrs. Stevens," Truman said. "And here I thought I was a cardsharp!"

Mrs. Stevens smiled graciously. "Well, I'm afraid I don't really play cards anymore. It's far too easy for me to calculate the probabilities of a given hand. Not much of a challenge these days!"

Hillenkoetter interrupted. "Anyway, let's get back to what you saw."

This time, Maggie stepped in. "We think it was an Enhancement of some kind."

"*What* was an Enhancement? Mrs. Stevens just got finished telling us you weren't inside Jim Forrestal's head," Truman replied, his demeanor changing quickly.

"I wasn't," Maggie said coolly. "I think there was another Variant affecting him."

"What's your proof?"

"For one, Jim Forrestal told us directly that he'd been plagued by shadow figures of some kind. It's why he didn't like to sleep, and why the staff at Bethesda had kept him on sleeping pills. He was seeing shadows move and whisper. And I saw one outside the window where he jumped, up on the wall in the corner above."

"What's more," Mrs. Stevens continued, producing a folder from her own little leather folio, "we have reports here from Commander Wallace, from his Damascus trip, that describe something very similar indeed."

Truman scowled deeply. "So, what are these shadows?"

Maggie shrugged, which struck Hillenkoetter as a bit too practiced. "Don't know. Given that both Danny Wallace and Jim Forrestal may have seen them, we can at least say that it doesn't take a Variant to see them. Maybe it's an Enhancement from an unknown Variant out there. Maybe it's something else entirely. The world gets stranger every day."

"Of course, Secretary Forrestal's death could just be part of his psychosis," Mrs. Stevens added. "The MAJESTIC-12 program could've been wrapped up in that too. He was certainly concerned enough to tell others about it."

Truman leaned back on the sofa and ran a hand across his face. "Yes, indeed. And while we're on the subject, the last person I ever wanted to know about this whole mess was Hoover, and now we have a recording of him talking about it with Frank Wisner. Oh! That reminds me." Truman opened a file folder and flipped through typewritten transcripts. "I'm betting your 'Joe on Capitol Hill' could be Joe McCarthy. Senator from Wisconsin. Pugnacious fellow, that one. I know he and Jim Forrestal were social."

Maggie and Mrs. Stevens traded a look, the latter smiling wide. "That's good to know. How do you want us to proceed?"

"Well, I'll be honest with you, ladies: I'm not sure I want you to proceed at all," Truman said. "Forrestal may have double-crossed me a couple times over, but that's just

Washington for you. I still considered him a friend. I appreciate your candor, but that doesn't exactly clear you of suspicion, you realize."

Mrs. Stevens looked taken aback at this, but Maggie's mask was firmly in place once again. "So, let us clear our names, Mr. President," she said. "We still need to track down the extent of Jim Forrestal's security breach around MAJESTIC-12. More importantly, we need proof of these shadows. If we get that, then it corroborates our report. If not . . . well, then. We're in your hands."

Hillenkoetter watched Truman closely as he thought about it. There was a lot on the President's plate—continued tensions with the Soviets, the Red Chinese on the march, money flowing out the door to help rebuild Europe, and any number of domestic battles that Hillenkoetter didn't know about or care to know about. And once again, Truman had a very sticky situation with the Variants to contend with.

Finally, the President stood, and everyone rose with him. "All right. Ladies, clean this mess up. I want to know exactly who knows about our operation here, and I want proof of this . . . phenomenon . . . you may have seen. Plus, if there are *any* more so-called suicides or accidental deaths in connection with this mess, I'll have no choice but to hold you both responsible. I don't need to tell you what that means for you and your fellows. Are we clear?"

Maggie nodded grimly. "Very. Thank you, sir."

Everyone shook hands again, and the ladies were ushered out the door. "I don't like it, Hilly," Truman said. "You sure she didn't mess with my head while we were talking?"

Hillenkoetter couldn't help but smile a bit. "Mr. President, you just threatened to throw her in a deep, dark hole along with all the other Variants. I don't think she was in your head one bit."

Truman was not amused. "I meant it, Hilly. I'm starting to see a little bit of what got Jim so worked up. We're letting these people walk free out there among us. And I don't know if I can trust them."

"I trust them, sir," Hillenkoetter said, officially putting his career on the line. "They'll find out what's going on."

"They better," Truman said. "Otherwise . . . " The rest was left unspoken.

19.

June 12, 1949

The man standing in Beirut's Martyrs' Square was thin, not very tall, starting to bald a little. His suit looked a little big on him, frankly, and Frank thought he kind of looked like somebody's bookkeeper, maybe. But as the man stood on a bench next to the Martyrs' Monument—a big, modern sculpture of two people, their arms raised—Frank saw the crowd's rapt attention. Antoun Saadeh could give one hell of a speech.

"You have lived at the mercy of others for far too long," Saadeh said in the Lebanese Arabic dialect, which Frank could piece together well enough. "The Ottomans, the French, now the Americans and English, perhaps. Or will you give your loyalties to the Muslims? The Christians? The Jews?

"I say to you that none of these are deserving of your loyalty, because none of these will give you the freedom to be who you really are. We, the people of Greater Syria—of Lebanon, Syria, Palestine, Transjordan, Iraq—yes, we are all one people! We are Christians and Muslims and, yes, even Jews. We are all Greater Syrians. For a thousand years, we were at the forefront of civilization! Our cities were home to learning and innovation, and we were a powerful yet tolerant people. We can bring this about once again!

"Our nation, our Greater Syrian nation, is the key to solving all the things that divide us. We will not be divided by religion! We will not be divided by politics or economics! We will unite as one people and take our place among the world's great powers! We will show these Americans, these

Russians, the Christians and the Muslims and the Jews, we will show them all the power of true social justice, of a nationalism that brings us together, not divides us!

"Some say we are fascists. Some say we are communists. How can we be both? We do not easily fall into these little boxes. Once again, I say that the system of the Syrian Social Nationalist Party is neither a Hitlerite nor a fascist one but a pure social nationalist one. It is not based on useless imitation but is instead the result of an authentic invention—which is a virtue of our people. We are a Syrian nation, one that embraces a unique philosophy born of centuries of civilization. And we will forge our own path as one nation!"

The crowd, at least two hundred strong, went nuts. Saadeh jumped down from the bench and began glad-handing the masses, while a couple flunkies began passing out copies of his newspaper, *Al-Jil Al-Hadid*, or "The Iron Generation." *What is it with nationalists and iron, anyway?* Frank wondered. He immediately regretted it, as no fewer than three voices in his head began explaining the iconography. At least he was getting better at shutting them down quickly.

Frank spotted Cal walking over to him, now dressed as any other worker bee in the city; there were small Sudanese and Ethiopian communities in Beirut, so he didn't stand out too much. And to Cal's delight, nobody paid him any heed at all, for good or ill.

"They're taking names," Cal said quietly as he leaned against an iron fence near Frank. "Looks like addresses and phone numbers, too. Heard a lot of folks saying, '*Alrrabie min yuliu. Kunn Jahiza.*' Something like that."

Frank nodded. "'July fourth. Be ready.' I think they got something going. Maybe another rally, or a march or something. Maybe more." Frank was about to say something more when he noticed a familiar figure walking over toward him. "I'll be damned."

"What?" Cal asked.

Frank just nodded at the slightly pudgy man in the bad suit and tie, puffing away on a cigarette as if it were a snorkel. Karilov smiled as he approached, and Frank gave a half-smile back. "You get around, Mr. Karilov."

The Russian just shrugged. "Beirut is a very interesting city. Vibrant cultural life here. Though a bit too bourgeois for my tastes. The proletariat has much to do here, yes?"

Frank just laughed. "What, you don't like Damascus anymore?"

Karilov's smile ebbed a bit. "I am disappointed in recent events there, I have to say. But I remain impressed by your work, Mr. Smith. Or rather, I am impressed with your success despite your bumbling colleague."

"I'm sure I have no idea what you're talking about, Mr. Karilov," Frank replied. "Except maybe for the colleague thing. Civil service being what it is and all."

"And now I find you here," Karilov said. "I cannot help but wonder why."

"I could say the same."

Karilov nodded and took another greedy pull on his cigarette. "So, what do you make of this Antoun Saadeh?"

Frank shrugged. "He gives a fine speech."

"Yes, he does. I find his politics . . . interesting. Can you cross true social justice with nationalism, I wonder? Marxism-Leninism argues that Communism is international in scope, uniting all the workers of the world. Your American capitalism is likewise global in its pursuit of profit at the expense of those workers."

"Says you." Frank grinned. He had to admit he was kind of enjoying all this.

"We can argue this all day if we wish. Maybe we will someday, you and I," Karilov said, equally amused. "But here, this Saadeh believes that the distinction between people is not economic, political, or religious but simply geographic. That there is something special about these people here in Syria and Lebanon."

"Maybe there is, *tovarishch*. They may be the best folks around, for all I know."

Karilov chuckled and dropped his cigarette butt, grinding it into the stones of the square. "The 'best folks' are never what they seem at first. This is why the workers are always underestimated, because nobody believes they can rise from nothing, that they have no gifts to bring to bear. But we know better, you and I. Don't we, Mr. Smith?"

Frank froze for a moment too long, wondering if the implication meant that Karilov was on to them as Variants, or if he was just going fishing for something. Frank chose the latter and prayed he was right.

"Absolutely. Like me with languages. And you with . . . well, talking, I guess." Frank smiled a perfectly un-genuine smile. "What is it you do again, Mr. Karilov?"

Karilov opened his mouth to say something more, then seemingly thought better of it. "I'm sure I will, as you say, *see you around, pal.* That is what they say, yes?"

"Not bad," Frank allowed. "See you around."

Karilov sauntered off, lighting another cigarette as he went, while Cal leaned in a bit closer. "I think we just got our pictures taken, Frank." He tilted his head a fraction toward a couple of tourists in the square, in different directions, each lugging a different style of camera. "Couple others watching too. We've been made."

"And we made them," Frank replied. "Hopefully, Meade got some photos too."

"You think they know who we are?" Cal asked as they began to casually walk toward a side street. "What we are?"

Frank grimaced. "Depends. Anderson didn't give up our names or photos to the Russians last year—just the fact that we existed and what we could do. Small blessings, right? But I bet the MGB is really keen on putting names and faces on us. And then there's the question of whether an operator like Karilov would even be cleared for something like a Variant program." With a sigh, Frank threw his hands up in frustration. "Hell if I know."

Twenty minutes later, they met Stephen Meade at their rendezvous, a little café with some of the best espresso in the whole goddamn Middle East. Frank eagerly worked on his cappuccino as they quietly gave each other an update; Meade had gotten photos of Karilov as well as three other

Russians in the square, and he recognized one of them as a goon from the Russian embassy in Damascus.

"Makes sense," Cal observed. "If this Saadeh fellow and our Colonel Za'im want the same thing—putting Syria and Lebanon together, right?—then sure, the Russians would be interested. Maybe they try to back up Saadeh, too. Play him against Za'im."

"So, Saadeh's the wild card," Meade said. "The Russians want to play him off Za'im, and we want him because Za'im wants him in his corner. And the Lebanese just want him to go away. They're cracking down on SSNP members daily now. This situation's gonna blow any day now."

"On July fourth, maybe," Frank said. "Cal overheard something about it in the square from Saadeh's people. Maybe some fireworks in store."

"Good day for a revolution," Cal agreed. "Course, we gotta protect Saadeh if he fails. How are we gonna do that?"

Frank downed the rest of his cappuccino. "We go talk to him. Now."

"Frank?" Meade asked warily. "What are you thinking?"

"You'll see. Come on."

The three men left the café and began walking through Beirut's warren of closed-in side streets, bisected every so often by broad, tree-lined thoroughfares. It was a pretty city, and Frank was heartened to see mosques, churches, and even a synagogue together as they walked. Lebanon was trying to do something interesting there at the inter-section of millennia-old religious tensions and new post-war political strife. He hoped they'd pull it off. Maybe even Saadeh might help them do it.

Frank arrived at a small intersection that had become familiar to them all during weeks of surveillance—Saadeh's newspaper offices were there, in a small, old stone building that looked ready to fall over. Revolutionaries rarely had a budget.

"Frank," Meade said again, warningly. He didn't listen.

Instead, he walked right up to the newspaper offices and went inside, Cal following. Meade had apparently had enough by this point, because he kept walking down the street—probably not to blow whatever cover he had left. It was probably a smart move.

"What do you want?" asked a man at a desk at the front of the building. He wasn't quite a receptionist, in that he was far too big, muscular, and menacing for that job. His French, though, was pretty good.

"We wish to see Mr. Saadeh," Frank replied in perfect Arabic. "We are Americans and we want to help."

Perplexed, the man nonetheless picked up the phone at his desk and spoke in rapid-fire Arabic for several long moments. At one point, the man asked if a representative of Saadeh's would be sufficient; Frank assured him it would not. Finally, the man hung up and glared at them. "Sit in that room," he said, pointing to an unoccupied office down the hall.

Frank and Cal walked into the office and sat down, situating their chairs so they could take in the door, the window, and everything else in the room between them. There they sat for a good thirty minutes, mostly in silence, until Antoun Saadeh came into the room in a burst of energy, his hand extended before him.

"I am so sorry to keep you," Saadeh said in accented but otherwise very good English. "It is a busy time for us. Please, please, sit down. They tell me you are here to help, yes? I will take all the help I can get." Saadeh sat down at the desk and looked the two of them over quickly and efficiently. "You're not the usual Americans I get here."

"What are the usual ones like?" Cal asked.

"Not African like you. That's one," Saadeh said with a smile. "The way you are treated in your country is an international disgrace. I hope your presence here is a sign of changing times. Especially since, unlike the other Americans who arrive here hoping to help, you are not students or idealists or castoffs. So, you are different."

Frank noticed three men in the room outside the office, all with pistols at their sides. They weren't taking any chances, which was good.

"Yes, we are," Frank said. "And we're here to help in more concrete ways."

"I'm listening," Saadeh said, leaning back in his chair and steepling his fingers.

"You're about to do something, something big, and the fact that we've put it together over the past few weeks means that everyone else has too—the Russians, the Israelis, the Syrians, and most definitely your own government here in Lebanon. You may want to rethink some things, for starters, though I doubt you will."

Saadeh smiled. "You're probably right on that. What else?"

"When this goes south and your revolution fails, we want you to know you have friends. We'll help you get out of Dodge."

"Get out of where?" Saadeh asked, his brow furrowed.

Right. "We'll help you escape if need be. We'll keep you safe and alive. Live to fight another day."

Saadeh frowned a little at this. "And?"

"And . . . you have friends here in the region. They want to see you succeed."

"So, what will they do to help us succeed? What will *you* do to help us succeed? Because I only hear how you will help me if we fail. And we cannot fail. It is not an option."

"Failure's not only an option; it's a likelihood in most circumstances," Frank retorted. "You see enough of these things, you know what kind of odds you face. Something somehow is gonna go wrong. And if you don't adapt to that, then you'll be happy we're around."

Saadeh nodded and looked thoughtful for a moment. "So, you are my guardian angels, then, and nothing more?"

Frank and Cal traded a look, and Cal smiled. "Something like that, sir, yes," Cal said.

The revolutionary stood and extended his hand again. "I appreciate your visit," he said, shaking both men's hands. "But I will not be looking to you in the case of failure. I will be looking for ways to turn that failure into success."

Frank nodded. "We'll be around, just in case," he said.

They were quickly ushered out of the room, but Frank nonetheless caught wisps of conversation between Saadeh and another man as they climbed up the stairs to another floor of the building.

"First the Russians, now the Americans. Everyone wants to help me survive, but nobody wants to help us succeed!" Saadeh said in French.

Frank hustled out of the building and headed back to the café rendezvous, with Cal hurrying to keep up. "What'd I miss?" Cal asked. "What'd you hear in there?"

Frank turned around to look back at the way they'd come. "Looks like everyone wants a piece of Antoun Saadeh. Guess we can only hope to be the first in line when it hits the fan."

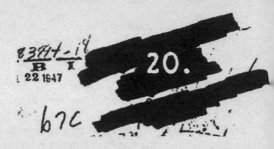

20.

June 17, 1949

Zipporah Silverman walked through the Parliament building in the Syrian capital of Damascus with purpose, now fully used to being in the halls of power and representing the United States.

Oh, and *The Jerusalem Post*. And the Associated Press. And . . . well, she was Jewish in a land that now hated Jews. So, there was that, too. Long story short, she was busy.

By now, she was a familiar figure in Za'im's inner circle—one of his pet reporters. Word was that he was cultivating her to keep a channel open to Israeli thinking, which many seasoned politicos in the capital felt was wise. Given that Za'im was America's man—or at least Miles Copeland's man—she felt she was doing her part.

And she was grimly determined to make the very most of her position now.

She was patted down and searched at the door to the conference room Za'im had taken as his own; the treatment was commonplace, and to her surprise and delight, the male guards hadn't taken any liberties. Maybe they could tell she'd whack 'em but good. Maybe they really didn't like Jews, even young, female, shapely ones. Either way, she'd rack up whatever small victories she could en route to the larger ones.

Smoothing out her blue dress and adjusting her red hat, she nodded at the soldier manning the door, who opened it to allow her into the gilt, ornate room. Za'im sat at the head of the table, looking sluggish and bored. She noted several new decorations on his military uniform since the last time she'd seen him; she'd just written about his plan to assume the military rank of marshal. Because ... why not? *Men and their ranks and baubles.*

Al-Hinnawi and al-Shishakli were already there, sitting to Za'im's right, while that strange little boy was reading a book in a chair against the far wall. You'd think a nation's senior military commander could afford a nanny. The kid looked up at her with his big brown eyes, then went back to his book. The two other army officers rose, as did Miles Copeland, who'd arrived separately.

"Please, gentlemen, don't let me interrupt," Zippy said, waving them back down and taking her seat. "Miles will catch me up later."

Al-Hinnawi grimaced slightly as he turned to her. "We were just talking about Israel, in fact," the Syrian said, his face florid; he looked like he'd been upset a moment ago. "Mr. Copeland here is urging us to make overtures to the Israelis."

"To what end?" she replied.

"Peace." Al-Hinnawi practically spit the word out. "They come in, invited by the British and the Americans, take over all of Palestine, create a massive refugee crisis, and now they want us to be the ones to try to make peace."

Za'im raised his hand, and al-Hinnawi fell silent. "I know you feel strongly about this, Sami," Za'im said. "We fought hard against the Israelis. And you know what? They were tough."

"Because we didn't have the equipment!" al-Hinnawi replied.

"Because they had the better army!" Za'im snapped back, staring the other man down into silence. "We blamed the equipment because it made the old president look bad, and because we need the army to have pride in itself. But you know it's true: we were beaten." Za'im turned to Zippy and smiled. "And that is enough of that argument. What do you think of reaching out to Israel, Miss Silverman? You are a Jew, are you not?"

Zippy's eyes widened a bit. "I'm an American, sir. You know who I work for."

Za'im waved her argument away. "Yes, yes. I know this. But you're also a Jew. Your fellow Jews suffered terribly in Europe under Hitler, yes?"

"*Terribly* doesn't even begin to describe it," she replied quietly. "It was genocide."

"And in recompense, the Americans and English invited you to try to reclaim Palestine," Za'im insisted. "Your people fought bravely and well, and Israel is a country now. One that we can't wish to go away just because we don't like it very much."

"I would agree with you there, sir," Zippy replied. "Israel fought for the territory and won."

"So, I will make an overture to Israel," Za'im said broadly and a little too loudly. "We have such plans for Syria, for Greater Syria. And I do not want an enemy at my southern flank if I can help it. There is no need to worry about Israel right now when Lebanon and Iraq are on either side of us. So, Mr. Copeland, what do you recommend?"

Copeland leaned back in his seat and smiled, giving Zippy the distinct impression that he was really enjoying his newfound role as kingmaker and advisor. "I can certainly get a message to the Israeli government that outlines your desire for . . . well, what exactly?"

Za'im shrugged. "We cannot call it peace, of course. Perhaps an armistice. A suspension of hostilities. Something with a name people here in Syria will tolerate. And you are willing to facilitate this?"

"To a point," Copeland replied. "We shouldn't be seen as being overly involved. You'll need someone within your government to manage that."

Za'im looked thoughtful for a moment. "What about al-Barazi?"

Zippy remembered the name: Muhsin al-Barazi. He was an advisor and minister under al-Quwatli, the old president, and Za'im had kept him on to help with the transition.

"Do you trust him?" al-Shishakli asked, his brow furrowed. "He worked for al-Quwatli, after all!"

"I trust him enough to do this," Za'im replied. "He has served faithfully. A government is a large thing, Adib! Muhsin has been faithful in keeping everything running. Mr. Copeland, tell your contacts in Jerusalem that al-Barazi is your man."

Copeland nodded, then turned to Zippy. "You know, we can do a little something in the *Post* about this, too. Place an article there about unnamed Syrian government officials hoping to discuss an armistice. Something that will make Syria look good and start driving public opinion there."

"I can do that," Zippy said. "Without anything official or quotable, I don't think it'd make the front page, but if I had to rely on unnamed sources, I could get it in the first five or six pages, I'll bet."

Za'im nodded. "I like this."

Zippy smiled. "Then, President Za'im, what does your government have to say *officially* about a possible armistice with the state of Israel?"

"No comment," Za'im said. Everyone laughed. "All right, there is one other thing, Mr. Copeland, but I will discuss it with you alone. Thank you, Miss Silverman."

Zippy rose and shook hands with all three men, her gloves off. It was her way of keeping tabs on them, what they'd seen and done lately.

First, al-Hinnawi. She clasped his hand and saw flashes of arguments and anger, of time spent at a firing range to relax, of yelling at his wife, of getting drunk. This wasn't particularly new—al-Hinnawi was volatile. But it seemed he was getting worse.

Next, al-Shishakli. These images and sounds were more soothing, at least. Reading, smoking cigars, conversations with other officials, and the boy, always the boy, talking to him and taking care of him. If nothing else, Adib al-Shishakli was a doting father.

Finally, Za'im. She smiled as she clasped the President's hand, excited to be part of something that might turn out to be historic—peace and security for Israel. They weren't her people, per se, but yes, they really *were*. And it was powerful stuff.

Then the images came.

Darkness. Crying out. Feeling trapped. Powerlessness. Clawing at air. A man gasping to breathe. No . . . gasping to be heard. To *exist*.

Zippy managed to keep her smile on as she dropped Za'im's hand. And with a quick "thank you," she made a beeline for the door.

It was only when she reached the outer hall did she realize Copeland had followed her. She nearly jumped out of her skin when he put a hand on her shoulder.

"Hey! Whoa! Sorry! Take it easy there. What's going on? What happened?"

He doesn't know about Variants, she reminded herself. "I just . . . I'm getting the sense that Za'im is a little . . . off. Not himself. You getting that?"

Copeland put his hands on his hips and regarded his shoes for a long moment. "Yeah, I suppose, maybe," he finally said. "He's been eccentric lately. This al-Barazi thing isn't sitting well with the other two in there. They want a completely new government, and they think al-Barazi may undermine them. Assigning him this new portfolio isn't going to help."

"What else?" Zippy pressed.

"Well, he's erratic, like I said. Named himself marshal. More medals. He's been throwing some pretty big parties. Delegating a lot of important things to unimportant people. I think he's just tired, you know? Been going hard at it ever since March, without a break. I don't think it's serious."

Zippy eyed him closely. "I do. Call it years of training and careful observation, call it a gut feeling, women's intuition, whatever. Maybe it's my psychic powers, right?" This got a smirk out of Copeland, as intended. "But something's wrong with Za'im, and I don't know that it's gonna get better any time soon. You better be ready to jump in."

Copeland nodded wearily. "I hear you. I am. It'll be OK."

Zippy nodded and, with a pat on his arm, left. She didn't have the heart to tell him just how much she disagreed with the notion that it'd be OK.

June 30, 1949

Danny Wallace reviewed the reports from Lebanon and Syria with pride—the Variants were doing a fantastic job. Frank and Cal were busy keeping the U.S. one step ahead of the Reds in Beirut, and Zippy's concerns about Za'im were getting the attention they deserved. The two OPC men in charge, Copeland in Damascus and Meade in Beirut, were downright effusive in their praise for the "elite operatives" provided by CIA. Hillenkoetter had given all three of them citations on their records and ensured Truman got a copy.

Sadly, that latter bit was necessary. Maggie and Mrs. Stevens were busy tailing J. Edgar Hoover and Frank Wisner around Washington, and had just added Joe McCarthy to the list. They'd tried asking for more resources but were turned down flat—CIA really shouldn't be in the business of domestic activity to begin with, they were told, and the kind of surveillance they were doing was of questionable legality even for law enforcement. Sure, they were ostensibly "Secret Service agents" by order of the President, but Danny knew Truman would revoke that at the first sign of trouble.

Danny knew that between the two of them, they were well equipped to sniff out all the leaks in MAJESTIC-12 and plug them up. He trusted them. Besides, he couldn't spend too much time worrying about them; he had bigger fish to fry.

Danny and Bronk had spent weeks poring over Schreiber's notebooks, but it was only in the past few weeks, at Hillenkoetter's urging, that they had looked at the idea of shadows. It seemed to be a recurring theme lately—shadows in Damascus, in Bethesda; the guards watching over POSEIDON had even mentioned that the Russian was talking to himself so much that he seemed to be having conversations, complete with pauses for responses. Plus, there was Schreiber's "Vanda" to contend with, too.

So they went over the notes again, and found several instances of the words "*schatten*" and "*schemenhaft*" in Schreiber's notes—particularly in dealing with experiments on the vortex.

Shadows. Shadowy.

They pulled out their German-English dictionaries again, going over each note in minute detail, trying to parse out every possible meaning. Dictionaries were shit for colloquialisms, but the two of them were getting pretty good at it after a while. And that was when they found the connection in a couple of sentences that took fifteen painstaking minutes to translate.

> "*When we conducted the latest experiment with the blood, not only did the data appear shadowy, but I actually saw what I believed to be shadows within the vortex. I would swear that they were human shadows.*"

Now, Schreiber wasn't the most reliable of sorts, but he'd have to be some kind of criminal mastermind to put a bunch of red herrings in scientific notes, just on the slim chance they'd be read by someone else. Both Danny and Brock agreed that there was something about the blood—they assumed it was POSEIDON's blood—that had prompted a unique reaction within the vortex.

They just needed to confirm it.

Danny started by going back to Schreiber, who seemed to be enjoying his enforced vacation. His house arrest seemed to look homier each time Danny visited. There were books everywhere now, from scientific treatises to something called *Rocket Ship Galileo* by Robert A. Heinlein. There was Nabokov next to Mickey Spillane, Agatha Christie next to Einstein. His phonograph record collection was getting extensive as well, with everything from jazz to opera. The German had also asked for, and received, a set of dumbbells, and Danny could see more sinew on his thin frame.

"How are you getting all these?" Danny asked incredulously as he leafed through a short story collection by someone called Ray Bradbury.

"You mean you don't know?" Schreiber chided. "How interesting. When I was first brought here through your PAPERCLIP program, I also asked for permission to relocate my mother to America. She's now in upstate New York, and she mails me books and records—almost every other week, in fact. Normally, when I'm finished, I deposit them in the camp library. But seeing as I no longer can leave, I keep them here."

That jogged Danny's memory; both Hamilton and his traitorous predecessor had mentioned it, and each package—funneled through three other military installations around the United States to protect Area 51's security—was thoroughly inspected, the letters translated from German. "Right. You want someone to come take these out of here for you?"

"You'll forgive me, Commander, if I am feeling less than generous toward my fellow man these days. I am content to leave them here at the moment."

Danny smirked. "Spoilsport."

Schreiber frowned slightly. "And so what brings you to my home today?"

"Shadowy data," Danny replied. "It was something you mentioned in your notes, along with seeing actual shadows in the vortex during one of your experiments with Variant blood. Care to elaborate?"

The German stared at Danny for several long moments before issuing a reply. "No. I do not."

It took Danny a bit to recover from that; usually, Schreiber was at least willing to play word games or mock Danny. Not this time. This time, he just shut the hell down. "Interesting. I guess we'll just have to see what our comparison studies come up with, then. Shame, though. You could've saved us a lot of time."

"Again, Commander, I am not feeling particularly generous," Schreiber said, ice in his voice.

Danny nodded and headed for the door. "Well, by the way, we've got a bit of POSEIDON's blood left." He turned to face the scientist again. "Hate to let it go to waste. Anything we should know before we throw it in there?"

Schreiber tensed at this, his whole body coiling up as if he were ready to leap out of his chair to . . . do something. Attack Danny? Run? Ask to join up again? But nothing else came of it, and he settled back into his chair without a word, turning his attention to the window overlooking the Nevada desert.

"Well?" Bronk said as Danny left the apartment block where Schreiber was kept under house arrest. "Anything?"

Danny smiled up at the tall, lanky scientist, who had stood waiting in the hot desert sun. "Nothing and everything. We're absolutely on to something. He clammed up so tight, he won't shit for a week. Let's get to the data."

That was the problem, of course, and why they'd approached Schreiber in the first place. They'd been recording data on the vortex almost continuously since Danny discovered it in Hiroshima in late 1945. Even with all of the "no event" days removed, there were still thirty-two known spontaneous emissions from the vortex, along with 117 different experiments conducted at Area 51 since 1947. Furthermore, each experiment and event was recorded on at least two dozen different pieces of equipment, measuring more than a hundred different factors. There were audio and film recordings, broad-spectrum radiation readouts, seismographic tracks, you name it.

The files on each event were the size of a New York City phone book, and that didn't count the film or audiotape.

And so they got started. Instead of investigating each and every event, they began with those spontaneous emissions and experiments where Schreiber was *not* present. It was easier to create a baseline that way, a bias-free look at what the vortex could and would do.

Danny and Bronk had considered bringing in a handful of scientists—Schreiber's assistants, by and large—to assist, but the request to do so was knocked down by Hillenkoetter; it didn't seem that he'd even run it past Truman, given the rapid-fire response. Bronk's specialty was in the new field of biophysics, and his role in MAJESTIC-12 was to evaluate and study the Variants themselves, not the vortex. Meanwhile, Danny had been a mere low-level intelligence analyst during the war, and his knowledge of physics was much more on-the-job than anything else.

So, it was slow going. But ultimately, they recreated and confirmed much of what Schreiber had found. And the implications were frightening.

Any experiments with non-living matter or energy— heating or cooling the vortex, launching various objects into it, adjusting the lighting, broadcasting radio waves or other energy into it . . . none of that mattered. It was as if the object or energy in question wasn't even there. The vortex spun on.

In 1948, the MAJESTIC-12 team had authorized Schreiber to take the vortex to a point just miles away from an atomic test on an island in the Pacific. The island itself—a lush little speck of land, full of trees and plants, birds and lizards—was leveled. And for the first time, the needle had moved. The energy signature around the vortex had changed, edging closer to the readings it gave off when it made a spontaneous emission—and, apparently, created a new Variant.

The movement wasn't much, but it was enough for Schreiber to try new avenues. He sent lab rats, cats, dogs, even a chimpanzee through the vortex. While the animals came out unharmed, there were miniscule changes in emissions—in a few cases, just a microsecond burst along one narrow band of radiation—that seemed to imply that the vortex was reacting to the presence of life.

That was when Schreiber's efforts grew darker. The results of the research correlated well to the timing of Montague's decision to allow Schreiber his nuclear test—the one Danny had stumbled upon when he came back from Vienna. The one where a man died.

This lit up the data more than any other single experiment. There were several spikes in broad swaths of the radiation spectrum, and even some grainy visuals of the vortex itself behaving oddly, its rotation changing, new eddies within it. Danny and Bronk watched the film together, slowing the projector and examining it frame by frame.

From there, after Danny had left for Damascus, Schreiber's experiments became more like pagan sacrifices. All those animals used in previous experiments were killed in the presence of the vortex. Once again, there were miniscule changes but more pronounced than when the living animals were used. Death, it seemed, had an impact on the vortex.

Schreiber then introduced a new factor into the equation—blood. He placed a vial of his own blood on a cart and pushed the cart into the vortex. While the reaction wasn't as pronounced as when he killed a man with an A-bomb, the vortex reacted strongly—far stronger than when animals were outright killed within it.

Danny and Bronk had saved the POSEIDON experiment for last. The radiation data was all there—huge spikes, even bigger than the nuclear-fire death at the start of the year. There were even minute seismic changes, which absolutely defied any conventional understanding of modern physics. The vortex, after all, was a creation of pure energy, and with the amount of energy needed to create a seismic event, well . . . Area 51 should've been vaporized. And yet it wasn't.

Even more interesting—the spikes in radiation emissions almost perfectly mimicked a spontaneous event, even though they were perhaps only 75 to 80 percent of the energy usually released. And unlike a spontaneous emission, this one was more diffuse—not "launched" in a given direction.

They also discovered the "shadowy" part after some intensive analysis. Not only were there spikes in certain kinds of radiation and in the seismograph, but other parts of the radiation spectrum were actually . . . obscured. Certain bands of radiation that, in "normal" events, were baseline or only slightly elevated had fallen precipitously, only to perk back up again to normal seconds later. The effect, Danny and Bronk agreed, was as if a shadow were flitting across the radiation spectrum.

They confirmed it in both the audio tape and the film. There were strange high-frequency bursts on the tape—so high that they were barely detectable—and the film showed actual darkening along the disc of the vortex as it swirled.

But even all that wasn't the strangest thing. On film, they could see Schreiber placing a vial of blood—POSEIDON's blood—on the cart used in their experiments. He then wheeled the cart into the vortex and walked out of the frame. Danny could see the visual shadows slip in and out around the ring of the vortex, and could even see the wisps of light becoming more . . . animated, somehow. It was disconcerting.

And then it stopped.

He could hear muted discussions on the audio portion of the film and see some movement around the edges. Finally, after about thirty seconds, Schreiber reentered the frame and pulled the cart away from the vortex. One of his assistants used a Geiger counter on the vial and, after a moment, gave Schreiber a nod.

The German picked up the vial, examined it for a moment and then, smiling, turned to the camera with the vial in his hand, extended toward the camera.

"The blood in the vial has been destroyed," Schreiber intoned, looking into the camera lens. "It appears to have been corrupted or incinerated somehow."

This caused Bronk to start rummaging through his papers. "Which was it?" he muttered.

"What's it matter?" Danny asked absently, his mind pre-occupied. If the vortex actually somehow destroyed Variant blood, what would it do to an actual Variant like himself?

"Because of the energy," Bronk said, still shuffling through reams of data and notes. "If the blood is incinerated, then obviously the vortex is emitting energy that only affects Variants—not surprising, given that the energy it emits creates Variants in the first place.

"But if the blood was 'corrupted,' we need to figure out how. Because if it's an entropic effect, that means the vortex is *taking* energy from the Variant blood in a more passive manner. And that's a whole other set of questions."

Finally, Bronk threw up his hands in disgust. "Nothing. Whatever Schreiber found, he either didn't write it down or he destroyed it. Either way, it's likely significant."

Danny stood up. "Sounds like it could help crack something. And we have one vial of blood left. So, let's get cracking."

"What if we need more?" Bronk asked. "I'd like to replicate the experiment a few times."

Danny gave him a sidelong glance. "Gee, wherever might we find another Variant who won't ask questions about getting blood drawn?"

Bronk smiled; he was the only other person currently at Area 51 who knew that Danny was the famed "Subject-1," the first identified Variant and the key to finding other Variants. "Right. Sorry. Let's get to it."

Now it was time. Danny walked out of the administrative building and to the massive hangar where the vortex was kept. He'd given three vials of blood—enough for now— but they would use the last vial of POSEIDON's blood first. After they analyzed the data, they would conduct the experiment again, after a few days, to see if Danny's blood had a similar reaction.

Once Danny got through security—three separate checkpoints that involved photo identification, passwords, and a thorough frisking—he entered the lab to find Bronk scurrying around the various control panels, getting all the equipment up and running. Typically, there would be several other technicians present, but Hillenkoetter had insisted that only Danny and Bronk be present, even though the other scientists on base had been thoroughly vetted and cleared several times over. Schreiber, to his credit, had likewise kept his experiment on POSEIDON's blood limited to one other person, and they were able to confirm this by having Hamilton thoroughly question the staff as part of a "regular security review." Schreiber's assistant was undergoing debriefing; he'd never hold a security clearance again.

"How are we doing?" Danny asked.

The biophysicist gave a wan smile. "Took me a while to figure out how to turn everything on, but I think we're good. Just start the camera when you're ready, and I'll take care of the rest."

Danny walked over to the massive film camera and, after puzzling over the controls for a moment, got it up and running, the soft whir of the film confirming his efforts. He then stepped in front of it. "This film is classified TOP SECRET-MAJIK, eyes only. Any personnel sharing this film with others of lesser clearance will be prosecuted to the fullest extent of the law." It seemed dopey, but Danny wanted to cross all his *T*s and dot his *I*s on this one.

He then took the vial of Variant blood from Bronk's outstretched hand and placed it on the wheeled cart, a standard government-issue cart most commonly found in mess halls and hospitals. Slowly, he wheeled it over to the vortex, which was spinning languidly in the middle of the room, about three feet from the ground. It looked exactly like it had the first time Danny had come across it in the ruins of Hiroshima, a pure white swirl of wisps and eddies, reminding him of a hurricane as seen from the air. It gave off a white but subtle light, not enough to be blinding but enough so that other lights in the cavernous room weren't needed.

Then it started to change.

"You seeing this, Det?" Danny asked as the vortex seemed to speed up, the currents and tendrils of light becoming more animated.

"Confirmed," Bronk replied quietly. "Looks like we're getting some increased radiation readings too, wide spectrum, non-ionized."

"It knows," Danny said. "It can sense the blood or something. Sweet Jesus."

After pausing for several moments, Danny pushed the cart farther, until the vial of blood came into contact with the edge of the vortex.

The vortex, for want of a better word, went nuts.

The eddies of light swirled violently, and the wisps and tendrils snaked out across the room. It seemed the vortex had grown bigger, slightly brighter, and much more animated.

And then Danny felt something.

Normally, his Enhancement was subtle. He would "feel" the presence of another Variant in a city, as if that person were somehow an extension of his five senses. Once he was locked on, he could then, slowly but surely, find his way to that Variant, even if the other person was moving around, or even got on a bus. It was an instinctual knowledge, deep inside, a subtle pull that seemed to tug at his core.

This, though . . . this was more. A lot more.

Danny felt the tug of hundreds—*thousands*—of others within him, all coming from within the vortex. It was as if an entire army of Variants were somehow inside it, making themselves known to him. He closed his eyes as a subtle jumble of voices encroached on the edges of his hearing, as if trying to listen to a crowd of people from three rooms away.

They were there, wherever *there* was. And they seemed to know he was there, too.

Without any conscious thought, Danny reached up with his left hand toward the vortex.

"Dan!" Bronk shouted. "What are you doing?"

Danny barely heard him. Before he knew it, he had touched the vortex—and a thousand voices exploded in his head, a thousand yearning invisible hands grabbing at his very soul.

That was the last thing he remembered.

```
••••••••••••••
• TOP SECRET •
••••••••••••••
```

FROM: DETLEV BRONK
TO: DCI HILLENKOETTER, POTUS
CC: LCMR WALLACE USN
DATE: 1 JULY 1949
RE: VORTEX EXPERIMENT FOLLOW—UP
CLASSIFICATION: TOP SECRET—MAJIK

LCMR WALLACE IS AWAKE AFTER 17 HOURS UNCONSCIOUS.
HE SHOWS NO SIGNS OF MENTAL IMPAIRMENT FROM HIS
ENCOUNTER WITH THE VORTEX. HOWEVER, HIS LEFT
HAND REMAINS SEVERELY INJURED. THE APPROPRIATE
SECURITY—CLEARED MEDICAL PERSONNEL REPORTED
THAT ALL FOUR FINGERS, HIS THUMB, AND TWO—THIRDS
OF HIS HAND HAVE BEEN SEVERELY WITHERED, AS IF
PREMATURELY AGED TO THE POINT OF DECREPITUDE—
MUMMIFIED IS PERHAPS THE BEST WORD FOR IT. HE IS
UNABLE TO USE OR EVEN MOVE THE HAND AT THIS
POINT. PHOTOS OF THE INJURY WILL BE SENT VIA
SECURE COURIER AS SOON AS POSSIBLE.

I INTERVIEWED WALLACE AFTER HIS MEDICAL EXAMINATION.
HE IS OBVIOUSLY TROUBLED BY HIS PHYSICAL INJURY,
AND EXPRESSED HOPE THAT MR. HOOKS MIGHT BE ABLE TO
ASSIST WHEN HE RETURNS FROM ASSIGNMENT. OTHER THAN
THIS UNDERSTANDABLE CONCERN, WALLACE APPEARS TO BE
LUCID AND IN CONTROL OF HIS FACULTIES. THE FOLLOWING
IS A SUMMARY OF HIS REPORT. HE IS COPIED HERE FOR HIS
FUTURE REFERENCE.

WALLACE REPORTS THAT HIS ENCOUNTER WITH THE VORTEX
WAS SIMILAR TO THE USE OF HIS ENHANCEMENT, IN THAT IT

WAS A SENSORY EXPERIENCE NOT UNLIKE HIS ENCOUNTERS
WITH OTHER VARIANTS. (REF. REPORTS #21, #37, #84, AND
OTHERS IN HIS FILE.) HOWEVER, HE SAYS THAT THE EFFECT
WAS MULTIPLIED A HUNDRED- OR EVEN THOUSAND-FOLD IN
HIS ENCOUNTER, AS IF THERE WERE NUMEROUS VARIANTS
INSIDE THE VORTEX.

WHILE WALLACE REMEMBERS REACHING OUT, HE MAINTAINS
THAT THIS WAS NOT A VOLUNTARY ACTION, BUT MORE
AKIN TO A REFLEX. "LIKE GRABBING FOR SOMETHING
THAT YOU'VE DROPPED." HOWEVER, HE ALSO RAISED THE
QUESTION OF WHETHER THAT IMPULSE WAS HIS OWN, OR HE
WAS UNDER THE INFLUENCE OF SOMETHING ELSE. HE SAYS
HE CANNOT BE SURE, AND WAS VISIBLY DISTURBED WHEN
CONTEMPLATING THIS.

THIS PROMPTED ME TO ASK WHETHER HE BELIEVED THAT
HE WAS IN CONTACT WITH OTHERS WITHIN--OR ON THE
OTHER SIDE OF--THE VORTEX. AFTER SEVERAL MOMENTS,
HE CONCURRED THAT THIS WAS A POSSIBILITY, AND AGREED
AS TO THE PROFOUND IMPACT THIS MAY HAVE ON ALL
VARIANTS AND THE MAJESTIC-12 PROGRAM.

CONCLUSIONS AND RECOMMENDATIONS

PREVIOUS WORK BY DR. SCHREIBER'S TEAM SUGGESTED THAT
THE VORTEX MAY BE A GATEWAY TO ANOTHER PLACE, OR
DIMENSION, AND GIVEN WALLACE'S ENCOUNTER, WE MUST
TAKE THAT POSSIBILITY SERIOUSLY. WE CANNOT KNOW HOW
TO EXPLORE THIS OTHER SPACE, AND WALLACE'S ENCOUNTER
WITH THE PHENOMENON SUGGESTS IT MAY BE HAZARDOUS
TO DO SO.

IN THE INTERESTS OF NATIONAL SECURITY, WALLACE
AND I AGREE THAT UNTIL OTHER EVIDENCE IS FOUND
TO THE CONTRARY, WE MUST ASSUME THAT THERE IS AN
INTELLIGENCE, OR MULTIPLE INTELLIGENCES, WITHIN OR ON
THE OTHER SIDE OF THE VORTEX PHENOMENON. WALLACE
POINTS TO HIS EXPERIENCE AS ONE POINT OF EVIDENCE,
AND POINTED TO LT. LODGE'S POST—MORTEM RETENTION
EMPOWERMENT——IN WHICH HE INTERACTS WITH THE
RECENTLY DECEASED IN HIS MIND——AS ANOTHER POSSIBLE
PIECE OF EVIDENCE.

FINALLY, GIVEN WALLACE'S PARTICULAR ENHANCEMENT AND
HIS REACTION TO IT, I MUST RAISE THE QUESTION AS TO
WHETHER VARIANTS HAVE BEEN CONTACTED BY, OR ARE
EVEN UNDER THE INFLUENCE OF, UNKNOWN INTELLIGENCES.
WALLACE DISAGREES STRONGLY ON THIS POINT, STATING
UNEQUIVOCALLY THAT HE HAS NEVER FELT UNDER SUCH
INFLUENCE. I AM CURRENTLY WORKING TO DETERMINE
WHETHER THERE IS AN EXPERIMENTAL PRAXIS POSSIBLE TO
DETERMINE THE TRUTH OF THE MATTER.

HAVING BEEN IN CHARGE OF THE STUDY OF VARIANTS
SINCE THE BEGINNING OF THE MAJESTIC—12 PROJECT AT
AREA 51, I HAVE PERSONALLY SEEN NO EVIDENCE OF ANY
KIND OF POSSESSION, FOR WANT OF A BETTER WORD, OR
INFLUENCE BY AN OUTSIDE FORCE. WE HAVE DONE MULTIPLE,
CUTTING—EDGE STUDIES ON THE VARIANTS, AND ASIDE FROM
THEIR ENHANCEMENTS, THEY SHOW NO OTHER MENTAL
OR PHYSICAL ABNORMALITIES. FURTHERMORE, THEY HAVE

PROVEN LARGELY TRUSTWORTHY, AND THOSE CURRENTLY ON
ASSIGNMENT HAVE SERVED WELL.

THAT SAID, GIVEN THESE NEW POSSIBILITIES, I BELIEVE WE
MUST CONSIDER A SUSPENSION OF ACTIVE DUTY FOR ALL
VARIANTS CURRENTLY IN THE FIELD AND RETURN ALL OF
THEM TO AREA 51 FOR FURTHER STUDY AND REVIEW. CMDR
WALLACE WISHES IT KNOWN THAT WHILE HE SHARES MY
CONCERNS ABOUT THE POSSIBLE INTELLIGENCES WITHIN OR
BEYOND THE PHENOMENON, HE DOES NOT FEEL THAT IT
IS NECESSARY TO CURTAIL THE CONTINUED SERVICE AND
LIBERTY OF VARIANTS.

(SIGNED) DETLEV BRONK

MR. PRESIDENT——ONLY TWO TEAMS OF VARIANTS ARE CUR-
RENTLY ON ASSIGNMENT, IN SUPPORT OF THE DAMASCUS
OPERATIONS AND IN THE FORRESTAL MATTER. THE REST
CONTINUE TO TRAIN AT AREA 51. I'VE ASKED VANDENBERG
TO STEP-UP SECURITY THERE. IN ORDER TO PRESERVE THE
SECURITY OF BOTH MJ-12 AND THE DAMASCUS MATTER, I
SUGGEST THE VARIANTS IN THE FIELD BE ALLOWED TO
COMPLETE THEIR ASSIGNMENTS. WE CAN WATCH STEVENS
AND DUBINSKY EASILY ENOUGH HERE AT HOME. I RECOM-
MEND FLAGGING COPELAND AND MEADE TO HAVE THEM KEEP
AN EYE ON THE OTHERS ABROAD. WE CAN COUCH IT HOW-
EVER YOU LIKE——STRESS ON THE JOB, PROBLEMS AT HOME,
EVEN SUSPECTED COMMUNIST INFLUENCES FROM THE HOUSE
UN-AMERICAN ACTIVITIES COMMITTEE (WHICH WE CAN OF
COURSE DENY). BUT IF WE PULL THEM NOW, I THINK IT'LL
CREATE MORE PROBLEMS THAN IT SOLVES.——HILLENKOETTER

FINE, BUT LET'S GET DAMASCUS WRAPPED UP ASAP, IF POS-
SIBLE, AND GET EYES ON OUR TWO INVESTIGATORS AT ALL
TIMES FROM HERE ON OUT. THE IMPLICATIONS OF THESE
"UNKNOWN INTELLIGENCES," IF THAT'S WHAT THEY ARE,
ARE PROFOUND. ARE THEY EVEN HUMAN? THIS IS TERRIFY-
ING TO THINK ABOUT——AND IF IT GETS OUT TO THE PUBLIC,
THERE'LL BE A PANIC LIKE WE'VE NEVER SEEN. ESPECIALLY
IF THEY'RE IN CONTROL OF PEOPLE WITH DAMNED SUPERMAN
POWERS. DIVERT WHATEVER YOU NEED TO FIGURING OUT
WHAT'S GOING ON AND WHETHER OUR PEOPLE ARE UNDER
ANY KIND OF INFLUENCE. MEANTIME, GET THE REST OF
THEM LOCKED UP FOR NOW.——HST

22.

July 4, 1949

Stephen Meade reached across the café table and handed Cal a telegram paper. "You care to tell me anything about why I should be keeping an eye on you?"

Cal took the paper and gave it a quick read. The wording was clipped and awkward, but the gist was clear: *We don't fully trust Hooks and Lodge. Watch them carefully.*

"Well, I don't rightly know," Cal said with a sigh, putting the paper down on the table. "I suppose maybe something's going on back in D.C., some kinda turf war between your folks and mine?" It was a bit of a gamble, pinning it on squabbling between bureaucrats at CIA and OPC, but it was the first thing that came to Cal's mind—other than the truth.

Meade frowned as he folded up the paper and stuffed it in his jacket pocket. "I suppose. But I guess I gotta keep an eye on you regardless. Try not to do anything too scary, OK?" The words came with a smile, but Cal could tell the former soldier—*officer*, he remembered—had a little bit of fire in his eyes about it.

Obviously, the good Lord thought Cal didn't have enough going on as is.

"I'll do my best to behave, sir," Cal replied. "Besides, I just had a call with my wife this morning. My boy did well in his first year of school, so I'm not of a mind to mess that up any time soon."

Meade's eyebrows went up. "College?"

"Grambling," Cal said. "Though he's looking to transfer to Howard so he can be closer to home when I'm away."

"Agency set that up for you?"

Cal stirred a little in his chair and tried not to feel too defensive. "Boy got in on his own. Agency just made it possible to pay the bills."

Meade smiled, and this time it seemed genuine—though he looked a little puzzled, too. "Well, that's pretty swell. Hope he does well. Though I gotta say, you look awfully young to have a boy in college."

Inwardly, Cal cursed himself for sharing too much with Meade, even if it was to get his suspicions back down; he'd forgotten how young and strong his Empowerment made him. Some mornings, he even startled himself when he looked in the mirror, in those moments before he remembered the strange journey he'd been on the last few years. "Well, I'm gonna take that as a compliment, sir. Started young, hard work kept me strong."

Thankfully, Frank Lodge arrived at that moment, preventing Meade from asking any more questions. Frank plopped down a package of the doughy, sweet, sticky *batlaywee* snacks that Cal had taken a shine to while in town. Cal in turn waved over the waiter to bring a coffee, while Meade excused himself to use the facilities.

"Meade got a cable from his bosses," Cal said quietly. "Said to keep an eye on us, like they don't trust us."

Frank frowned. "Think it's because of the program?" *The program* was their shorthand for MAJESTIC-12 and all things Variant that were too classified to discuss aloud.

"That'd be my guess, but I can't say for sure. I just passed it off as bickering between the Foggy Bottom folks. Hope that holds, but I think he's taking it seriously."

"Maybe it's just that," Frank said, shrugging. "I'll send a cable to Danny and ask what's up. Meantime, we—"

He stopped short to watch Meade dash past. "I think it's happening!" the man shouted as he ran out the door of the café and onto the street—where Cal could see several young men thundering by.

"Here we go," Frank muttered, downing his coffee in one gulp as he rose to his feet. Cal stuffed a piece of *batlaywee* in his mouth and shoved the rest of the package in his suitcoat pocket as he followed.

Outside, Frank pointed to a satchel next to Meade. "You got your radio?" Frank asked.

Meade nodded. "I'll get the car. You find Saadeh and let me know where to go." He sprinted off, away from the stream of men heading down the street. Frank and Cal joined them, going as quickly as possible and taking side streets wherever they could. Frank led the way—he'd sat with a dying Beirut deliveryman the week prior and now had a local's map of Beirut in his head.

Their route took them once again to Martyrs' Square, where a large crowd had gathered and was chanting in what Cal took to be Arabic. Not only was Martyrs' Square the central-most open space in the city, it was also just a short walk to the Lebanese Parliament building—and where else would you stage a coup, if not at the center of government?

Given the line of heavily armed police Cal saw in front of the Parliament building, the government knew it too. He wondered if the growing mob was armed, or if they were getting reinforcements. And if so, from whom. Revolution, Cal thought in that moment, was one hell of a messy business.

"Find Saadeh and stick with him," Frank said as they pulled up and began surveying the crowd. "Tap in if you find him."

Cal nodded and felt for the small cigarette case radio in his pocket, then turned toward the edge of the square, where a number of streetlamps lined the edge of the walkways. He ran over and began climbing the pole, his long arms and ropey muscles making easy work of it. He couldn't help but feel a little satisfaction at the way his rejuvenated body tackled the job, as easy as climbing a tree had been when he was a boy. A few moments later and he was hanging off the top, looking down on the crowd, searching for Saadeh's gray, frizzy pompadour.

There. Near the center of the square, slowly making his way toward what Cal assumed was his favorite park bench.

Saadeh was waving and shaking his fist, and while Cal couldn't hear over the crowd, he was pretty sure Saadeh was getting them good and riled up.

Hanging off the arm of the lamppost, Cal reached into his pocket and pulled out the cigarette case radio, giving it two urgent taps. A moment later, a tinny voice came through. "Where is he?" Frank said.

"Usual spot. Crowd's thick on him. You seeing weapons down there?"

"Nothing useful. Only a few guns. Bunch of broom handles and tire irons. Some idiot brought a cricket bat."

"Cricket's a dumb sport," Cal remarked. "I'm coming down. Gonna make my way to him."

"Stay on him," Frank said. "If he gets himself wounded, keep him stable until we can get him out of there. Don't compromise yourself."

"Try not to. Out."

Cal swung down from the lamppost with all the vigor and nimbleness his youthful body could provide and started running toward the center of the square. The crowd was moving now, an undulating and living thing, pushing toward the line of police in front of the Parliament building. The cops had helmets and rifles like soldiers, but even as the crowd surged, they seemed unsure as to what to do—despite being armed to the teeth, they were severely outnumbered.

Don't shoot, don't shoot, don't shoot, please God, don't let them shoot, Cal thought as he pushed and shoved his way closer to the center of the swirling mob, toward Saadeh. He had to be forcefully rude to a few people on the way as he cleared himself a path—even muttering "sorry" as he man-handled someone aside to push ahead—but he had orders. Za'im wanted Saadeh safe, and the U.S. wanted Za'im as a happy partner. Simple enough.

Finally, Cal saw a familiar face, one of the goons from their little visit a few weeks back. "I'm a friend, I'm a friend," he panted, getting up close. "Here to help. Keep him safe." The goon had an automatic pistol in his hand and glowered at Cal with disdain but ultimately shoved him into what seemed to be Saadeh's inner circle, a group of tweedy-looking older men who looked an awful lot like college professors. That seemed to fit the bill of revolutionaries these days—bunch of older college boys trying to convince the worker bees to follow along.

As Cal fell in beside them, he couldn't help but think that the American Revolution had been kind of the same thing, though—college-educated men getting a bunch of farmers and dockworkers to go along with a radical idea.

The edges of the crowd reached the line of police and started to move to the sides, allowing Saadeh and his entourage to get closer. Cal was now just about four or five people away from Saadeh as the revolutionary approached the police line, shouting something long and wordy in Arabic. Cal didn't understand—but the crowd immediately cheered loudly when he was done. *No wonder Za'im likes this guy,* he thought. The policemen holding the line began to fidget and look at each other for support as Saadeh continued to exhort them, presumably, in the name of unity and prosperity or whatever it was they wanted.

There were others in the crowd talking to individual policemen, trying to argue their case or plead with them. A few even put their hands on the cops' shoulders, which Cal couldn't help but tense at the sight of; where he was from, touching a cop was a good way to get your nose broken. Yet the police here did nothing; in fact, a few started to relax and lower their weapons in response.

And then, one by one, members of the crowd started walking past the police line, in between the individual officers. The trickle soon became a wave, and all of a sudden, Cal was walking with Saadeh past two armed policemen looking out at the crowd with tears in their eyes.

"Cal, come in," came the tinny voice from his cigarette case.

"I'm here, Frank," Cal said. "Just got past the police line."

"I know. I circled 'round. It's a trap. You need to get Saadeh out of there."

Cal looked around for several long moments, trying to see what Frank was talking about. "Frank, come again. I don't see nothing out here."

"I'm telling you, it's a trap," Frank said. "I got army troops around the back of the Parliament building and—shit, they're moving! They're moving, Cal! Get him out of there!"

Cal reached out with a long arm towards Saadeh, who was walking briskly toward the Parliament building, the bulk of the crowd at his back. "Mr. Saadeh! Mr. Saadeh! You got to come with me, sir. It's a trap up ahead."

Saadeh turned to give Cal a bemused look. "The only trap here is laid by men like you, Mr. American," he said with a smile. "Watch as we take back Syria for the Syrians."

But then Saadeh stopped cold, his smile evaporating as several columns of soldiers emerged around each side of the Parliament building, carrying rifles. Officers on horseback shouted at the armed men in Arabic, and they formed a new line, several rows deep, in front of the building.

"Like I said, Mr. Saadeh, this here's a trap. You need to come with me," Cal insisted, taking him by the arm.

Saadeh wouldn't move, but the crowd around him slowed as well, the shouting and hollering dying down almost instantly.

One of the men on horseback drew his cavalry sword and shouted—and with his orders, the lines of soldiers began to shift. They were three deep, and the first two ranks immediately knelt down and raised their weapons. Two hundred rifles were suddenly pointed out at the crowd.

"Sweet Jesus," Cal muttered, grabbing hold of Saadeh's arm again, this time tighter. "Sir, we got to go *now*. You understand me?"

"They will not fire," Saadeh muttered in disbelief. "They cannot."

The man on horseback shouted again, and two hundred rifle bolts clicked into position.

First ready, now aim. "They sure seem like they're gonna, Mr. Saadeh. You need to get out of here. Come *on*." Yet nobody around them was fleeing, and Cal suddenly understood—these folks weren't gonna move until Saadeh did, and Saadeh was frozen still. "Sir, you're gonna get a whole lot of people killed if you stay here," Cal said, trying a different tack and moving around to place his body between Saadeh and the rifles—because that, he figured, was his job at the moment.

Finally, Saadeh raised his fist in the air and shouted something in Arabic, then again in French. The crowd cheered once more.

"Aw, Lord," Cal said quietly as he screwed his eyes shut and waited.

The cavalryman barked orders a final time.

Two hundred rifles erupted as one.

"Aw, Lord," Cal said again, a bit louder, pulling Saadeh to him in a bear of a hug and using his body to shield the revolutionary.

Cal's upper thigh blossomed into agony as a bullet pierced him with a roar of pain. He staggered forward, pushing Saadeh along with him even as men began dropping all around him and screams erupted from the crowd. Cal tried to put weight on his leg, but it gave way from under him in a searing white-hot blast of agony, sending him to the cobblestoned plaza.

Next to him on the ground, Cal found himself face to face with another man staring back with the glassy-eyed look of the freshly dead, blood pooling in the cracks between the cobblestones under his head. In his haze of pain, Cal reached out and touched the man, praying to God that he was indeed dead instead of merely injured, and pulled as much healing life out of the man as was left.

The pain subsided somewhat as he felt himself grow stronger, and Cal looked up to see Saadeh surrounded by his own men pushing him away from the lines of soldiers. Knowing there would almost certainly be a second volley, Cal pushed himself up onto his hands and knees. His thigh still throbbed, but he managed to get to his feet and hobble after Saadeh, pushing his way through the now chaotic, panicked throng.

There was shouting all over, and another round of shots pierced the air. Cal winced but somehow missed getting shot again. The young man next to him—no older than his own boy—wasn't so lucky, falling to the cobblestones with a cry of agony. Cal paused, wanting to reach out and help, or at least alleviate the pain, but caught himself— God help him, that wasn't his job right now. His job was Saadeh.

The knot of burly men with Saadeh in the middle was falling back toward the edge of the plaza, away from the Parliament building, and Cal managed to get there just as they reached an alleyway—a dead-end one at that.

Cal shoved through the mob around the revolutionary. "Mr. Saadeh, this ain't no good. You got to come with me if you want to live. Come on!"

Saadeh made eye contact from behind the line of men protecting him. "Where?" he shouted.

"We got a car. Come on!" Cal raised his radio and keyed it on. "We're in the alleyway off the plaza, next to the shops. Where are you?"

"I'm almost there," Meade replied. "It's a madhouse here."

"Hurry up," Cal said, looking over his shoulder to see the line of government troops now systematically marching into the square, using truncheons to beat up anyone damn fool enough to confront them. They had two, maybe three minutes. "Frank, you better get over here."

His reply was a tap on the shoulder. "Right here, Cal," Frank said, panting from exertion. "Let's get these boys lined up." Frank turned to Saadeh. "Too many men in here. Get them to stand at the street. They may have to buy us some time."

Saadeh looked dismayed, and for a moment, Cal wondered if he was going to play ball after all. But finally, Saadeh barked out some orders in Arabic, and several of his bodyguards fanned out back through the alley. Some of them pulled pistols, which Cal figured wouldn't do anything except piss off the soldiers and turn the alley into a shooting gallery. "Tell 'em to act scared, hide behind things," Cal said. "If they look like they're gonna fight, the fight's gonna come to them."

This time, it was Frank who gave the orders, and to Cal's relief, Saadeh's men obeyed. They now had a clear path to the street—so long as Meade showed up with the damn car.

Finally, with the soldiers now marching into the middle of Martyrs' Square, the trusty blue Packard screeched to the curb, Meade behind the wheel. "OK, Mr. Saadeh, you keep your head down," Cal said. "Get your jacket up over your head so they don't see you right away. Ready?"

Saadeh, wide-eyed and sweating, nodded quickly and pulled his suit jacket up. "Ready," he said quietly.

Cal looked over to Frank, who had his Regina .32-caliber pistol out, the suppressor already screwed on. Cal thought to reach for his own, but figured against it—the man next to Saadeh shouldn't be a target. Wasn't like Cal had it loaded anyway.

"OK, go!" Frank yelled.

Cal grabbed Saadeh by the arm and took off fast as he could down the alley toward the street, his thigh getting more painful with each step. Meade reached back and opened the rear door, and they quickly shoved Saadeh into the back seat, Cal right behind him. Frank clambered in up front, and Meade was driving again before the doors even closed.

"My men!" Saadeh yelled as he sought to untangle himself and sit upright. "What about my people?"

"You're a wanted man now, Mr. Saadeh," Frank said. "And—hell, keep your head down! We can't have anybody seeing you in this car. Better you get out of town than get arrested with the rest of them."

"But I need to regroup! This isn't over!" Saadeh protested as he nonetheless slouched down in the backseat.

Meade swerved onto a side street. "Sir, I just drove across town to get here, and let me tell you, it's over for now, OK? There are troops at every major intersection. They're looking for you. I think you had a leak in your ship."

"Leak? Ship?" Saadeh asked impatiently.

Cal put a hand on the man's shoulder. "Means the government had someone on the inside, spying on you. We got to assume they know everything you got going. All your bolt-holes and safe houses. Everything. That's why you got to go, leave Beirut, figure things out away from everything."

Saadeh looked miserable, on the verge of tears. "My own people. I cannot believe it."

"Honestly, sir, your security was shit," Frank said, no recriminations in his voice. "If we could wander around and figure out what your plans were, no doubt the government could too. Or the Russians. Anybody, really. Next time, you have to be smarter."

Saadeh looked as though he wanted to strangle someone but instead just closed his eyes and rested his head against the back of the seat. "So, where are we going now, Americans?"

Cal smiled at him. "Don't you worry, Mr. Saadeh. You got friends in Damascus. We're going to take you there."

"I don't have friends in Damascus," Saadeh said quietly.

"None that you know of," Cal replied. "But you do."

July 5, 1949

It took six long hours to drive from Beirut to the outskirts of Damascus—a trip usually done in well under three. Instead of taking them east along the main road, Meade chose a more winding path that led them south through farm country, then over the cedar-lined Mount Lebanon range on a road that seemed more like an ambitious goat path. Frank looked down at one point and saw the Packard's tires were inches from a precipice that would've ended them, but Meade drove as efficiently and automatically as a New York City cabbie in rush hour. Frank just closed his eyes and leaned his head back, praying for flat land.

They were in the Beqaa Valley by sunset. As they drove, Saadeh inexplicably began talking about Lebanese wines—apparently, they were the best in the Middle East. Frank really felt for the guy; his pride in his homeland was palpable, and the sadness and weariness in his voice felt like his soul was in a vise. Saadeh even offered to have them stop for a meal at a vineyard owned by a friend, but that was quickly vetoed. Instead, they found a lonely looking gas station at a major intersection—they had to cross a well-traveled road at *some* point—where Meade had to barge in on the proprietor's dinner to fuel up but managed to wrangle some bread and grapes out of him as well. Meanwhile, Frank took the opportunity to use the phone to dial a nondescript number in Damascus.

"Yes?" came a tired voice in Arabic-accented English.

"Mr. Hawley, please," Frank said, using one of the code phrases Copeland had established.

That perked up the man on the other end of the line. "Yes, of course. One moment."

There were several clicks and a bit of static, then a phone that rang six times before it finally picked up. "Yes?" It was Copeland's voice.

"Hawley!" Frank said in his best salesman voice. "It's Jack Rittenhouse! I know it's late and all, but are you up for a drink tonight? I'm coming to town and got my hands on some actual Scotch. Had to practically wrestle a bear for it, but it's the real deal." *We're coming in, and we have Saadeh with us. Things went south in Beirut.*

"Oh. Oh! Yes, hello! How are you?" Copeland said, and for a minute there, Frank thought he wouldn't keep up with the ruse. "So, you're on your way?"

"Might take a bit—customs, you know, but yes. Shall I come by the house? Or maybe Morty's in town and would like a drink?" *On our way, still in Lebanon. Meet at the consulate or go straight to Za'im?*

"You know, I imagine Morty would love to see you. Let me ring him up. You can meet me at the house and we'll go from there." *Za'im wants him. Pick me up at the consulate before you go.*

"Right, then. See you soon. Bye, Hawley!" Frank hung up with a grimace. He hadn't been in the spy game for long, but amateurs rankled him as if he were a pro.

Back in the car and munching on bread and grapes, they crossed the Beqaa Valley on a dirt road, still heading east and headed for Mount Hermon, which straddled the Lebanese-Syrian border and was within spitting distance of the heavily fortified Israeli border. Frank wasn't worried about his own safety should Meade take a wrong turn, but he was pretty sure the Israelis wouldn't mind keeping Saadeh for themselves, what with his whole vision that a newly formed "Greater Syria" would also include all of Israel. But Meade had mapped out his escape routes even before they arrived in Beirut, and the crossing over Hermon into Syria

was uneventful—though Frank really wished someone
would've put some goddamn guardrails up.

Once in Syria proper, with the Packard now heading
northeast toward Damascus on the main road, everyone
relaxed a little bit. Well, Frank and Meade did—Saadeh was
still looking forlorn, staring out the window blankly, while
Cal had managed to go right to sleep about an hour outside
Beirut.

"So, why does Colonel al-Za'im wish to ally himself with
me?" Saadeh said finally. "I feel as though this is not, as you
say, a fit like a glove."

"How come?" Frank asked.

"He gained power through a military coup, against a
president elected by the people. I wished to empower the
people of Lebanon against the government that ruled them.
I would simply think he would wish to side with that government instead."

Frank thought about this a moment before replying.
"Well, I suppose you have a point there. But I also think
Za'im thinks the same as you about the whole Greater Syria
thing. He's more, I guess, cosmopolitan when it comes to
religion and social issues, kind of like how you've described
it. Maybe you have more common ground than you think."

"I guess that depends on what sort of man he is," Saadeh
allowed. "Have you met him?"

"Yep."

"And?"

"You're asking what, exactly? If he's a good guy?"

"I suppose that's a place to start," Saadeh said.

Frank sighed. "He's an army officer. You served in the
army, Mr. Saadeh?"

"I have not."

"The army's rough. Not a lot of room for debate or
thoughtfulness when bullets are flying. You make a decision, you expect it to be carried out, no questions asked.
I think he's a good example of that sort of mentality. He
wants stuff done and makes it happen. And that's what he
did in Syria, I guess."

Frank looked back to see Saadeh smiling. "Either you don't know him well at all, or you are trying not to tell me something."

"Look, we're not pals, so I can't tell you if he's good to his wife or goes to church every week," Frank said. "He took Syria without firing a shot. Isn't that saying something?" Frank left out the part about Za'im nearly murdering the old president.

"Yes, that is a good thing," Saadeh said, but he didn't sound convinced. "I suppose I will have to meet him myself."

It was well past midnight when the glow from Damascus's lights were spotted over the horizon. Frank nudged Cal awake so they'd have an extra set of eyes as they entered the city, then told Saadeh to hunch down again. Saadeh's SSNP no doubt had some friendlies in town—and Frank figured the Lebanese might have some folks stationed there as well. Maybe it was paranoid, but more and more, it had been paying off to play it safe.

The trip into the city center was blessedly uneventful, and soon the Packard pulled up in front of the consulate. Meade ran inside to fetch Copeland, who came out looking disheveled and generally tired, a sight that amused the hell out of Frank. "We mess with your beauty sleep, Miles?" Frank said as Copeland crammed into the back seat with Saadeh and Cal.

"What the hell happened?" Copeland said, then caught himself and extended a hand toward Saadeh. "Miles Copeland, U.S. State Department."

"Mr. Copeland," Saadeh said, shaking his hand. "Unfortunately, it seems the Lebanese government knew of our intentions and sent soldiers to deal with us—truly a sign of their animosity to the people of Lebanon!"

Copeland looked over at Cal, who just shrugged. "They tried a revolution. Didn't work."

Saadeh looked as though he was ready to punch Cal but seemed to think better of it.

"All right," Copeland said. "We're going to Mezze."

"What?" Frank said. "Why there?"

"Well, we can't just march him into the presidential palace, now, can we?" Copeland said impatiently as Meade hit the gas. "Za'im's refurbishing one of the buildings there as a kind of retreat for these kinds of meetings."

Yeah, that's convenient, Frank thought, but held his tongue. Why the hell would a country's president want a safe house at a prison? On the other hand . . . well, it was pretty well secured and it was the last place you'd look. Maybe it was a sharp move, even if it was creepy.

The Packard rolled out of the city center toward the hills outside town. Mezze Prison was situated on a particularly forbidding hillside overlooking a poorer neighborhood. A wide swath of land separated the prison from the barbed wire and walls that set it off from more respectable sorts. Meade drove up to the gate, and Copeland rolled down the back window to give some kind of password to the guards; they were let in without any hassle at all. Another guard inside pointed them toward a separate building set apart from the main prison. It looked like some kind of administrative building. Outside, Frank saw al-Hinnawi there, looking as brutish and pissed off as ever.

"Colonel al-Hinnawi," Copeland said as he practically jumped out of the vehicle. "I assume the President is here?"

"He is, Mr. Copeland," al-Hinnawi said gruffly. "Do you have him with you?"

"We do, yes. Shall we?"

Al-Hinnawi held up a hand. "Just Mr. Copeland and Mr. Saadeh."

Frank walked over to the Syrian and stood just close enough to make his point. "Colonel," he said in Arabic, "with all due respect, we work for the United States, not you. My colleagues and I went through a lot to get him here safely, and we're going to make sure he's safe and sound inside, God willing."

The colonel narrowed his eyes and tried to stare Frank down for several long moments, and Frank had to admit, al-Hinnawi looked like one tough bastard. Finally, though, the colonel just turned on his heel and stalked inside. Frank motioned for everyone to come along. "Let's go. It's fine."

Cal looked at Frank with an eyebrow raised. "Don't seem fine." But he followed nonetheless, as did the rest of the Americans; they practically surrounded Saadeh on all sides as they entered the building and proceeded down a short, nondescript hallway lit by dusty lightbulbs from above, toward a nondescript door.

When al-Hinnawi opened it, though, it was as if they were transported to a different world.

The room they entered—likely once a conference room or some such—had been turned into something out of *Arabian Nights*. There were a couple of couches, several overstuffed chairs, and enough throw pillows to start a pillow fight. Tapestries hung from the walls and helped curtain the windows, and the lights came from beautiful Tiffany lamps. A hookah sat idle in one corner, and incense wafted through the air. In the middle of it all, seated in a leather club chair with his back to a massive bookshelf, Za'im was reading a book and smoking a cigarette. And on one of the couches . . .

"Miss Silverman!" Cal breathed. "What are you doing here?"

Zippy smiled. "Good to see you, Cal. The President asked me here."

Frank had to pick his jaw up off the floor. Immediately, he wondered how Zippy had managed to get into Za'im's good graces so quickly, and was quickly ashamed of where his mind went. He didn't know Zippy all that well but knew enough to figure she wasn't the type to use her feminine wiles that way. Besides, she was dressed in a pretty plain dress suit, like you'd expect a reporter to wear—not a gun moll or something.

"Did he, now?" Frank said. "Interesting."

Zippy merely shot him a look and moved her hand a fraction. *I'll explain later.*

Meanwhile, Za'im looked at Frank and Cal with surprise—and displeasure. "What is this?" he quietly asked al-Hinnawi in Arabic.

"They insisted on accompanying him," the colonel said, his frown deepening.

To Za'im's credit, his smile instantly returned. "My American friends," he said in English. "I thank you, on behalf of the people of both Syria and Lebanon, for delivering our friend from danger. And Antoun Saadeh! Welcome, my friend!"

Za'im got up and walked over to Saadeh, wrapping him up in a bear hug. Saadeh shot Frank a perplexed look but returned the hug nonetheless. "You do me honor, Mr. President."

"You honor me, Antoun," Za'im said, his hands now on Saadeh's shoulders. "I am saddened to hear of what happened in Beirut. Come, we have tea here. I wish for you to tell me all about it so that we may decide what happens next."

Tentatively, Saadeh allowed Za'im to lead him over to one of the couches, seating him next to Zippy, and the Syrian leader personally poured tea for the revolutionary. Copeland cleared his throat. "President Za'im, would it be all right if I stayed for this conversation? Perhaps I can offer further assistance."

Za'im looked over at Copeland and smiled. "I believe your compatriot here can best represent the interests of the United States in this matter. Do not worry. Mr. Saadeh is my guest, and I simply wish to hear his thoughts on the Syrian Social National Party and Lebanon." Za'im handed Saadeh his tea, then walked over to Copeland, hand extended. "You have done Syria a great service, and I thank you. The friendship between the United States and Syria will endure for many years to come, thanks to you."

Meanwhile, Frank was staring holes into Zippy's head, and she most definitely noticed. "I can do this, Frank," she said in Hebrew, knowing that they were likely the only two Hebrew speakers in the room. "Long story. I'll tell you later."

"You better," Frank replied, then looked over to Copeland, who was staring back, seemingly looking for guidance. All Frank could do was nod.

Copeland smiled and shook Za'im's hand. "Very well, Mr. President. I'll make an official visit in a few days. Thank you."

And with that, Copeland turned to go, pulling in Meade, Cal, and Frank with a look as he left. Frank turned around for one last glance at Za'im, sitting across from Zippy, and a more relaxed Saadeh, smiling and chatting in Arabic.

"All right, then," Frank said quietly as he closed the door behind him. "Hope you're right."

LEBANON EXECUTES WOULD-BE DICTATOR

Antoun Saadeh Pays Ultimate Price for Fascist Rebellion

BEIRUT, Lebanon, July 8—The leader of the Syrian Socialist Revolutionary Party, Antoun Saadeh, was executed early this morning by firing squad after trying to mount a rebellion against the elected government of Lebanon.

Saadeh's revolutionary party, which had adopted a mythic "Greater Syria" racial platform similar to European fascism, attempted to overthrow the Lebanese government in an action on July 4, but expected support from mountain tribes and Druze separatists never arrived, and Saadeh was driven from the capital toward Syria, where elements of his party still exist.

Saadeh was arrested outside of Damascus the next day by police under the direction of President Husni al-Za'im, and was returned to Lebanon, where he was immediately placed on trial for high treason against the government. Authorities here report that at least 500 of Saadeh's followers are now under arrest, and several of them testified against him at the trial, confirming that the rebellion, which cost the lives of at least one military officer, was conducted under Saadeh's instructions.

Saadeh's defense attorney had asked for a delay in the proceedings in order to study the government claims, but the request was denied and the matter brought before a military tribunal. The guilty verdict was rendered last night and confirmed by Lebanese President Bechara El Khoury.

The trial and execution were conducted in secrecy, with the news of Saadeh's conviction and death announced only today. Authorities here explained that this was done for security reasons.

A representative of President El Khoury thanked the Syrian government for their cooperation, stating that the removal of Saadeh and his "fascist party" would help foster peace in the Middle East. Syrian President Za'im, speaking to reporters in Damascus, echoed the sentiment.

"The governments of the region must come together in mutual trust and support," Za'im said. "War recently ravaged Europe under fascist regimes. We will not allow this to happen here."

24.

July 9, 1949

How well do you know Zipporah Silverman?" Hillenkoetter asked Maggie and Mrs. Stevens as they sat in his cramped, surprisingly plain office in Foggy Bottom.

The two women looked at each other and shrugged almost simultaneously. "Not really well, but I did some ops with her," Maggie replied. "Nice enough. Good for intel work, not so much the rough stuff. Kind of a natural actress, and her Empowerment is really useful. Why do you ask?"

"You're not cleared for it," Hillenkoetter replied. "All I can tell you right now is you might be heading back to Syria soon."

Maggie nodded, then pointed to the newspaper on Hillenkoetter's desk. "Looks like something went down in Beirut," she noted. "Zippy's involved?"

Hillenkoetter smirked. "See, why can't you break open the Forrestal ring as quick as that?" he asked. "Speaking of which, how's that coming along?"

Maggie looked over at Mrs. Stevens, who referred to the legal pad on her lap. "They're being careful. No documents are changing hands. We've got some interesting conversations on tape, but actual evidence that Forrestal was leaking confidential information about MAJESTIC-12 is thin and mostly circumstantial. They'll just claim them to be unsubstantiated rumors or something silly like that. And you know, of course, that we can't be the ones to catch them in the act, with us being Variants and all."

Hillenkoetter nodded. "Who's in on it that we know of?"

"Hoover and Wisner for sure. Trying to get more dirt on McCarthy, but nothing solid yet,'" Maggie replied.

"Might be able to help you there," Hillenkoetter said. "Just got a call from General Vandenberg today. One more for your list—Louis Johnson."

"The new Defense Secretary?" Mrs. Stevens asked. "Isn't he already cleared for MAJESTIC-12?"

"Nope. The President specifically kept him out of it," Hillenkoetter said. "Louis was nominated as a budget-cutter, not a war-fighter. Everything's very political with him, and more politics is the last thing we need to throw into this equation."

Maggie smiled. "You don't trust him with this."

"No, I don't, and thankfully, neither does the President. But apparently, Johnson's caught wind of it anyway. Sent a memo to Vandenberg this morning requesting more information. Vandenberg told him to take it up with the President, which was the exact right response."

Mrs. Stevens looked down at her legal pad a moment, then shut her eyes. Maggie knew that this was a sign that her wheels were turning. She looked up and smiled. "You're thinking McCarthy tipped off Johnson."

"Not bad, Mrs. Stevens," Hillenkoetter replied. "Louis has met with Joe several times up on the Hill, part of the dance he has to do to get a budget passed. Joe also knows Hoover pretty well."

"And you sound like you have a plan, sir," Maggie noted.

Hillenkoetter leaned back in his chair and smiled. "I just might. Care to help me pull it off?"

Maggie and Mrs. Stevens traded a look. "Will it get us closer to being exonerated in Forrestal's death?" Maggie asked.

"Can't hurt your chances."

Before Hillenkoetter could continue, there was a rap on the door; a young, bespectacled woman poked her head into the office. "Sir, I have Commander Wallace on the line. You're really gonna want to take it."

Hillenkoetter nodded and picked up the phone. "Go ahead, Commander." Maggie could hear a tinny, rapid-fire voice on the other end of the line but little else.

"What do you mean, he's *gone*?" Hillenkoetter barked. He then looked up at the two women. "Out. Now."

* * *

Danny hung up the phone and wiped the sweat from his brow with his good hand. It wasn't from the desert heat. "Well, that was horrible," he said, looking over at Hamilton. "Tell me you have something, because a former Nazi scientist under house arrest doesn't just up and disappear from the most secure military facility in the world."

Hamilton stood in front of Wallace's desk in formal at-ease position. "I have an unconfirmed report of . . . something unusual. Sir."

"Shit, just tell me," Danny groused. "It's not like the unusual is . . . well, all that unusual around here." Danny held up his injured hand for emphasis. He'd taken to wearing a glove on it just to keep the staring to a minimum.

Hamilton cleared his throat. "One of the MPs on duty last night said he saw some kind of . . . shadow . . . moving oddly around Schreiber's door."

That prompted Danny to jump to his feet. "What kind of shadow?"

"Very dark. And . . . kind of man-shaped."

"Did he think to check on Schreiber after that?" Danny demanded.

"No, sir. He thought it was just a trick of the light. The other MP didn't see it. I almost wasn't going to mention it to you at all, sir. It just sounded so . . . ridiculous."

Danny came around the desk and headed for the door, clapping Hamilton on the shoulder and pulling him along. "All right. That's something, at least. Are all the Variants accounted for?"

"Yes, sir," Hamilton replied. "I've got every team locked down; null-fields are on."

"Good. If I had to bet, I'd say we had an outside Variant visitor last night," Danny said as he hustled down the hallway toward the door. "How many more null-generators do we have?"

"Only a handful. We're spread pretty thin."

Danny stopped at one of the labs, where Bronk was testing blood samples—Danny's blood. "Det! I need you to stop what you're doing. Gather every set of hands you can find. We need more null-generators, stat. I need the entire base covered."

"What's happening?" Bronk asked, brow furrowed.

"Don't know yet, but we need this place secured," Danny replied before rushing down the hall again, Hamilton keeping pace behind him. "Deploy whatever we have left around the vortex. I don't want anybody sneaking in there. We need a car with a radio. Not a jeep."

"Where are you going?"

Danny burst out of the administrative building and headed for the motor pool. "*We* are going to Vegas."

"Why?"

"Because it's the only place within a full day's drive that has a bus station and an airport. Let's just hope our scientist doesn't have too much of a head start."

* * *

Every single thing that is wrong with America is in this very room, Kurt Schreiber thought as he looked behind him at the throngs of people, drinks in hand, surrounding slot machines and gaming tables, taking their hard-earned money and throwing it away on the slim chance they'd be rewarded with instant riches.

Some, certainly, didn't *need* instant riches but rather entertained themselves with the notion that they had enough money to throw away on gambling, expensive meals, Cuban cigars, and alcohol—so much alcohol. These men and women, in fine suits and whorish dresses, grew fat and drunk and cared for nothing except their own debaucheries.

And then there were the desperate ones. The men whose suits were threadbare and stained, plugging pennies into mechanisms that ate them greedily, only spitting out just enough winnings to keep the poor souls in their chairs, to prolong the agony of losing their pittance salaries or, worse, their last dollars. And the women were doing the same when they weren't trying to make "friends" and earn a few dollars.

How in the name of God did these . . . people . . . manage to defeat the greatest army ever assembled? How did these mongrel bands of malcontent wastrels reduce Berlin to rubble? How did they even manage to conceive of the atom bomb, much less build one without destroying themselves in the process?

Schreiber sipped at his ginger ale, unwilling to join them in their descent. He had better things to do. And yet his contact was late, and he was getting worried.

"Why so glum, chum?"

Schreiber turned to his right to see two men in tuxedos sitting down at the bar next to him. One was tall, handsome, and ruddy, with a smile that no doubt made the ladies there swoon. The other—the one who'd spoken in a rather squeaky, grating voice—was shorter and more awkward, with a prominent nose and teeth that looked like they wanted to escape his face somehow. Schreiber had half a mind to oblige them.

Schreiber sighed. "I'm waiting for someone," he said, trying to bury his accent.

"I bet it's a girl," the other man said in a soothing baritone. "Hope she ain't stood you up, pal. Hey, barkeep! Coupla gin and tonics."

"Yes, me too," Schreiber said neutrally. "It's been a very long day."

"Aww, it'll be OK, pal," the short one said. "If she comes, then she's worth the wait. And if she don't, she ain't worth nothin', right, Dino?"

"That's right," the tall one said. "And when she does get here, you play a little hard-to-get with her, all right? Let her know it ain't good to keep you waiting. You gotta keep these dames on their toes; otherwise, they'll walk all over you."

The short one laughed. "Hey, you should know. What's that on your back?"

Dino contorted himself trying to look over his shoulder. "What? What's on my back?"

"Footprints. High heels, size six!" The short one burst out laughing, making perhaps the most grating noise Schreiber had ever heard in his life.

To his surprise, Dino laughed as well. "Hey, that's not bad! You gotta write that down."

But the other man had already produced a small note-book and pen from his jacket pocket and was scribbling away. "Definitely. Lemme work on it some. Timing's not there yet."

Schreiber downed his drink like a shot. "If you'll excuse me, gentlemen."

"Aww, wait a second, pal!" the tall one said, reaching into his jacket and pulling out a couple slips of paper. "We owe you for the joke. Here! On the house!"

If for no other reason than to be rid of these men, Schreiber took the slips and stuffed them in his coat pocket. "Yes, thank you." He then quickly walked off before the two buffoons could engage in any more mindless banter.

It didn't seem like his contact would show up after all, which left only plan B. That meant going from the Fabulous Flamingo, where he'd spent his entire day sipping sodas, and heading to the bus station. His ultimate destination would be New York, a city perfect for anonymity, where he would have his pick of international consulates to choose from.

But he never made it to the front door. Instead, someone tapped him on the shoulder amidst the slot machines. "Mr. Schreiber?"

Steeling himself, he turned to find a short, round fellow in an ill-fitting suit. "Can I help you?" Schreiber asked.

"I apologize for being late," the man said, sporting a light Slavic accent. "I think it's best if we conduct our discussions elsewhere. If you'll come with me?"

Schreiber looked around suspiciously for a moment but couldn't see anyone who looked odd or out of place. And this man looked the part well—a slightly rumpled, off-label suit, scuffed shoes, monochrome tie. It was a look designed to be inconspicuous. Just another lost soul in America's cultural wasteland, with only the accent to give him away. And yet . . . would there not be a little more conversation before this? Would this man not wish to determine Schreiber's bona fides? It made Schreiber feel uneasy. "Why don't we have dinner?" he asked. "I admit, I'm starving."

"Not here," the man replied. "I have a car. Let's go."

Schreiber frowned, standing very still for several long moments and looking the man in the eye. The bus to New York was looking better now; he wished he had gotten more information from his contact. On the other hand, he knew that Wallace—that ignorant pup—would already have begun searching for him. Finally, Schreiber nodded and followed the man through the casino. He couldn't help but wonder if he was trading one prison for another. But on the bright side, he imagined the Soviets were much further along in their Variant program than Wallace, Bronk, and the bumbling idiots they called a team.

Just before the front door, Schreiber felt another tap on the shoulder—but the man was still in front of him. "I thought there was just going to be one of you," he said, then turned . . .

. . . to find Danny Wallace behind him, smiling.

"Don't even think about it, Doc," Danny said, grinning.

Four other men suddenly appeared among the masses of gamblers, weapons drawn and aimed at Schreiber and his contact.

He turned to the Russian. "This is why you should've been on time!" he shouted, all pretense of civility gone.

"Oh, please," Danny said, pointing at Schreiber's contact with his one good hand. "This guy? He's from Brooklyn. It's only his family that's from Leningrad."

"St. Petersburg," the would-be contact said in a suddenly very American accent. "The Reds just changed the name."

"Right," Danny said as the other man began frisking Schreiber. "Anyway, lucky me—he's an MP on base. Figured you'd sell us out, and the Reds are really the only game in town. Vegas P.D. had eyes on you four hours ago. Sloppy, Doc. Very sloppy." Schreiber was thoroughly patted down, and his wallet and other belongings were handed off to Danny, who dumped them on an unused blackjack table to rifle through them. And then the damned Navy man laughed. "What's this? Taking in a show?"

Danny held up the papers the two men at the bar had given him—tickets.

"And what if I was, Commander?" Schreiber said. "There is only so much house arrest one can take."

Danny just shrugged and put the tickets in his pocket. "Whatever, Doc. OK, let's get him out of here."

Schreiber was marched toward the front entrance of the casino by two burly men, each gripping an arm. He could feel the eyes of bystanders and pedestrian gamblers all around him, which infuriated him—he was just one more spectacle in their evening, nothing more.

"Hey, what'd he do?"

Schreiber looked up to see the two men from the bar approaching, but Danny stepped in front of them. "Sorry, gentlemen. Please step back. He's a dangerous guy."

The two men craned their necks to look over at Schreiber. "Him? Why, Jerry here is more dangerous than that pencil-neck. Aren't you, Jerry?"

The short man, apparently named Jerry, put up his fists in a mock fighting stance and gave a ludicrously buck-toothed grin. "I'm the most dangerous man here!" he squeaked. "Put up your dukes!"

Danny smiled. "I think I've seen you guys on the television," he said, pulling Schreiber's show tickets out of his pocket. "I don't think he'll need these anymore, fellas."

"You keep 'em," Dino said. "You can make the late show."

Danny extended his hand farther. "Sorry. Wish I could. But your friend's given me a whole lot of work to do."

July 15, 1949

When Cal had first arrived in Damascus, back when the days were temperate and the nights cold, he had wondered why folks seemed to be scarce during the best part of the afternoon. Now, in the heat of the summer sun, he understood completely. *Too many years on second and third shifts*, he thought to himself. *Forgot what summer felt like. And it's sure a hellacious summer around here.*

The one benefit to the heat was that with fewer people on the streets, it was easier for the Americans to meet with Za'im—and with Zipporah Silverman. Apparently, while Cal and Frank were busy in Beirut, she'd burrowed herself deep into President Za'im's confidence—so much so that it was almost impossible to get in touch with her these days. Needless to say, the radio silence had folks back in Washington all kinds of worried about her—and wondering about what exactly she might be up to. So was Copeland, though for different reasons; the OPC man thought Zippy was after *his* job, trying to take over as the go-between with Za'im and Washington.

Course, she'd have to actually be in regular contact with Washington to do that, and she was only barely making her weekly scheduled dead-drop reports. Copeland was, of course, out of his mind about this, but her report after seeing Cal and Frank at Za'im's little harem room was spooky once they decoded it.

Helping Za'im with Israel question. He's increasingly paranoid. I'm being followed. I think there's something wrong with his mind. Split personalities? Like working with two people. Al-Hinnawi frustrated. Watch him.

Frank was still mighty angry about what Za'im had done to Saadeh, and Cal was right there with him. You don't save a man from being shot, promise him friendship, then stick a knife in his back, try him for treason, and hang him.

Cal had heard that SSNP stuff for a month while they were in Beirut, and while he wasn't a political scholar or anything, he was pretty damn sure Saadeh was no fascist or Nazi or anything like that. The man had just been trying to unite his people—Syrians, Lebanese, Palestinians, Druze, folks with the same color skin. Unite them against the Europeans who'd given them back their freedom but still tried to tell them what to do.

Cal could definitely relate to that.

He shook his head, dodging a cart of produce being pushed up the street by a bunch of young Syrian boys. He had to keep his mind on the game, especially with D.C. getting antsy about Zippy. Copeland had gotten the same note Meade had about keeping an eye on the CIA folks, which had only seemed to give the man *more* reason to be paranoid. In fact, Copeland had told Cal and Frank that he was feeling good about Za'im at this point, despite what had happened to Saadeh, and was going to cable Washington to let them know that everything was under control and Cal, Frank, and Zippy could all go home.

Frank wasn't having any of it, though, pointing out that things weren't as tidy as Copeland was making them seem. Zippy had finally made contact and explained how she'd gotten close to Za'im—apparently, she was more adept with her feminine wiles than she let on but insisted it was just flirtation, along with the promise of better press in Israel. Frank and Cal had both felt bad for not trusting her—it was getting harder to trust anyone, it seemed—but they still insisted on more regular meets with her, if only to keep tabs and offer help as she got in deeper with Za'im. Frank wanted to be damn sure he and Cal were there for her, and reminded Copeland that having someone that close to Za'im was a great asset. Copeland had backed down after that, but Cal didn't have to be told outright when someone was getting tired of having him around.

Making matters worse, they'd gotten a cryptic cable from Danny the other day. Something about shadows? Danny had a problem back in Nevada—a security violation of some kind—and Maggie sounded like she was wrapped up in something similar in Bethesda—which Cal wasn't cleared to hear more details on. So on top of worrying about Syria's stability, Lebanon's revolutionary party, Za'im's mental health, and Zippy's safety, well . . . there was one more thing to put on the list.

This spy stuff was stressful. California was starting to look real good.

Cal arrived at the Syrian parliamentary building and availed himself of a service entrance—even in the Middle East, a Negro would always get a lot more grief going in the front door, no matter his diplomatic passport. Even so, he got stopped three times in the building before he made it to Za'im's offices. At least the folks there recognized him, and he was ushered into a waiting area. To his surprise, he was the first to arrive—Copeland and Frank were expected as well, and he assumed Zippy would be there now too.

Cal happily availed himself of a glass of water from the ewer on the coffee table, and picked up a magazine to read. It was in Arabic, but at least there were photos. In fact, he was so engrossed in looking at the details of a mosaic in some mosque that he failed to notice another person enter the room until they were a few feet in front of him.

It was Zippy. *Some spy I am!*

"Hey there, Miss Zippy!" Cal said as he rose, smiling at her. "Been a while. You doing all right?"

She looked . . . tired. Rings under the eyes, a little thinner than usual, though she wasn't all that curvy to begin with. "I'm OK, thanks, Cal," she said with a weak smile. Then her voice dropped to a whisper. "Za'im is in trouble."

Cal nodded and waved her to the couch next to him and poured her some water. "You gotta tell me. And make it fast."

"You won't believe me," she whispered.

Cal actually smiled at that. "You'd be surprised."

"I think he's possessed."

Cal turned that over in his head for a few minutes. It wasn't outside the realm of possibility for a Variant to do something like that, he figured, since Miss Maggie could already screw around with folks' emotions. And without Danny around, Cal supposed a new Variant could've shown up—maybe a Russian, maybe someone else, and who knew what they might be capable of.

"What makes you think that?"

Zippy simply took off one of her kid gloves and wiggled her fingers, and Cal understood at once. She'd been shaking hands with him and catching something from it with her Enhancement.

"Who's doing it?" Cal asked.

"I don't know. But the weird side of Za'im—the one I'm not sure is Za'im at all—that's the one that cut a deal with Lebanon for Saadeh, and the one pushing for peace with Israel," Zippy whispered. "That one's erratic but very single-minded about getting what it wants."

Cal nodded and had a million questions, but right then, Copeland and Frank entered the room in the company of al-Shishakli, chatting amiably. Zippy put her hand briefly on Cal's knee to cut off any further conversation.

Copeland grimaced at Zippy, but Frank immediately made his way across the room. "You OK?" he whispered.

She nodded. "Yeah. Cal can fill you in later. Be careful."

Al-Shishakli walked over as well, hand extended, his smile tight. "Miss Silverman, our liaison with the Israelis. I trust you're well," he said.

"I am, thank you, sir," she replied, taking his hand with her ungloved one. "And really, all I'm doing is passing along messages."

The Syrian colonel nodded. "Of course you are. Shall we go in? I think the President is in another meeting elsewhere at the moment."

Cal followed the rest of the group into Za'im's ornate meeting room. The only person there was that boy that kept hanging around the three Syrian Army officers. Still odd, Cal thought, that the men running the whole damn country couldn't get a maid or a nanny or someone to take care of that child. And why was he never in school?

While the others sat down at the conference table, Cal went over to where the boy was sitting along the wall. "Hey there, son," he said quietly. "You OK?" The child looked at him blankly, and for the umpteenth time, Cal kicked himself for forgetting the language barrier. "No English, huh? English?"

The boy just stared, his hands fidgeting slightly.

Cal pulled a coin from his pocket, a little Syrian one, and thought back to his spycraft training at Area 51. In particular, he remembered his sleight-of-hand session with the stage magician John Mulholland. "OK, I got something I can show you here, something my daddy taught me. You see this?" Cal held the coin between his two fingers and then, with a flick of his wrist, made it vanish.

The boy's eyes widened slightly, and the faintest ghost of a smile briefly crossed his face. Cal wondered just what made a child so sullen like that. Even growing up poor and black in the South, Cal had never felt that listless.

"Well, all right. Let's see if we can find that coin now," Cal said, reaching for the boy's ear. Immediately, the child shrank back. "Oh, hey, hey, it's OK. It's OK. Look! It's here!" Cal gently tapped the boy's ear, and once again produced the coin. "See? There you go." Cal offered him the coin, which he took gingerly.

"Well done, sir," al-Shishakli said from behind him. Cal rose and turned to see the colonel smiling—a genuine smile.

"I've seen him around a few times now, just wanted to say hello," Cal said. "He your boy?"

Al-Shishakli cocked his head a bit. "I help take care of him. He's a Bedouin, part of the Hasana tribe. He is . . . different from the others."

"I see that," Cal said, his heart breaking for the child.

"His father, one of the sheikhs of the tribe, brought him to us a year ago, asked for our help. The support of a major tribe was critical to our success, and so we agreed. We have tried, sought out many specialists," al-Shishakli said.

Cal nodded. "Hope I didn't disturb him, sir."

Al-Shishakli put a hand on Cal's shoulder. "Kindness is never disturbing. Come, the President is on his way."

Cal joined the others at the table, taking the seat Zippy pulled out for him. A moment later, a small, tightly folded slip of paper fell into his lap. Cal snatched it up quickly and made it disappear just like he had with the coin earlier. A few discreet movements later, and the paper was tucked safely away in his jacket breast pocket. He was sure it would make for fine reading later on.

Then the doors to the room burst open, and President Za'im entered at a brisk pace, smiling and energetic and speaking in rapid-fire Arabic. He moved his hands as he talked, and he seemed absolutely bursting with energy.

What's more, Cal noticed the man's military uniform was all kinds of shined up and decorated now. The last time he'd seen him he was wearing a plain, kind of Spartan-looking uniform, but now there were multiple medals and badges, extra piping, fringed epaulets, and even a sash.

Cal glanced over at Zippy, who gave a nearly imperceptible nod. *That's the crazy personality.*

"My friends!" Za'im bellowed, switching to English. "You are well? You look well." He then looked from Cal to Frank and back again. "I must apologize to you both. Mr. Copeland tells me what happened with Saadeh did not sit well with you. Understand that I did what I had to do in order to preserve the integrity of my nation, and that of Lebanon. These are not easy choices a leader must make, and know that I did not make this one lightly."

Frank opened his mouth as if to say something, but seemed to think better of it. Instead, he gave Za'im a curt nod, and for want of anything better to do, Cal did the same.

"Good. Thank you. Now, Miles, I know you've worked very hard on my behalf, and I know the United States wishes to maintain the security of the State of Israel, is that right?" Za'im asked.

"That is correct, Mr. President," Copeland said genially. "And we appreciate your recent efforts, facilitated by Miss Silverman, to assist in that regard."

"We need peace, first and foremost," Za'im said as he began to pace behind his chair. "And we cannot have peace in our lands if we continue to fight Israel. That is not because I am in support of the Jewish state—it was taken from the Palestinians, make no mistake! But tell me, which were the first two countries to recognize the State of Israel as a legitimate nation?"

Copeland replied: "The United States was the first, of course."

"And the Soviet Union was the second," Zippy added.

"Precisely! How can we, Syria, recently independent and still finding our way after a period of inept rule, defy both the Americans and the Soviets?" Za'im said. "How can anyone in this region—all of our nations, recently freed from the shackles of European colonialism—how can any of us defy the two great powers in the world?" The President turned to look at al-Hinnawi, who was sitting with his arms folded, grimacing in his direction. "Sami, you know this to be true. If we move against Israel, we move toward our own destruction."

To Cal's surprise, al-Hinnawi suddenly sprang up like a bolt had hit him. "Then why did we fight last year? Why did we seize power this spring against a government we saw as weak against Israel? What are we even doing here?"

"We are preserving Syria!" Za'im bellowed, marching over to al-Hinnawi. "Do you think the Soviets will last forever? Do you think the Americans will have a thousand-year empire? The British and French are reduced powers, and the Americans and Russians soon will be as well, and *then*, if there is still an Israel, we can liberate it from the Jews! But until that day, do we fight a war we cannot win? Do we?"

The two men stared hard at each other, fists clenched, and Cal wondered who'd take a swing first. Instead, Zippy rose from the table and quickly pushed herself between the men. "Mr. President, Colonel! Please! Enough of this!" She put her hands on each man's chest and literally pushed them apart.

Her bare hands, Cal noted. *Smooth.*

Za'im turned on his heel and, without another word, made his way back to his seat, while al-Hinnawi glowered at Zippy with pure hatred in his eyes. "I do not like the fact that you are here, an American and a Jew and a woman advising our president."

"I am here at the President's invitation," Zippy responded curtly. With that, she went back to her seat and al-Hinnawi sat down again. Cal pulled a little notebook out of his jacket pocket and made a couple of notes to himself—al-Hinnawi bore watching. Cal could tell when someone was gonna be up to mischief, and the Syrian colonel seemed like he was just about there.

Meanwhile, Za'im sat and pulled out a folder. "I propose that the Syrian nation take on three hundred thousand additional refugees from Palestine and resettle them here. In exchange, I ask the Israelis to adjust the border to include the areas here on this map."

Za'im handed the map to Copeland, who looked it over and nodded. "This seems fairly reasonable. Does this proposal include a peace treaty and recognition of Israel?"

Za'im actually laughed. "Miles, my friend, you ask far too much. I would be willing to discuss an armistice at most. A suspension of hostilities. But there will be no peace treaty or recognition. You ask too much. Not even with the Soviets by your side, asking this, could I do such a thing."

"I understand," Copeland replied, handing the map across the table to Zippy. "Miss Silverman will send this along to her contacts in Israel."

"Miss Silverman has *already* sent this along to her contacts in Israel," Za'im replied. "But I thank you regardless."

The President then quickly and deftly moved to other matters on his agenda, including another request for military aid that Cal figured would get nowhere fast. Neither the U.S. nor the U.S.S.R. seemed to be in a big rush to send armies down into the area, preferring instead to play with proxies. Cal knew from his briefings that the Russians were busy indeed, trying to make friends with Egypt, Iraq, and Iran, besides supporting Israel.

Cal figured that would have to change at some point, especially as he looked at the petulant al-Hinnawi. Folks here didn't just dislike Israel; they actively hated the idea that a bunch of Jewish folks had come in and taken over Palestine. And Cal knew that no side was completely in the right. The Jews had gone through hell and back during the war; Cal had seen the files detailing the genocide. And yet the Palestinians weren't the ones who had done the deed.

Arab nationalists and Greater Syrians were one side, with some real religious Muslims on the other, planning to reestablish a caliphate. Then you had the Americans and Reds, all pushing for everyone else to get off the fence and pick a team.

Cal glanced over at Copeland, who'd clearly been startled earlier to hear of Zippy's activities but now seemed to be chatting amiably with Za'im. He'd often marveled at how a college man like Copeland could manage to nearly singlehandedly overthrow an entire government, and it was obvious the man had imagination and guts. But this thing . . . this thing was gonna get ugly, and Cal had spent enough time with him to know Copeland wasn't going to be able to keep the peace all by himself.

Zippy flicked another note into Cal's lap. It was just a slip of paper with a few words on it, but they rattled Cal to his core.

Hinnawi wants to kill Za'im. He's working on a plan.

Apparently, this thing was gonna get ugly faster than anyone thought.

26.

July 24, 1949

Danny Wallace paced the cell and looked down at Kurt Schreiber, who was lying on his cot with his eyes closed. At least they'd managed to stick him in a proper prison this time, with no fewer than four guards on him at any one time, twenty-four hours a day, seven days a week.

Oh, and the lights were on full bore. Danny had didn't give a rat's ass whether Schreiber slept well—the man had used up the miniscule amount of goodwill Danny had left for him. For once, everyone involved with MAJESTIC-12 agreed with him, even that know-nothing Montague.

"You know, Kurt, you're pretty much done for. Hope you realize that," Danny said. "You'll never go back to your research. You won't go back to *any* research, in fact. The only thing keeping you from a firing squad at this moment is my generosity."

"And for that I thank you," Schreiber said with a smirk, eyes still closed. "Though I think there's more to it than that."

"Do you, now?"

Schreiber sat up and swung his legs around to the floor, looking up at Danny. "You likely have many talented individuals here, yes? But what you don't have is what's up here"—he tapped his forehead with a finger—"in my mind; otherwise, you would have employed them immediately, or at least sooner than this. And so we wait for you to slowly accept that even if you no longer trust me, you know I'm the only hope you have. Which means your threat of a firing squad is an empty gesture."

The worst part, of course, was that Schreiber was right. Danny had no idea how he had escaped, beyond some kind of literal shadow, some kind of under-the-radar Variant ability—though he couldn't even be sure of that. Maybe it wasn't a Variant in fact, maybe it was something or someone Schreiber had contacted through the vortex. But there had been eyes on the phenomenon nearly every minute since it had been brought to Area 51 two-plus years before. How could something have slipped by? Or maybe the shadow was just an incredibly talented operative, as Hamilton had suggested. Danny dismissed that idea largely due to logistics—if someone had managed the near-impossible feat of breaking into—and then out of—Area 51, why then just send Schreiber out without a better escape plan than to hitchhike his way to Vegas?

"Who is Vanda?" Danny pressed.

"The Wicked Witch of the East, of course," Schreiber taunted. "Or was that the West? I can never remember. How is your hand, Commander?"

Danny involuntarily looked down at his gloved hand. If things hadn't been so fucked up at Area 51, he would've strongly considered heading to Damascus to see Cal for some healing. "What about my hand?"

"From what I can see, you have recently lost the use of it. You have not flexed it, which means you have lost muscle control, and since you choose to hide it from sight, I can assume it does not look particularly pleasant, either. Now, these are perhaps leaps of deduction, but for a long time, I have wondered why *you* of all people have been placed in such a powerful position here.

"Given what we both know that I know about the phenomenon and its impact on those of Variant blood, I think it's likely you reached out and touched the vortex with your hand, and your hand has become useless, likely desiccated from the destruction of blood and tissue. And of course, this would confirm my long-running suspicions that you are a Variant yourself. A Variant with a very potent Enhancement, one that makes you extremely valuable to those in charge of this program. A shame they have no idea how truly incompetent you are."

Danny stared hard but knew deep down that his face had given away the game a while earlier. Danny had only killed one man in his entire life—that traitor Anderson—but he felt disturbingly inclined to end Schreiber right then and there, circumstances be damned. Only his military training—and the increased scrutiny on Variants throughout the MAJESTIC-12 program—stayed his hand. For now.

"Sorry, Kurt. That's a fine story you've deduced, but that's all it is: a story," Danny said. "And since you're not going to talk, I guess I'll wait for one of the others to get back so I can either cripple you emotionally or just shoot you in the head. Honestly, I'm hoping it's the latter."

Without a backward glance, Danny turned and left the cell, allowing the MPs to lock up behind him. Bronk met him outside the brig area.

"Why do you insist on doing that?" Bronk said. "He's not going to say bupkus."

Danny shrugged. "I don't know. Glutton for punishment. What's up?"

"Electrical problems again at Training Area 1. We've had to use portable nulls for now. The ones we have wired to the generators are getting fried. But that's not the worst of it. I saw some worrisome things in Group 1's blood tests this morning."

That stopped Danny in his tracks. "Define 'worrisome.'"

"All four of them are showing lower white blood cell levels than is normal. I went and tested some of the MPs who put in a lot of time there, but they're fine. It's only the Variants."

"Cause?"

Bronk ran a hand over his face and let out a sigh. "Training 1 is where we keep the highest number of null-generators, to keep the trainees in line."

"The generators are causing a lowered white cell count?"

"Possibly. They throw off radiation, after all. We've been operating under the belief that the radiation was largely harmless, a unique but otherwise harmless combination of emissions that happened to disrupt Variant Enhancements. But there could be something in there degrading their immune systems. I'm afraid if we keep this up, their immune systems could be severely degraded, if not worse."

Danny stood with his hands on his hips for several long moments before kicking at the desert dust in a burst of frustration. "Fuck! Goddamnit! We need those null-fields shut off ASAP."

"If we do that, how do we contain them?" Bronk asked. "I'm thinking of Julia especially. What happens when she realizes her Enhancement is completely unchecked?"

"I don't know. I don't know, Det. But we're injuring them right now, and that's completely unacceptable. Tell Hamilton to shut 'em down. I want two sets of eyes on each of the Variants at all times, and bed checks every fifteen minutes at night—install a peephole or something if you have to, privacy be damned. And have Julia Meyer brought to my office. I'll have a chat with her. Meantime . . ."

Danny's voice dropped off as he saw a small cargo plane on approach to the lakebed landing strip. It was one of Montague's from Albuquerque.

Bronk saw it too. "This day keeps getting better and better. I'll talk to Hamilton. You go deal with that."

Danny simply nodded, his head down, hands on his hips as he tried to gather his wits about him in the hot afternoon sun. He then made his way to the admin building, where air traffic control was housed in a small radio room. Two airmen and a master sergeant were on duty.

"Sergeant, who's on that plane?"

The NCO, a grizzled-looking, wiry fellow, just shrugged. "No manifest, sir, and they ain't sayin'. But they have clearance and the right code words, so I'm letting 'em land. Could be the Radio City Rockettes, for all I know."

"We ain't that lucky," one of the airman muttered.

Danny left the room and jogged out of the building toward the motor pool, where he grabbed a jeep and sped out to the plane, arriving just as it was finished rolling to a halt near the tent awning they used as a welcoming area.

The plane door opened, and Gen. Montague came out, followed by a bear of a man in a crisp-looking suit. He was tall and balding, his face broad and flushed from the heat, but well put-together, like a rich guy or a politician.

Danny briskly walked over to the general and saluted; Montague returned the salute with a disdainful little smirk. "Commander, I sure hope you're getting your security back together here," Montague said without preamble.

"We are, General," he said simply, then looked over at the man in the suit. "For example, I need to know who this is so that I can determine whether or not he's cleared to be here."

Montague's guest walked over with a grin, his hand extended. "I'm Louis Johnson. I'm the Secretary of Defense."

Well, fuck. "Sir," Danny said, saluting again before taking Johnson's hand. "Welcome to . . . our facility. General, I have to ask, has there been an update with regard to clearance for our project that I'm unaware of?"

Montague's smirk turned into a frown pretty quickly at that. "Did you hear the man, Commander? This is Secretary of Defense Louis Johnson, and he's here to inspect this facility—a facility, need I remind you, under my personal command."

"I heard him, sir," Danny said, unmoving. "However, because of the nature of our work here, I'm going to have to confirm that Secretary Johnson here is appropriately cleared to conduct his inspection. Once I have word from Washington, I'm sure we can—"

Montague looked down at Danny. "Commander Wallace. Given your recent difficulties managing security at this base, I am relieving you of duty as executive officer of Area 51, effective immediately."

"That's . . . that's your prerogative, General," Danny managed to stammer. "However, I remain the principal investigative and training officer for . . . um, any CIA projects based here at Area 51. And since I'm currently seconded to CIA, only an order from Director Hillenkoetter can remove me from that position. And thus, before Secretary Johnson gains access to any part of any project, I *will* clear his presence here with Washington."

Montague's mouth hung open for several long seconds, while Johnson just looked at Danny with disbelief. "Are you disobeying a superior officer, young man?" Johnson said in disbelief.

"No, Mr. Secretary, not at all," Danny said, feeling slightly more confident now. "I've been relieved as executive officer on the base, which means that I no longer have authority in terms of the base operations. However, I remain an officer of the Central Intelligence Agency, and I remain in charge of any CIA projects underway here. So of course, you and the general are more than welcome to inspect the base. However, since I have yet to confirm your clearance for any CIA projects here, there will be some areas to which you won't have access. I do apologize, sir."

Montague stepped forward and pressed a meaty finger into Danny's chest. "I swear, I am going to bust you down to a goddamn mess cook before we're done here," the general muttered. "Now, you will take us on a full inspection of this base *and* your project, or I will have you arrested for disobeying a direct order."

To his surprise, Danny felt a calm moment of clarity at this, and he even managed a slight smile. "Yes, sir, General," he replied smartly. "This way."

Danny didn't even bother looking back. Instead, he just walked briskly to the jeep and waited for the other two men to clamber aboard. Wordlessly, he sped off for Area 51, trying his best not to smile.

Five minutes later, he pulled up directly in front of the main research hangar. "If it's all right with you, General, I need to alert Major Hamilton to the change in my status, since that makes him acting executive officer in my place."

Montague climbed out of the jeep and stared down at Danny again, disdain on his face. "You're dismissed Commander," he said finally. "Mr. Secretary, let's go."

Danny watched a moment as the two men walked toward the MPs guarding the entrance to the facility, then hit the gas and sped off toward the admin building, no longer bothering to hide his smile. Back in his office, he picked up a phone and dialed the long string of numbers he had committed to memory years before.

It took the better part of two minutes before someone picked up. "Yes?"

"This is Commander Wallace. Password MAJIK one four eight three."

"What's wrong, Commander?" The voice on the other end grew quickly worried.

"I need a clearance confirmation for Secretary of Defense Louis Johnson. He just landed with General Montague for an inspection of both the facility and the project. Does Secretary Johnson have TOP SECRET-MAJIK clearance?"

There was a long silence on the line before President Truman responded. "He sure as hell does *not*, repeat, *does not* have clearance for that operation. Not in any way, shape, or form."

"Very well, sir. Shall I tell him to call you?"

"No, Commander. I'll wire you new orders. Where are they now?"

"Well, they're about to attempt entry into the main research hangar."

"And you left them there?"

"I did, sir. General Montague relieved me of duty as executive officer of the base prior to that, sir, so I was under no obligation to inform or advise further."

Another silence, followed by a sharp bark of a laugh. "That's rich. You're reinstated. Orders are coming. Carry on, Commander."

"Thank you, Mr. President."

Danny hung up with a smile, then lazily got up and walked to his door, opening it and sticking his head out to address his clerk. "Airman, I have a secure communication coming in the next few minutes. Gimme a shout when it's here."

The airman was on the phone; he covered the mouthpiece to respond. "Yes, sir. Uh, sir, we have a situation—"

"Tell the MPs to follow their orders to the letter," Danny replied.

"Yes, sir. I have Julia Meyer waiting for you in the conference room as well," the clerk said.

Danny nodded and walked over to the meeting room next to his office. Inside, Julia was sitting at the table, idly looking out the window while passing her hand through the table repeatedly, up and down.

"That's some fine control you have there, Julia," Danny said. "When you came here, you would've sunk through that chair if you'd tried to do that."

She just shrugged. "We practice when your men let us. And the rest of the time, we don't."

Danny pulled up a chair next to her. "I know it's distressing to be cut off from your Enhancements like that."

She turned to him with a fierce look on her face. "What do you know of it, Navy man? It isn't just 'distressing.' Your little devices cut us off from ourselves. It is like you blind us or cripple us whenever you like. And for what? To keep us under control?"

So, it's gonna be like that, Danny thought. "Yes, actually. To keep you under control. If you and your teammates expressed more of a willingness to play ball, we wouldn't have to do that. In fact, all the other Variants I've worked with have really found a place for themselves working on behalf of America. They're good people, burdened with extraordinary and dangerous abilities, and they've *chosen* to make a difference, to help people."

"They've chosen to be lapdogs, just like you," Julia replied. "What happened to your hand?"

Interesting. "Little accident, that's all," Danny said, brushing if off. "Now, I got several Variants out in the world doing great things. I want to be able to trust you and the others to do that, too. Have you ever stopped to think about what you'd be doing if we hadn't picked you up?"

Julia actually laughed at this. "I'd be sunning myself on the Riviera in front of my very own mansion."

"That's quite a way to spin being on the run from the authorities."

"At least it would be my choice."

Danny regarded her hard for a long moment. "I've been clear with you from the very beginning: either you play ball with us and get to live your life as you see fit with a few important but reasonable limits, or you don't and you're stuck here. Probably for good. And that's not just you. That goes for the others, too. You know damn well they have families. I for one would like them to be able to see them again, wouldn't you?"

Julia stared daggers at Danny but said nothing.

"I'm going to take a leap of faith with you, Julia. I'm shutting down the null-fields for a while. You and your team will be able to use your Enhancements again as you wish, though always within the rules Dr. Bronk set up for you. I'm giving you this as a gesture of goodwill," he lied. "Don't make me regret it."

Danny stood up and left the meeting room without waiting for a response. He figured the others on Julia's team could be easily contained even without the null-fields on, but Julia . . . she could conceivably take off at any time. He'd have to figure out a way to get some kind of null-field going at a moment's notice. Maybe . . . He pulled a little notebook from his jacket and made a quick scribble. He'd ask Mrs. Stevens about it later—whenever Hillenkoetter deigned to give her back.

On his way back to his office, Danny stopped by the small, secure closet where the telex from Washington was kept, and saw that the little red message light above the door was on. It took a key and two combination locks for him to open it—only three people at Area 51 even had keys. Once inside, he pulled the paper off the printer, scanned it quickly . . . and smiled.

Danny took it slow, pouring himself a cup of lukewarm coffee and sitting down in his office to read the orders

carefully. After about fifteen minutes, he got up and sauntered to the door, orders in hand, and made his way out of
the administration building. For once, the sun felt good on
his face as he walked over to the security outpost, where
two MPs saluted smartly as he entered.

The desk sergeant inside looked up and grunted.
"Commander, you mind telling me what the hell is going
on?"

"Where are they?" Danny asked.

"Back in the cell where we keep the drunk and disor-
derlies," the sergeant said. "They told me working this post
would be crazy."

"They weren't lying," Danny said as he walked through
the office door and into the holding area.

Major General Montague and Defense Secretary Johnson
were locked inside the cell. Montague bolted to his feet, his
face red with fury. "Wallace, you got five seconds to unlock
this cell before I have you shot for treason!" Montague
shouted.

Danny saluted smartly but didn't bother waiting for a
response. "Secretary Johnson, General Montague. I apologize for the inconvenience, but your detention is in line
with standing security orders given by National Command
Authority."

Johnson also stood and looked at Wallace with a politician's smile. "How is it exactly, Commander, that detaining
the Secretary of Defense is in line with orders here?"

I'm glad you asked, Louie. "All unauthorized personnel
attempting to access the main research hangar at Area 51
are to be immediately detained and held until such time as
their clearance can be verified. And that's what happened
here."

"I'm cleared for MAJESTIC-12!" Montague roared.

"Yes, sir, you are, but Secretary Johnson is not. And by
attempting to allow him access, you violated orders, orders
which can only be overturned by National Command
Authority. Also, pursuant to those orders, I contacted

National Command Authority to determine the security clearance of Secretary Johnson with regard to the project— the name of which, I should add, I can neither confirm nor deny as being the one the General just mentioned."

"You're enjoying this, you little shit!" Montague snarled.

"Fulfilling my duty is its own reward, sir," Danny replied, straight-faced. "In contacting National Command Authority, I received a secure wire with new orders. They are as follows." He then read directly off the fax.

1) SECDEF JOHNSON IS NOT CLEARED FOR ACCESS TO ANY PROJECTS UNDERWAY AT AREA 51. HIS PRESENCE AND ACCESS IS LIMITED ONLY TO NON—PROJECT AREAS UNTIL SUCH TIME AS HE DEPARTS THE FACILITY.

2) SECDEF JOHNSON IS ORDERED TO RETURN TO WASHINGTON IMMEDIATELY. ONCE ARRIVED, HE IS TO REPORT DIRECTLY TO THE PRESIDENT.

3) MJG MONTAGUE IS RELIEVED OF DUTY AS COMMANDER, AREA 51. LTG VANDENBERG IS APPOINTED ACTING COMMANDER, AREA 51, UNTIL PERMANENT APPOINTMENT IS MADE.

4) MJG MONTAGUE IS NO LONGER CLEARED FOR ACCESS TO ANY PROJECTS UNDERWAY AT AREA 51. HIS PRESENCE AND ACCESS IS LIMITED ONLY TO NON—PROJECT AREAS UNTIL SUCH TIME AS HE DEPARTS THE FACILITY.

5) MJG MONTAGUE IS TO RETURN IMMEDIATELY TO ALBUQUERQUE AFB, WHERE HE WILL AWAIT FURTHER ORDERS FROM LTG VANDENBERG.

6) CMDR WALLACE IS REINSTATED AS EXECUTIVE OFFICER, AREA 51, AND IS TASKED WITH ASSISTING IN THE FULFILLMENT OF THESE ORDERS.

(SIGNED) TRUMAN

Danny finished reading and handed off the paper through the bars; Montague, now looking ashen, snatched it from his hand and huddled with Johnson to read it. Meanwhile, Danny poked his head through the door and addressed the desk sergeant. "Let's get these gentlemen out of here, Sergeant, and have them escorted back to their aircraft. Note in the log that General Montague is no longer cleared for any project matters on base."

When he turned back, he saw both men looking angry—and maybe a little scared.

"Son, if you had simply talked to us about this," Johnson said, "we might have avoided all this nonsense."

"I tried, Mr. Secretary," Danny said. "Nobody listened. Now, if you'll excuse me, I'm sure the paperwork on all this is gonna be a bitch."

Danny saluted once more, turned, and walked off, relishing at least one decent-sized victory.

27.

July 26, 1949

Maggie waited outside President Truman's office, Mrs. Stevens fidgeting nervously next to her on the well-appointed couch. Both wore their Sunday best, and both were armed to the teeth with briefcases full of transcripts and reel-to-reel tapes. Neither of them wanted to be there—but they both knew their futures teetered in the balance.

"It's not fair," Maggie muttered.

"What's not fair, sweetie?" Mrs. Stevens said in her best maternal voice.

Maggie cast a quick look over at the President's secretary, who was busy typing away, and at the Secret Service man at the door. "This whole investigation—it wasn't just about patching a leak. It was about testing us. Clearing our names. All of us. Making sure we're trustworthy."

"And we are! I think we've done that," Mrs. Stevens said. "You should be proud of what we've done, not just for us but for everyone else, too."

"Yeah, but we'll have to do it again. And again. It won't stop," Maggie said. "Every single time something goes wrong with a Variant, we'll be under the gun until we prove we're in the right. No benefit of the doubt, no innocent before proven guilty. None of that stuff. We're guilty until we can prove otherwise. And God forbid if one of us *actually* fucks up."

"Language!" Mrs. Stevens whispered quickly. "We're in the White House!"

Maggie rolled her eyes hard. "Five bucks says the President's said worse."

"Well, sure, but he's a *man*. And he's in a stressful job. Even the best of us can slip up from time to time," she replied.

"Point is, even if we're cleared now, I think it's only a matter of time . . ."

"Until?"

Maggie didn't get a chance to answer; the door to the Oval Office opened and Hillenkoetter appeared. "Ladies, let's go."

The two got up, smoothed their skirts, and picked up their briefcases before entering Truman's office. Inside, Truman and General Vandenberg were sharing a laugh about something. Two Secret Service agents were posted off to one side, fully alert. That was new—usually Truman didn't have them around during meetings. They typically peered through a little keyhole from another room instead.

"Don't mind the agents, Miss Dubinsky," Truman said as he came around his desk to shake their hands. "You never know how these things will go sometimes."

Maggie smirked a bit. "That'd be interesting."

"Yes, it would. Though I imagine you'd have a handle on it before they could draw," the President said.

"Maybe. How fast are they?"

"Let's hope we don't find out. How are you, Mrs. Stevens? That portable recorder of yours is impressive, to say the least."

"Oh! Well, thank you, Mr. President! You know, I think with the right application of solid-state technology, we might get a lot of our electronics smaller. And I've been tinkering with some ideas on batteries that could—"

"Yes, yes, that sounds swell, Mrs. Stevens," Truman said quickly. "Why don't you and Miss Dubinsky have a seat here? I believe everyone else is cooling their heels in other parts of the building. Hilly, let's get 'em all in here."

Maggie watched with bemusement as, one by one, the targets of their investigation came marching through the door of the Oval Office. Louis Johnson was first, Frank Wisner right behind him. Both men were greeted brusquely by the President; no handshakes were offered. Next came Senator McCarthy, who at least received a handshake from Truman and a comfortable armchair. J. Edgar Hoover was the last to enter, all swagger and business, walking right up to Truman with his hand extended; the two shook, and the FBI Director took the chair right next to Truman's desk— where Hillenkoetter had been sitting just a moment before.

Maggie reached out with her mind to take the President's temperature, so to speak. He was angry and a little nervous, and he had an undeniably deep-seated hatred of Hoover. Maggie decided then and there that if Truman ran for a second full term in '52, he'd have her vote. She'd even wear a button.

"All right, gentlemen, let's get to it," Truman said, sitting down behind his desk. "You know how I keep saying, 'The buck stops here,' right? Well, it applies to everybody in this room right now. If I hear any excuses or alibis or passing the buck, I'll have your resignations on your way out the door. And yes, Senator, that goes for you, too. Don't think I can't do it."

McCarthy looked surprise. "Now, Harry, what's going on? I—"

Truman sat bolt upright. "Senator, I am the President of the United States, and you will address me as such, you hear me? This isn't the Senate floor, and this certainly isn't the Capital Grille, where I know you've been spending some time with these gentlemen here."

Hoover's eyes narrowed. "Mr. President, have you placed us under surveillance?"

Truman actually smiled at Hoover, and Maggie got the sense he was enjoying this a bit. "For the government to conduct surveillance over citizens within the United States, there would need to be an appropriate warrant, and the surveillance conducted by a proper law enforcement agency.

"So, to answer your question, yes," Truman added, taking out a thin blue paper from a folder on his desk. "This is the warrant from D.C. Circuit Court. And these two ladies are with the Secret Service. Maybe you recognize them?"

All four men gave Maggie and Mrs. Stevens a good hard look. Only McCarthy had a spark of recognition that Maggie could sense, but he kept his mouth shut.

Truman continued. "Each of you has been recorded discussing something that you've been calling MAJESTIC-12, and doing so in some detail. This meeting is not for me to confirm or deny the existence of this project or its nature but is instead to determine whether I order the Secret Service to arrest anybody for mishandling classified information and, quite possibly, treason. Now, let's start with Mr. Wisner here. Where did you first hear about this alleged project?"

Wisner was sitting stiffly, a bit of sweat at his brow that had little to do with the summer heat outside. "I first heard about the operation from Senator McCarthy in private right after a Foreign Relations Committee briefing, Mr. President."

Truman turned to McCarthy. "Same question, Senator."

Shifting in his chair, McCarthy seemed to ponder his words before speaking. "While I hate to speak ill of the dead, Mr. President, I have to say, it was Jim Forrestal who first told me about it."

"I see. Director Hoover?"

Frowning as he fidgeted with a pen, Hoover simply said, "Forrestal."

"And Secretary Johnson, who told you about this project before you stormed off to the desert this past weekend on a fool's errand?"

By this point, Johnson was hunched forward in his seat, looking down at his shoes; Maggie could sense the genuine panic in the man's chest and wondered if he was going to have a heart attack on the spot. "I was invited to a meeting a few weeks ago with these three gentlemen. They wanted to brief me on the project."

Truman walked forward toward Johnson. "A project you're not cleared for. A project *none* of you are cleared for."

Johnson finally looked up. "Sir, with all due respect, you appointed me Secretary of Defense. The Senate confirmed it. Why would you keep something like this from me? After all we've been through together."

Truman actually put a hand on Johnson's shoulder. "Louis, you did a lot to help me over the years, especially with the election. And I'm grateful for that. But you and I both know you're a politician, first and foremost. I appointed you to cut budgets and battle Congress, not fight wars or oversee classified projects. And both of us know you got a big mouth."

Truman turned to the others in the room. "I'm going to ask you, each of you, one more question, and by God, you'd better tell the truth. Did any of you have anything to do with the death of Jim Forrestal? If you don't fess up now and we find out later, I'll make sure you get the chair."

Each of the men in the room registered shock at this, and Maggie probed their emotions carefully as they spoke. All denied their involvement, and while Maggie wasn't exactly a lie detector, she didn't sense anything off about their reactions. Maggie glanced over at Mrs. Stevens, who'd made a quick study of body language and reactions over the past few weeks. Mrs. Stevens shook her head. *They didn't do it.*

Truman looked over at Maggie, who simply nodded.

"All right," the President said. "I believe you. Now, you likely heard a lot of nonsense about little green men or superheroes or whatever nonsense Jim Forrestal told you. Jim was my friend and a courageous, loyal American. But the job took a toll on him, and I'm willing to bet he told you a couple of humdingers about this MAJESTIC-12 thing."

"Mr. President—" Hoover began, but Truman cut him off with a hand.

"In the interest of national security and the public trust, I know each of you will refrain from discussing any of this nonsense moving forward. If you do—and don't think we won't find out about it—we have ample evidence already to ensure you'll each do jail time for violating national security. Do I make myself clear?"

All four men nodded; none of them had words at this point.

"Mr. Wisner, I've decided the Office of Policy Coordination within the State Department will be folded into the Central Intelligence Agency. As of this moment, I'm placing you under the direct command of Director Hillenkoetter here. I'll let Dean Acheson know myself. It'll be up to Hilly here to figure out what you'll do after your office is merged. That'll be all, thank you."

Wisner nodded nervously and stood; Hillenkoetter walked over to the door and let him out, closing it behind him.

"Senator," Truman said, turning to McCarthy. "I suggest that you focus your attentions on Capitol Hill elsewhere. Otherwise, you might find yourself facing very well-funded opponents when you're up for reelection. Primary *and* general."

McCarthy stood. "Mr. President, these people . . . Our country is in danger."

"Yes, it is, Senator. Which is why we have talented people to help us defend it. Now, again, not a word of this to anyone, or so help me, I'll make your life hell. I won't enjoy doing it, but don't think for a minute that will stop me. Thanks for coming by."

Mouth agape, McCarthy paused for a long, confused moment before finally storming toward the door. Hillenkoetter closed it behind him with a smirk.

"Louis, if I ever catch you sticking your nose into something you're not cleared for again, I'll fire you on the spot. As it stands, General Vandenberg here tells me there's been some irregularities regarding acquisitions for the Air Force under your watch. Something about a company you're tied up with?"

"Now, Harry—"

Truman stood right up to Johnson, looking up at the man with controlled anger on his face. "If you don't fix it, Louis, I'll be asking you to resign soon enough. You have one more chance. Otherwise, you'll be done here and done with politics. Understood?"

Johnson's face visibly sagged. "Yes, Mr. President."

"Thank you, Louis. Now, if you'll excuse me, I need a word with Director Hoover here."

Johnson trudged out of the office. Hoover was simply sitting and watching, his bulldog face alert but yielding nothing. Inside, Maggie could sense he was nervous, though not as much as the others. She figured J. Edgar was probably a fine poker player.

That reminds me, I need to get to Vegas, she thought idly. Meanwhile, Truman went back to his desk and sat. "So, Director, what are we going to do about this?"

Hoover gave a slight smile. "Mr. President, the FBI has a mission to investigate federal crimes in the United States. That won't change."

"No, but I imagine you'll be on the lookout for some unusual ones from here on out," Truman said, his friendly face masking his anger. Maggie thought the President might be an even better poker player.

"You never know where an investigation will take you, Mr. President."

Truman finally let the mask slip. "I can tell you this, Director. Your agency will immediately alert Director Hillenkoetter here the moment you have information on any individuals exhibiting unusual characteristics. And then you will remove your agency from that investigation. Are we clear?"

Hoover remained steady. "Mr. President, the CIA has no jurisdiction over criminal cases within the United States."

Truman looked over at Hillenkoetter. "Hilly, can you and the ladies step out for a moment?"

Maggie quickly stood and followed Hillenkoetter and Mrs. Stevens out the door, closing it behind her. Curious, she reached back to scan the emotions of the two men left in the Oval Office. Truman was triumphant. Hoover quickly went from mildly nervous to absolutely terrified in the space of about twenty seconds.

Moments later, Hoover barged through the door and hustled through the anteroom as if his ass were on fire. Hillenkoetter smiled. "Let's go back in."

The President had one of his patented grins on his face. "Well, that was fun."

Maggie couldn't help herself. "What did you say to him, sir?" she asked once the door was closed.

Truman shook his head side to side. "Miss Dubinsky, some matters should remain private. In fact, that's exactly what I told Director Hoover just now."

Hillenkoetter folded his lanky body back onto the couch. "He'll hate you for this, sir."

"Aw, he hates me already, Hilly. That's fine. Honestly, I wouldn't want to do it—God knows he's not the only one in this town with those kinds of skeletons in his closet. But if it's a choice between his private life and a global panic about Variants, well . . . I think even he knows that I won't hesitate to make the right decision for this country."

Maggie thought about that for a moment while the two men chatted further. The kind of panic and fear she'd felt out of Hoover was existential in every sense of the word. She'd only felt that from people facing death or the loss of a loved one. Or . . .

"He's gay," she blurted out.

"Excuse me?" the President said.

Maggie realized what she'd said, and felt her face go red. "Sorry, sir. Never mind."

Truman frowned. "Whatever you may think you know about the director is just a rumor, nothing more. J. Edgar Hoover has served for years with distinction. Understood?"

Maggie nodded but was surprised at her distaste for such a tactic. "Yes, Mr. President." *Maybe he's not getting my vote after all.* "But why not just fire him?"

"Because J. Edgar Hoover has dirt on everybody in this town," Hillenkoetter responded. "He's been at this for twenty-some years now. Cut him down completely, he'll spill on everyone. But he who lives by the sword—"

Truman held up his hand to stop Hillenkoetter from saying more. "All right, now, where are we with this shadow business?"

Hillenkoetter opened a folder from his briefcase. "From what we've been able to determine from interviews and the like, the description these two provided regarding their encounter at Bethesda is materially different from what Wallace mentally received during his encounter with the vortex, and also different from the eyewitness accounts reported before Dr. Schreiber's escape. However, we have identified potential similarities with what Wallace believes he observed in Damascus back in March."

Truman looked disgusted. "Christ, Hilly, let me try to get this straight. You're suggesting that now we got, what, three or four different kinds of shadowy bullshit going on?"

"Appears to be, sir. I'm hoping to send my best agents to look into it ASAP."

"You mean your best people aren't already on this?" Truman snapped.

Hillenkoetter looked over to Maggie and Mrs. Stevens, and smiled. "My best people are sitting right in front of you, and you've kept them pretty busy, sir. But if it's all right with you, I'd like 'em back."

Truman relented and even offered the two women a tired smile of his own. "Permission granted. Ladies, thank you for your service."

Maggie and Mrs. Stevens nodded and, taking their cue, rose as Hillenkoetter walked them to the door. "Mrs. Stevens, have my secretary back at the shop get you on the next flight to you-know-where to assist Wallace in his investigations. Maggie, you're heading back to Damascus to check on something for Wallace. I'll brief you later this afternoon."

Maggie nodded and followed Mrs. Stevens out the door. To her surprise, she turned and gave Maggie a big hug, right there in front of the President's secretary.

"We did it," she said quietly. "I'm gonna miss you."

Maggie felt the genuine emotions pouring out of Mrs. Stevens—pride, a little sorrow, and real affection. She broke off the hug and managed to give Mrs. Stevens a smile. "I'm gonna miss you too, Rose. I will. Now go fix Danny's mess. I need to see about Frank and Cal."

Mrs. Stevens smiled and headed off, leaving Maggie standing there a moment, wishing she could feel as vibrantly and intensely as Rose Stevens did about . . . anything at all, really.

August 14, 1949

Frank was just about ready to pack it in—for the night, for the week, for the mission, you name it. It was 2 a.m. and sleep wasn't happening. The week had been fruitless and frustrating; Copeland had been fretting endlessly about Za'im's increasing . . . eccentricities . . . but refused to allow Frank, Cal, or even Meade to investigate. The last time Frank had seen the President, only al-Hinnawi was with him; rumor had it al-Shishakli was on the outs. Even Zippy was starting to get frozen out of Za'im's increasingly small circle; her fears about the Syrian president's mental fitness were starting to make more sense.

Over the past few weeks, Za'im had taken to wearing a far more ostentatious marshal's uniform, decking himself out with everything from a feathered fez to gold-buckled riding boots. He'd thrown a couple of really over-the-top parties, too; Copeland had snagged an invitation to one and reported a scene right out of a bad *Arabian Nights* knockoff, complete with belly dancers, that would've felt right at home at a burlesque, and enough alcohol—a taboo for many Muslims in Syria, let alone many of those in attendance—to drown the Fifth Fleet.

The biggest issue, though, was Za'im's public announcement of negotiations with Israel, which were definitely more taboo than any amount of Scotch around these parts. Without warning or any kind of discussion beforehand, he just up and talked about it on one of his radio addresses, a series of increasingly rambling, nonsensical homilies about the greatness of the Syrian people, the need for a united

Middle East, the shiftless youth of the souks, the cleanliness of the streets, and the necessity of no longer wearing the fez because of its Ottoman legacy.

Which made it all the more confusing that he'd shown up with the feathered fez the next day, but Frank had stopped trying to make sense of Za'im after he had Saadeh sent back to Beirut. Frank, Cal, and Meade had risked a whole lot to get Saadeh to Damascus, and ultimately Za'im used the guy's life to score political points with Lebanon. Frank could see the logic in it—if Saadeh had succeeded, then sure, maybe he'd have wanted a united Greater Syria under *his* rule instead of Za'im's—but it was a cold, hard thing to accept. And that bullshit about Saadeh being a Middle Eastern Hitler? Please.

Frank ran a hand over his face and, grabbing a bathrobe, headed out to the Copelands' courtyard. That was one thing Frank felt American houses needed—courtyards, with fountains in them. Shady and cool during the day, inviting and quiet at night. Frank idly thought about where a house with a courtyard might make sense—Nevada, for one. He'd heard nice things about Albuquerque, or maybe Phoenix. Maybe his time in Syria had given him a taste for the desert—or maybe he was just hankering to be alone with his thoughts, without the voices in his head chiming in about every little thing.

Odd noises coming from the street, said the former O.S.S. officer in his mind. *Multiple bogeys, clustered near the door.*

"Christ, it's probably just some toughs out there," Frank muttered, plopping down on a chair near the fountain. "Gimme a break."

You should check the door.

"No, goddamn it!" Frank hissed, a little louder than he wanted to. "Shut the fuck up!"

Frank leaned forward and put his head in his hands. Maybe he was wrong and being alone would be the absolute worst thing for him. Without stimuli, maybe the voices would get antsy, start telling him how to cook his meals, trim the hedges, maybe even offer ideas for hobbies. Model trains, maybe, or collecting commemorative souvenir tea-spoons. Maybe Damascus had a shop for those.

The sound of splintering wood shook him out of his rut, and fast. *The door! Multiple bogeys entering the building!*

Frank immediately dashed toward the staircase leading up to the second floor. His first priority was supposed to be Cal—the safety and security of Variants was always mission number one—but he found himself at the door to the kids' room instead. Security be damned; there was a baby in there.

Only three ways down from here, all with line of sight to the front door, said one of the many voices in Frank's head; it was getting hard to tell who was who anymore. *Grab the kids and get them to Copeland's room.*

Frank entered the room and did his best to gently lift the baby from the crib, then woke little Miles as gentle as he could. "C'mon, kid. Wake up. Your dad needs to see you," he whispered.

Young Miles rubbed his eyes. "Daddy?"

No time! Grab him! Jim said, practically shouting inside Frank's skull. With one arm, Frank scooped the boy and threw him over his shoulder like a sack of flour, then did his best to run down the hallway toward Copeland's room.

Thankfully, the break-in had awakened Lorraine, who was just opening the door. "Frank! What is it?" Then she saw her children in his arms and her eyes grew wide.

"Take the baby," Frank whispered. Lorraine, however, was already scooping the child out of the crook of his arm. He put little Miles down at the door. "Lock this door. Put all the furniture in the room in front of it. Then call the office for help. You understand? Lock the door, move the furniture. Call for help."

Lorraine looked dazed, but nodded. "Door . . . furniture . . . help. Come on, Miles. Come with Mommy, then? Come on."

Little Miles walked into the room, while Lorraine gave Frank one last, panicked glance. He waited until she shut the door and he heard the click of a lock before turning back to the hallway. "OK, guys, tell me everything," he muttered as he started moving back down the hall.

The voices came all in a rush.

At least six different people inside, telling from their voices.

With that many inside, high probability of backup on the street.

They're speaking Arabic, and one of them addressed the other as "Captain." Police or military, likely the latter.

If they're Syrian regulars, expect bolt-action repeating rifles, revolvers as sidearms, and a short, curved dagger for each of them.

Sounds like they're moving through the courtyard now.

Moving in twos. Smart.

Get your firearm. Use the suppressor. Only chance of picking off enough of them to escape.

Behind you!

Frank hit the deck immediately, a rifle butt missing his head by inches. He kicked upward, entangling the legs of his assailant, then grabbed the man's belt and pulled him down. The soldier—or at least someone wearing a Syrian Army uniform—fell squarely on his ass and lost his grip on his rifle, which Frank then scrambled for.

"Stop!"

Moving in twos, remember?

The second soldier had his bolt-action trained on Frank's forehead from a range of about a yard. Frank froze in place, hoping for any great ideas to come bubbling up.

Surrender for now.

Hands up.

Try to start a dialogue.

You're fucked.

"Very funny," Frank muttered as the first man got to his feet and angrily grabbed his weapon off the floor.

This time, the rifle butt landed squarely on the side of his head, and all the voices went quiet.

* * *

"There you go, Frank. There you go. Come on now."

Frank opened his eyes and saw Cal hovering over him, looking mostly like the late-twenties young man he'd been lately, though maybe a little worse for wear. Frank braced himself for one hell of a headache, but it never came.

"What happened?" Frank asked, slowly sitting up. He'd been lying on a stone floor, and when he noticed the bars on the window, he figured he was back at Mezze Prison. Given what had happened to Saadeh, Frank figured their odds weren't so great.

"They woke me up, grabbed me, pulled me out of Mr. Copeland's house. You they carried out. Then they drove us here, tossed us in the cell, and that's it. Soon as they were gone, I figured I'd heal you up and get you awake," Cal said. "Probably just knocked you out some. Didn't take much to get you going."

"Copeland? The family?"

"They weren't taken. Other than that, don't know."

"Recognize anybody?" Frank said as he looked around.

Cal shook his head. "No, just a bunch of soldiers, young fellows, led by a captain. Though I did hear someone mention Hinnawi."

Za'im's right-hand man, came the political scientist. *Likely acting on his orders.*

"No shit," Frank muttered, then looked up at Cal's confused face. "Sorry. Someone was stating the obvious. Anyway, good ears, Cal. Anything else?"

"Just that it's been busy here. Lots of folks moving about. Everybody looks worried as hell. And I sure wish they'd give us some clothes."

Frank did a double take at that, realizing that Cal had been taken in his undershorts. Frank at least had a T-shirt on.

"All right, we need a plan," Frank said quietly. "Guard patterns?"

"Ain't been here long enough," Cal said. "But when we got here, they put us in a cell block with guards at either end of the hall, by the two doors. Plus the guards that brought us in."

"Assume six minimum, all armed. Not good. Maybe if we . . ."

Frank's idea died off as keys clanked against the metal door. A moment later, it opened to reveal two guards. "Get up. Move it," one said in Arabic.

"We are diplomatic representatives of the United States government and entitled to fair treatment," Frank replied in the same language. "We will not accompany you until the leader of our delegation, Mr. Keeley, is called."

The guard laughed and pulled his revolver. "I was told you might try that, *spy*. Get up or I will kill you where you sit."

Frank sighed and hauled himself to his feet. "Well, at least we know this all isn't some innocent mistake," he told Cal. "Play nice for now."

The two were led out of the cell—there were actually eight guards in the hallway—and marched out one of the doors and right out of the building. It was still pitch-black outside, and Frank figured there were at least two hours before sunrise. They headed toward one of the soldiers' barracks—the same barracks, Frank remembered, where Za'im had taken the former president to kill him in the shower, before Cal had talked him out of it.

He looked over at his partner, who'd clearly put two and two together as well. Frank imagined it'd be tough for even Cal to survive a shot to the head, but he hoped and prayed he'd make it out somehow. He was the one with a family, after all.

The two Americans were marched inside the barracks and, as Frank feared, taken directly to the soldiers' shower room. "Guess Za'im went and got antsy again," Cal whispered. It was gallows humor, but Frank couldn't help but crack a smile.

The voices in his head were silent, and for once, Frank missed the chatter. Perhaps they knew a lost cause when they saw one. Or maybe they were just still thinking. He hoped they'd hurry up with something, *anything*, because Frank himself was drawing a blank.

Za'im was already in the shower room, waiting for them.

But he was in casual clothes, kneeling on the floor with his hands on his head, looking terrified. Next to him, pointing a gun at his head, was Colonel al-Hinnawi.

And next to al-Hinnawi was Karilov, the Russian.

"Mr. Lodge," Karilov said with a smile. "I knew we'd meet again. Hello, Mr. Hooks."

Frank's stomach turned slightly; Karilov knew his real name.

Cal gave the man a confused nod. "Don't know if this is the best thing for anybody to be doing right now," he said. "Seems like it could cause a real big fuss for everyone."

Frank admired Cal's attempt at diplomacy but figured it for what it was—a fool's errand. And both al-Hinnawi and Karilov ignored him, with the latter turning to the former. "Where is the third one?" Karilov asked in Arabic.

"She's coming," the colonel replied. "We have her."

Frank and Cal traded a look. *Zippy.*

"What's going on, Comrade Karilov?" Frank asked in perfect Russian.

Karilov smiled. "Ah, finally. The tongue of Tolstoy and Lenin! I cannot tell you how it pains me to speak in churlish Arabic. Tell me, Comrade Lodge, where did you study Russian?"

Frank ignored him. "You do realize that the United States government isn't going to let this stand."

"They will, because to contest your capture carries great risk, does it not?" Karilov replied. "Better to lose three than to risk the world knowing what you are, what you can do."

Frank calmly turned to Cal. "Cover's blown," he said in English. "You, me, and Zippy. He knows. All of it."

Cal's face showed a sad resolve. "Always figured this job was more trouble than it's worth."

Suddenly, Zippy was shoved into the room, dressed in an ill-fitting Syrian Army uniform, probably a spare given to her to cover up. She looked shellshocked, and her expression changed to outright fearful when she saw Za'im and al-Hinnawi.

"Are you satisfied?" al-Hinnawi asked Karilov.

Karilov nodded. "You may proceed. I'll take these three, as agreed."

Without another word, al-Hinnawi turned and shot Za'im in the head at point-blank range.

Zippy screamed, and Cal's hands flew to his mouth. Frank just closed his eyes and turned away. "Syria is now an ally of the Union of Soviet Socialist Republics," Karilov said in Russian.

"For now," Frank replied. "I think you just saw how quickly things can change."

"You have no idea," Karilov said. "Follow me."

Frank looked around, searching for something that might trigger some advice in his head. Eight guards, plus an armed Syrian Army colonel who had already proven he had the balls to shoot a man in cold blood.

Karilov walked off, and Frank gathered Cal in with a wave, then went up to Zippy. "Come on, Zip. We gotta go."

She nodded and stood up straighter, sniffling and rubbing a sleeve of her uniform across her face. "Never seen a man killed before."

"Yeah. Let's go."

They walked out of the shower room—an improvement in odds from when they'd walked in, Frank had to admit— and out of the barracks toward a waiting army truck. The drivers, Frank noticed, didn't look Syrian in the least.

"So, where are we going, Comrade?" Frank asked.

Karilov turned back and smiled. "Far away from here, Comrade Lodge. Far away indeed."

They were ushered around the back of the truck, which was covered with a tarp. Inside were eight armed men dressed in Syrian Army uniforms—but their pale, long faces and shaved heads told a much different story.

"Good morning, comrades," Frank sighed in Russian as he climbed into the truck.

* * *

The first sign of trouble for Maggie was when she got off the plane at the Damascus airport and her ride wasn't there.

In fact, nobody's rides were there. Instead, she and the rest of her fellow passengers on the flight from Istanbul were left standing on the curb in the early morning light, wondering just what the hell was going on.

Finally, one of the police officers guarding the airport entrance—and Maggie noticed there were far more than usual on duty—made an announcement. "There is a curfew today," he said in broken English after presumably giving the same spiel in Arabic. "You will be taken on bus to area for interviews."

Well, that won't do. She walked up to the man after he'd finished speaking—he'd thrown in some French as well. "Sir, you know, I hate to trouble you, but I work at the U.S. embassy here. I really think I should give them a ring, let them know what's going on."

She reached out with her Enhancement, trying to give the man a little nudge in the right direction—helping out a young woman, a little fear of annoying an American diplomat—and he responded accordingly.

"Telephone inside. You tell them OK from me," he said with a smile.

"Aren't you so sweet! Thank you!" Maggie said, touching his arm and trying to channel Mrs. Stevens. A few minutes later, she was on the phone, dialing Copeland's house.

"Yes! Tell me what you got!" Copeland answered quickly—and nervously.

"Miles, it's Maggie Dubinsky. What the hell is going on?"

"Shit, Maggie. There's been a coup. Al-Hinnawi took over. Za'im's been executed as a traitor."

Maggie paused as she took it all in, as well as Copeland's complete abandonment of discretion on the phone—a sure sign that things were bad. "OK. Let me speak to Frank."

"Maggie, they took Frank and Cal. Al-Hinnawi's men. I can't reach Zippy, either. I got a guy at the airport who said the three of them were seen there just after daybreak with Sergei Karilov, the Russian attaché."

Maggie looked around quickly. "OK. I'll try to find them."

"Wait! Maggie!"

"What?"

"They took off. On a plane. A Russian plane heading east."

Without another word, Maggie hung up, pondered things for another moment or two, then picked the receiver back up and dialed a long string of numbers.

After a pause, a prim-sounding British woman picked up. "Amalgamated Exports, to whom may I direct your call?"

"Victor Davies," Maggie replied. *Agent down. Director's office. Now.*

"I'm sorry, I didn't quite get that. Come again?" *Request confirmation.*

"Victor Davies." *No, really, get the director's office now!*

"One moment, please."

There was a long series of whirrs and clicks, the telltale signs of trans-Atlantic phone lines switching. Finally, Hillenkoetter's tired voice picked up the line. "This is Mr. Davies."

"Mr. Davies, this is Miss Davenport calling from Damascus. Unfortunately, it seems three of your shipments aren't here at the moment." *Three agents down in Damascus.*

"I see, that's . . . well, that's unfortunate. Were these the special shipments you were sent to assist with?" *All Variants?*

"I'm afraid so. They seem to have been loaded onto a different plane here at the airport. I'm afraid they may be headed elsewhere, and I'm not sure where." *All three Variants assigned to this theater of operations have been captured and taken out of theater.*

"Well, that's not going to work. Did you happen to catch which plane?" *Who took them and where?*

Maggie swallowed hard before answering. "No, sorry, but someone here thinks they were loaded onto a plane with red livery. That's all I know." *Soviets. Destination unknown.*

"All right. Why don't you head into the office over there? I'll get folks working over here on my end." *Report to the nearest U.S. diplomatic post immediately and do not leave. Await further orders from Washington.*

"Very well. Thank you, sir." Without any further ado, Maggie hung up the phone. The consulate was the safest place for her to be, of course, if random Reds were kidnapping Variants.

But of course, if that were the case, all bets were off.

FROM: DCI HILLENKOETTER
TO: LCMR WALLACE USN
CC: POTUS, LTG VANDENBERG USAF, DR BRONK
RE: SEARCH AND RESCUE OPERATION
CLASSIFICATION: TOP SECRET—MAJIK
DATE: 16 AUGUST 1949

AGENTS HOOKS, LODGE, AND SILVERMAN ARE MISSING AND
PRESUMED CAPTURED, POSSIBLY BY SOVIET AGENTS OR THOSE
AFFILIATED WITH THE SOVIET UNION.

THE LAST CONFIRMED SIGHTING OF AGENT HOOKS WAS
APPROXIMATELY 2200 ON 14 AUGUST AT THE RESIDENCE OF
AGENT COPELAND OPC IN DAMASCUS.

THE LAST CONFIRMED SIGHTING OF AGENT LODGE WAS
APPROXIMATELY 0200 ON 15 AUGUST AT THE COPELAND
RESIDENCE. LODGE HAD TAKEN COPELAND'S CHILDREN TO
THEIR MOTHER AFTER SOUNDS OF A BREAK—IN AT THE
RESIDENCE. COPELAND CONFIRMS FORCED ENTRY AT THE
RESIDENCE. BOTH HOOKS AND LODGE WERE REPORTED MISSING
AFTER THE BREAK—IN, AT APPROXIMATELY 0230.

THE LAST CONFIRMED SIGHTING OF AGENT SILVERMAN
WAS APPROXIMATELY 1900 ON 14 AUGUST, AT THE
DAMASCUS BUREAU OF THE JERUSALEM POST, WHEN SHE
LEFT FOR THE DAY. HER WHEREABOUTS SINCE THAT TIME
ARE UNKNOWN.

THERE WAS AN UNCONFIRMED SIGHTING OF AGENTS HOOKS,
LODGE, AND SILVERMAN TOGETHER AT THE DAMASCUS

AIRPORT AT APPROXIMATELY 0530 ON 15 AUGUST, WHERE
THEY BOARDED AN AIRCRAFT IN THE PRESENCE OF SERGEI
KARILOV (SEE FILE). THE AIRCRAFT WAS LAST SEEN TAKING
OFF ON AN EASTWARD BEARING.

AGENT DUBINSKY ARRIVED IN DAMASCUS AT APPROXIMATELY
0800 ON 15 AUGUST, AND HAS BEEN ORDERED TO SHELTER
IN PLACE AT THE US CONSULATE, WHILE DIRECTING
CONSULATE STAFF TO ASSIST IN LOCATING THE MISSING
AGENTS. THERE HAVE BEEN NO FURTHER UPDATES AS OF
THIS WRITING.

YOU ARE HEREBY ORDERED TO SURRENDER OPERATIONAL
COMMAND OF AREA 51 TO MAJ HAMILTON USA AND
OPERATIONAL COMMAND OF MAJESTIC-12 TO DR BRONK FOR
THE DURATION OF THE FOLLOWING OPERATION.

YOU ARE HEREBY AUTHORIZED TO FORM VARIANT GROUP
TWO, WITH AGENTS MEYER, SORENSEN, VANOVERBEKE, AND
YAMATO UNDER YOUR COMMAND, AND DEPLOY TO DAMASCUS.
AGENT DUBINSKY WILL JOIN GROUP TWO UPON YOUR
ARRIVAL.

YOU ARE HEREBY ORDERED TO LOCATE AGENTS HOOKS,
LODGE, AND SILVERMAN. IF OPPORTUNITY PRESENTS ITSELF,
YOU ARE TO CONDUCT RESCUE OPERATIONS. IF RESCUE IS
IMPRACTICAL OR IMPOSSIBLE, YOU ARE TO ELIMINATE ANY
VARIANT OPERATIVES IN SOVIET HANDS.

IF NEITHER OPTION IS PRACTICAL OR POSSIBLE, REPORT TO
DCI HILLENKOETTER FOR FURTHER ORDERS.

TOP SECRET / MAJIC
EYES ONLY
* TOP SECRET *
****

003

YOUR TOP PRIORITY IS TO PREVENT ANY VARIANT--THE
MISSING OR THOSE UNDER YOUR COMMAND--PERMANENTLY
FALLING INTO SOVIET HANDS.

(SIGNED) HILLENKOETTER

29.

August 16, 1949

Danny Wallace was throwing clothes hastily into a duffel bag when the knock came at his door. "Commander!" He smiled, knowing the voice. "Come on in, John."

Major Hamilton entered and Danny's smile vanished in the face of the man's hurried concern. "Julia Meyer is missing."

Danny dropped his shirt to the floor. "Come again?"

"We went to assemble Group Two, as you ordered. She's nowhere to be found."

Danny screwed his eyes shut and reached out with his Enhancement. There were thirteen other Variants on base he could sense. The first was just one building away—Mrs. Stevens, back puttering in her labs—and the captive Russian POSEIDON was in the main research facility under lockdown. There were supposed to be four others in each of the three training areas—but one area only had three. How?

Danny immediately hustled for the door, dragging Hamilton with him by the arm. "What about the others?"

"All accounted for, waiting in the staging area," Hamilton said as they headed out the officers' quarters block toward a waiting jeep. "Nobody's seen her since lunch. Just locked down the entire base."

"The rest of the Variants know she's gone," Danny said as he jumped into the passenger seat. "Or at least they have suspicions. They have to."

Hamilton gunned the engine and took off for the training area. "How can you be sure?"

"Because they're Variants, John."

They spent the rest of the ride across the lakebed coordinating security efforts via radio. There were teams of at least four MPs with eyes on every critical asset there—the vortex, POSEIDON, Schreiber, Bronk and his lab, and each Variant. Searchers in Bell H-13 Sioux helicopters began an overlapping grid search of the base and surrounding mountains, while soldiers on the ground methodically fanned out around the buildings across the main base and training areas.

They arrived at Julia's training area to find the three others on her team in the mess tent, under armed guard. There was no sign of a fourth.

"Major, if we could have the room," Danny said, but it was more an order than a request. Hamilton motioned for the MPs to get out, leaving Danny alone with Tim, Rick, and Christina, all of whom looked scared and properly chagrined. He sat down in front of them and gave them a small smile. "All right. We have a problem. What I need to know from you is information on where she went."

The three other Variants looked at each other pointedly until Rick finally spoke. "She didn't tell us about any immediate plan to escape," he said haltingly.

Danny nodded. "But she had plans," he prompted. "You all did. You probably still do."

Tim seemed to get his nerve up at this, looking Danny straight in the eye. "I don't know what you're talking about, sir."

"Well, the last four Variants who lived here did. They plotted and planned and eventually figured out more about this place and themselves than you four ever have. They asked the right questions of themselves, made the right choices, and proved themselves to be curious, smart and capable. And they graduated to field operations and did well.

"But now they're in trouble, and they need our help," Danny continued. "We think that several of them have fallen into enemy hands. Soviet hands. And I've seen firsthand these Soviet Variants. They're brutal. I know a little of what they went through to become that way, and it makes what you've been doing here at Area 51 look like a garden party. The Russians will study our Variants. They will use them. They'll seek to brainwash them, and if they can't do that, they'll probably torture them for information and eventually kill them. Is that what you want to see happen?"

Christina narrowed her eyes at Danny. "*Our* Variants?"

Goddamnit! Danny hung his head for several long moments, trying to think of a way out, but ultimately his silence became his answer. "Yes," Danny admitted. "*Our* Variants. *American* Variants. Like you. Like me. And like I've been saying over and over again, you will be stronger together and working with this program than you will be on your own. I know. If this program didn't exist, they might have hunted you down and locked you away with the rest of us years ago. They might have just killed us. Instead, we have a chance to do some good and to stick up for one another.

"I'm going to head out to go get *my* fellow Variants," Danny said, standing up. "And I need you with me to help *your* fellow Variants as well."

One by one, the three remaining members of Group 2 looked to one another and began nodding. "All right," Rick said. "What do you need?"

"For starters, I need Julia."

Once again, they glanced at each other for guidance until, finally, Tim spoke up. "She knows about the vortex. That German scientist told her. I think she went to turn him loose. Him and the Russian Variant you got over there at the base."

Danny actually staggered backward at this, words failing him and his hands instinctively reaching for a sidearm that wasn't there—yet. "How?" he asked.

"The electrical for those null-generators you got. They were jury-rigged together pretty slapdash, frankly. Easy for me to keep the 'on' light working when the rest of the thing was shut off," Tim said with an apologetic half-smile on his lean face. "I was even able to whip up a little device from old radio parts that could counteract the fields for a while. I can get it to last a good thirty minutes now."

Danny cursed himself for thinking too much about Enhancements and simply not enough about the regular skills and ingenuity these folks brought to the table. "All right. Thank you. I mean that. Get your gear and be ready to move. I'm going to find Julia."

The three other Variants nodded as Danny purposefully strode out of the room, only to break into a dead run for the jeep as soon as he was out of sight. "Hamilton! Back to base! *NOW!*" He jumped in the passenger seat and grabbed the radio, setting to a base-wide broadcast.

"Attention, attention! Lock down Area 51 completely! Seal the main hangar and all facilities. Any nonessential personnel seen outside a building will be shot. Repeat, any nonessential personnel seen outside a building *will be shot.*"

Then he flipped the channel to the MP band. "All security personnel, we need a room-by-room sweep of the base. Each team will need a null-generator and tranquilizer guns. And double the guard around POSEIDON and Schreiber."

Hamilton clambered into the driver's seat as the affirmative responses came in, and minutes later—after a wind-whipped, high-speed ride back across the lakebed—they came to a jolting stop in front of the main research hangar. "Report," Hamilton barked at one of his junior officers, a lieutenant who seemed fresh out of officer training.

"We're working through the area now. Administration and personnel quarters are clear—all base personnel are sheltering in place, and nobody is out of place at the moment."

"Schreiber? POSEIDON?" Danny asked.

"Secured, sir. I think—"

The lieutenant was interrupted by the sound of tearing metal from above their heads. Danny looked up to see the sheet-metal wall of the hangar beginning to cave in, as if someone had grabbed it from the inside and pulled . . . .

"POSEIDON is loose!" Danny yelled. "Swarm the building!"

Danny rushed inside with the rest of the security men, even though that was technically violating orders. Nobody would be standing on ceremony now. Overhead were more sounds of screeching metal; it sounded like POSEIDON was trying to rip apart the entire base. Someone offered Danny a tranquilizer pistol, which he gratefully accepted. He took a moment to concentrate, and finally sensed the two Variants he was looking for. "Second floor! Research labs! Go!"

The men rushed up the stairs, but Danny felt his perceptions shift—the two targeted Variants had just left the building through the hole they'd created, even though it was a good twelve feet off the ground. "They're outside now! Move!"

Danny was the first out the door, and saw just what POSEIDON had been planning. The Russian, dressed in a simple olive-drab uniform, had his arms around Julia and Schreiber, one on each side, and was using his telekinetic pulling enhancement to move incredibly quickly through the base, pulling himself through the air from building to building.

"Fire!" Danny shouted, running after them. A flurry of darts launched from a dozen guns, but POSEIDON was moving too fast for them.

But he was also running out of buildings to use. Soon, they'd have to hit the ground and run—at least until he got close enough to the mountains, at which point he could pull them up faster than a jumped-up billy goat.

Danny dashed toward a jeep and hopped in the driver's seat, slamming it into gear and tearing off even as Hamilton and two of his MPs were still climbing in. They hung on for dear life as Danny sped off toward the fugitives. They were in the desert valley now, too far from the base buildings for POSEIDON to anchor his Enhancement but still about two hundred yards away from the first foothills—close enough for him to latch onto them.

"Take aim!" Danny shouted above the wind. "If tranqs don't work, then use firearms. Shoot to injure, not kill, if you can help it."

POSEIDON was running full tilt now, reaching back with his Enhancement to pull both Schreiber and Julia along, as neither seemed to be as fast or enduring a runner as the MGB man. Danny floored it, quickly gaining on them.

And then the jeep began to rise.

"Shoot! Now!" Danny yelled.

But it was too late. The jeep, despite Danny's best efforts behind the wheel, began to overturn and fly through the air as POSEIDON pulled it toward him. Hamilton was thrown from the vehicle, while Danny and the other MPs clung on to whatever they could find.

POSEIDON slammed the jeep down on the valley sands on its side, continuing to drag the vehicle toward him on the ground. Danny wanted to reach for the tranq pistol in his belt at the small of his back, but it was too much just trying to hang on to the steering wheel and brace himself inside the jeep so he wouldn't fall out. Both MPs finally lost their grips and tumbled out, leaving only Danny in place as the jeep finally skidded to a stop in front of POSEIDON.

"You!" the Russian Variant shouted. "You I will kill with my bare hands!"

Dazed and bruised, Danny let go of the wheel, slumping out of the jeep onto the sand, then looked up to see POSEIDON, his fists balled and rage writ upon his face, about twenty yards away.

"Come and get me," Danny whispered.

He felt the pull of POSEIDON's ability, completely helpless as he was dragged across the desert sands, rocks battering his ribcage and sand stinging his eyes. Then he was airborne, moving faster than ever.

It was the only thing he could think of to do, and in the mere seconds he had to spare, Danny reached for the tranq pistol, pulled it, and fired it at POSEIDON's chest at a range of about four yards.

The dart broke the Russian's concentration, and Danny landed hard on the sand, skidding to a halt. He looked up and POSEIDON was coming for him, fists raised, but then the man staggered and fell to his knees, collapsing just inches away.

Danny heard a scream. Julia.

He slowly got to his feet, his legs almost buckling with the effort. Kurt Schreiber and Julia were nearly ten feet away—Schreiber holding a gun to the Variant's head.

"That's close enough, Commander," Schreiber said. "Drop your weapon."

Danny looked from Schreiber's grim, determined expression to the panicked, anguished look on Julia's face. It took a few seconds for the incongruence to register in his head, but once it did, Danny had to force himself not to smile.

Instead, he calmly reloaded the tranquilizer pistol. "You know, Doctor, I think I'm actually genuinely insulted right now," he said.

A flash of confusion passed over Schreiber's face, quickly replaced by anger. "I will kill her, I promise you, Commander. I will kill her and then I'll kill you."

Danny finished loading as Hamilton—dirty, bruised, and bleeding from a cut on his forehead—walked over, his automatic pistol pointed at Schreiber. "Drop it, Doc," Hamilton said. "She's a lot more valuable than you are."

"Which is why you will call for another jeep which will take us away from here, and you will not follow," Schreiber said, pulling Julia's body in front of his. "I mean it. I will shoot her."

"Not if I shoot her first, Doctor," Danny said. He raised the tranquilizer pistol, aimed it at Julia's heart—and squeezed the trigger.

Julia immediately turned immaterial, and the dart passed right through her, sticking into Schreiber. The scientist gasped and staggered backward as Danny threw the other object he'd been carrying right at Julia.

The active null-generator landed at her feet.

She gasped, then turned and began to run. A tranquilizer dart from one of the MPs took her down in a matter of steps.

Danny walked over to the bodies now lying on the desert floor and picked up the anti-null device next to Julia's inert hand. It was about the size of a dime-store novel, and it looked burned out. Sorensen's. Not a bad bit of work, really. Danny shoved the device in his pocket; he imagined Mrs. Stevens would be very interested in analyzing it.

"Get an ambulance over here, and activate more nulls just in case they wake up," Danny told Hamilton.

"You want me to put Meyer in with the Russki until we figure out what to do?" Hamilton asked.

"Nope. I want them both doped up, nulled at all times, and ready to travel."

"What about Schreiber?"

Danny entertained the notion of just tying him to a pole in the middle of the desert lake bed and leaving him there to die. Not a very kind idea, admittedly, but then Schreiber wasn't exactly deserving of Danny's good Christian charity at that moment.

"Throw him back in the brig," he muttered. "But don't feel you have to be nice about it."

30.

August 17, 1949

Cal looked idly out the window of his plane at the rolling steppe below, fighting nerves and trying to stay alert as best he could. Frank said they were aboard a Soviet military Lisunov Li-2 transport—a Soviet-made knockoff of a DC-3 passenger plane—and Cal supposed that wasn't the worst plane they could be on, given the stories he'd heard about the subpar machinery the Soviets designed themselves.

They were prisoners, but at least they weren't gonna fall from the sky. For now.

They'd been taken from Mezze Prison to the airport and put on a nondescript cargo plane headed for Yerevan, the capital of Armenia—part of the Soviet Union. Once there, Karilov had handed them off to a bunch of soldiers who hustled the Americans onto the plane they found themselves on now. They'd taken off and landed several times, and Frank had been calling out the names of places as they flew into them: Yerevan to Baku, Azerbaijan, and then a bunch of towns in some place called Kazakhstan. Fort Shevchenko, Shalkar, Astana, and now to some other place. It was hard to keep up.

Kazakhstan was part of the Soviet Union just like Armenia and Azerbaijan but a lot bigger—the same way Texas was a lot bigger than Rhode Island, Cal figured. They'd flown over mountains and desert and now grasslands, and it was all sparsely populated as far as he could tell. Frank—or maybe it had been one of the people taking up residence in his head—figured they were headed to a remote military facility of some kind, since they were headed well away from Leningrad, home of the Bekhterev Institute, where the Reds studied their own Variants. They were also pretty far from Moscow, for that matter. In fact, they were getting to within spitting distance of Mongolia— which meant they were the farthest Cal had ever been from home.

Thoughts of home were hard. Cal had last called his family a whole eight days before, so he knew Sarah and Winston—the boy was done with college and working at *The Washington Post*'s printing presses for the summer— would be worrying sick about him. The government folks had given Cal's family a number to call in case he was out of touch for a while, and he hoped the CIA would take care of them after . . .

. . . after whatever happened to him.

Frank and Zippy had talked a lot about what-ifs during their journey. There had been a lot of initial plotting about overpowering the guards, maybe seizing control of the aircraft. But then Cal spotted the other planes off in the distance to either side of theirs—fighter aircraft. Frank identified them as Yak-9s, and apparently they were fast and pretty good in a scrap, and it was safe to assume they were there to shoot down their plane if it deviated off course. Their presence also made a parachute escape highly unlikely.

After that, the talk turned to what their lives might be like under the Soviets. Zippy was the most outwardly worried, concerned about rape and torture and all kinds of dark ideas—and while Cal had put a fatherly hand on her shoulder and said the right things to calm her down, he truly had no idea what would befall them. Would they be recruited? Cal knew Frank wouldn't flip, and Zippy seemed grimly determined to give them nothing. For himself, Cal figured the Russians couldn't touch his family, and they were a Godless lot besides. So, between family and God, they had nothing to bargain with him. They could do their worst.

That was easy to say, of course, without knowing what the worst might be. As Variants, they were mighty valuable, and when Zippy wasn't thinking the worst, she'd wondered if they might be treated well enough because there simply weren't that many Variants around—the Russians couldn't afford to be cruel to them. Frank, however, had reminded the two of them that if they didn't play ball, then the Soviet Variant program—whether it was at Bekhterev or wherever else—could almost certainly use some experimental subjects. "Those who can't be suborned can be dissected," Frank had said. Grim thoughts indeed.

Cal told himself he was ready to make his peace with God, and to see Sarah and Winston again at the Second Coming—but he wasn't. He desperately wanted to go home, to kiss his wife and hug his boy and write off all this spy-game nonsense once and for all. And if he ever got out of all this, maybe he'd do just that—so long as the MAJESTIC-12 folks let him. There was that to consider as well.

The plane suddenly pitched forward, and a Russian voice came over the intercom. Cal turned to look at Frank, who was busying himself with his seatbelt. "Strap in," Frank said. "Coming into Semipalatinsk."

Cal buckled up. "Where's that?"

"Middle of nowhere, Kazakhstan. Ought to be a real garden spot," Frank said.

But it wasn't quite nowhere. They'd flown over a handful of small villages—collections of thatched huts and small stone buildings—and now were descending toward some kind of outpost. Cal looked out the window and saw clusters of buildings surrounding a modest airstrip, and there were jeeps—or whatever the Russians called their versions of jeeps—and people going about their business. Honestly, with the prefab buildings and aircraft hangars and such, the place looked a whole lot like Area 51, except it was situated in a much nicer-looking grassland, with a decent-sized river flowing nearby.

"Could be worse," Cal said with a smile.

Frank smiled back grimly. "How do you do it?" he asked.

"Do what?"

Frank nodded to the window as the plane swooped lower. "We're captured Americans in Soviet territory. We might not get home again. And you, with the optimism. How do you do it?"

Cal thought about this for a moment and found himself thinking back to his time working in the Firestone plant back in Memphis—the daily insults, the weekly fistfights, the sabotage by his white coworkers, and the docked pay from his white foremen that led to less food on the table and postponed promises to his wife and boy. "Because I've seen worse," he said finally. "When it gets *really* bad, I promise I'll let you know."

Frank nodded and went back to looking out his own window. At first, when Cal had talked about working conditions for Negroes in the South, Frank had looked shocked and in disbelief. Cal figured it wasn't Frank's fault per se. He was the rare white man who treated black folks well enough, even though he'd never spared much of a thought for the folks around the country—not just in the South—who saw things very differently. Most of the people in MAJESTIC-12 were pretty good about it, though he imagined they were under orders. After all, Cal had seen a black woman, a Hispanic-looking fellow, and an Asian kid around the base, and was sure they were Variants too. No reason for a black woman to be out in the middle of the Nevada desert otherwise.

Cal's thoughts were interrupted by tires on tarmac, and the plane landed with a jarring thud and a screech of rubber. Cal had been on a fair number of planes over the past couple years—never having flown his entire life before that—and he already could tell these Russian pilots didn't have half the skill of the American boys. He actually took a little pride in that for some reason.

Immediately, the Russian soldiers unbuckled and stood up, and while their weapons weren't trained on the Americans, they were certainly in hand. "*Vstavay. Poyekhali.*"

Frank was already rising. "We're moving. Let's go," he said.

Cal waited for the two of them to go ahead before following; he and Frank had agreed early on that they'd work to protect her. Wasn't like she wasn't trained up—she was—but Frank carried with him the skills and knowledge of a half dozen top-notch fighters, while Cal could drop a man with a touch. Zippy's Enhancement was great for gathering intelligence, but Cal knew he and Frank would have to take the lead in a scrap.

Of course, they couldn't stop bullets, and a full squad of Russian soldiers was a bit too much to handle at the moment, so they had little choice but to walk out of the plane and into a warm, sunny August day. It was a dry heat—not as bad as Area 51 but still pretty warm. The air smelled clean, and Cal wondered if there were farms nearby, based on the slight whiff of mown grass and manure in the breeze. The prefab buildings were clean and new, and it looked like the base was kept in fine order. Cal had seen photos and heard reports about other Soviet bases, and this one seemed far better. That meant funding, and it probably meant the people in charge had decided whatever was going on here to be pretty important.

Once they set foot on the ground, the soldiers threw a pair of heavy work gloves at Cal's feet, and at Zippy's as well. "*Naden'te perchatki,*" one of the soldiers said.

Cal didn't need Frank to translate. He picked up the gloves and put them on, as did Zippy. Only then did the soldiers come and put handcuffs on each of them. *They definitely know what we can do,* Cal thought. *They already got us pegged. But how?*

Hands cuffed behind their backs, they were marched to a waiting cargo truck and forced to sit in the back, along with the soldiers who had accompanied them on the plane. Again, their weapons were held at the ready, and an officer barked at them for a good thirty seconds straight before the vehicle began to move. Cal assumed he was warning them that they'd be shot if they so much as blinked wrong, so he sat tight and waited for the next thing. The back door was shut, and a couple flashlights provided the only illumination. The Russians were apparently pretty good at keeping folks in the dark.

The drive was a good twenty minutes, but it felt longer without being able to see where they were going. Paved tarmac turned into gravel, then to a bumpy dirt road. There were a few turns here and there, and then finally the truck came to a complete stop. The back was opened, and everyone was ushered out with shouting and a few shoves. Once Cal set foot on the ground again, he looked around and saw that the base and airfield were no longer anywhere in sight.

Instead, they were in a cluster of three older buildings in the middle of a kind of dirt courtyard. One looked to be a crumbling old home, a stone structure that maybe had once been fine indeed but was long past its glory days. The second building was a big old barn, weathered and gray, with closed doors and no straw in sight on the ground; Cal had five bucks it wasn't holding livestock. The third looked to be some sort of stable, but again, there was no evidence it was still being used for its original purpose. All three buildings were old, and Cal imagined that they'd withstood a lot through the years on the steppe. No trees around, no shelter at all. Great for farming, he imagined.

The large sliding door to the barn wheeled open, and Cal could see that he was right; there were a concrete floor and electrical lights inside. In fact, it looked like they'd put a prefab *inside* the barn, complete with barebones furniture like desks and chairs. A man in a lab coat and a grim-faced, pale soldier wearing an officer's uniform waved them in; the shoves at their back provided incentive to accept the welcome.

"Officer's an MGB colonel," Frank whispered as they walked toward the barn. "Scientist seems civilian, though. Joint ops like this are rare. This is big."

Cal nodded briefly, trying to take in as much as he could. They were moved past a security desk in the front room, and then through a smaller door into an area with worktables lining the walls and all kinds of scientific equipment scattered around. Chalkboards covered in graphs, equations, and Russian script filled up the back of the room, where a man sat on top of a desk with his arms folded, looking at the newcomers with a smile.

He was a slight, balding man with round spectacles on a round face, wearing a suit and tie over his thin frame, but all the Reds entering the room immediately saluted him. Cal felt he'd seen the man's face before but couldn't place it.

"Please, sit," the man said in accented English, pointing to three stools in front of him. Slowly, each of the Americans took a seat, Cal and Frank still bookending a wide-eyed Zippy. Frank also looked surprised, which Cal took to mean that this guy was someone big.

"Thank you for being here," the Russian said. "I know, of course, you did not *want* to be here, but we are nonetheless grateful. I believe you have met some of my friends before, yes?"

Cal looked around, and saw two more people enter through a side door—a severe-looking middle-aged woman and, incongruously, a girl who couldn't have been more than eleven. Both wore MGB uniforms, both highly decorated. Cal recognized both of them immediately. The woman was Maria Savrova, a Variant who could track a single person across the globe once she'd touched them; the little girl was Ekaterina Illyanova, and Cal knew from personal experience she was as strong as Superman and mean as a rabid dog.

They'd fought a year earlier in the woods outside Prague. The Soviets had set a trap for the American Variants, and Cal, Frank, and Maggie had barely gotten out alive. Ellis Longstreet hadn't.

"Good to see you ladies again," Frank said. "You're looking well."

The little girl spat out something in Russian that didn't sound like she was returning the kindness, and she glared daggers at Cal. The girl's older brother had also been a

Variant, someone who could move like lightning itself, but Cal had gotten his hands on him, aged him something fierce. He wondered, given the girl's reaction, if the Illyanova boy was even still alive.

"I'm sorry about your brother," Cal said as gently as he could. "I truly am."

The top dog chuckled. "The funny thing is that I believe you, Comrade Hooks. From what I have read of you, you are a kind man. A gentle man. You do not belong here."

"Well, then. If it's all right with you, I'll just be on my way, then," Cal ventured with a smile.

The man's chuckle evolved into a short bark of a laugh. "Americans! So full of vigor. Full of confidence. But sadly, since you've allowed yourselves to be used by your imperialist masters, your presence here is no fault but your own now. And we have such plans for you." The man in the suit got up and began to pace. "We have very good intelligence on your Empowered program—that is what we call the people you call 'Variants.' We know you have a very effective means of locating your Empowered, far better than what we are capable of. So, the first thing I'd like to explore, once you've been tested and settled here, is how exactly you manage this."

He's talking about Danny, Cal thought. *They ain't got anybody like Danny. But they sure as hell have enough folks up in our business back home.*

A third figure entered the room—this one far different from the rest. It was a vaguely human-shaped inky shadow, moving in a manner that could only be described as half-walking and half-floating, and it paused to "look" at the American Variants. Cal assumed it was a look, but only because something vaguely head-shaped turned towards him.

"*Ochtet,*" the suited man said.

The shadow's voice replied as a whisper, but one that seemed to be right in Cal's ear. He wondered if everyone heard him that way. Of course, Cal couldn't make out a word of it, but when he looked over to Frank, there was pure shock on his face.

The guy in charge smiled at the Americans once more. "I think you understand now, Mr. Lodge, how we know so much."

Frank nodded slowly. "That's a Variant. He's not even here. He's a shadow—and he can be anywhere he wants to be, more or less."

"Very perceptive," the man said. "He cannot track, of course—that is Comrade Savrova's gift. But yes, when conditions are right, we can have a presence wherever we need to be, including at your Area 51. Or in Washington. We can whisper in ears, even."

Cal nodded slowly. "You knew about Area 51 from your plant, Captain Anderson, which allowed you to send your Variant there."

The Russian nodded, then turned back to the shadow and spoke to it in Russian again. The shadow nodded . . . and promptly disappeared.

"You'll notice that we do not use your null technology here," the man said. "We have no reason to distrust the Empowered working alongside us here. We will, of course, take other measures to ensure you do not use your gifts upon us—this is why we asked you to wear the gloves. But we will not cripple you the way you have crippled your own fellow Empowered at your training facility."

The man rose and put his hands on his hips. "You are loyal Americans, and for that I commend you. Loyalty is important. But as you spend time here, as we begin to study you, I would simply ask you this: To whom are you loyal? To people who fear you? To a country that enslaves you? Or is your loyalty better suited toward each other? Should you not be loyal to your fellow Empowered instead?"

That wasn't the sales pitch Cal had expected. When they had been training him up, the Area 51 folks had been sure to warn them about how they might be tempted if they fell into enemy hands—money, sure. But class, race, and gender, too. Cal had been told all about the Russkies' crazy ideas that the Soviet Union was a paradise free of racial and religious strife.

Loyalty to the Empowered, though? To Variants? That was something else. Cal had long felt a bond with his fellow Variants—shared experiences and all. Apparently, the Russians felt the same way about theirs.

The man left the room, followed by his two Variants, and Cal looked over to Frank questioningly. Frank looked back, wide-eyed.

"That was Lavrentiy Beria, Stalin's number two guy," Frank said quietly. "And I'm pretty sure he's a Variant, too."

31.

August 19, 1949

There was something out there; Danny was sure of it. It was something at the very edge of his consciousness and perception, but it skittered away like a roach when the lights came on every time Danny tried to focus on it. He couldn't tell if it was consciously avoiding his Enhancement or whether it was a kind of automatic reflex.

He didn't even know what it was, but he was sure of one thing: there was something else in Damascus—a Variant, perhaps, or something related to the vortex and what he had felt inside it back at Area 51. It was in Damascus and, more importantly, it didn't want to be discovered. And that made for the most tantalizing mystery Danny had encountered since the MAJESTIC-12 program had begun.

Unfortunately, there was something far more important to do first. And that would likely take him away from Syria for a while. He could only hope that the presence in Damascus would be there when he could return.

"Eyes on target," a voice crackled over the small Handie-Talkie. "Heading out of the café."

Danny keyed his own radio. "Roger that," he replied to Sorensen, who was using his natural camouflage plus another of Mrs. Stevens's "Enhancement suits" to stay far closer to the target than anyone else could be without detection. "Chris, get into position."

A shadow crossed the street above, and Danny looked up to see Christina Vanoverbeke leaping from building to building to keep pace. Thankfully, the night sky of this warm Damascus evening was doing a fine job of keeping her hidden—the last thing they needed was a bunch of locals reporting a strange blonde woman making superhuman leaps across their city.

"Looks like he's following the pattern," Christina reported. "Same as every night so far."

Danny acknowledged the report. Ever since Maggie had landed in Damascus again, her job had been to tail Karilov, to learn his every movement. Naturally, the Soviet agent had taken a whole lot of meetings with al-Hinnawi of late, and given the Russian's involvement in the coup against Za'im, that wasn't surprising. Yet nearly every single night, Karilov would make his way toward a single café in the oldest part of town, one that only served local fare. It seemed the Russian had acquired a taste for *shawarama* and *manakish*, because they were all he ordered.

But it was patterns like those that would get Karilov in trouble. The Soviet probably figured that with Za'im dead and the American agents captured, Copeland and Meade weren't much of a problem—and indeed, the two OPC men still seemed to be at a total loss as to how to proceed. Their strongman was dead and most of his allies had quickly switched sides. Nobody in Syria's power structure was very open to chatting with Americans these days.

"Eyes on target," Maggie chimed in. "He's headed for the box. Over."

"Roger," Danny said, moving a little quicker down the street now. "Rick, report."

"In position," the young man replied. "Right by the transformer, the one Tim pointed out."

"Roger that. Tim, call it."

As the one closest to Karilov, it was up to Tim to give the signal—three quick clicks on the radio—once the Soviet was in position. The "box" was a choke point in the Russian's walk back to his residence, a narrow, high-walled alley that was only about ten yards long and with just one exit on either end.

If I were his trainer, I'd rip him a new one, Danny thought as he moved into position. *I can only imagine what*

Hamilton would do to him. It was a comforting thought, for sure.

The three clicks came over the radio, and Danny broke out into a run. "Go!"

The lights went out first.

Sparks flew overhead as Rick sent a surge of electrical power into the transformer, blowing through its safeguards and knocking out electricity over a six-block area. Danny was immediately plunged into darkness, only the full moon above shining the faintest of light down on the shadowed alley below.

He arrived to take position behind Karilov, who was in the middle of the alley with his hand against one wall, moving slowly through it in the blackout. Sorensen was nowhere to be seen, but that wasn't surprising—between his Enhancement and the darkness, he could be a hairsbreadth away from Karilov and the Russian wouldn't even know it.

A shadow flickered ahead of Karilov at the mouth of the alley. That would be Christina, jumping down to block the exit, as planned. Just ahead of her, Maggie emerged from behind a few crates.

"Hello, Sergei," she purred. "Got a minute?"

Danny saw the Russian pause, then turn and start hustling back up the alley. He got about three feet before he was clotheslined by an invisible force across his chest—Sorensen's arm, most likely—that sent him tumbling to the cobblestones.

Danny hustled forward, meeting Maggie in the middle over Karilov's prone body. "Mags, shut him down," Danny whispered.

Maggie smiled, and at Danny's feet, Karilov's eyes grew wide as saucers, the whites reflecting the moonlight. He choked out a gurgling, stunted scream before fainting, a wet stain spreading at his crotch.

"God, you're scary," Sorensen said from somewhere behind her, his voice coming out of thin air.

Maggie nodded. "Damn right I am."

* * *

Karilov bolted upright and screamed in terror, then looked around the shabby little hovel, confused and concerned, his Enhancement-powered terror replaced with a very real fear that was just beginning to simmer away.

"Where am I?" he demanded in Russian, his voice seemingly swallowed by the shadowy, dimly lit room.

Danny, sitting in the shadows behind Karilov, replied briefly in the same language. "You're not cleared for that, Comrade."

Karilov turned around and looked for Danny's face, hidden largely in darkness. "You're American," the Russian said in English. "You realize you have committed an act of war against both the Soviet Union and the Republic of Syria by detaining me here."

Danny shrugged. "You've already committed an act of war against the United States by illegally detaining several of our diplomatic personnel. However, we're willing to concede this might have simply been done in error, given the change in government here in Damascus, and so long as we get our people back, we'll let it slide. This time."

Karilov stood up from the rickety cot they'd placed him on. "I'm sure I have no idea what you're talking about."

With a sigh, Danny stood and looked around the hovel, rented just two days prior and chosen for its privacy and proximity to the alley where they'd grabbed Karilov. "All right, we can play it that way, Comrade. But then we'll have to go to work on you. See, I don't know how much you know about us, but I imagine you've seen enough to know that the folks of ours you grabbed were different. Special." Danny walked over to the door and knocked; it opened to reveal Maggie and Rick on the other side. "And frankly, we're kind of angry that you took our friends."

Karilov stumbled backward at the sight of Maggie; maybe she was already working on him, maybe he was just remembering the fear in the alleyway. Hard to say, but it didn't really matter. Whatever they were doing to him, it was working.

"Now, I don't really condone torture, Comrade. I really don't. However, when you kidnap American diplomatic agents and take them to Russian soil—and I assume that's where they went, yes?—then I think the usual international norms are thrown out the window," Danny said. "So, you're going to tell us where you sent our friends, one way or the other."

Rick walked toward Karilov and placed a hand on the Russian's shoulder. Karilov let out a scream, practically jumping out of his skin and falling to the floor in a heap.

"Too much?" Rick asked, a few sparks still jumping around his fingertips.

Karilov looked up at Rick from the floor, his fear in full bloom now.

"No, that was a good start," Danny said, crouching down next to Karilov and looking him in the eye. "We don't want to electrocute him right off the bat. You see, Sergei, we want to give you a chance to do the right thing. Otherwise, we may have to fry you bit by bit." Danny took off his left glove, revealing his still-withered hand. Karilov could only imagine *how* it had happened. "Do you want this to happen to you?"

Karilov looked up at Danny's hand as tears began to form in his eyes. "No," the Soviet said feebly. "No."

"Then tell us where our friends are."

"And after?" Karilov said. "What then?"

Danny smiled. "Then we'll give you some interesting options."

* * *

Two hours later, Danny was on the phone, waiting for "Victor Davies" to pick up.

"Yes?" Hillenkoetter said over the line.

"Mr. Davies! This is Mr. Walters. I hope you're well. How are the kids?"

"Fine, fine," Hillenkoetter said impatiently. "You have some news on those missing packages for me?"

"Yes, sir. I believe we tracked them down to a place called Semipalatinsk. It's in eastern Kazakhstan."

There was a long pause and a rustling of paper; Danny figured the boss was digging for a map, just as he himself had done a half hour before. "Well, that's quite a diversion, isn't it?"

"Yes, it is, sir. Amazing how things can get fouled up."

"So, are the folks in Semipalatinsk willing to send the packages back directly? I'm willing to pay for shipping, even throw in a bonus or two." *Can you do a trade? Ours for POSEIDON and maybe even Meyer?*

"Well, the shipping agent I talked to here really isn't authorized to make that sort of arrangement, sir. I'm afraid we'd have to work with the folks there directly. Is that something you want to handle, or shall I do it?" *Karilov can't deal; only the bigwigs in Russia can. You want to reach out, or should we proceed with Plan B?*

"Unfortunately, I don't really have the kind of export licensing I need to get packages out of Kazakhstan from here," Hillenkoetter said. "Since you're already halfway there, why don't you finish it out?" *There's no way the United States is going to talk Variants directly with the Soviet Union. It's your show.*

"I may have to go directly to Semipalatinsk to make that work, sir. Do we have the budget for that?" *Reminder: we would be invading the Soviet Union to effect a rescue.*

"Budget isn't an issue, Mr. Walters. Just need to be sure those packages are secured, and I stress this, one way or the other." *Do it. And remember, whether you trade or invade, either get our people back or make sure they're dead.*

Danny frowned. "Of course, sir. Thank you, sir."

The line went dead, and Danny went back to his map again, looking over the terrain. The Semipalatinsk area bordered Russia proper, Mongolia—a puppet state of the Soviet Union anyway—and the Xinjiang region of China. Not a lot of great options—the nearest remotely friendly area was Pakistan or India, at least eight hundred miles away.

But Xinjiang might not be a lost cause. The Kuomintang and some pro-Russian forces were holding the area against the encroaching People's Liberation Army, and large parts of the area were pretty deserted anyway. They just had to find a friendly Kuomintang commander . . . and avoid the inevitable Soviet advisors surrounding him.

Danny sighed. Nobody had said this was going to be easy. But at this point, it was bordering on ridiculous.

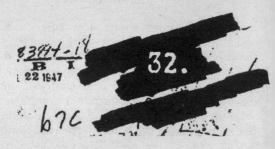

32

August 28, 1949

Frank was getting goddamn tired of the strange bits and pieces of food that had made up his rations over the past week and a half. Twice a day, a bowl of meat and broth was shoved into his cell through a floor-level slot in the door. The broth was salty as hell, the meat was largely on the underdone and chewy side, and Frank found himself actually getting excited when he found a bit of carrot or onion in the mix.

The meat is likely sheep, and it looks like a fair amount of offal in there—hearts, kidneys, tongue. Might be a bit of actual beef, said Kirill Suleimenov, a hapless young Kazakh soldier Frank had absorbed early on during his stay. The Reds were already well aware of Frank's enhancement and had decided to use Kirill in an experiment. They'd hooked Frank up to a host of machines and medical monitors, and then marched Kirill into the lab in cuffs. They'd shot him in the chest just five feet away from Frank and then observed as the transfer took hold.

Frank had tried to use the horrible opportunity to learn more about the base, or anything else, but the Russians were smart. Kirill had been stationed in Semipalatinsk, the town nearby, and knew nothing of use. He'd barely known his duties in the town itself. He'd just followed orders and hoped to fulfill his compulsory service in the army so he could go back and take over his aging father's horse farm.

Frank had cried for Kirill that night.

But he'd nonetheless picked up some Kazakh, which was handy, along with a working knowledge of how Red Army grunts comported themselves. Oh, and he could probably run his own horse farm someday, if he ever needed to—and cook up some fine horsemeat dishes, something Kirill really enjoyed.

At least Frank wasn't truly alone, not with Kirill and everyone else in his head. He knew Cal or Zippy weren't so lucky. After Beria's little pep talk a week and a half earlier, the three Americans had been separated. Frank was taken to a holding cell in the old stables. The wooden-walled cell was cloying and smelled like horseshit, and he had no doubt that the once-every-three-days shower he was permitted wasn't much of a help. His civvies had been taken and exchanged with what looked like Red Army surplus—olive-drab shirt and pants, threadbare boxers and socks, a pair of old parade shoes that had probably lost their luster sometime around the rise of Lenin.

Each day, Frank was marched into one of the Russians' labs. They took blood, made him run a treadmill and exercise—they even watched him eat, monitoring his vitals as he chewed leathery sheep's heart. And they constantly asked him questions: how he was feeling, how he was responding to the various little tests they ginned up. They questioned him extensively after he absorbed Kirill, going so far as to have one of the bigger guards work him over pretty good when he refused.

It didn't work. Every stimulus, every question, everything they threw at him, Frank was determined to remain silent. And for the most part, he did—when the meaty-fisted Cossack used him as a heavy bag, his hands shackled above his head and chained to a roof beam in the barn, Frank did nothing but swear at his tormenter. A lot. In fourteen languages.

That was a week before, and they hadn't tortured him since. The meals came in the morning and in the evening, and he did lab time after the morning meal. They'd occasionally let him into a shoddy little exercise yard behind the old manse, just a penned-in area with some kettle weights and medicine balls. Frank had already developed a cell-bound exercise regimen—sit-ups, push-ups, running in place, pull-ups on an overhead beam—so he just took the opportunity to take long, slow circuits around the perimeter of the yard, looking out over the grassy steppes of Kazakhstan. Maybe he'd been letting Kirill narrate a bit too much in his head—the young man liked to wax poetic about his country and the land—but Frank actually found himself appreciating the grasslands and the herds of horses and sheep that he'd spot off in the distance.

He'd also seen something else the day before. It looked like some kind of tower—too far away to see whether it was steel or wood—rising off in the distance. It was easily at least five miles off, but the manse was up on a hill with fantastic sightlines. Honestly, it might have even been farther, because there were very few reference points among the grasses. But it seemed pretty tall, and it was kind of in the middle of nowhere, no buildings or anything around it for miles.

This information produced a panoply of opinions in his head.

Observation post monitoring approach to the manse area.

Fire watch tower—it's been dry here.

A well of some kind. Water, or oil.

It looks like the shot tower for the Trinity test.

That last notion was particularly interesting. Back in 1945, during the Manhattan project, the scientists in New Mexico had built a hundred-foot-high tower and placed the Trinity test weapon on top. They let it drop from there—and the subsequent mushroom cloud was the very first nuclear bomb detonation in history.

Shot tower.

It made sense. Thanks to the work of the Bekhterev Institute, the Russians knew that the vortex phenomena had been created in part by the detonation of a nuclear weapon at Hiroshima. Frank had been on patrol in Berlin at the time and had seen a similar vortex appear in the labyrinthine bowels of the former Reich Chancellery, all thanks to the efforts of a mad scientist employed by the Nazis—Kurt Schreiber.

Frank hadn't worked with Schreiber at all and had only spotted him at Area 51 once, but was pretty sure that five minutes alone with Schreiber would result in a new voice in Frank's head. But he couldn't be comforted by such thoughts now, because if the Russians were preparing for a nuclear test near where Variants were being housed, it meant they were keen on exploring the link between nuclear detonation and Variant Empowerment.

If there was one, of course. Maybe they'd all just get blown to hell and back and that would be that.

Or maybe that was all just crazy talk. Maybe the Reds were just giving Smokey Bear his due and watching out for grass fires. Frank cautioned himself to not get overly excited about things. Chances were he'd be there for a good while, a prisoner of Beria's Empowered troops in for the long haul.

Frank finished his bowl of stew—there was always a sheet of pasta dough at the bottom for some reason, which was the tastiest part of the whole damn thing—and shoved the bowl back under the door. He heard it hit something, and crouched down to look through the slot.

There was a pair of shining cavalry boots now flecked with leftover broth and tiny bits of meat.

Ah, hell.

Frank stood and moved away from the door as it suddenly swung open. A pair of guards flanked an MGB major in a pristine uniform—well, except for the boots. The man looked familiar, but it took several moments before one of the voices in his head, the double-agent once known as INSIGHT, produced the name. "Boris Giorgievich Illyanov," Frank said with a nod, then continued in Russian. "I trust you are well."

The man grimaced. "I am old, Frank Lodge."

Frank nodded sadly. Frank's team had encountered Illyanov with the other Russian Variants in the woods outside Prague last year. He'd been young at the time—barely a teenager—and his Enhancement made him freakishly fast. That was until Cal came into contact with him, aging Illyanov greatly in order to heal his own grievous wounds. There was never any definitive evidence as to whether Boris could have snapped back from the encounter, or had even lived very long after it.

The man in front of Frank now appeared to be nearly seventy. But looks could be deceiving.

"Come with me," Illyanov said. The two guards entered the cell and prodded Frank with the butts of their new AK-47s. Not really seeing an option, Frank followed the Russian Variant out of his cell and out into the sun.

To his very great surprise, Frank saw Cal and Zippy being marched in similar fashion into the courtyard between the buildings—Zippy from the manse, Cal from the barn/lab building. Frank shared a look with each of them, and they nodded in response. They were OK, as far as Frank could tell, and holding the line as best they could. Cal, though, was considerably older looking—at least mid-fifties, if not more. They'd been working on him, too, no doubt.

Frank also saw a small cadre of similarly uniformed MGB officers in the courtyard. Boris's little sister—Ekaterina, the super-strength girl—was there, as was Maria Savrova. There were two others Frank didn't recognize, but given how they stood together with Savrova and the Illyanova kid, Frank imagined they had to be Variants as well.

When the strange shadow figure showed up next to Ekaterina Illyanova, Frank's suspicions were confirmed.

"Looks like we got a little tent revival going here, Frank," Cal said by way of greeting. "Gang's all here." *Was it all Variants?* Up close, Cal still looked hale, despite his aged appearance, but he hadn't been given the benefit of an old uniform—his clothes were nothing more than castoff rags, and they hadn't even bothered to give him shoes, the bastards.

"Appears to be," Frank confirmed. "Zip, you OK?"

Zippy spared him a smile. "The food's shit. I've been trying to have a word with the staff about it." She was dressed in what Kirill confirmed was Kazakh peasant garb—poofy-looking trousers and a broad white blouse. At least she'd been given some decent shoes.

Savrova turned to the guards and barked in Russian: "Leave us. Fetch the director."

The guards immediately scattered—Savrova clearly had pull. In fact, it seemed that the Russians had integrated their Variants directly into the MGB, giving them ranks and authority within the overall military-intelligence hierarchy. That likely had to do with Beria's influence, Frank figured; his voices agreed.

Speak of the devil.

Beria walked out of the barn, dressed in the uniform of a Marshal of the Soviet Union. Frank knew Beria was deputy premier, and former head of the secret police, and . . . well, there were any number of jobs and titles the man held that would let him wear whatever the hell he wanted. And yet it seemed he wanted to be cut from the same cloth as his . . . fellow Variants?

"My friends," Beria said in English as he approached, arms outstretched. "I had hoped to thank you for your cooperation over the past several days, but that is unfortunately not how you have decided our time together will be. Surely, you understand why we have thus had to keep you as prisoners of war."

So, Cal and Zippy had sealed their lips and taken their punishment right alongside him. Frank felt immensely proud of them.

"Nice try, Comrade," Frank said. "Once again, we are American diplomats, accredited to the U.S. Consulate in Damascus, and we demand to contact our embassy immediately."

Beria stopped and looked positively murderous for a moment, then burst out laughing. "Mr. Lodge, can we please, for a moment, stop with the charade?"

To make his point, Beria held up his hand—which immediately burst into flame.

Well, that settles it.

"We are all Empowered here—Variants, as you would say. But I think this term you use belittles your status and your gifts," Beria said as his hand burned. "*Empowered* is more apt, wouldn't you agree? After all, we have been given power, and we, as the champions of the proletariat, should use it to usher in a new age of socialist peace and security."

Beria waved his hand, and the flames immediately extinguished. His hand appeared unaffected by the fire.

"Well, that's impressive," Cal said. "Must be handy up there in Leningrad. I hear they got some cold winters."

Illyanov moved toward Cal with his hand raised, ready to strike, but Beria put a hand on the man's shoulder. "No, Comrade. This is fine," Beria said in Russian. "They are like us. We can allow them some freedoms, can we not?"

Illyanov sneered at Cal. "He is a subhuman dog, and he has refused to fix what was done to me," the man responded, also in Russian. "He will never join our brotherhood."

"Then he will be destroyed," Beria said gently, pulling Illyanov back into the fold. Beria turned to Frank and smiled. "Yes," he said in English, "that is the choice we now offer you."

Frank rolled his eyes. "Seriously? You're going to play that hand?"

"You have resisted all our efforts to reach out to you," Beria said. "All of you. You had many opportunities to share the details of your Empowerments, and here with us now, you could have cooperated with our experiments. Yes, you could have healed Boris Illyanov, Mr. Hooks, and been treated far better than you have been."

Frank gave Cal a little smile. *Good man. Good job.*

"But we want you to understand something," Beria continued. "You are American, and yes, we are Soviet. But what we are—Empowered—is far bigger than politics, than this Cold War. We all believe, all of us here, that the future will be claimed by the Empowered. We have a duty to lead the proletariat to a better future. And we invite you to join us to lead all nations—the United States, the Soviet Union, all of them—into a new era of prosperity."

Frank thought about this a moment. "So . . . basically, you want us to help you . . . what, rule the world?"

Beria's smile grew wider. "That is the language of the imperialists," he replied. "Of course you would believe this, because you cannot even comprehend a world in which capitalistic dominance of the weak isn't present. But there is a difference between rulership and leadership, one which we can teach you. The Empowered are stewards of humanity, not tyrants. We protect, nurture, and grow the proletariat. And as we unlock the secrets of the phenomena—the ones from Berlin and Hiroshima—we may yet spread the blessings of Empowerment to those who understand the responsibility of such a thing and join the ranks of proletarian champions."

Frank blinked several times, trying to cut through the word soup. The other Russian Variants gazed at Beria with looks ranging from grim determination to utter rapture—but they all seemed to buy what Beria was selling. "So, uh . . . OK. Is the proletariat going to have a choice in the matter?" he asked.

"There is a reason, Mr. Lodge, why your superiors have kept your existence a secret in the United States, and it is the same reason that the Empowered work quietly within the Soviet system," Beria replied. "People fear that which they do not understand, as you well know. If we reveal ourselves too soon, without the proper preparation, the opportunity to lead humanity to its next great evolution will be wasted, and we shall have to hide—or worse, openly fight those who would use us for reactionary, fascist aims."

Cal cleared his throat and stood up a bit taller. "So, way I see it, sir, you're gonna be in charge, and nobody will have a say in that? Sorry, but I can't go along with you there."

In the blink of an eye, Illyanov rushed up to Cal and backhanded him across the face, sending him sprawling onto the ground. "Stupid ape!" the old Soviet roared in

Russian. "How is it you are even Empowered? You are not even human!"

Suddenly, the shadowy figure materialized in front of Illyanov and somehow turned solid enough to put his hands on the speedster's shoulders, stopping him. "This is not how it is to be done, Boris," the shadow said quickly and quietly, the sound entering into Frank's mind like the memory of a whisper. "He is Empowered, like you. He is greater than human, like you. Leave him be."

Frank and Zippy converged on Cal, helping him to his feet. There was a nasty cut on his lip, but he seemed otherwise unharmed. Frank turned to Beria. "Can you get our man a live animal of some kind? A sheep headed for slaughter?" he asked in Russian. "It won't take much, but it will help him immensely."

Beria, however, was staring hard at Illyanov, who had reluctantly allowed himself to be led back to the group by the shadow figure. "We will speak later, Boris Giorgievich," Beria said, sotto voce, before turning to Frank and addressing him in English. "If you want to help your man, then I suggest you cooperate, Mr. Lodge. That goes for all of you. You have until sunrise tomorrow to decide whether you will continue to live like sheep and allow yourselves to be used as pawns by the rich and powerful, or if you will take your rightful place, here with us, as the champions of working people everywhere. That is all."

Zippy finally spoke up. "I think we can save you the trouble, Comrade," she replied, a little too loudly and forcibly; she was definitely working up her courage. "We're not joining you. So, you can take your supervillain shtick and shove it up your ass."

Beria turned and smiled again. "We'll see if you feel any differently in the morning."

THE SECURITY SERVICE

TRANSMISSION INTERCEPT TRANSCRIPT—MI6
29-07-49 0217 GMT
LISTENING STATION KABA
CLASSIFICATION: TOP SECRET

VOICE 1: (Russian) Yes?

VOICE 2: (English) You really need a better phone system, Comrade. Took us less than an hour to get this number.

VOICE 1: (English) Who is this?

VOICE 2: An interested party. I believe you have something of ours. Three somethings, in fact.

V1: Ah. I am impressed. Though perhaps I should not be surprised, given the capabilities of your people.

V2: Well, I have to say, your past efforts surprised us quite a bit. We're overdue for returning the favor.

V1: Finding my private telephone is not quite the same as driving one of your top ministers insane. Or releasing two of your greatest assets. Suborning one of your top scientists. But I am pleased you have at least decided to join the game. It's been terribly boring until now.

V2: Careful what you wish for, Comrade. Meantime, I'm calling to suggest a trade.

V1: Really? A trade? Do tell me more.

V2: You have three of ours. We have two of yours, plus an untrustworthy scientist. Seems like a fair trade to me.

V1: And how would you even begin to conduct this trade?

V2: We know where you are. Just tell your border people to stand down, and we'll hop on over in a 'copter. In and out, ten minutes.

V1: You want me to stand down the border guard? This ridiculous request tells me you're not serious.

V2: There's only one man in the Soviet Union you can't boss around. So don't pretend you can't manage a simple covert border crossing, Comrade.

V1: You're in China.

V2: Of course we're in China. That's no big secret. I'll tell Mao you said hi.

V1: I want to meet. Face to face.

V2: Not this time. This is just a quick prisoner exchange. Then we're up and out. You want a sit-down, we can discuss after everybody's back where they belong.

V1: All right. I assume you will want to bring others with you.

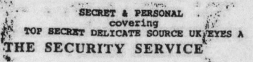
V2: Well, I can't fly a helicopter myself. And yes, we'll be bringing a small party to ensure security.

V1: No more than six.

V2: I can live with that.

V1: You may cross at Tomar. It is roughly 450 kilometers south—southeast of Semipalatinsk. I assume you know where you're going after that?

V2: Of course we do.

V1: You must be here by six o'clock in the morning. Otherwise, there is no deal.

V2: We'll make it work. I have your guarantee of safe passage?

V1: You will not be harmed in Soviet airspace.

V2: See you in the morning, then.

(V2 line disconnects, V1 open line redials)

V3: (Russian) Yes, Comrade?

V1: (Russian) Come see me in my office immediately. We are having guests tomorrow. We will need to welcome them.

(line disconnects)

THE SECURITY SERVICE

WHAT THE BLOODY HELL IS THIS, JACK? ISN'T THAT THE
BIT OF KAZAKHSTAN WHERE UNCLE JOE SET UP HIS TESTING
AREA? WHAT ARE THE YANKS UP TO? MAKE THIS A PRIORITY.
I WANT ANSWERS.——M

33.

August 29, 1949

The banging at his cell door woke Cal up from a fitful sleep. He'd spent half the night staring up at the ceiling, trying to compose himself, to get right with God. He knew he wouldn't join Beria's circus, so he'd figured it might be his last night on Earth, and his last opportunity to make amends.

The Russians had started treating him better after that little meeting in the courtyard. He'd gotten a hand-me-down army uniform and some better shoes. They'd let him bathe, fed him a decent meal for once. He'd asked for a pen and paper, hoping he might write a note to his wife and son, but either the Reds didn't know English well enough to understand, or they'd just ignored him. He'd also been hoping for some livestock, anything to get him a bit healthier and younger, but that wasn't meant to be either.

Then again, a whole lot wasn't meant to be. Hence the late night, talking to the Lord.

Cal had managed to spend a year of active duty in MAJESTIC-12 without killing anybody. That had been one of his most important goals when he'd first signed up, and he had to shoo away a bit of pride when he thought about it. Nobody got extra credit for avoiding murder, he figured; the straight and narrow was narrow for a reason, even more so when your government asked you to be a spy for your country. But he'd managed it, and had still served the United States well, by his count. There were stories about how his great-grandfather came north through the Underground Railroad, then joined the Union Army when it came time to fight the South; he figured he was just doing the same as his ancestors did, and that was enough.

Still, he wanted to see his wife's face one more time. He wanted to tell Winston all he could tell him about life, and walking with God, and how to be strong in the face of everything the world would throw at you. Cal wondered if the MAJESTIC-12 folks would ever divulge even a little bit to his family about how he'd served his country. Even just say that Calvin Hooks died in defense of America. Wouldn't that be grand?

Life was unfair, though. And so Cal waited for dawn, not holding his breath.

His wait was cut short by the knock on his cell door; it seemed whatever charade remained left in his life, however long or short it would be, would commence before daybreak. He was taken out and moved at gunpoint into the courtyard, where a large cargo truck sat idling. The cargo bed was covered with canvas, as was the back gate, so Cal figured they were going for a ride. He looked around the compound one last time, figuring he should remember the place where he'd spent his last night alive.

Frank and Zippy were already inside the cargo area, along with a couple of Red soldiers who looked to be no older than sixteen—but they were armed with nasty-looking rifles, so he figured to behave.

"'Morning, Cal," Frank offered quietly.

"Frank. Miss Zippy," Cal replied. "Guess nobody went and flipped."

Zippy smiled. "I don't think they had any intention of welcoming us into the fold. I think yesterday was more for the Russian Variants' benefit than ours."

"Yeah, Beria knew," Frank said as the truck began to move. "We're gonna be the justification for whatever he's got cooking next. I'm sure he's got it all planned out."

Cal opened his mouth to say something but thought better of it. Cal had orders—unique orders, given to him by Hillenkoetter himself—about what to do should they all be captured. He hadn't had a chance to put them into effect yet because they'd been separated. It was an order Cal had sworn he'd never follow, one that probably meant ending up on the wrong side of the gate with St. Peter.

But now, maybe he'd have to do it.

"If you're captured and it looks like they're going to separate you for good, I'm ordering you to use your Enhancement on however many other American Variants are with you. We cannot let them fall into enemy hands," Hillenkoetter had said on a brisk fall morning in Foggy Bottom.

"Come again, sir?"

The director had smiled sadly at Cal. "I know it doesn't sit right with you, Mr. Hooks, and I'm sorry to have to give you this order. But if it's the difference between letting a Variant fall into Soviet hands or not, then I expect you to carry this out. Deny the enemy any Variants who are with you. I don't care if it's Maggie or Frank or anyone else. Send 'em home to God, son."

Cal frowned. At the time, he'd just nodded. Hadn't had the guile to lie or the courage to resist. Now he'd have to choose, and God help him, he didn't know if he could do it.

Or if he *should* do it.

After several minutes of silence, the truck rolled to a stop with a screech of badly maintained brakes; Cal couldn't help but notice that the Russians didn't do a great job of caring for their machinery in general; seemed like the workers' paradise didn't leave much time to get any real work done. A few moments later, the back flap of the truck was opened, and the two boys with guns stood and motioned the Variants to exit.

The sky was starting to lighten off to the east, and Cal found himself hoping to witness a sunrise just once more. He wasn't usually this pessimistic, or romantic for that matter, but he supposed that was just what folks did and felt when their end arrived. He looked at Frank and Zippy as they stood there, Zippy hugging herself for warmth, Frank looking around earnestly, taking in everything, probably still trying to find them an escape route.

Not yet. He wouldn't yet. Not until Frank gave them a chance at something. Nonetheless, Cal went and stood between his friends, just in case.

They were out in one of the big grassy fields well away from the old buildings, though Cal could see some lights up on a rise far off in the distance and figured that was where they'd come from; the drive was short enough. There wasn't much there, just a rutted dirt road and a whole lot of grass.

And a tower of some kind, made of wood. Had to be a hundred feet high, towering over them. At the top, there was a little shed, with power cables running out from it down the tower to a purring generator on the ground below. And it was busy. There were men in white coats climbing up ladders to the top, going inside the shed. Others were on the ground, standing around a series of makeshift tables, taking notes and watching a few different instruments with moving needles and dials and such.

Cal looked over at Frank, who looked pale. Cal raised an eyebrow, and Frank mouthed a single word: "A-bomb." Cal looked up again at the tower and saw a metal cone protruding from the bottom. An atomic bomb? Probably—Frank had enough expertise in his head to identify what was going on.

Oddly, it was kind of comforting. If the Russians wanted to drop an A-bomb on them, Cal didn't have to worry anymore about murdering his friends so they wouldn't fall into Soviet hands. The Soviets weren't interested in having them around anyways, it seemed.

"Good morning, my fellow Empowered," Lavrentiy Beria said, walking over to them. He had on one of his workers' jumpsuits, and despite the early hour, he was animated. "I trust I don't need to tell you what is happening here."

Zippy held her head high. "Somebody ordered a mad scientist kit?"

Beria laughed. "Something like that. This morning, we change the world forever. Not only do we make the Soviet Union the preeminent power in the world, but we come to an even greater understanding of the Empowered condition."

Cal looked around again and saw that shadow figure off to the side, leaning against the tower in an oddly normal way, like it was waiting for the bus. A few of the other Variants—that scary girl, the speedster he'd aged last year—were also hanging around, observing.

"I think I know what's gonna happen," Cal said. "Either we join up with you, or you're gonna drop that bomb on us, see if there's any changes in that white light you got locked up in Leningrad."

Beria nodded, smiling at Cal. "Very good, Mr. Hooks. You and your colleagues have obviously made the connection between nuclear blasts and the arrival of Empowerment. And yes, perhaps you even have a sense that death itself is a key. But what of actual Empowered deaths? We of course have not tested this yet, because we value the lives of our Empowered. And if you valued your own lives and sought to bring them to their full potential to help humanity, you would join us and avoid such a fate." Beria's face grew serious. "But yes, I do not think you will do this, as much as I would like you to. It gives me no joy to destroy such rare, talented people. But since you would oppose us, we should at least make your deaths a benefit to our scientific inquiry."

Beria looked Cal right in the eye, and Cal stared back. He desperately wanted to live. He had so much to live for, and he wanted to see his wife and boy again. But he was also tired of folks claiming to be better than other folks, something he'd dealt with his whole life. And this charming, smiling Russian was as Godless as they came, seeking to replace the Good Shepherd with his own oversight.

"Best get your equipment ready then," Cal said. "Ain't signing up."

Beria looked over at Cal's fellow Americans, who let their hard stares and silence do the talking. With a shrug and a look of sadness that almost seemed genuine, Beria stalked off toward the scientists. The three Variants were then manhandled over to the wooden tower—and placed directly under it, each one of them tied to one of the tower's legs.

Cal saw Frank's head was still on a swivel, constantly looking and assessing, still trying to find a way out. Zippy was starting to look a lot worse for wear, though, as if the impact of her situation was just hitting her.

"What you got, Frank?" Cal called out.

The former Army man grimaced. "Not a lot. Ropes aren't horrible; we could probably be free right after they pack up and leave. The trick, of course, is getting clear." Cal nodded. Tough to outrun an atomic bomb. "Shelter nearby?"

"Been looking, nothing really helpful. We'd need to put a lot between us and that bomb, whether it's distance or shelter." Frank shrugged. "We're on an empty steppe."

"What can I do, Frank?" Cal asked.

"Just . . . get ready. We'll give it a shot. Help Zip when the time comes."

Cal looked over to Zippy, who had just begun to shed some quiet tears. "Don't you worry, Miss Zippy. We gonna be moving soon."

She gave a brave nod and a half-smile, but Cal could tell her heart wasn't in it.

In the distance, Cal heard a helicopter. It was getting closer.

He looked up into the brightening sky . . . and saw *two* helicopters. Coming from different directions.

Cal turned to Frank, who had a look of disbelief on his face and maybe just a glimmer of hope in his eyes. "Frank?"

"That's American," Frank said quietly. "Looks like a HUP-1, if I'm not mistaken. Navy bird."

"Ain't no Navy out here, Frank," Cal said.

"Trust me. Got a guy in my head who says he was overseeing the prototype testing a few years back. Question is, what's she doing out here?"

The other helicopter—Russian-built, Cal assumed, given the big red star on it—landed pretty close to the tower and all the scientists, while the first one circled about, as if to get a good look at things, before landing a bit farther away. It was unmarked, which certainly lent credence to Frank's claim that it was American made. Couldn't have a U.S. Navy aircraft enter Soviet airspace all marked up with the red, white, and blue.

Several Russian jeeps approached from over the low ridge, each packed with soldiers. It definitely felt like the welcoming committee for that helicopter. Beria, meanwhile, was yelling out orders and the scientists were packing up quickly, at the same time as the soldiers present began to check their weapons. The Russian Variants were spreading out, and Cal lost track of a few of them in the hustle and bustle. Not good.

"Work your ropes," Frank said. "We gotta be ready."

"For what?" Zippy asked.

"If I knew, I'd tell you."

Cal began wiggling his wrists around, ignoring the rope burn as he tried to loosen his bonds. Meanwhile, the hatch on the side of the American helicopter opened up, and two people emerged, making their way toward the Russian encampment—and the big atomic bomb.

"Well . . . I will be damned," Cal muttered as the sun peeked over the ridge and illuminated the newcomers.

It was Danny Wallace and Maggie Dubinsky.

Cal was about to call out to Frank when he felt tugging at his ropes. He looked over his shoulder and saw . . . nothing? A little blur of movement?

"Cavalry's here," came a distinctly American voice, seemingly out of nowhere.

For a split second, Cal saw a white man in his thirties crouched behind him, untying his bonds. Then it was all blurry again.

"You one of us?" Cal whispered.

"MAJESTIC," the voice responded. "Get ready to move."

August 29, 1949

Maggie walked across the grasslands a step or two behind Danny, surveying everything she could and bringing all her training to bear. There were at least thirty people surrounding that derrick—which Danny had said likely contained a goddamn A-bomb—and six jeeps speeding down the road toward them, so anywhere from twelve to twenty-four more bodies in the mix. That would be too many for one go-round. She'd have to work in batches, and work fast, to incapacitate that many people. And the odds were good that at least two, maybe as many as four, would chose the fight option of "fight or flight" and make things even harder.

"If this deal goes south, this is gonna get ugly. There's too many," she said quietly.

"They're not gonna deal," Danny replied. "And I got a bead on . . . six other Variants besides our people. Confirming one of them appears to be Lavrentiy Beria."

"Super," Maggie replied. "Any idea how they'll affect the plan?"

"Nope. 'Best-laid plans' never accounted for new Variants."

The Russian troops spread out across the field, rifles aimed, but at a considerable distance. At least half were beyond the reach of Maggie's abilities, which was a pretty smart move, she had to admit. Of course, the more they walked, the more it looked like the Russians might catch themselves in a crossfire. Were they that dumb? Possibly.

Or perhaps Beria didn't care how many people died, so long as the Variants were killed or captured.

Maggie felt her anger rise. This wouldn't end well for them.

"Maggie, ease up on the rage," Danny hissed. "I . . . I can't afford to just punch Beria in the face when I see him."

Maggie closed her eyes and made a conscious effort to rein in her emotions. After all this time, shit like that still happened. Frustrating. "Sorry."

"Not to worry," Danny said. "I'm seeing movement at the tower. Looks like Sorensen is doing his job. If we make it out of here alive, we gotta figure out how to extend his camouflage to others."

"Shut up," Maggie whispered as Beria began walking toward them, surrounded by at least six armed guards and officers. "It's show time."

The two stopped about fifty yards from their helicopter—and a good hundred yards away from the tower and the Soviet scientists. The Red Army guys were taking positions about thirty yards away, with at least a dozen rifles aimed at them. Soon, Beria and his people were only about ten feet away. Danny held up four fingers—there were four Variants in total in front of them. Maggie instantly recognized the Illyanov siblings from their encounter in Czechoslovakia, but the abilities of the other two, including Beria, were a mystery.

"You must be my mystery caller," Beria said simply.

Danny nodded. "That's right. Your people are in our helicopter. Where are ours?"

"Secured. I'm sure you know what's going on here today."

"About time you guys caught up to us," Danny replied.

Beria frowned and looked down at his shoes a moment, as if collecting his thoughts. "Your people are stubborn," he said finally. "I would make the same offer to you I made to them, but I feel as though this would be a waste of time."

"Let me guess," Maggie chimed in. "Join up? Rule the world in the name of communism?"

"Something like that," Beria said, a half-smile appearing. "And I assume you have a plan to rescue them and leave, given that I have no intention of releasing them or you."

"Goes without saying," Danny said as he evened out his stance. Maggie did the same, appreciating Beria's lack of bullshit, if nothing else.

"Many Empowered people could die because of this," Beria cautioned. "There are too few of us to be wasted in such a way. We are stronger together than fighting each other."

Danny shrugged. "You and yours are more than welcome to come with us if that makes you feel any better."

"No, thank you," Beria said. "*Teper!*"

Beria raised his arms and a giant gout of pure yellow flame exploded out of his hands toward Maggie and Danny. Both of them hit the ground immediately and Maggie let loose with both proverbial barrels, sending abject fear out from her in waves of pure red terror. Danny moaned next to her—she was going more for brute power than accuracy, and no doubt he'd caught a whiff.

Then the screaming started, and Maggie smiled, even as shots began zinging past overhead. The flames sputtered and died, and she looked up to see Beria running away as fast as he could.

Maggie grabbed Danny and moved forward, away from the grass now completely engulfed in flames, diving to the right to use the remaining tall grass, the stuff that wasn't yet on fire, as cover. The Russians that had been in front of them moments earlier were nowhere to be found.

"Let's go," she said, letting the fear slough away.

* * *

Frank saw the flames erupt about a hundred yards off and knew that whatever Danny had planned, it had either just been shot to shit or it was going perfectly. He hoped for the latter.

Weapons, then sabotage. Move.

His hands free, Frank grabbed one of the distracted guards from behind and snapped his neck in one fluid motion—an incredibly hard move that he wouldn't have been able to pull off without the instruction in his head. Frank grabbed the poor soldier's rifle before he hit the ground, and turned to find Cal gently laying another boy on the ground, looking a little bit younger for it. Cal handed the rifle to the blur—only to realize that this new Variant's camouflage didn't actually hide whatever he was carrying.

"Zip, grab the rifle," Frank said, quietly as he could. "Everybody down." Frank hit the deck along with everyone else, then looked around. "New guy, where are you?"

"Right next to you," came a voice to Frank's left. "Sorensen."

He's good. "What's the plan?"

"The deal was to trade a couple other Variants for you three, but Danny always figured the Reds wouldn't play according to the rules. So, it's a rescue now."

When did we get two tradable Variants? "Who else you got?"

"Yamato, who controls electricity, is working it from the left side there. Christina's a leaper—she's working her way around on the right to help us from behind. We also have null grenades."

"Come again?"

"Null grenades. That crazy housewife managed to create grenades that'll create those null zones on impact. Each one lasts about a minute."

Frank smiled, then gave a listen to the multitude of voices coursing through his head.

Even the odds.
Create distractions.
Sabotage.
Kill Beria if possible.

"OK. We need distractions. Blow up a jeep or two, send some others running free. Take out as many soldiers as you can. We meet at the helicopter you came in on. If that's damaged, head for the Russian bird. Do *not* damage either 'copter. Got it?"

"Got it." A moment later, Frank saw the faintest blur heading off toward one of the jeeps.

"Cal, how we feeling?"

The black man smiled at him. "A lot better than a few minutes ago."

"I'm putting you on Variant duty. Find 'em, drain 'em, take 'em out."

"Frank, I ain't gonna—"

"I know, I *know*. Just take 'em out of the game. Move. Pick up as much juice as you can along the way."

Cal nodded and hauled himself up and over to one of the legs of the tower, using it as cover. "Zip, you and I, we got trained for this. You can do it."

The young woman nodded nervously.

Scared.

First combat.

Liability.

"Shut up," Frank hissed, then glanced back at Zippy, who was looking at him strangely. "Sorry, not you. You stay behind me as we go forward. You cover the right flank and the back. I'll take left and front. These are AK-47s, thirty rounds, don't waste bullets. You see some ammo on the ground, grab it."

Zippy held up a cartridge and managed a weak smile. "On it."

"Good. Let's go."

Frank crouch-ran toward another of the legs. Three Red soldiers were rushing toward the field where Beria had let loose; Frank stopped them in three shots, then swiveled and took out a scientist who'd been yelling, "They're loose!" in Russian. *Just what we didn't need.*

Quickly checking to see if Zippy was still following, Frank then dashed over to one of the bigger cargo trucks, laying down cover fire as he went. They managed to get behind the truck just as bullets pockmarked the ground behind them.

The truck.

"Get in," Frank said, yanking open the passenger door and motioning for Zippy to lead. She dove for the driver's seat with the good sense to keep her head down, and Frank jumped in after.

There was a shadow waiting for them inside.

"What the—"

A hand materialized and sent Zippy's head into the steering wheel, knocking her senseless. Frank reflexively reached out to grab the arm it was attached to, only for it to dissolve into shadow once again. Then a fist caught him squarely in the jaw, sending him back out of the truck onto the grass.

"You can't fight me," the shadow's voice hissed in Russian as it climbed out of the truck. "You can't even lay a finger on me."

Frank got up off his ass and, staggering slightly, began to throw punches at the shadow; all he got for his trouble was laughter.

He may not risk materializing if you keep at him.

Frank kept swinging, and the shadow kept laughing—but at least there were no more fists for the time being.

Now it was just a question of what to do next, before his arms got tired. All the voices were pretty silent on that point.

* * *

Danny followed Maggie as they dashed across the steppe, crouched low. Bullets continued to whiz past overhead, but an explosion from around the tower told him that Sorensen had freed Frank, Cal, and Zippy—and that they were doing as expected. Danny figured he didn't need to tell Frank what to do, given that he had a bunch of top military minds already in his head.

A bolt of lightning grabbed Danny's attention; Yamato had just fried several soldiers to their right. Immediately, Danny and Maggie took off at a dead run toward the light and met up with the young man just as he was gathering the dead Russians' weapons. He tossed an AK-47 to Danny but hesitated when he came to Maggie. "You know how to use one of these?" Yamato asked incredulously.

Maggie grabbed the rifle out of his hands, checked the action, then raised it and fired toward a soldier a good seventy-five yards off. He went down. "I think I got this, kid," she said impatiently.

Danny looked up quickly—there was a Variant coming toward them, and fast. "Down!"

Too late. Yamato cried as a gunshot rang out and a blood-red stain appeared in his gut. "Fuck! Oh, fuck!" The teen-ager fell, and Danny fired his weapon off in the general direction of the Variant, the rapidly parting steppe grass giving him a feeble target.

"He's heading for the helicopter!" Danny yelled. "He's going to get the others!'

He took off at a dead run, leaving Yamato behind in Maggie's care. The gut shot would be painful as hell, but he'd linger long enough for Cal to reach him. Probably. Maybe.

As Danny ran, the rotors began turning. Boris Illyanov likely was in the pilot's seat. If nothing else, at least that would keep the speedy bastard in one place.

Just as the runners left the ground, Danny made it to the door and jumped in. Suddenly, there in front of him, was Ekaterina, the little girl with the big goddamn muscles.

She smiled and threw a fist at his gut.

It barely registered.

Danny smiled back as her grin evaporated.

"Null-generators," he said, not bothering to find the right words in Russian. "Otherwise, our friends here would be free to escape."

Pushing her aside toward the still-bound captives in back—he kind of felt bad about that for a brief moment—he moved up to the cockpit and held his rifle to Boris's head. "Take her up," he said. "We have things to do."

* * *

Cal moved through the shadows, relying on his Area 51 training and plain old luck to attack from the fringes of the chaos. He'd managed to lay six people low—just enough to age them a year or two and knock them out cold, while giving him the vigor of a healthy man in his thirties, give or take. Most of them were soldiers, though a scientist who turned around at the wrong time ended up aged a little more than Cal would've liked. But he'd live, and that was the most important thing.

The problem was Beria was nowhere in sight. That was someone Cal wouldn't mind grabbing more than a few years from, but with all the people running about—and a few jeeps careening around the camp—Cal could barely identify anybody.

"*Ne dvigat'sya!*"

Cal turned to see another young soldier—why did the whole damn Red Army look like a bunch of high school kids?—about ten feet away, pointing his rifle at him, his hands trembling. He didn't need a translation to get the gist: if the kid wanted him dead, he'd be dead. Instead, cursing himself for not paying attention, Cal slowly raised his hands. "OK, son. I got my hands up," Cal said quietly and, he hoped, soothingly. "You got me dead to rights. Let's just take it easy, now."

The boy raised his rifle and started yelling in Russian—until a woman came out of nowhere and landed right on top of him, driving him into the grass. Hard.

"What in God's name?" Cal blurted.

The woman—a petite young blonde wearing a flight jumpsuit and boots and carrying an assault rifle, just smiled. "I figure you're one of us, yeah? Not many black men in the Russian Army."

Cal ducked as bullets whizzed by. "Get down!"

Instead, the woman jumped high—about fifty goddamn feet high—and sprayed a nearby area with automatic fire.

She was back on the ground in two seconds. "Sorry about that," she said, finally crouching down next to Cal. "I'm Christina."

"Cal Hooks," he replied. "You see Beria from up there?"

"Hang on." And up she went again, this time making it to the derrick holding the Soviets' A-bomb. She grabbed hold about forty feet off the ground and looked around for several moments before leaping back down next to Cal once more. "Spotted him! Heading for the Russian helicopter!"

"We just gotta get him before he sets us on fire," Cal said. "Lord help me, never thought I'd say that."

Christina just smiled. "You just get over there, fast as you can," she said, holding up an unusual-looking grenade. "I'll take out his Enhancement."

And then she jumped once more—so high and so fast, Cal lost sight of her.

Cal started running, dodging from cover to cover—behind trucks, tables, equipment. There was less gunfire now, for some reason. Maybe the others had put a nice big dent in the Russian numbers. Of course, somebody would have a radio, so they couldn't bet on having the advantage for long. No doubt there was already backup on the way.

Finally, Cal saw the helicopter and Beria's balding head as he ducked and ran toward it. Swearing slightly under his breath—he knew he'd feel bad about it later, if there even *was* a later—Cal took off at a dead run.

Bullets skittered ahead and behind him, and Cal did his best to zigzag across the steppe, trying to cover the thirty or so yards quick as he could. He looked up just as Christina fell from the sky, landing right in front of Beria and dropping her grenade. There was a flash—and his power was gone.

Then Cal saw the Russian pull a pistol and shoot Christina in the head.

"NO!"

Cal ran faster, fast as he could, and came up behind Beria just as he began heading into the helicopter, tackling the man to the ground. Cal put his hands on Beria's face and willed his Enhancement to the fore with a prayer for justice . . .

. . . and nothing happened. The grenade was still active.

Beria lashed out with a fist, catching Cal squarely on the jaw, sending him reeling backward onto his ass.

"You . . . you killed that girl!" Cal stammered as he struggled to get to his feet, his head swimming.

Beria laughed and reached for his holster—but his gun had been jarred loose by Cal's tackle. Turning, the Russian jumped into the helicopter. It began to rise into the air, leaving Cal no choice but to duck for cover as the gunners opened fire on him. Pain lanced through his leg—a stray bullet had caught him, sending him crumpling to the ground in agony.

Cal crawled over to Christina's body, hoping beyond hope that she'd survived, but the bullet hole in her forehead left no debate about it. Whispering a quick prayer for her soul, he drained her of what life he could—and felt the wound on his leg close up somewhat. The grenade's effects must've worn off. He'd be limping, but he'd be mobile.

He looked around to see much of the area deserted. There were bodies everywhere, mostly those Russian Army boys and a few scientists. And off about thirty yards, Cal could see Frank Lodge getting the living crap beat out of him by what looked like a demonic shadow from hell.

Cal looked back at Christina, saw the pouch at her belt, reached inside, and found another of those queer grenades. He flipped a little thing on the side—it was the only button or switch he could find—and it gave off a shrill beep. Getting up on his knees, he flung it toward Frank as hard as he could.

A moment later, the shadow coalesced into a very surprised-looking white man in his thirties. Frank wiped the look off his face with a right hook that looked like it could've downed a horse.

Staggering to his feet, Cal limped over as quick as he could, watching as Frank sank to his knees, utterly spent. When he finally reached him, he could see Frank's face was a welt of cuts, bumps, and bruises. He looked like he'd been fifteen rounds with Joe Louis.

"Come on, Frank," Cal said. "We gotta get up, get moving."

Dazed, Frank nonetheless managed to rise. "The others?" he mumbled.

"We lost that girl, Christina. Where's Zippy?"

Frank nodded over to one of the trucks. "Inside there. Knocked out."

Cal rushed over to the truck, trying to ignore the pain in his leg, and found Zippy in the driver's seat, woozy and sporting a cut on her forehead. "OK, Miss Zippy. Time to get you out of there. Gimme your hand."

With some effort—including having to weather a great deal of pain from his leg—Cal managed to get the girl out and on her feet. Frank joined them at the truck; he'd even managed to pick up a stray AK-47 off the ground.

"Now what?" Cal asked.

Frank looked at the Russian 'copter heading off toward the horizon. "We need our ride. Let's go."

It didn't take long. Once they got out from under cover, they saw the American bird about forty yards off, Maggie and a now-visible Sorensen covering the door with rifles. Maggie spotted them and started waving and shouting.

"*Cherez dve minuty i podscheta golosov.*"

The Russian voice came from loudspeakers mounted on the tower.

"Frank?" Cal asked.

"Two minutes and counting," Frank said, the color receding from his face. "Move!"

Cal grabbed Zippy's hand and ran—harder than he'd ever run in his life.

35.

August 29, 1949

Maggie watched as her fellow Variants took off at a dead run. She wasn't sure what the broadcast was all about, but she had an idea—and it wasn't good.

"Get ready to take off once they're on board!" she shouted over the din of the rotor. "I think we're in for it."

"*Odna minuta, tridtsat' sekund i podscheta golosov.*"

"Danny! What is that?"

Danny poked his head out of the helicopter door. "Ninety seconds. Get in here and put a gun to Boris's head. Now!"

Maggie switched places with Danny, marching up to the cockpit and putting the barrel of her rifle right against Illyanov's temple. "When I give the all clear, you get us out of here as fast as you can, you read me?"

The recently elderly Russian just looked at her sadly. "I don't want to die either."

The helicopter jostled as the rest of the team piled aboard. Faintly, she could hear the loudspeaker again.

"Go! Now!"

Boris needed no encouragement, pulling up on the controls and sending the helicopter into the air with a lurch, heading straight away from the bomb. It didn't seem nearly fast enough.

Maggie went back to check on the others. Yamato was sweating profusely and barely conscious, while the others looked a lot worse for wear.

"Cal, we got wounded," Maggie said, kneeling beside him. "Can you help?"

He nodded, trying to catch his breath. "Null-generators," he gasped.

Maggie reached over to the hull of the helicopter and flipped a switch. She felt her emotional senses immediately snap back into action.

"Maggie! No!" Danny cried out. But it was too late.

The side door of the helicopter crumpled and flew across the compartment, barely missing Danny as it slammed into the wall.

POSEIDON and Julia Meyer were still aboard, and Maggie had just let them loose.

Immediately, Maggie latched onto the emotions of the two Variants, but they almost immediately disappeared out of range. POSEIDON flew out the open hatch, likely connecting with the ground using his telekinetic pull, while Julia just sank right through the floor of the helicopter, leaving her bindings and clothes behind.

"Shit!" Maggie yelled, then wheeled around and flipped the switch back once again.

But Boris Illyanov was gone, the pilot's seat empty.

A shot rang out inside the cabin.

Maggie turned once more to find Frank Lodge with a rifle in his hand—and Boris Illyanov on the floor in front of him.

Ekaterina screamed, as only a terrified little girl could.

Danny pushed past Maggie and headed for the cockpit. "We got thirty seconds." He settled into the pilot's seat and pushed the 'copter forward as much as he could. "Everybody brace!"

Maggie hunkered down onto the floor—they had stripped out the seats of the helicopter—and pulled the Russian girl close. It was the only thing she could think to do.

* * *

Julia Meyer sank deep into the earth from her fall, and had to claw her way up, finally reaching the steppe and gasping for air. About fifty meters away, she could see the Variant they called POSEIDON shaking loose from his shackles.

She didn't know why the Americans were so keen to leave, and didn't really care. The scary woman, Maggie, had slipped up—and both she and POSEIDON had been ready to take advantage. They were free, and that was the most important part.

"*Desyat'.*"

The loudspeaker was faint—they were a good kilometer from the tower that had interested the Americans so much. Julia didn't understand Russian.

"*Devyat'.*"

POSEIDON had stopped and was staring at the tower now.

"*Vosem'.*"

Suddenly, the Russian began frantically pulling at the remaining bonds around his legs.

"*Sem'.*"

He was shouting something at her now, but she had no idea what he was saying. He seemed pretty agitated.

"*Shest'.*"

Finally, he seemed to give up and started flying through the air toward her, using his Enhancement.

"*Pyat'.*"

He landed next to her and grabbed her arm. A split second later, they were airborne.

"*Chetyre.*"

"What is it? What are you doing?" Julia demanded in English.

"*Tri.*"

They crashed to the earth some fifty yards away. Julia felt a bolt of pain in her arm—it felt broken.

"*Dva.*"

"Damn it! What are you doing?" she said, this time in German.

"*Odin.*"

They were airborne once more, the Russian nearly pulling her arm out of her socket, causing her to scream.

But the sound never made it out before they were swallowed in light and heat. And then they were gone.

* * *

Danny pulled up higher as the sky went bright yellow all around him, then just as quickly darkened. He knew the shock wave would come at any—

The helicopter surged forward and pitched hard, spinning round like a top. Danny jerked back on the controls, hoping that they'd at least stay airborne. He could feel the temperature around him rising quickly, even as the air suddenly became impossibly dry and harsh.

And then everything went black.

What the hell?

Danny tried to move, but there was nothing *to* move. He tried to speak, then scream, but he had no mouth, no voice. Nothing.

Jesus. I just died.

There was a white light ahead, swirling in the darkness, growing brighter. Maybe that was the tunnel of light he'd heard about in church. His first thought was to go toward it, but as much as he willed himself to move, he was still formless.

Instead, the light started to come to him. As did . . . voices.

So *many* voices. As if the entire world was trying to whisper to him at once.

Danny looked into the light as it neared, and saw it for what it was—the vortex. But now, he could see forms in the formlessness, swirling bodies of some kind inside it.

Bodies.

That's what they were. Bodies. People. *Inside the vortex.*

The voices grew more intense. They were talking, not whispering. Some were shouting. More and more of them, all at once.

They were angry. If Danny could've pressed his hands to his ears to keep them out, he would've. But there were so many that it probably wouldn't have mattered.

The vortex washed over him, and Danny prepared himself for the intense pain he'd felt when he reached out to touch it back at Area 51. But there was nothing.

Instead, he was on a rolling plain, something like the steppe that had been under him a moment earlier. But this was pure white, and the sky was gray. And there were . . . shadows . . . on the plain. Dark shadows in the shape of people.

In that moment, Danny knew. He knew and he was horrified.

Then the shadows rose up from the plain and began hurtling toward him. Hundreds, thousands . . . *millions.*

And then all was black again.

* * *

Frank saw Danny go limp just as the 'copter began bucking, and knew something had going terribly, horribly wrong. He let go of the straps he'd been clinging to and found himself flying toward the cockpit—as planned, but it was a helluva way to go. He slammed into the back of the copilot's seat and reached for the now-gyrating stick, grabbing it and yanking it upward in an attempt to steady things out.

Didn't work. They were spinning well out of control.

"Anybody ever fly a helicopter?" Frank muttered as he managed to squeeze himself into the seat.

Full speed on your tail rotor, ease back on your main rotor speed. Level off—going higher isn't going to help you, came the voice of Lt. Reginald Cooper, U.S. Army Air Corps— who had never, to Frank's knowledge, ever flown a helicopter. But it was better than nothing—at least someone was talking to him.

Doing as instructed, Frank managed to wrestle the bird back into control—just as a second shockwave hit, sending debris surging around the aircraft.

Just put her down. If you're not dead now, you'll probably survive.

"Probably?" Frank yelled.

Just do it.

Frank eased the aircraft lower. He could barely see the ground with all the crap flying around him but caught enough of a look to pull up hard and land with slightly less force than an actual crash. He cut the engines immediately and reached over to check Danny's pulse on his neck—his heart was beating incredibly fast.

"Well?" Frank asked, but none of the voices replied. *Something new.*

Frank turned to check on his passengers. Maggie and Sorensen were shaken but generally OK. Cal had seen better days. Yamato, though—he didn't have long.

And then there was Ekaterina, who shoved Maggie aside with enough force to send her flying into a wall. And that was when Frank realized that the null-generators were down altogether—that was why the voices were still in his head. The radiation from the blast must've knocked them out of commission.

Frank grabbed a rifle from the floor and leveled it at the kid—but she already had Cal in a headlock and seemed quite furious enough to snap the man's neck.

"Ekaterina, I am sorry about your brother, I truly am," Frank said in Russian, training the rifle at the girl's head. "But killing someone else will not bring him back."

"I should kill all of you!" she cried out. "You are all dogs! You could've been champions of the people, and you selfishly chose yourselves instead!"

Frank lowered the gun slightly. "Ekaterina . . . where is Lavrentiy Beria now?"

"How should I know?" she answered petulantly.

"Exactly. Because instead of coming for you, he left you and your brother behind. He left you where he had set off an atomic bomb. He left you to die."

"Liar!"

Frank shrugged. "Then where is he? All his talk of 'Empowered unity,' and where was he when you needed him most? We were supposed to be rare, gifted people, people to be saved and nurtured so they could lead. But he sacrificed you. You and Boris. He left you there."

"No!" Ekaterina's face was an anguished mask now, and tears were sliding down her cheeks.

"He didn't know you and Boris would be on board our helicopter. He didn't know if you'd escape. And he didn't care. He could've waited to detonate the bomb, and he didn't."

Ekaterina began crying in earnest, choking back sobs and loosening her grip on Cal, who gently moved her arms from his neck—then took her into his own arms.

"Um, Cal, you know . . . you could be . . . " Frank said as he lowered his weapon, hoping he'd get the hint.

He did, but he wasn't going to play it that way. "Ekaterina, honey, I need to go save this young man over here, OK? Just give me a minute here and let me help him. He's one of us, and he needs me right now."

Frank translated, and Ekaterina nodded slightly. Cal then leaned over to touch Rick Yamato on the leg. Almost immediately, Cal's hair began to grow gray, then white. His skin began to sag, and his muscles became ropy. Yamato, meanwhile, began to breathe easier.

"Cal?"

"Boy was close," Cal said, speaking in the dry, cracked voice of an old man. "Should pull through. But I'm done for a while, Frank. Need to rest."

Frank nodded, then turned back to Ekaterina. "We do take care of each other, Ekaterina," Frank said in Russian. "And we would take care of you. But if you want to get out here, or somewhere else in Kazakhstan, I will let you go."

The girl's eyes widened, and she seemed to think about things for several long moments. Ultimately, she simply leaned back against the bulkhead of the 'copter and closed her eyes.

Frank turned to Maggie. "Help me with Danny. Let's get out of here."

FIELD REPORT—ADDENDUM
AGENCY: Central Intelligence Agency—State Department
Office of Policy Coordination—Department of Defense
PROJECT: MAJESTIC—12
CLASSIFICATION: TOP SECRET—MAJIK EYES ONLY
TO: POTUS
FROM: DCI HILLENKOETTER CIA
CC: LTG VANDENBERG USAF, LCMR WALLACE USN, DR BRONK
CIA
SUBJECT: KAZAKHSTAN OPERATION
DATE: 3 SEP 49

The following serves as an addendum to CIA Intelligence
Report #743 dated 3 Sep 49 and makes reference to said
report throughout.

OPERATION SUMMARY

A strike team led by LCMR Wallace, and including Variant
agents Sorensen, Yamato, Vanoverbeke, and Dubinsky,
infiltrated Soviet territory (Kazakh SSR) early on 29 Aug
49 to rescue Variant agents Hooks, Lodge, and Silverman.
The operation was a qualified success.

MAJESTIC—12 Variants encountered several Soviet
Variants, along with at least two squads of Red Army
regulars, and witnessed the successful detonation of the
Soviet Union's first atomic weapon, confirming suspicions
that the Soviets' progress in creating such a weapon was
far more advanced than NATO forces believed.

The strike team and rescued Variants also confirmed that Soviet Deputy Premier Lavrentiy Beria appears to possess Variant Enhancement, a potentially destabilizing factor in bilateral relations going forward.

SOVIET VARIANTS AND DISPOSITION

The following Soviet Variants were identified during the course of the operation.

— Lavrentiy Beria: The deputy premier was seen generating flames without an evident source. The flames were projected up to ten feet away and engulfed up to five feet square. The extent of his ability remains unknown. He is believed to have escaped and remains at large, presumably still in power.

— Boris Giorgievich Illyanov: The MGB officer remained at the advanced age inflicted upon him by Hooks last year (ref: MAJIK report 25 Jun 48), but also retained his speed Enhancement. Illyanov was critically wounded by Lodge in the engagement and did not survive.

— Ekaterina Giorgievna Illyanova: The MGB officer, aged 11, retained her strength Enhancement. She was successfully captured during the engagement.

— Maria Ivanova Savrova: The MGB officer was present during the engagement, but did not apparently make use of her tracking Enhancement. It is unknown whether she escaped the engagement or the test detonation.

— Unidentified Variant 1: This Russian male, approximately 32 years of age, can become an insubstantial shadow, and phase parts of his body into form while the rest remains insubstantial. From the description given by Hooks, Lodge, and Zimmerman, this appears to be the same unidentified form seen by Dubinsky and Stevens at Bethesda Naval Hospital on 22 May 49. We believe his Enhancement may also include a type of projection or spatial displacement, allowing him to appear, as a shadow, at great distances. It is unknown whether he escaped the engagement or the test detonation. This Variant was previously unknown to subject INSIGHT, according to Lodge.

— Unidentified Variant 2: Male, late 20s, detected by Subject-1 during the engagement. Enhancement unknown. Disposition unknown. Unknown to subject INSIGHT.

— Unidentified Variant 3: Male, late 40s, detected by Subject-1 during the engagement. Enhancement unknown. Disposition unknown. Unknown to subject INSIGHT.

— Subject POSEIDON: Captured trying to escape Area 51 with assistance from Julia Meyer and Karl Schreiber (ref: MAJIK report 17 Aug 49). Brought to Kazakhstan for potential prisoner exchange. Escaped and believed to be killed during the test detonation.

- Julia Meyer: Former MAJESTIC-12 Variant, believed to have communicated covertly with POSEIDON and Schreiber while at Area 51. Brought to Kazakhstan for potential prisoner exchange. Escaped and believed to be killed during the test detonation.

MAJESTIC-12 VARIANTS AND DISPOSITION

Agents Dubinsky, Lodge, Silverman, and Sorensen returned safely to U.S. territory with only minor injuries. As for the rest:

- CMDR Wallace: Wallace awakened on 1 Sep 49 from a comatose state, apparently brought on by the inter-action of Variant deaths and the test detonation (see below). He has since been cured of any linger-ing injuries from the operation, as well as the hand injury suffered on 30 June 49, thanks to intervention by Hooks.

- Calvin Hooks: With a stop at a farm in Kuomintang-held northern China, Hooks was able to heal his injuries suffered in the engagement and treat oth-ers. I've authorized compensation for the 77 sheep and 4 cows lost by the landowner.

•••••••••••••
* TOP SECRET *
•••••••••••••

- Richard Yamato: Yamato suffered a critical gunshot wound to the abdomen during the engagement, but was successfully evacuated and subsequently treated by Hooks. He has made a full recovery.

- Christina Vanoverbeke: According to Hooks, Agent Vanoverbeke was shot and killed by Beria as the latter escaped the engagement. Her body was not recovered and is presumed lost in the subsequent test detonation. We are developing a cover story and will notify her family accordingly, providing full death benefits. A star will be added anonymously to the proposed Central Intelligence Agency's Memorial Wall in her honor.

All surviving Variant assets have been deemed to be fit for duty and are available for assignment.

OTHER ASSETS AND DISPOSITION

Dr. Karl Schreiber remains in custody under heavy security at Area 51. He has yet to cooperate with any inquiry into the events of 17 Aug 49 or previous encounters with Meyer. Recommend interrogation by Dubinsky at the earliest opportunity.

STATUS OF VORTEX PHENOMENON

At roughly 16:42 on 28 Aug 49, sensors monitoring the vortex phenomenon at Area 51 detected a notable but

TOP SECRET / MAJIC

EYES ONLY

000

....
* TOP SECRET *
....

short spike in non-ionized radiation discharge. At roughly 16:47, a second spike--much more intense and longer-lasting--occurred. Our analysts are still study-ing the data to determine how these spikes differed from other past discharges.

It's worth noting, however, that the first spike may well correspond to the time we believe Agent Vanoverbeke gave her life for her country. We also believe that the second spike corresponds to the time we believe the Soviets detonated their atomic weapon. Past U.S. test detonations had little or no effect on the phenomenon, but we believe that the presence of at least two, if not more, Variants within the Soviet test detonation zone may have prompted increased activity.

As a result, we believe that fatalities--whether caused by nuclear detonation or not--may have an impact on the vortex. We also believe that the deaths of Variants themselves have an even greater effect.

NEW HYPOTHESIS OF VORTEX AND VARIANT PHENOMENA

The following is highly speculative, and has yet to be tested. In fact, we're not entirely sure how to test for it. But in the interest of full disclosure, I'm including it here.

Wallace awakened from his comatose state and almost immediately demanded a secure line to my office. After about an hour, I was able to take his call, and was informed that Bronk was in the room with him as well.

Once we began, Wallace described a vision he received immediately after he became comatose, while escaping from the Soviet test detonation blast radius. In this vision, he believed he heard—and then later saw—numerous shadowy figures within the vortex phenomenon. He believes that these figures and corresponding voices represent distinct intelligences that somehow reside within or beyond the vortex. If within, then the vortex represents a kind of "pocket" within normal space, and if beyond, the vortex could represent a kind of gateway to another space entirely, possibly an entire dimension.

When pressed as to the nature of these shadow figures, Wallace could only say that they sounded human, and that they looked roughly bipedal.

Both Wallace and Bronk have further conjectures as to what these figures might be, but unless there is greater interest on your part, I suggest more study is needed before making any further conclusions.

RECOMMENDATIONS

As noted above, I suggest Dubinsky be given the opportunity to interrogate Schreiber at the earliest possible opportunity.

I further recommend that, given the advanced state of
the Soviets' Variant program and, in particular, the
theoretical capabilities of the Soviet "shadow" Variant,
operations at Area 51 be moved elsewhere, at the earliest possible opportunity. I suggest Mountain Home AFB
in Idaho.

I further recommend that all MAJESTIC-12 Variants be
housed at the new facility until further notice. Julia
Meyer's activities at Area 51 were disruptive and potentially devastating to operational security. As much as I
would prefer to allow our Variants as much of a normal
life as possible, I believe monitoring their activities to
be more important at this stage. We can make allowances
for those Variants with families to have their families
join them in base housing.

I further recommend that Wallace be given authorization
to form a team which will return to Syria to further
investigate the potential for Variant activity there.

Finally, I recommend that all surviving Variants involved
in this operation receive commendations from the
President, at his discretion.

36.

September 4, 1949

"S o, basically, you want me to give 'em medals, then tell 'em they're being shipped off to a remote base in Nowhere, Idaho?" President Truman asked as he finished reading Hillenkoetter's report, tossing it down on his desk.

"I don't think we'd do it consecutively like that." Hillenkoetter smiled as he relaxed on the couch in the Oval Office. "We're not cruel."

"But that whole thing you wanted about getting them a normal life. That's gone," Truman said as he rose from his desk and began to pace—a sure sign he wasn't happy.

"Sir, there are some very sneaky Variants out there. Julia Meyer couldn't be controlled. That Russian shadow, he might be able to pop up in this very room if we didn't have a null-generator in here. Until we figure out more security measures, we need to keep our assets secure."

Truman frowned. "What about those devices? Those null things? Can't they just wear 'em like a collar or something? Shut down their abilities until we need them?"

Hillenkoetter shifted in his seat a little; he knew this would be a hard sell. "The null-fields may produce some health problems after long-term exposure. We're looking into it, but I'd like to minimize their use whenever possible."

Putting his hands on his hips, Truman exhaled and looked at the floor for a moment. "Fine," he said. "But you make damn sure they're set up nicely out there in Idaho. They get officer housing, all of 'em. Full base privileges. And if they want a vacation, then give 'em one. Send along some chaperones if you have to, but I want them taken care of."

"Yes, sir."

"They didn't ask for this. Any of it," Truman said, pacing once more. "Jesus, can you imagine? You get hit with these strange powers, you get all kinds of side effects, and then your country rounds you up and puts you out there in the field. These people nearly got an A-bomb dropped on them."

Hillenkoetter coughed a bit to interrupt Truman's rambling. "On the bright side, we have excellent intel on the Soviets' weapons program now. And their Variant program."

Truman smiled a little and flopped down on the couch opposite Hillenkoetter. "Yeah, we need to brief Congress about their A-bomb. Probably go public soon."

"Actually, sir, I recommend we wait on that."

"Why?"

"The only way we'd know if the Reds tested an A-bomb out in the middle of Kazakhstan as of *this* date would be because we had an asset there. Which we did. But the rest of the world—including the parts of the MGB and Red Army that aren't in on their Variant program—doesn't know that."

"You want us to look dumb."

"Exactly," Hillenkoetter said with a smirk. "Hell, you can even leak to the press that you're pissed at me for taking so long to find out."

At this, Truman barked out a laugh. "I just might do that. But what about your career?"

"What about it? You fire me as DCI, I'll just go back to the Navy. Maybe command a nice quiet carrier group somewhere. Sounds nice, actually," Hillenkoetter said.

"You're not going anywhere," Truman said, jabbing a finger in his direction. "Does CIA have awards or commendations yet?"

"We're working on a few things."

"Get 'em up and running, and then I'll sign off on 'em for your people. The move to Mountain Home is approved along with the rest of your recommendations. Let me know what that Dubinsky girl gets out of the PAPERCLIP man. I already feel sorry for him."

"I don't."

"True enough. Anything else?"

Hillenkoetter stood. "Just one more thing. Didn't want to put it in the report. You remember Mrs. Stevens?"

"How could I not?" Truman said, rising from his seat. "Fine lady. Kind of an odd duck, though."

"Geniuses are like that. I want to put her on the vortex study in place of Schreiber."

Truman's good humor evaporated. "She's a Variant."

"She is. But she's also the smartest person we have. She might just be the smartest person *ever*."

"And if . . ." Truman paused, searching for the words. "Look, if there are people of some kind—aliens, whatever—on the other side of that white light, and they're actually responsible for creating Variants, how do you know she won't be compromised?"

Hillenkoetter picked up his briefcase from the floor, then just shrugged. "Mr. President, none of them have been compromised by any outside influence that we know of. But yes, that can happen. But if that's the case, I can think of several other Variants far more dangerous than Mrs. Stevens. And I genuinely think she's the best one we got to try to crack this nut."

Truman locked eyes with Hillenkoetter for several moments, leaving the DCI feeling like he was a midshipman again, undergoing inspection. "Fine. But she answers to Bronk, and all major experiments or whatnot go through all of us—you, me, Bronk, Vandenberg, everyone. Clear?"

"Yes, sir."

Truman extended his hand. "Well done, all around, Hilly. Thank you."

"Thank you, sir."

Hillenkoetter walked out of the Oval Office, past the secretary, and out onto the veranda. He took a seat on a bench and sat down to admire the Rose Garden for a bit, trying to feel better about it all. The operation had been a success, and his people had landed him several prime intelligence coups. His position as DCI and the *de facto* head of MAJESTIC-12 was assured, for at least a little while longer.

But there were shadows everywhere now. The Russians and their A-bomb, Lavrentiy Beria and his "champions of the proletariat." And even his own Variants . . . If he was being honest with himself, Wallace's little revelation had cast a long shadow of suspicion over them as well.

Which was why they were all going to be moved to Idaho.

* * *

October 12, 1949

Frank walked out into the crisp morning air with a cup of coffee in hand, taking his now-customary seat on the porch of his little craftsman cottage. Idaho was warmer than he'd expected, and even in mid-October, he only needed a sweater to stave off the chill.

His house was one of many on a little block in a little neighborhood just off the main road inside Mountain Home Air Force Base. The units had been slapped together during the war, and there were enough little maintenance jobs to keep Frank busy, at least for the first few weeks. Now it was actually feeling like a home. He had even picked up a couple of knickknacks at the post exchange for decor, which Maggie—living three doors down—mocked him for incessantly. If she wanted to keep her house bare—"minimalist," as she called it—that was her business.

They'd moved in about a month before. At first, Frank had resented MAJESTIC-12 for corralling them all together like this; they called it "operational efficiency," but he and the others knew it for what it was—mistrust. They didn't want all the Variants roaming around unsupervised. Even now, Frank had to check in with Detlev Bronk before driving into Mountain Home itself—population maybe two thousand on a good day—or making the hour-plus trek to Boise to get a decent restaurant meal. And he knew full well he was being followed, of course. It didn't take CIA training to spot a government-issue vehicle in your rearview on the empty roads of southern Idaho.

But now, having settled in, Frank much preferred base life to his shoddy D.C. apartment. He'd made friends with a couple of the Air Force sergeants who ran physical training, and wrangled himself an invite to join up whenever he liked, as some of the younger officers did. He'd also got approval to work with Major Hamilton on training new recruits, and had been working with a team of four new Variants over the past couple weeks. He found himself enjoying the process of whipping them into shape while he waited for his next overseas assignment.

Cal seemed to be settling in pretty well too. Frank had just been over to his house, a block away, two nights ago for dinner. It all seemed very civilized, and Cal's wife Sarah was an amazing cook. The community wasn't all that welcoming—there were still some people who felt Negroes shouldn't be posted in officers' quarters—but Sarah was busy volunteering at the base hospital, and Cal of course was actively working with MAJESTIC-12. He seemed to be Mrs. Stevens's go-to guy for experimental help these days.

Mrs. Stevens was being kept incredibly busy with her new responsibilities studying the vortex, which had been moved to Idaho using the same electromagnetic rig that originally got it out of Japan. She was so busy, in fact, that Frank would see her walking home down the street toward her house at nine or ten o'clock. This wasn't really a problem for Mr. Stevens anymore, though. Word had it that he'd filed for divorce before the move to Idaho. Frank felt bad for her, of course, seeing as she was a devoted wife and all. But Frank could certainly understand the problems that might crop up, being married to a genius. It was a shame all around, but Frank figured that was how it was going to be for all of them. Being a Variant meant being different. Being normal was no longer an option.

Mrs. Stevens shared her house with Zippy Silverman, who had been an instant hit at the officers' club on base, what with her being young and attractive and all. She'd become quite the regular there, already at the bar every time Frank stopped in for a drink. She'd wear a nice skirt, get all dolled up, and have those kid gloves on all the time—couldn't blame her for the gloves, given her Enhancement. Frank had ended up walking her home a few times when she'd overdone it. He figured she was in the hopeless, get-drunk phase of coping with her ability. At least, he hoped so.

Maggie jogged by the house and waved at Frank, which he returned with a smile as he sipped his coffee. She'd been the most vociferously opposed to relocating, alongside Danny, but ultimately came around. She still spouted off now and then about unfair treatment and "Variant rights," which Frank imagined could become a real thing at some point if more of them continued to crop up, but overall, Maggie seemed to be rolling with it now.

Of course, she had a much more interesting job at the moment than most of them.

* * *

"Good morning, *Herr Doktor*. What are we gonna talk about today?"

Maggie walked into Schreiber's cell and plopped down on a chair, smiling right at the German scientist as he immediately retreated to the far corner of the room, opposite his government-issue bed, and balled himself up on the floor.

"Go away," he whimpered quietly.

"Why?" she asked sweetly.

Schreiber pulled his legs closer to his chest and began rocking but didn't answer. If he wasn't a Nazi scumbag, even Maggie might have started to feel bad for him. But as it stood, she was perfectly fine with things the way they were. In fact, over the past five weeks, she'd rather enjoyed seeing just what her abilities could do.

They could do a lot, actually.

Kurt Schreiber, to his credit, had been a really tough nut to crack. His emotional discipline was absolutely impressive—so much so that Danny had had him tested to see whether he was actually a Variant, even though Danny couldn't mark him as such with his Enhancement. But no, Schreiber was just a steely guy.

It had taken three weeks of intensive emotional manipulation to break him.

First, Maggie tried anger—anger at her, at MAJESTIC-12, at Variants, at the Nazis, at anybody she could think of. Anger and vengeance were powerful motivators, but while she managed to get Schreiber to rail at just about everybody she brought up, he didn't spill. He even attacked her in a fit of rage, but her training was more than up to the task of fending off a pissed-off pencil-neck.

Then there was fear. So much fear. Even Maggie started having nightmares after a solid week of inflicting terror on the poor guy. He screamed, cried, soiled himself on several occasions, tried begging for his life, even begged for her to *end* his life a couple times. But when she asked him to spill his guts in exchange for safety, he shut down. He'd scream more or pass out entirely. But he wouldn't budge.

The less said about lust, the better. Maggie only tried two days of that before she felt the need for a month-long shower.

Finally, she'd hit upon love. At first, she'd kind of gone for romantic love, but when that didn't work, she tried a more maternal bent. Lo and behold, Schreiber responded just a little bit, giving a few details about how Julia Meyer had come to him during his house arrest, how they'd compared notes about the Variant condition, how they'd sought to escape together. It wasn't romantic with Julia, Maggie found, just a shared interest.

More and more, Maggie had used that maternal approval thing to draw him out. It quite obviously messed with Schreiber's head completely—he'd tried to cut his wrists with a sharpened toothbrush last week after Maggie had expressed her utter disappointment in him—but it was working.

In fact, she'd managed to piece the whole thing together at this point. Julia Meyer had just wanted out—she wasn't a Soviet spy, just a manipulative opportunist looking to get back to robbing banks and living large. She'd convinced Yamato and Sorensen—not the sharpest tools in the shed, to be fair—to help her disable the null-generators at their Area 51 training area, then moved under the earth incorporeally to shuttle between POSEIDON and Schreiber. She'd even managed to convince Schreiber that a Soviet agent would meet him in Las Vegas so he could sell out for a ton of money, which they'd split and then go their separate ways. There was no agent, though. Their best guess was that Julia just wanted an ally on the outside, someone she could leverage to sell secrets to the Russians later on after her own escape.

Danny and the others had undertaken an exhaustive search but found no trace of any contact with a Soviet agent. It was suspect, of course, but Maggie believed Julia had played Schreiber's greed and vanity like a Stradivarius. And when she'd told Schreiber that, alongside a healthy dollop of motherly disapproval, the man had folded like a bad hand.

Nazi as mama's boy. It was only because Maggie was a Variant that she'd seen stranger things.

"I don't think I'm gonna fuck with your head today," Maggie said. "I need a break. And you, pal, you *really* need a break."

Schreiber's eyes darted toward her briefly before looking down at the hard, concrete floor once more. "Then why are you here?"

"I want to talk to you about your theories. About the vortex."

There was a long silence for several seconds . . . and then Schreiber started to actually chuckle.

Maggie tamped down hard on her annoyance. "What's so funny?"

"You have no idea. You really don't," Schreiber said amidst the little laughs. "Oh, no. You really don't know."

"Oh, I think you'll tell me."

Schreiber looked up, scared for a moment, but to Maggie's surprise, he held her gaze. "You know, I think I'll tell you anyway. It won't make a difference either way."

"Tell me what?" Maggie asked, trying not to sound concerned.

"The vortex is death."

The words hung in the air for long moments as Maggie tried to wrap her head around it. "Come again?"

"The vortex . . . is death. It is death."

Maggie frowned. "You're gonna have to be more specific than that, Doc. Otherwise, I'm gonna have to go heavy on you again, and nobody wants that."

Schreiber leapt to his feet suddenly, laughing and shouting. "Death! It's death! And it will come for you! For us all!"

Before Maggie could react, Schreiber screamed incoherently and ran headfirst toward the metal cell door. Ran headfirst *into* the metal cell door.

There was a sickening crack and then silence. His body slumped to the floor.

Reeling, Maggie slowly got up and made her way over to him, bending down to take his pulse. There was none. For once, she was glad of the camera in the room recording everything, because she doubted anybody would believe her otherwise.

She stood up and banged on the cell door to get the attention of the guards outside. "We're done here," she called out, then looked down at Schreiber once more. "Probably for the best."

December 24, 1949

Christmas in Damascus was a surprisingly genial affair, Danny thought, given the numerous religions all vying for attention in the city. It seemed the Muslims had ceded the past few weeks to their Christian neighbors, allowing both tasteful manger displays and garish plastic Santas to be proudly shown off in homes and storefronts. There were even strings of electric Christmas lights here and there, and as Danny walked down Al Hamra Street, he stopped short when he spied an evergreen in someone's window. Fake, undoubtedly, but still.

"I can't believe he's finally seeing us," Miles Copeland said excitedly as they made their way toward Syria's Parliament building. "I'm hoping we can maybe jumpstart something good here."

Danny just shook his head sadly and walked on, Maggie and Frank bringing up the rear and, as usual, keeping an eye out for trouble. "Miles, Syria just had its third coup of the year. This whole thing has gotten way out of control."

Copeland frowned but let the matter drop. They were on their way to see Colonel Adib al-Shishakli, the new leader of Syria. Last week, al-Shishakli had officially deposed his fellow Syrian Army officer, the Soviet-backed Sami al-Hinnawi, the one who had deposed—and killed—Husni al-Za'im over the summer.

Za'im had been America's man, of course, while al-Hinnawi had definitely been in the Soviets' pocket. But nobody knew where al-Shishakli stood yet—and that was on Copeland and Stephen Meade, who had been trying

desperately to regain a foothold in Syrian politics after
Za'im's death. Their failure had them on a short leash in
Washington, though they'd managed to buy a little bit of
time as construction began on the Trans-Arabian Pipeline
within Syria. If nothing else, al-Hinnawi hadn't canceled
it, and no doubt Copeland would try to impress upon
al-Shishakli the importance of honoring Syria's agreements.

Normally—if anything could be called normal in Syria
anymore—Copeland, Meade, and/or Keeley would be the
ones going to see the new strongman. Al-Shishakli, however, seemed to have other ideas, not to mention a keen
grasp of who was doing what in Damascus.

The invitation for an audience was specifically addressed
to Copeland . . . as well as Danny, Frank, and Maggie. That
in and of itself was highly disconcerting and had prompted
a furious round of cables between Damascus and Foggy
Bottom before they were finally given the green light to
accept.

Danny had been in Damascus for six weeks now, looking desperately for whatever had crept onto the edges of
his Enhanced perceptions back in the spring. Normally,
when Danny sensed a Variant, that person stood out in his
mind like a beacon, giving him an unerring sense of his
or her nature as well as a general direction to follow. That
was how he'd been able to find so many Variants back in
the States—they'd get a few odd reports in the papers, then
Danny would go to whatever city it was, close his eyes, and
home in on the signal, so to speak.

The signal in Damascus was directionless and sporadic.

He'd spent the first week just walking the streets, playing
tourist, even hauling a camera around for show. He'd stop
in cafés and restaurants to sit and concentrate, extending
his senses over as wide an area as he could—and he could
manage a hundred miles, give or take, when he put enough
brain power into it. There was nothing.

Then one evening, while enjoying dinner at the
Copelands' house, a tiny flicker had appeared. He'd bolted
upright and practically fled the house, running about the

nighttime streets like an idiot—but he couldn't pin it down at all. And after an hour, it was gone.

That sporadic sense came and went over the course of the next several weeks, popping up here and there, anywhere from three times a day to a week apart. Danny would go haring off in a direction but would ultimately lose the trail. He started fastidiously noting times and dates, cabling Mountain Home to see if there was any corresponding change in the vortex. There wasn't.

Finally, two weeks before, there had been a massive flare-up, and Danny had finally caught a bead on the Variant in question—and it was a Variant. For a few brief minutes, that flickering sense had bloomed to life as a fully formed Variant, and Danny had dashed toward the center of Damascus as fast as he could—at first by taxi, then by foot when traffic jammed up.

Then the Variant had disappeared completely, as if winking out of existence entirely. It had been like nothing he'd ever sensed. That was when he'd called Frank and Maggie to come join him. There was definitely something going on.

Immediately after Frank and Maggie had arrived, al-Shishakli deposed al-Hinnawi—something Danny swore had to be related. Somehow. The three of them scoured Damascus for a full week, tracking down every single person who'd been arrested or "disappeared" since al-Shishakli had taken power. To be fair, there weren't that many such people. It seemed Syrians were pretty happy to be rid of al-Hinnawi, and there wasn't much dissent.

Then again, Danny figured if his own country had just had its third coup in a year, he'd be keeping his head down too.

Their activity must've prompted al-Shishakli's invitation. Frank had spent months in Damascus and was well known to al-Shishakli, and even Danny and Maggie were known quantities, though to a lesser extent. Maybe the new boss just wanted to set some ground rules. Or maybe it was something else.

The Parliament building—long a hub of politicking and gathering at seemingly all hours—was largely deserted now, except for the Syrian Army soldiers staked out surrounding it. Since the coup, al-Shishakli had been busy consolidating power and meeting with various legislators from an office in the building, and given Syria's instability, the heavy army presence wasn't surprising.

Copeland led the way to the checkpoint, speaking in rapid-fire Arabic. After producing their diplomatic passports, they were allowed inside the perimeter. There was a second checkpoint at the doors of the building, and there they were escorted by four armed soldiers up into the highest recesses of the building. Finally, they were frisked in a small office before being led into an opulent meeting room.

"Za'im used to hold court in here," Frank whispered. "Interesting."

Adib al-Shishakli was sitting at the end of a long table, a stack of papers on either side of him. A few other military officers were helping him file paperwork, while another pair of armed soldiers covered the other door out of the room. Their presence was announced, and al-Shishakli looked up and gave a tired smile.

"Mr. Copeland," the new Syrian leader said. "We meet again."

Copeland smiled and walked over, his hand extended. "Indeed we do, sir. I'm pleased to see you again."

Al-Shishakli didn't get up and didn't shake Copeland's hand. "Please, all of you, sit. I have tea coming."

Danny took a chair on al-Shishakli's left side, with Maggie next to him, while Copeland and Frank sat across. A valet came in with an ornate silver tea set, and there was silence as the tea was poured. Danny shifted in his chair nervously—he was no diplomat and was probably the least important person in the room.

Or so everyone else thought.

"You are different, Mr. Wallace," al-Shishakli said without preamble. It was a casual statement with no accusation or questioning.

"Sir?"

Al-Shishakli smiled briefly. "That was unfair, but it has been a rare thing to have 'one up' on you Americans, as you say. I suppose I should explain."

Danny cleared his throat. "Perhaps Mr. Copeland and all other nonessential personnel should leave the room?"

The Syrian seemed to consider this a moment, then spoke in rapid-fire Arabic. Immediately, all of al-Shishakli's aides packed up and walked off, along with all but two of the guards. "Mr. Copeland, I apologize, but it seems as though this matter should be discussed privately. If you'll excuse us?"

Copeland looked from al-Shishakli to Danny, his mouth slightly open, his eyes wide. Then, without a word, he simply rose and walked out of the room. One of the guards closed the door behind him.

"Now, Mr. Wallace, you are different. You and Mr. Lodge and Miss Dubinsky here," al-Shishakli said.

Danny looked to Frank, who simply shrugged in disbelief, and to Maggie, who leaned over and whispered in his ear. "He's calm. Confident," she said.

After taking a sip of tea to calm his nerves and find the right words, Danny said, "Without confirming or denying anything, sir, I'm curious as to what makes you believe so."

Al-Shishakli slowly rose from his chair and began walking aimlessly around the room. "As you likely know, I have a ward—a young Bedouin boy. He has been with me for nearly a year and a half now. His father asked me to look after him because of his particular needs. He has an odd affliction, and I sought to gain the support of his father's tribe for the struggles to come. He has been . . . more of a problem than I believed, but also a surprising asset."

"And how can a boy be an asset?" Maggie asked, almost rhetorically.

"He is different, like you. In fact, it is through the thing that makes him different that we discovered your own unique place in the world," al-Shishakli said.

Variant. Danny took another sip of tea. "And so you used his affliction, as you say, to your benefit."

"I confess, we tried," al-Shishakli said. "His father believed him to have the soul of a djinn, one of the ancient spirits that haunt the deserts. He would . . . leave his body behind and travel to the soul of others. Once inside them, he would assert control, pushing the other soul out for a time."

Frank sat up and put his tea down. "Za'im. When Za'im got weird . . . that was your boy."

Al-Shishakli nodded. "Sami and I backed Husni in his takeover because we felt the President and Parliament were failing the people of Syria, keeping us from asserting our rightful place in this region. But then Husni allied himself too closely with Mr. Copeland and you Americans, and Sami and I feared we would simply become puppets in your Cold War."

Danny nodded. "And so you had the boy supplant Za'im, forcing him to act more and more erratically."

"Well, we simply wanted him to act in Syria's best interests," al-Shishakli said, shaking his head sadly. "But the boy is still, at heart, just a child. All of Za'im's excesses were simply the whims of a youngster, a boy's idea of what leadership should be."

"And so al-Hinnawi took over and shot Za'im."

"The boy shot Za'im, using Sami's hand."

This hung in the air for several long moments before Maggie spoke up. "You couldn't control him."

Al-Shishakli sat down again, slumping in his chair. "The boy, he would move from Husni to Sami, using them to play off one another, like a great game. He would tell Copeland things with Za'im's mouth, then court Karilov with Sami's. And I realized, after a time, that his control over Sami was just as awful as before. So, we had to restrain him. I briefly succumbed to his power before he was finally subdued."

Danny leaned forward. "So, what was it like? His power?"

The Syrian looked hard at Danny before answering. "I do not like to discuss it, but I will, so that you know. When he took over my body, my soul traveled . . . somewhere else. I could only see a barren white plain, with the souls of others wandering it. Back when the boy was still new and still listening to us, he would describe it as traveling the land of the dead. And he said that certain other souls would stand out while he was traveling. He identified them as you three, plus your Mr. Hooks and Miss Silverman." Al-Shishakli smiled briefly at the stunned looks in the room. "We have our own intelligence agency, my friends. We know who comes and goes out of our own country. And the boy saw each of you at one point or another."

And his presence would seem to be displaced when he was bopping around other bodies, Danny thought. *That's why I couldn't find him!* "So, where is this boy now?"

Al-Shishakli looked down at his hands. "He has been sedated. For two weeks now. We feed him through a tube. He wastes away, despite our best efforts. But if we let him awaken, he may take over my body, take over the country, do anything, really."

Maggie actually looked taken aback, even a little sad—a rarity for her. "I'm sure you didn't have a lot of great choices," she said quietly.

"I have horrible choices now," the Syrian snapped, looking up at her. "I am a soldier and I have seen death, but I cannot consign this boy to die, either slowly, the way he is now, or quickly. And yet here you are, all of you . . . people. I do not know what you are, what you can do, but I know you work for your government. And only a fool would not assume the Russians would have similar people they are using. And so, once again, Syria is a pawn, this time on a larger chessboard. It is disgusting."

Another uncomfortable silence descended on the room until Danny, practically ready to jump out of his skin, spoke up again. "I'm sorry, sir. I really am. What would you like to do?"

Al-Shishakli idly shuffled a manila folder around the table in front of him. "I can tell you want him, Mr. Wallace. The boy. You want to take custody of him, to bring him into your . . . agency or program or whatever it is. Use him, as we tried to use him. This is madness. You cannot use someone with such power."

"We have the means to subdue his power without harming him," Danny said quickly, putting aside the concerns about the null-generators' long-term health effects for the moment. "We can help him to understand his ability, use it responsibly if he can. If he can't, we can at least keep him safe, away from others, where he can't harm anyone. And we can learn from him. There's a lot we're still trying to figure out, but what you told us sounds a lot like what others have reported. Maybe we can figure out how all this happened, how we can bring it under control."

Al-Shishakli shook his head sadly. "Control. You are always trying to control. But yes, I believe what you're saying, and I believe you have a genuine concern for those like you, Mr. Wallace. So, I will allow you to take him—but with conditions."

"Name it."

"The United States must recognize the legitimacy of my government, but more importantly, I want assurances that Mr. Copeland is done trying to play kingmaker in my country. Send him somewhere else. Anywhere else. I don't care."

Frank smiled at this. "Can't guarantee that, but we'll certainly make your position crystal clear with the folks in Washington."

Al-Shishakli nodded. "I also want your assurances that the boy will be well cared for, and not killed if at all possible."

"Of course," Danny said.

"Finally, I want you all out of the country tomorrow morning. And any of your kind . . . I do not want you to return. We know what to look for now, and I promise you, we will be looking. All of the nations here in your 'Middle East' have been colonies and puppets for too long. We do not need to be the puppets of people with your abilities as well."

Danny looked at Maggie again, who raised an eyebrow at him. *Might be bluffing on that last bit.*

"Understood, sir," Danny said. "Anything else?"

Al-Shishakli rose, and the Variants followed suit. "There is an ambulance outside. The boy is in it. Take him where you must tonight. Fly him out of the country tomorrow. That is all. And now, if you'll excuse me, I believe I need to see Mr. Copeland. If you do not wish me to tell your secrets to the world, I suggest you do as I say."

Danny turned again to Maggie, who had both eyebrows raised. *Not a bluff, that.*

With a nod toward the new leader of Syria, Danny headed for the door, his fellow Variants behind him. The world had just gotten a whole lot stranger, and a lot more dangerous, he felt, with an independent state like Syria in on the Variant secret.

It wasn't just about Americans and Russians anymore.

Acknowledgments

First, I would like to thank everyone who bought and enjoyed the first book in this series, *MJ-12: Inception*, as well as my other work. I get to make stuff up, write it down, and sell it because of you, and I am eternally grateful for it. So many reviewers, fans, and fellow authors have contributed to the success of this series, and all my work, and it's getting difficult after five novels to list you all out. But I remain thankful for everyone who has ever given me a leg up, a space to write, a kind word, and a stiff drink. I will work hard to pay it back, forward, and sideways whenever possible.

I'd like to thank the folks at Borderlands Books in San Francisco for having me over to help launch the first book in this series. If you like science fiction and fantasy, I strongly urge you to visit them, either in person if you can, or online. The folks at both Phoenix Comicon and Dragon Con in Atlanta also helped immensely in getting the word out on this series, and if you find yourself looking for great cons to go to, I recommend them wholeheartedly.

A special shout-out to the *real* Christina Vanoverbeke, winner of a prize I sponsored in the raffle benefitting Kids Need to Read at 2016's Phoenix Comicon. The prize was to have a character in this book named after her—and to give that character a noteworthy death. I can only hope that being unceremoniously shot by a historical villain, and then having a nuclear weapon dropped on her corpse, has sufficed in fulfilling my end of the bargain.

As always, editor Cory Allyn at Night Shade Books has done incredible work in making this book better—and calming this writer's nerves. And my thanks to Jason Katzman and Brianna Scharfenberg at NSB for all their support as well. Richard Shealy remains the best copyeditor in the business; he's a big part of why this book makes actual sense.

My agent, Sara Megibow, has been a firm believer in my work, and any alleged talent I may possess, for six years now. She is a most excellent advocate and a lovely person, and I wouldn't be here without her.

Finally, my wife Kate and daughter Anna needed a little extra patience with me as I wrote this one, and I am especially grateful to them for dealing with a particularly harried version of myself. They continue to make everything in life better. I love you both.

Michael J. Martinez
2017